THEY WERE SISTERS

Persephone Book N° 56
Published by Persephone Books Ltd 2005
Reprinted 2007, 2009, 2012 and 2016

First published 1943 by John Murray
© The Estate of Dorothy Whipple
Afterword © Celia Brayfield 2004

Endpapers taken from
'Pattern of Anemones', a 1935 printed cotton
crêpe dress fabric manufactured by
Calico Printers' Association,
Manchester

Typeset in ITC Baskerville by Keystroke,
Wolverhampton

Printed and bound in Germany by
GGP Media GmbH, Poessneck
on Munken Premium (FSC approved)

ISBN 978 1903155 462

Persephone Books Ltd
59 Lamb's Conduit Street
London WC1N 3NB
020 7242 9292

www.persephonebooks.co.uk

THEY WERE SISTERS

by

DOROTHY WHIPPLE

with a new afterword by

CELIA BRAYFIELD

PERSEPHONE BOOKS
LONDON

THEY WERE SISTERS

CHAPTER ONE

Lucy, reading Vera's letter at breakfast, smiled. Vera would come when Charlotte came and they would all be together. Once more, like old times, they would all be together. She must break it tactfully to William. Across the dazzle struck from the cloth and the silver by the sunshine of the September morning, she looked at him. Should she tell him now or later?

William was engrossed in the paper, folded beside his plate. He bent over it, eating porridge with a reckless hand, splashing his tie as usual. He knew he was splashing, too, because from time to time he made absent dabs at the tie with his free hand, rubbing the porridge in under the delusion that he was rubbing it away. This was a concession to Lucy. He didn't care about his tie, but he knew she did and Lucy felt a faint pride. After eleven years of marriage she was still secretly gratified by any evidence of her influence over William, because William was less influenced by other people than seemed humanly possible. If William didn't go his own way, which he usually did, he went hers; but never, if he could help it, other people's.

This characteristic had brought him, in the old days, into frequent trouble with the Board of Education, which he

1

served as Inspector of Science and Technology over an area of several counties. Nowadays, however, there was truce. Time had proved William to be, if, in the Board's opinion, odd, nevertheless a highly efficient and indefatigable servant. The Board now mostly let William do as he liked.

After the way of wives, Lucy decided that she wouldn't tell him both about the splashing of his tie and about the impending visit of her two sisters. She must withhold rebuke about the tie, she decided. But when William, bending still lower over the paper, poured porridge backwards from his spoon into the milk on his plate and bespattered freely a large area of waistcoat, she could not suppress a groan. Whereupon William, without removing any attention from the paper, rubbed his tie for something like half a minute.

Lucy turned her head away so that she shouldn't laugh out loud and disturb him. Let him read his paper. Her thoughts were flowing to her sisters, to the future when she would see them again, to the past which she had shared with them.

Sitting at the breakfast-table in her little old house in the midland country, mature, almost forty, she was back at 'home', a girl again, trying to manage that chaotic house where no one was in time for meals but her father and herself, where the piano was always going, where you couldn't get a room or a corner to yourself to read in, even if there had been any time to read, which there wasn't. Not for Lucy at any rate, because at night, when there was an end at last to the bustle of the day and she might have got an hour with a book, she generally had to listen to her father.

Mr Field liked, towards half-past nine in the evening, to lay aside his paper, grasp the lapels of his coat, stretch out his legs and, as his children put it, hold forth. So at half-past nine there was never anybody there, except Lucy. Charlotte and Vera escaped without a scruple, the boys were always out; but Lucy felt her father must be lonely since her mother's death, so she listened.

She remembered how her mother used to listen, if listening it could be called. She sat with her knitting, not really paying any attention, smiling at anyone who came into the room, welcoming all interruptions, communicating round the side of the chair by signs and nods, but never getting too far away to say, when her husband paused: 'Yes, dear?' and set him off again. It was a piquant situation, because if she did not listen to him, neither was he talking to her. He was just talking. He needed to talk. He fired himself by talking and after a talk he was a new man, refreshed and able to face once more the anxieties of professional – he was a lawyer – and family life.

But Lucy had not her mother's powers of self-protection. She really listened, with youthful courtesy, her eyes on his face. He talked about the office, about the state of the country, always, according to him, bad. He talked about the money it took to keep the house up; it seemed to Lucy that they were always on the verge of bankruptcy. But most of all he talked about the necessity, which she must share with him, of keeping the boys straight and of watching continually over the girls. There was a strain of wildness or weakness in the family.

'From your mother's side, you understand,' he said. 'Not from mine. My people, Lucy, are and always have been a steady, upright, God-fearing lot.'

They were. There was no denying it. But unfortunately nobody wanted to be like them. Her father's family were worthy and charmless; her mother's charming and worthless, or nearly so, according to her father. Lucy had joined with her brothers and sisters in admiring her mother's family and poking fun at her father's, but when the responsibility of the household fell upon her, she came to know what her father meant. She saw the dangers.

She couldn't fail to see them with Harry and Aubrey about the house. Harry was the eldest of the family, two years her senior, but he had no more sense of responsibility than a fly. In Lucy, the sense of responsibility grew heavier as her sisters grew older. There was no need for her father to point out to her the dangers of the family strain and the boys' bad example. She saw it clearly enough. But he could not resist pointing things out, even the most obvious. By talking he lessened his own burdens and increased Lucy's. After listening to him, Lucy felt more than ever anxious and oppressed.

When her mother died suddenly, from influenza, Lucy was eighteen and had just left school, where she had lingered as long as they would let her because she hadn't wanted merely to remain at home and help in the house. Lucy liked to be quiet, to pursue her own paths, to read a great deal and that was impossible at home. She had mapped out a plan for herself. She had persuaded her father, against his will, to give

her an unused room in his office building and there she installed herself to read for a scholarship for Oxford. But her mother died and Lucy, grief-stricken, gave everything up to plunge into the management of a household made up of her father, Harry, herself, Aubrey, Jack, Charlotte and Vera, the two little sisters then thirteen and eleven years of age.

Looking back, Lucy didn't know how she had managed; probably she hadn't. They must all have just scrambled through the years somehow. When the war came in 1914, although they were always anxious about Harry and Aubrey in France, there was more quiet in the house. War abroad and peace at home, thought Lucy. Then Harry and Aubrey came back, bringing chaos with them.

Mr Field had sent all his sons into the law, intending to choose a partner from among them and put the other two into the way of becoming, he hoped, Town Clerks. He had long ago chosen as partner Jack, the youngest, his favourite and the most amenable. But when the two elder ones came home from the war, they hilariously declared that the law was not for them. They would look about, they said, for something less deadly. In the meantime, they had their gratuities.

'We'll all have a good time now,' they said, and bought a car to take the girls to the races and the dances.

Charlotte was by this time twenty-one and pretty enough, but Vera at nineteen was beautiful. She was slender, pale, her hair was ashen-gold, her eyes dark blue, her lashes long and dark. There was something in Vera's face that touched your heart. Not when she was gay and queening it about the place, as she often was, but when she was reading under a lamp, or

asleep, or thought herself alone. It might be nothing but the effect of the faint hollowing of her cheek, or the shadow of her lashes, but at such times it seemed that in lovely, reckless Vera there was someone who was lost, seeking, who wanted something that wasn't there, something undefined, but lacking, and Lucy had to suppress a strong desire to ask what it was so that she could comfort her. She didn't ask, because she knew Vera would never tell. Even if she knew, she would never tell, and probably she didn't know, thought Lucy. Her face was cast in such a lovely mould that what it expressed seemed more haunting and significant than the expressions of more ordinary faces. 'I look worried,' thought Lucy, 'but Vera looks touched by all the sorrows of the world, yet it's probably about the same sort of thing.'

She was often angry with Vera, bewildered by her and ashamed of her. Vera told lies when it suited her. She went for what she wanted with a complete disregard of others. She was contemptuous of her father, mimicking him with merciless brilliance. She did things that made Lucy wince. For instance, when old deaf Mrs Parker called, Vera would make rude remarks, sure of not being heard.

'Tell me what you're laughing at, my dears,' said Mrs Parker once. 'I like to laugh too and you don't find much to laugh at when you are old and deaf, you know.'

Vera blushed then, Lucy was glad to see.

Vera was unselfconscious. She walked across a ballroom as if there were nobody in it and out of a hotel dining-room in the same way. The family tacitly let her go first, ranging themselves behind this star.

People, not men only, but women young and old, and children, were seized with violent admiration for her wherever she went. The post brought anguished letters, offerings of all sorts; the boy next door had given her his treasures through the years: birds' eggs, the *Travels of Mungo Park*, his best catapult, boxes of chocolates, bottles of scent bought with his first earnings. If this boy had not been killed in the war, Lucy thought Vera might in time have married him. As it was, she was scornful of the rest.

'The fool,' she would say, throwing down a letter, leaving a soul's anguish exposed on the breakfast-table to any gaze.

'I thought . . . ' one would unwillingly catch sight of. 'I don't understand . . . You said . . . Why? . . . '

When the maid announced an admirer, Vera would say: 'Why did you let him in? Lucy, you'll have to go. Or Charlotte. I won't see him.'

Most men were reduced to humble adoration for Vera, but there are men who don't like to be reduced by love and can't bear to feel humble. Charlotte had her following among these and Geoffrey Leigh was one of them. Geoffrey liked to be the centre of a group, the life of a party. He began by trying to impress Vera, but when he found he couldn't, he tried to impress Charlotte and succeeded.

Charlotte was gentler than Vera, more amenable, blinder, warmer-hearted. Her hair was more golden, her eyes bluer, rounder. She was gay in those days, with a delighted childlike gaiety and far younger, in spite of her two years seniority, than Vera. One of her endearing qualities was that she was never in the least jealous of her beautiful sister.

It was the penalty she had to pay, Lucy supposed, for being the eldest, the one in authority, the one from whom permission had to be asked in the early days, the judge of clean hands and suitable hair-ribbons, but she often felt a wounding hostility in her sisters when they were growing up. They would stop talking when she came into a room, or glance at each other as if to say: 'Be careful.' Sometimes they told her lies, at the instigation, she knew, of Vera. 'It's nothing to do with *her*,' she could almost hear Vera tell Charlotte. They kept things from her and deceived her as if she were a parent. They made her weep into her pillow at night, because she loved them with all her heart. They were her responsibility, her anxiety and her happiness.

Sometimes, when there were no young men about and Harry and Aubrey were out of the house, the three sisters were happy together, happier than at any other time. There was complete confidence among them then. At these times, Vera would suddenly disclose things she had decided not to tell Lucy. They would clear up misunderstandings, make everything straight. Vera burst out into imitations and they laughed till they were weak. They put on the gramophone, kicked off their slippers and danced wildly about the rooms, whirling each other round when they met in the hall, their eyes alight, their hair flying, smiling, smiling all the time.

Lucy was not out of it then. There was a charm about Lucy, but she had to be confident before it could show itself. When all barriers were down, it worked on the other two. When they flung themselves into chairs, relaxed after dancing, she could hold them rapt, telling them about what she was reading.

In bed at night she read all she could lay her hands on about Napoleon, the Brontës, Joan of Arc, Mary Queen of Scots, Byron. She could take her sisters out of their girlish world and put them in another, of grandeur, solitude, genius. At these times when they told her what was in their hearts and she told them what was in hers, the sisters were completely happy together, the three of them drawn close in deep affection. If only they could have had more times like those, thought Lucy. But the girls were swept about on the tides of their reckless youth. They were swept away from her again by and by. They were always going off somewhere in those days after the war.

Lucy mostly went too, but when she went out with them and the boys she felt more like a chaperone than a contemporary. She was twenty-seven and looked older. She felt plain and out of things and must have looked both, she thought, remembering herself as she was then, mostly in a tweed coat and skirt, with a heavy hat made of the same material. A 'Storm-proof' hat it was called, though why she had worn a storm-proof hat to watch dancing she couldn't at this remote date think.

She used to have a good deal of trouble with her hair, which was dark brown, not fair like her sisters'. They were among the first to wear their hair in a 'bob' which suited them to perfection, but Lucy was too timid to cut hers. She thought it wouldn't be suitable. Years later she cut her hair and found it suited her in her way as well as it suited them.

But in those days she wore her hair in a bun, which was often coming down because she was usually driven to the last

minute in getting ready. While she bundled up her hair and pinned on her hat, the car would be in the drive, with Harry furiously sounding the horn and all the laughing faces turned up to her window.

One day, the day it was that Vera danced, Lucy ran down, snatching someone's gloves from the table in the hall, clambering into the car. She was hot and flustered with hurrying and when someone said: 'What an age you've been,' she said rather crossly: 'I've no time to come at all really.'

It was never safe to say things like that before Vera. She always pounced.

'Then why come?' she inquired.

Lucy turned her head to hide the tears of anger and resentment that stung her eyes. She was tired of it, she told herself, tired, tired. She didn't want to look after the house and them, but there was no one else so she had to. They took her and all she did for granted and when they were going to have fun, they didn't want her. Her heart burned all the way to Blackpool, whither they were bound that afternoon, with more friends of Harry's and Aubrey's coming behind in cars.

In those days everybody had to dance. Wherever you went to for the day you had to dance. If you went to London for two days only, you would spend both afternoons dancing. It was something that got into everybody. The young Fields were always giving dances in the attic. Long after he had gone to bed, poor Mr Field had to endure the sip-sip of feet over his head and the night-long sounds of a gramophone. In spite of the abundant refreshments provided by Lucy, the maids would come down in the morning to find that immense

meals of bacon and eggs had been cooked sometime before dawn. The maids frequently left, saying they couldn't stand the parties.

On this day when they reached Blackpool, someone suggested that they should go, for a lark, not to a *thé dansant* at a hotel, but to the Tower Ballroom. They went, and Lucy sat in the gloom under the balcony, watching the others dance. Vera and Charlotte with their partners skimmed out on to the floor. Lucy felt like a barn-door fowl watching two swans she had brought up take to the water.

When she first went out with the parties, nobody asked her to dance. The young men thought her much older than she was, they were shy of her and powerfully attracted by her sisters. Harry and Aubrey were generally too assiduous in picking up girls of their own to pay any attention to her, so there she sat, a wallflower.

Sometimes she was kept company by Brian Sargent, who was not a good dancer. He was too large to dance, a tall, solid, handsome young man who regarded the antics of the other young men with a solemn eye. His home was in the midland city of Trenton, but he made his aunt's house in Sefton his headquarters when he was in the north, as he frequently was, on the business of his father's very flourishing firm of accountants.

Brian liked poetry. At least, he usually had a book of verse in his pocket, though Lucy wasn't sure whether he really liked poetry, or whether he thought he ought to like it. Still, in such society, she was grateful to him for even seeming to like it. Lucy felt more at ease with Brian than with any of the other

young men. They might have talked, she felt, if Brian had been able to turn his eyes from Vera for a moment or two, which he never could. Brian did not want to talk about poetry or anything else with Lucy when he could watch Vera. So there he sat, mum, and never thought, any more than the others did, of asking Lucy to dance.

After two or three afternoons spent this way, Lucy put on a stout pair of brogue shoes to show that she came with no intention of dancing. When, remembering their manners or becoming aware that she was a girl too, the young men at last asked her to dance, she smiled stiffly, showed her shoes and said: 'Thank you, but I can't dance in these shoes.' She was sure the young men were relieved and resumed her fixed gaze at the dancers.

On this afternoon at the Tower, her heart swelled. She was angry with Vera, hurt, out of things. There was some strong pulsating excitement in the atmosphere which she felt, but could not share. It made her want to cry, sitting there on the plush sofa, watching other people dance. After all, she loved dancing too and she was not so old. Not so old, at twenty-seven, as all that.

The floor cleared after a waltz, and her sisters drifted back to where she sat under the balcony. In a few moments the orchestra struck up a tune nobody seemed to know. Nobody went out on to the floor, until suddenly Vera and Tony Carter skimmed out into the middle and began to dance. Everybody watched, fascinated. No other dancers appeared on the floor.

They had danced together a great deal, Lucy knew, and this must have been a dance they had practised. They were

perfect partners, but no one looked much at Tony. It was Vera who held all eyes. Lucy never forgot how she looked that day. 'The day Vera danced', they would say long afterwards. On that vast shining floor, Vera danced in a kind of ecstasy, the remote lovely look on her face, her black chiffon dress flowing over her limbs like smoke. When she parted in the dance from Tony Carter, smiling over her shoulder, one arm outstretched, her fingertips lingering to the last on his, and when she came to him again, it was like the parting and meeting of lovers. Even the boys were grave, looking at her, and Lucy, glancing once at Brian, saw that his eyes were full of tears.

When the music ceased and the dancers floated to a standstill, there was a silence. Then the orchestra itself led the applause. Tony and Vera hand in hand, sliding their feet over the floor, came back to the others. Vera sat down by Lucy, and Lucy gave her sister's hand a squeeze. Who could not forgive anyone so lovely? If she wished you to forgive her, you could not withstand her. Admiration warms the heart of the admirer as well as the admired. Lucy, glowing over Vera, cast off resentment and enjoyed the party as never before.

But it was after this afternoon that the general chaos seemed to increase.

For one thing, Vera announced that she was going to leave home and become a dancing partner in London; at the Grosvenor Galleries, or somewhere like that, she said. Tony Carter had told her she would have a marvellous time. He was often in London himself, and he would see that she did. Lucy was alarmed and horrified. She knew her father would never allow it, but she was afraid Vera would simply go.

Lucy exhausted herself in argument and persuasion. Every morning, as soon as she woke, she rushed into the girls' room to see if Vera was still there; she expected her to run away in the middle of every night.

For another thing, Geoffrey Leigh was now always in the house, disrupting everything. Geoffrey Leigh had come from London as agent for Bancroft's, the huge chemical combine. From the moment he walked into the bar of the *George*, a man from another, wider world, the young bloods of the town had rallied to him. He was lean, dark, sallow, with a quick, monkey face. Harry and Aubrey seized him and bore him home. He was after their own heart, even crazier, when he set out to be, than they were themselves. It was Geoffrey's power of keeping things up that won their admiration. After a night at the *George*, for instance, when they all climbed lamp-posts to hang over the cross-bars for fun for five minutes, Geoffrey hung there for hours. He could outhang anybody. He outhung their patience. They left him in the end, but it tickled them to wake up much later in their beds and think that old Geoff was probably still hanging there, doubled over the cross-bar. That sort of thing endeared Geoffrey to the boys, though Lucy could never see why. When she said so, the boys were disgusted. 'God, she's getting just like Aunt Phoebe,' they said.

Aunt Phoebe, needless to say, was on their father's side, a worthy, but boring woman. Lucy was told so often, when she showed disapproval of the boys or her sisters, that she was getting like Aunt Phoebe that she began to think it must be true.

The boys, though they could not impress Lucy by Geoffrey Leigh's exploits, were sure of an appreciative listener in Charlotte. She thought Geoffrey was wonderful. At first she said so, glowing over him, but when she found her sisters unsympathetic, she shut up like an oyster. She began to draw away from them and attach herself to him.

Geoffrey Leigh didn't like his rooms. He much preferred the Fields' house, where there was comfort, good food, lively company and plenty of people to play practical jokes on. He was either in such tearing high spirits that everyone, except Charlotte and the boys, found him exhausting, or else he was silent and moody. It soon became apparent that Charlotte reacted to Geoffrey's moods. Her sisters were amazed to see her hang on his looks as she did. She blushed, smiled, looked anxious or bewildered according to Geoffrey's behaviour.

'That's not the way to treat him,' said Vera with scorn to Lucy. 'If she shows him she likes him, he'll take it out on her. He's that sort of man. She's a fool if she has anything to do with him, Lucy.'

'That's all very well,' said Lucy anxiously. 'But how can we stop her?'

There was no answer to that.

Day after day Geoffrey came to the house and night after night, when the rest had gone to bed, the boys sat up with Geoffrey and a bottle of whisky. Lucy, an anxious housewife, got into the habit of keeping awake until the small hours, when Geoffrey, with a loud bang of the door, departed and her brothers came, stumbling, upstairs to bed. Then, chilly, tired and resentful, she went down to see that all was safe. Once a

cigarette had burnt a hole in the carpet, another time a glass of whisky had been upset over a polished table, another the lights had been left on. It was better to go down, Lucy found.

Then one night, coming back upstairs, she found her father on the landing. She had not seen him in the middle of the night since she was a child, and she was shocked to see how old he looked, with his long thin neck and long thin ankles.

'This has gone on long enough, Lucy,' he said sternly – strange how they all spoke to her as if she were responsible for everything. 'They'll have to go,' he said.

'Who?' said Lucy, startled.

'Your brothers,' he said. 'I can't do anything with them. They must go.'

'But where?' faltered Lucy.

'They can choose,' said her father, turning back to his room. 'But they're going.'

They took his decision with calm.

'We might as well go,' they said. 'There's nothing here.'

And with a large lump sum each and no decrease of spirits they went to Canada.

Though she loved them and wept, with her sisters, to see them go, Lucy certainly found things easier in the house. It was as though a strong wind that had been blowing for a long time had suddenly dropped. The calm felt, for a time, unnatural.

But anxiety soon began to beset Lucy again. It was not Vera who worried her this time. Vera had abandoned her project of going to London to dance; she was now practising

hard at her music. Vera would, at times, sternly withdraw to live laborious days, and this was one of those times. It was Charlotte Lucy worried about now.

The boys had gone but Geoffrey Leigh still came to the house, and it was plain that Charlotte was more in love with him every day.

'What on earth does she see in him?' Vera kept asking.

Lucy couldn't tell her. Uncomprehending and powerless, the sisters looked on while Charlotte moved away from them. When she wasn't with Geoffrey, Charlotte liked to be alone, and if they came upon her sitting with a rapt expression, she would get up and go away, to dream further.

One day after lunch, when the sisters were standing about as they usually stood after meals before dispersing each to her own activities, Geoffrey came in on them unannounced through the garden window. He was going, he told them. Leaving Sefton. He had been transferred to a much larger area. Three counties. No more touting for orders, he said exultantly. In the future he would supervise agents and direct all business without moving from his desk. His desk could be, and very probably would be, in his own house.

'I'm tired of rooms,' he said. 'I shall have a house of my own.'

It was a good appointment, it seemed, for so young a man. His firm, though Lucy and Vera could not imagine why, evidently thought well of him. Since he would go now, they thought, and they need never see him again, Lucy and Vera were able to be quite warm in their congratulations. But Charlotte went red, went white and stammered over hers.

Her sisters saw that she had suffered a shock and was trying to rally from it.

Lucy and Vera waited for Geoffrey to go, but he was very pleased with himself and in no hurry. He rose and fell on his toes on the hearthrug, jingling money in his pockets and smiling deeply.

'I wish Harry and Aubrey were here,' he said. 'By George, wouldn't we celebrate!'

His eyes gleamed to think what they would have done. Her sisters observed him coldly, but Charlotte looked up at him with all her love in her eyes.

He went at last. He left her to her anguish. For days he didn't come at all. The other two were both indignant and relieved, but they had to see Charlotte going about with a white face and reddened eyes without daring to say anything.

'I hope I never fall in love, that's all,' said Vera.

'I wish I could do something for her,' said Lucy. So often that Vera grew tired and said irritably: 'You know you can't, so do be quiet.'

Then Geoffrey came back, through the window as suddenly as before, giving Charlotte no time to get away. She had to stand where she was, with the evidence of what she had suffered plain in her face. She stood by the mantelpiece and, after a shamed smile in his direction, turned her head away, forgetting that she was reflected in the mirror. They were all reflected in the gilt mirror that stood behind the old white marble chimney-piece arching at an immense height to the ceiling. They were all there, grouped between the lustres that stood on each side, Charlotte with her reddened lids lowered,

Vera with her lovely profile turned coldly on Geoffrey, Lucy with her anxious expression, and far back, shadowy in the moted depths of the old glass, Geoffrey, looking at himself, smiling as if he had a joke on. He had.

Her sisters had drawn closer to Charlotte when he came in, interposing themselves between her and the man they disliked, but at a word from him she left them and followed him into the morning-room. There, it turned out that this was one of his very best practical jokes. He had meant to propose to Charlotte all the time, it appeared, but he thought it would be fun to let her think he wasn't going to. How he laughed when he told her and how she laughed, too, crying again and wiping her red eyes.

It had all been a joke, she told her sisters, laughing and crying again when he had gone. And hadn't it come off? she sobbed. She'd taken it for deadly earnest. Wasn't it just like him? she asked.

'Yes,' said Vera with sudden vehemence through her teeth. 'Yes, it's just like him. No one but Geoffrey Leigh would do a thing like that. And are you so infatuated you can't see it? Can't you see what you're in for if you're such a fool as to marry him? If you'd any sense, Charlotte, you'd run to the end of the earth to get away from him.'

'Stop!'

Vera, startled, stopped. Charlotte put her handkerchief into her waistbelt with an air of having finished with it, of having finished with showing her feelings, happy or otherwise, to her sisters. Her tear-streaked face set, she leaned forward from her chair towards them.

'If either of you,' she said, 'ever says another word about Geoffrey to me, you'll never see me again after I've left home. I warn you. When I marry him, I'll go away from here and I'll never even write. So keep your opinions to yourselves. What difference can they make to me? I love him.'

Before such a blaze, they shrank. She silenced them. They never dared to say again what they thought of him.

Not even at the wedding. Though, of course, it would have been too late then.

Charlotte's wedding was an occasion none of the family could remember without shame. Of all the disgraceful affairs . . . began Lucy's thoughts every time it occurred to them. The wedding took place in June and a marquee was put up on the lawn, which made it worse, thought Lucy afterwards, because everything was so public. People passing in the road climbed the garden wall to see what the noise was about. Geoffrey and his friends looked upon the day as an occasion for fooling on a vast scale. Geoffrey had played many practical jokes on his friends and now they took their revenge, or tried to. Geoffrey's ingenuity in turning their own tricks upon them was endless. The bride, pale in her pale tulle, satin and orange blossoms, was of no account, was almost ignored in the riot. She had to keep stepping aside to get out of the way.

At first, at the breakfast, the guests were amused, but they grew tired. They tried to go on laughing, but their laughter sounded hollow and finally died away. Poor Mr Field attempted to draw off the older guests to another part of the garden so that they should not witness what seemed to him entirely disgraceful horseplay. His side of the family, the

aunts, uncles and cousins, stood in dark disapproval, wondering that Joseph had been able to manage no better than this.

Mr Field kept going in search of Jack.

'Can't you stop this, Jack? It's shameful.'

'What can I do?' asked Jack. 'They're all tight.'

'For sheer bad taste,' said Vera in cold scorn, walking about with Brian Sargent, 'I've never seen anything like it.'

At last it was time for Charlotte to change into her going-away dress. Her sisters followed her upstairs, their arms full of her tulle and her train. She was trembling when they took off her wedding-gown. She stood in her petticoat, clasping her thin arms over her breast as if she were cold, waiting for them to bring her going-away dress. She smiled all the time in a fixed way that wrung her sisters' hearts. But they daren't say anything. They were all very quiet, while Geoffrey and his best man bounded about hilariously in the next room.

Lucy's fingers shook as she fastened Charlotte's dress at the back, and Vera's lips were set as she busied herself with Charlotte's case.

'Your new powder-puffs are in the pocket – you won't forget?'

'Now my shoes,' said Charlotte, bending to put them on.

'I'm ready now,' she said. But she paused at the door before she opened it and went to face the people again.

She was down first, but in a moment Geoffrey came skimming down the banisters behind her. His appearance was a signal for a concerted attack from his determined friends. They seized him, carried him spread-eagled round the lawn,

dumped him on the grass and proceeded to take off his shoes and – appallingly – his socks. At the sight of the bridegroom's pale feet kicking in mid-air a shudder ran over the assembled guests. Two ultra-sensitive ladies clasped each other convulsively. Charlotte, after standing uncertainly, looking at the struggling group on the lawn, got into the car, where she was mercifully almost hidden from view. Suddenly Geoffrey freed himself and made a dash for the car, leaving his shoes and socks with his friends. He scrambled into the car, banged the door and started the engine.

'Here, you can't go without your socks and shoes, you fool!' shouted his friends, holding them aloft.

'Can't I?' shouted Geoffrey, and shot off down the drive. The guests cheered feebly and waved their hands, but Charlotte did not look round.

'And that's the beginning,' said Vera grimly.

CHAPTER TWO

I

It was that same evening when everyone had left, the marquee gone slack, mopping and mowing like a tethered elephant in the dusk and the sisters sitting together in silence, that Vera said in a dreamy voice: 'I think I shall get engaged to Brian.'

'Vera!' Lucy sat up, flushing warmly with surprise and pleasure. 'Has he asked you?'

'Many a time,' said Vera coolly. 'But I think I'll say yes now.'

'Oh, darling, I'm glad,' said Lucy, rushing over to kiss her. Vera received the kisses. Lucy was the one who glowed.

'I like Brian,' went on Lucy, sitting on the arm of Vera's chair. 'He's so sound, such a contrast to Geoffrey, and he adores you, Vera.'

'Yes,' said Vera calmly. 'I think he's all right,' she said. 'I think I'll be all right with him.'

'Oh, I'm sure you will, darling,' said Lucy, with tears in her eyes. 'This is a terrific relief to me, after today. I do so want one of you to be safe,' said poor Lucy.

'I don't think anything could be safer than Brian,' said Vera.

Lucy was so relieved about this engagement that she did not realise until she had gone to bed and was alone to think, that she would now be left in the house without her sisters. Their upbringing had seemed so long and difficult, but it was over so soon. They had been a trouble and an anxiety to her, but a deep pleasure too. She was like one who has a piece of work on which she has been long engaged taken suddenly out of her hands – a work she was obliged to leave unfinished and which had turned out quite differently from what she had intended. She dreaded being left alone in the house with only Jack and her father. She felt there was no purpose in her life now. Her sisters had been her purpose. They had been like her children once, and later her dear companions. Their interests had been hers; she wondered if she had any interests outside theirs now. She had never had time to make any; they had kept her so busy. In the night, she wept, looking into a future that seemed blank without them.

She didn't know that William Moore, hitherto unseen, was already coming towards her through time. Within a month she met him at a tennis-party, the oddest man, she thought, she had ever come across. Odd, but strangely attractive; to her, at any rate. She smiled to see him sit in the unceasing flow of tennis-party talk that afternoon as indifferent as a boulder in a stream. But it was a good-humoured indifference; he smiled to himself, taking pleasure in the sunshine and his own thoughts and feeling no need whatever of communication with other people. From time to time he got up and played tennis with great vigour and enjoyment. He played twice with

Lucy and she felt she had made no more impression on this unimpressionable man than any other young woman. But she was wrong.

In the spring, soon after Vera married Brian Sargent and went away to Trenton, Lucy married her William, who had already been transferred to the midlands. The family melted from the old house like snow from the roof, leaving Jack in possession, for Joseph Field died that same year. The three sisters were dispersed, Lucy to her village, Charlotte to her northern, Vera to her midland city.

After her marriage, Lucy went through a strange time of repair. She was always falling asleep – in the afternoons, in the evenings.

'I'm so sorry, William,' she would say apologetically. 'I'm afraid I've been to sleep again.'

He only smiled and turned a page of his book. After her father's talks, the companionable silence of William was very soothing to Lucy. Little by little she repaired herself. She became much better-looking than she had been since early girlhood. William had married a tired young woman who had 'gone off early', so people said; but he soon found himself with a pretty wife. So pretty that her sisters, after not seeing her for some time, exclaimed at the improvement in her looks, at the change in her altogether. There was a serenity about Lucy now that, remembering her rather fussy anxiety in the old days, surprised them.

'You couldn't tell them, I suppose, that it is getting away from them that has done it,' remarked William caustically.

He was caustic about Lucy's family. He resented, in retrospect, the responsibility thrust upon her at so early an age.

'A housekeeper would have done just as well,' he said.

'Oh, no,' protested Lucy, shocked. 'The girls couldn't have been left to a housekeeper.'

'Were you able to do any more for them than a house-keeper could have done?' he asked.

William didn't mince truth; he offered it in ungarnished lumps. You could digest it as best you could or refuse it.

'Oh, William,' pleaded Lucy. 'I think I did more for them than a housekeeper. I hope so,' she said.

'Charlotte married Leigh in spite of you, didn't she?' asked William.

'Yes, but Vera's all right,' defended Lucy.

William said nothing.

'Vera's all right, William,' repeated Lucy.

'It depends on what you mean by all right,' said William cryptically.

'Brian's so good,' said Lucy.

William said nothing, and Lucy let the conversation drop since there was no use going on with it. William would not reassure her, she knew. At times there was something very un-cosy about being forced to face facts by William.

On her marriage, Lucy had come into harbour in more senses than one. She left the bustle of the full house at Sefton for a quiet house of her own where there was only William to look after; she left the crowded manufacturing town for the village of Underwood; she left the dark, rolling hills, the cold

rain of the north for the warmth, the comfortable, comforting country of the south midlands. Moreover, that she should live in the house and the exact situation she did live in, seemed everlastingly too good to be true to Lucy.

The house was a little old stone house with the date '1612' over the door and Colley Weston slates on the roof. All the garden was behind, with an orchard at the side where Lucy and William kept bees and hens. There was no more garden before the house than two strips of lawn each side of the cobbled path, but it was all that was needed, because the house was perfectly set, or so Lucy considered, on a small green away from the rest of the village, with the church to the left and, immediately in front, the gates, but not the main gates, of the big House. Beyond the gates lay the Park, where the small spotted deer fed, and far within stood the House, in remote classic beauty, no sign of life about its dreaming courts and terraces. Lucy, who was allowed the freedom of the Park in common with the rest of the village, took a sad pleasure in the House. It was so lovely and so unused, and what, she wondered, would happen to it? The Family came perhaps twice a year, sometimes not even that. They found it cheaper, it was said, to live in their London house. The Park and the House within it, the long deserted avenues, the little deer, had a lost, haunting, unreal beauty; the whole scene was like a painted drop-cloth which must soon roll up and vanish, to reveal the grim play of life going on behind it. After wandering in the Park, Lucy would turn home, thankful to have a house so small that it could be saved, surely, from the changes that threatened.

Lucy and William had no children. Life seemed determined, Lucy sometimes thought, to keep her an onlooker. She had looked on at the pleasures of youth without sharing them. She looked on at maternity through her sisters.

Charlotte kept the impending arrival of her first baby a secret. She said nothing until almost the last moment. 'By the way,' she wrote to Lucy, 'I'm going to have a baby next month.' Lucy, all tenderness and anxiety, sure that Charlotte would need her, took the first train to Denborough, where she found Charlotte very nervous, not of her own ordeal, but of its effect on Geoffrey. 'I do hope it doesn't upset Geoffrey,' she kept saying. Lucy stared at her in amazement. 'Geoffrey hates illness,' Charlotte explained to Lucy's unspoken comment.

'Even other people's?' Lucy could not help saying caustically.

'Oh, yes,' said Charlotte seriously. She had been sick and wretched the whole time, she told Lucy. Many a time she hadn't been able to go out with Geoffrey when he wanted her to, she said, gazing at Lucy as if that were a dreadful thing.

Lucy went home to worry silently, but when she went again after the birth of the child, a girl, she found Charlotte radiant. Geoffrey liked the baby, so everything was all right.

Charlotte had three children by the time Vera telephoned the news of her first child. 'I'm afraid I'm going to have a baby,' she called out from Trenton to Underwood. 'Isn't it a nuisance? We were going to Cannes. I'd got all my clothes.'

'Are you all right, though, darling?' asked Lucy anxiously. 'Shall I come?'

'Well, I'm all right so far,' said Vera. 'But I suppose I shall

look such a sight soon I shan't want to see anybody. You can come then, darling. Of course, Brian's delighted. I tell him he wouldn't be so delighted if he were having it.'

When Lucy went to Trenton later, Vera did nothing but sigh and wish it were over. Lucy kept telling her how happy she would be when the baby was born. 'I wish I could believe you,' said Vera. 'People keep asking me if I'm not excited. But I'm not. I know I ought to be, but I'm not.' She looked angrily at Lucy as if she were being done out of something she had a right to expect.

But again when Lucy went after the birth of the baby, a girl, christened Sarah, she found Vera, in her turn, radiant. Not about the baby, though the baby amused her, but at being restored to health and beauty. She held court all day, sitting up in bed in the loveliest negligées, the room massed with flowers. The only bore, she told Lucy, was that Brian's mother and sister Gertrude came every day. 'I used to be able to keep them down to once a week, but now they're here every single day. Of course, it's baby they come to see, not me, so I'm going to make Nurse take her into the nursery when they come and they can dote there. Old Mrs Sargent keeps telling us what to do. She keeps telling us what she did when Gertrude was a baby. Forty years ago!'

Maternity, at any rate to her sisters, hardly seemed the heart-stirring experience Lucy had expected it to be. She maintained, however, a secret conviction that to her it would have been.

She had not hitherto had much chance to be a successful aunt. She saw little of her sisters' children. Geoffrey did not

encourage his sisters-in-law's visits. Vera's children, except for periodic appearances in the drawing-room, were always with their nurses. Lucy was glad Charlotte was bringing her youngest child with her this time; it was nearly two years since Lucy had seen her.

Lucy sometimes tried to find out if William minded, too, that they had no children, but she could not. He was never one to bemoan or regret.

'We're very well as we are,' he would say.

It was true. Lucy was so happy that she sometimes felt she ought not to be.

'I feel I live a selfish life. I feel guilty,' she said sometimes.

'That's because you did as other people liked for so long that now you can do as you like you feel you oughtn't to. You must learn to like to do as you like, my child, and don't complain of it, either. In these days you never know how long you'll be permitted to live a quiet life, so you'd better make the most of it.'

Sitting opposite each other at the breakfast-table, Lucy had travelled backwards years in time, and William had progressed through porridge to bacon and was now at the marmalade stage. He liked marmalade and had absently nearly emptied the dish, leaving almost none for her. He was not at all like the conventional good husband, full of small attentions. He left her to look after herself and didn't see why she shouldn't. Sometimes, as now, she felt he needed reproof.

'William,' she said, and had to wait until he raised his head from the paper. 'May I have a *little* marmalade?' She looked with meaning at the denuded dish.

William looked too and grinned.

'As little as you please,' he said and, passing it over, returned to the paper.

Lucy laughed and scraped out what was left. She could have rung for more if she had wanted it. He knew that. His attitude was sensible, but her sisters would have looked at him with disapproval.

She must break it to him about the girls. It was not that he didn't like them, she thought, but that he didn't like visitors. He liked Lucy and the house to himself. He liked his own chair by the sitting-room fire, and he liked to read in peace with Lucy opposite in the evenings. When her sisters were there, he couldn't. They chattered. He had to take his book into the other room where the chairs weren't so comfortable and sit there without Lucy. The floods of talk and laughter that streamed out of the sitting-room distracted him. How they laughed! He felt slightly piqued that Lucy should be able to laugh like that with her sisters and without him. He was always hurrying to leave the sisters to themselves, as if to imply that he knew that was what they wanted. They wanted him out of the way, he implied, and he meant them to see that he hastened to comply with their wishes. He overdid it, in Lucy's opinion, and it made her cross. The girls never saw William as he really was, she lamented. Not that he saw them as they were, either. It was a pity, Lucy felt, that she could never really bring together the three people she loved most.

'Vera's coming too when Charlotte comes,' she said suddenly.

'Oh,' said William. He had begun to frown, but quickly made his face a blank. He pushed his paper and his chair aside.

'So the house will be pretty full,' he said, reaching for his shoes. 'Since Charlotte is bringing what's-her-name.'

'You mean Judith?' said Lucy, again with reproof. William should really attempt to remember the names of her sisters' children. It was not as if they were innumerable.

'I suppose so,' said William. 'Well, perhaps she'll be better than the other one.'

'You mean Margaret? Don't you like Margaret?'

'Oh, she's not like a child. I like a child to have some spirit.'

'It might be difficult to have spirit, living with Geoffrey,' said Lucy.

'You're probably right,' said William. 'But I must go. Goodbye.' He gave her a hasty, but warm kiss, reached under the table to pat Cora, the Golden Labrador bitch, who always lay at Lucy's feet no matter where she put them, and made for the door. 'I shan't be home for lunch,' he threw out.

'Oh, William,' protested Lucy. 'You didn't tell me.'

'I forgot,' said William, and was gone. By the time she had followed him out with Cora, he was in the car and driving away with a wave of the hand.

Lucy stood in the sunshine, smiling after him. A man of one occupation at a time, William. When he was reading, he read; when he was eating marmalade, he ate it; when he was going, he went.

Cora thrust her head under Lucy's hand.

'All right,' said Lucy. 'Come along.'

In her slippers she set briskly off to walk Cora round the great tree on the green, to go as far as the church gates, the park gates and a little way down the lane. There was no gate to the front garden; Cora could have gone for a walk at any time. But though the world was open to her, she could not enjoy any of it without her people. When she wanted to remind them that a walk was due, she took up her position on the green before the house, lying with her nose on her paws, her amber eyes on the door. Occasionally, during what was sometimes a long wait, she would sigh heavily, occasionally her tail would thump the grass, but she never took her eyes from the door. When at last someone came out, she would rush in search of a stick, scrabble wildly in the grass under the trees, whining with excitement and impatience, find one, toss it into the air, drop it, pretend not to be able to pick it up, pick it up, bring it to show, throw it aside and set off in earnest for the walk.

But after breakfast she knew there was no time for this demonstration. She stalked with dignity on the customary round.

The morning was golden, and still with the autumn stillness. Through the gates of the park the trees dreamed and the open spaces were dotted with the little deer. 'They give a Noah's Ark effect,' thought Lucy.

The sun was warm on her head, the stone coping of the low wall before the house was warm under her hand. She would have liked to stay out and bask in the blessed warmth

and light which every day now would little by little withdraw. But she must go in and break it to Janet that Vera was coming now as well as Charlotte. Another one to break it to, another who didn't like visitors.

In the kitchen, Janet was bent over the sink washing up the breakfast things. Her back view, broad expanse of blue print crossed with white apron strings, her stout legs and the small tight knot of hair looked even more uncompromising than usual, and Lucy fiddled about in the kitchen waiting her opportunity. On the subject of visitors Janet had to be approached with care.

Janet was forty, stout, downright, a one-man dog, so to speak, devoted and faithful to Lucy and William, but treating outsiders with hostility, especially if they approached the house. Janet was good, but difficult and from time to time, exasperated beyond bearing, Lucy gave Janet notice. From time to time, Janet gave notice on her own account.

'Now Janet really is going this time,' Lucy would announce to William.

William was unmoved, which annoyed Lucy. He said nothing. Sometimes he even smiled.

'A month from today she's going,' repeated Lucy. 'I can't stand her any longer. It's final this time.'

Janet always declared herself quite ready to go, wanted nothing better, in fact, had been thinking for a long time of making a change. But the fixed day, the month-end, always passed either unnoticed by mistress and maid, or, if noticed, without comment. Janet remained.

Lucy mostly 'managed' Janet. One of her ways of managing

was to let her talk. She felt that Janet had no one to talk to through the day but her. She must have some need to talk about her own life, about someone or something belonging to herself, instead of always of what concerned the house and its master and mistress, so, as Lucy had listened to her father, she listened, while she was cooking or working in the house, to Janet. And just as talk restored her father, so talk restored Janet. Talking about themselves restores most people. It was only exceptional people like William, thought Lucy, who had no need to talk about themselves.

Janet's talk was mostly reminiscent; a sad sign, thought the too-compassionate Lucy. As if nothing were going on now, being added to Janet's life *now*.

'There was a gentleman, a churchwarden in our church,' Janet would relate, having dwelt on it, apparently, for years, 'his daughter went farming. Nobody could ever understand why a young lady brought up delicate like that went milking the cows and cleaning out the shippons.'

Life, it seemed, had never solved for Janet the strange case of the churchwarden's daughter, for she referred to it again and again.

She talked about her cousins. Her relations seemed to be all cousins, nothing nearer. There were a great many of them, widely scattered, and Janet never called them by name, only 'me cousin'. So that, after five years' constant information, Lucy still could not sort them out. She hardly ever dared to inquire which cousin Janet was speaking of for fear of being entirely felled by Janet's genealogical tree, but if she did happen to say: 'Is that the cousin who lives in Yorkshire?' it

was sure to be wrong. 'Oh, dear me, no,' Janet would exclaim with surprise that Lucy should know so little. 'I'm talking about me cousin in Manchester.'

Janet disapproved of all visitors, even of the most casual caller. 'Mrs So-and-so's here,' she would announce to Lucy in the garden. 'I'm sure I don't know what for.'

So, knowing her, Lucy, who wished everything to be smooth for her sisters' visit, hesitated before making her announcement. Finally, however, she brought it out:

'I've heard this morning that Mrs Sargent is coming too, when Mrs Leigh comes, Janet.'

Janet half-turned, not looking at her mistress but in her direction, as if she had a stiff neck.

'So that'll mean three extra?' she said.

'It will.'

Janet gave one sniff, but it expressed all her displeasure. She returned to the pots. That Mrs Sargent made a lot of work. Came from a house where she was waited on from morning till night and expected the same where there was only one pair of hands. Never picked a thing up after herself. Everything thrown about. Powder all over the dressing-table. Last time, the wood was white for weeks after she'd gone.

'So we must get the little room ready for Mrs Sargent,' said Lucy.

'I suppose you'll want the bed airing?' said Janet, as if this piece of unreasonableness was now to be expected.

'Certainly.'

'It can't be damp,' said Janet.

'It must be aired,' said Lucy, and went out of the kitchen.
Finishing the pots, Janet threw down the dish-cloth. 'Now
I'll go and enjoy myself with that bed,' she said caustically.

II

William got out the car and drove Lucy to the station in the
town to meet Charlotte, who was to arrive first. Lucy was
excited; she kept smiling. William was not excited, but he tried
not to look too patently put out. This was his free half-day and
he might have been doing some very necessary work in the
garden, but he had to make this trip for Charlotte and the
child, and little more than an hour after they had arrived at
Underwood, he had to make another trip for Vera. Starting
with his half-day, which she had taken from him and given to
the girls, Lucy would give them everything from now on until
they went. That was what she had always done and she would
go on doing it, he supposed, to the end. But did they appre-
ciate it? William asked himself. Not they.

He swung the car round the semi-circular space before the
little station and drew up where he could; there were several
cars and lorries before the entrance. Lucy, without a word,
her cheeks pink, her smile deeper now, got out of the car and
disappeared through the booking-hall.

William sat on, gradually losing himself in the limbo
peculiar to those who wait in cars for others. His hands were
slack on the wheel, his eyebrows clomb his corrugated brow.
He stared absently up the hill where the little town clustered,
embosomed in trees, from which rose the magnificent steeple

of the Parish Church. By and by he turned his head and stared absently at a group that had appeared before the station, two women, one with a pale, fair little girl by the hand. The child yawned as if she had come on a long journey. When one of the women beckoned urgently, William came to himself and got hurriedly out of the car. He had failed, for the moment, to recognise his own wife.

'I thought you'd gone to sleep,' said Lucy.

That was another thing about these visits, he thought; Lucy was often slightly cross with him.

'Well, Charlotte,' he said, giving Charlotte a peck on the cheek. He bent and pecked the child's cheek, too.

'Say "how-do-you-do" to Uncle William,' prompted Charlotte.

'How d'you do?' said the child obediently, without a smile, raising her blue eyes.

Charlotte seemed paler and thinner than she used to be, thought William, holding the car door open for her. The sisters got in at the back. Judith was bidden to get in front beside her uncle.

William drove away. The sisters talked, but he could tell that the ice wasn't broken yet. This ice always seemed a strange thing to him; Charlotte and Vera brought it with them. To Lucy, it was the reappearance of the old hostility, the hostility of the two little girls who didn't want the elder even to *know* what they had been doing. The truth was that Charlotte and Vera were changing all the time, as we all change. Life was having its effect on them, but Lucy, ignorant, or nearly so, of their lives, was puzzled by the results. She had

to guess at everything. Some time had always to pass before the sisters really came together again.

'And how is Geoffrey?' Lucy was asking politely.

'Oh, very well,' said Charlotte, without enlarging.

'And Margaret? and Stephen?'

Their voices were merged. 'Couldn't very well leave Judith . . . . Oh, why should you? We love to have her. . . . She rather gets on Geoffrey's nerves . . . you see, with always being in the house . . . '

William drove in silence. They were out of the town now and Judith craned her chin and looked about her. She wore a minute pair of wash-leather gloves on her hands, which were clasped in her lap. William was tickled by the size of these gloves and smiled to himself.

'I like sitting in front,' Judith vouchsafed suddenly.

'Do you?' said William.

'You can see things,' she said.

'Can't you see things at the back?'

'Oh, no,' she said gravely. 'You can't see anything but the ones in front. Stephen and me only see the back of Mummy and Daddy, or the back of Daddy and Margaret. 'Course Stephen's bigger than me. He's getting to see the tops of things now.'

'But you take it in turns to go in the front, don't you?' said William.

'Oh, no,' she shook her head. 'Stephen and me don't go in front with Daddy. Margaret does.'

'Really,' said William, maliciously interested in this sidelight on Geoffrey as a father.

'Here we are,' said William, drawing up before the house. Judith stared out in astonishment.

'Is this where Auntie Lucy lives?'

'Get out, darling, get out,' urged her mother.

Judith obeyed.

'Have I been here before?' she asked, her face turned up to them in enquiry.

They were too busy getting out the bags and cases to answer, so she stood looking about in deep pleasure at the house, the gates, the church, the trees. She took a few steps forward to stand on the green and look at that.

'Is this *everybody's* grass what I'm standing on?'

Nobody answered, but she hardly expected it. Her life was full of unanswered questions.

'Come along, Judith,' said Lucy, smiling at her.

'Straight upstairs, Judith,' said her mother. 'You'll have plenty of time to stare at everything later. She always stares at things so,' she explained to Lucy. 'You can't get her along. It does annoy Geoffrey.'

'What little flat stairs,' said Judith with great interest. 'It wouldn't matter if you fell down these, would it? It wouldn't hurt, would it?'

'This way,' said Lucy leading the way into the bedroom they were to share. 'Which bed are you going to have, Judith? This one by the window?'

'Am I going to sleep in here with Mummy?'

'Yes.'

Judith stood stock-still. She went pink with pleasure and relief. Then she began to rush about the room, staking out her claim.

'Can I put my nightdress under the pillow? Can I put Angela on the bed to show it's mine? Could you get Angela out, Mummy? I'm sure she feels very stuffy in the case. Could you get her out, Mummy, please?'

'Do give me a minute, darling,' pleaded Charlotte, putting her hand to her head as if it ached.

'Can I get Angela? Where is she?' asked Lucy.

'In the blue case, if you wouldn't mind . . . '

Lucy extricated Angela, a faded beauty with a fuzz of fair hair, crushed pink ballet skirts and flaccid legs. Judith received her eagerly and pressed her into the pillow, which slowly swelled up again and rejected her. Judith, who was in a hurry, pressed her back and rushed to the window before she could come up again.

'Where do those gates go to? Oh, look at the little things under the trees, the little animals with spots on them! Oh, look, Mummy, look, look!'

'Darling, not so much noise. She gets so shrill,' said Charlotte. 'It does annoy Geoffrey.'

'It doesn't matter how much noise she makes here, you know,' said Lucy in a low voice in case she should seem to interfere in maternal discipline. 'We like it. It's a change for us.'

'Yes, but I can't stand much of it,' said Charlotte wearily.

'You look very tired, darling,' said Lucy.

'I am rather,' admitted Charlotte.

'You must have a good rest. I'll take Judith off your hands as much as possible. I shall love it.'

Charlotte smiled faintly at this enthusiasm. Looking after children always seemed fun to those who had never done it.

'Come along, Judith,' she said, taking up a towel. 'Bathroom, please.'

'I know what they are,' said Judith, talking to herself and turning reluctantly from the window. 'They're harts. Like in the fairy-tale. They're harts.'

A look of wonder and delight came into her face and Lucy, seeing it, remembered her own childhood. To find that something, like the little deer for instance, that you had read about, or, in Judith's case, been read to about, really existed, went about the earth and could be seen; was to make a wonderful discovery. Lucy's hand lingered fondly on Judith's head as she piloted her guests to the bathroom.

'Oh, let me smell,' said Judith, immediately reaching over the basin for the soap. 'Oooh, lovely.' She held the new tablet in her two hands enjoying the smooth hardness and the shape of it, absorbed.

'When you've finished,' said her mother, making an effort to speak lightly, 'we'll get on with our washing.'

Judith looked enquiringly into her mother's face and gave up the soap. Lucy hurried down to see that tea was on the table; she was sure Charlotte needed a cup of tea.

Judith came skipping down the little flat stairs, her face washed, her hair shining. She pulled out the chair set for her at the table, climbed on to it, sat, looked thoughtful and then announced, 'This chair's cold. And too,' she nodded at them, 'it pricks.'

'Oh, it's these old horsehair seats,' said Lucy self-reproachfully, and William got a cushion.

Lucy noticed how carefully he lifted the child on to it. She

noticed how he in his turn passed his hand over Judith's floss-silk hair before he sat down again. 'He minds, after all,' she thought with a pang.

But pleasure in Judith herself soon dispelled all pangs. It was strange and touching to see a look of both her sisters repeated in this child's face, though only fleetingly, because Judith was distinctly herself. She had a firm little chin of her own, deliciously squared at the base, and her eyes were different, not so shadowed as Vera's, wider than Charlotte's. Her eyes were grey and full of light. She was very fair, with a singularly pure childish fairness and with her shoulder-long hair turning under at the ends, her puff sleeves, white socks and ankle-strap slippers she had an Alice-in-Wonderland air that delighted Lucy, who could, in fact, hardly keep her eyes off her.

Judith ate biscuits made, she had been told, especially for her and ornamented with cherries. They were very good, she thought, and ate several. As she ate, she looked about her, taking everything in: the latticed windows open on the orchard where apples, turning red, hung among the leaves; the deep sills on which it would have been nice to climb, she thought, though Auntie Lucy, like Daddy, was probably very particular about the paint. She took another bite of biscuit and a look under the table at Cora, who was a darling dog, she thought. She smiled as if everything pleased her, and looking at her Uncle William, was moved to tell him something else that pleased her too. 'I'm going to sleep in Mummy's room,' she said, smiling shyly behind her biscuit.

'It's time we were going to meet Vera,' said Lucy soon.

'Charlotte, don't come. Let me take Judith and you rest until we come back.'

But Charlotte wouldn't hear of it and they all set off, since it was unthinkable that Judith should be left with the curmudgeonly Janet. They drove back to the station; Charlotte and Lucy, with Judith by the hand, disappeared through the booking-hall and William returned to his limbo as before.

'Aren't you excited?' said Charlotte, coming suddenly to life on the platform. Her face wore the look of gay expectancy it had worn when she was a girl. 'It's nearly two years since I saw Vera,' she said.

'It's nearly as long since I saw her,' said Lucy.

They stood looking down the line, Judith threading her way between them, in and out, in and out, playing some game of her own. The train appeared round the bend.

'Now,' said Lucy, her eyes shining. She secured Judith by the hand, remembering how Aunt Phoebe always used to do the same to her, saying that the train drew you in.

The train, like some powerful, kindly monster, lending itself to the activities of little human beings, drew up with its great chest towering above the platform. Its sides burst open, and people dragging bags and parcels got out, struggled away from the compartments, bumping into porters, into other people going in contrary directions. Charlotte and Lucy were drawn into the general confusion. They couldn't see Vera anywhere. They craned this way and that, trying to look over heads, round bulky bodies. 'D'you see her? Is that . . . ? No. Where can she be? I do hope she's come . . . '

Judith, low down, tacked like a little tender attached to her

aunt. People kept knocking her hat off. At last she put one hand on the top of it and followed blindly with her head down.

Far down the train, when most of the passengers had cleared away, the door of a first-class carriage opened and Vera alighted, with nothing in her hands. The stationmaster hurried forward, beckoning up a porter. Vera, smiling, walked towards her sisters with her inimitable grace. She was as lovely as ever, thought Lucy – and how like her to leave everything behind in the compartment. No anxiety, no fuss about Vera; she was always sure of being waited for and upon, and she always was. Lucy and Charlotte, with Judith between them, hurried towards her.

'Well?' said Vera, as they reached her.

The sisters kissed. Judith stared upwards. She couldn't remember ever having seen this aunt before. She looked lovely, and she wore flowers, lilies of the valley. Judith did not know how much it cost to wear lilies of the valley in September. Vera bent to kiss her, and Judith took a long sniff of the air about her.

'Oooh, lovely,' she said.

'Funny little girl,' remarked Vera, in detached amusement.

Lucy laughed and took Judith's hand again. Judith evidently liked sweet smells.

The sisters appeared at the front of the station. What a time they'd been, thought William, getting out of the car. Everybody else had got away long ago. Looking very creased, noticed Lucy, he advanced to greet Vera. All this kissing, he thought. He got her into the car; she had to be in front

beside him, he supposed, though he would rather have had the child. He got the others in, superintended the getting in of Vera's luggage, got in himself and drove off.

He was confused with feminine chatter. All very artificial still. Women talk to cover up, he thought; men keep silent. Well, both methods work, he supposed.

'And how is Brian?' Lucy was asking. Again. In the same tone too.

'Oh,' said Vera, raising her eyebrows. 'Just the same.' She spoke as if the poor chap suffered from something chronic, thought William.

Arrived again, Judith followed the grown-ups into the house. She was fascinated by her beautiful aunt. She gazed at her with grave interest, but now and again when Vera laughed a reflection of her laughter crossed Judith's face. They went upstairs and Judith went too. Lucy apologised for putting Vera into the little room over the door.

'Oh, but must I sleep here?' asked Vera. 'Can't I sleep in Charlotte's room? I see so little of her. I'd love to be in the same room, like old times. Judith wouldn't mind sleeping in here, would you, darling? You'd let Auntie Vera be with Mummy for a treat, wouldn't you?'

Judith went very pink and rubbed against the wall.

'Don't rub against the wall, darling,' said her mother. 'No, I'm sure she wouldn't mind sleeping in here, Vera. She'll sleep anywhere Auntie Lucy wants her to, won't you, Judith?'

Judith nodded, putting her tongue in her cheek, distorting it.

'And it's time she was going to bed, too,' said Charlotte. 'I'll undress her while you're unpacking, Vera. It's really much better for her to be in here. I shan't disturb her when I go to bed now!'

Lucy hurried down to the kitchen to see that dinner was going properly. As she looked into saucepans, seasoned, stirred, she strove to cajole Janet into a better temper, and so far succeeded that Janet began to talk about her cousins.

'Me cousin had no idea me cousin was such a big man,' she said putting brussels sprouts into the pan.

'Really?' said Lucy, who didn't know whether Janet meant physically or financially, but had no time to pursue the subject. 'China tea for Mrs Sargent, Janet, in the morning. You won't forget, will you? Indian for Mrs Leigh.'

Upstairs, Vera, dressing, was calling out to Charlotte, and Charlotte was calling back. Lucy rejoiced in the sound of their voices and their laughter, but she also hoped they weren't keeping Judith awake.

In the unfamiliar room, Judith chewed the sheet. The drawn curtains were lined with a dusky crimson colour; it made the light coming through like fire. Judith didn't like fire at the windows. If only Stephen were in the house, she could call out and tell him about fire at the windows. Her mother came in to kiss her on the way down.

'Go to sleep, darling.'

'I can't,' said Judith.

'Oh, yes, you can,' said her mother absently. 'You must try.'

Judith pressed her eyelids together to obey her mother and also to keep out the fire at the windows. But her eyelids

quivered; it was too difficult to keep them closed. She opened them again. She had forgotten her doll. It was still in her mother's room. She got out of bed and went for it.

The room, tidy before, was now strewn with all the paraphernalia of a beauty's toilet. The dressing-table was a forest of bottles and jars, silk underclothes spilled over the chairs, a pale green chiffon wrap lay like a pool on the bed occupied by the doll Angela. There was a pair of pale green slippers with ostrich feathers on them. Judith had never seen feathers on slippers before; she crouched down and blew on them.

What lovely things Auntie Vera had! The room smelled of her too; Judith sniffed up the faint, delicious scent. Auntie Vera was a wonderful sort of person, thought Judith getting up from the floor, but she had left the flowers she had worn on the dressing-table. Judith took them up and regarded them pitifully as they drooped over her palm. Their tender leaves were bruised and dark from Auntie Vera's diamond brooch. They had come on a long journey and no one had given them a drink at the end. In her long nightgown she padded to the bathroom and, reaching across the basin, turned the cold-water tap with an effort. She filled a tooth-glass, put the lilies in and carried them back to the dressing-table. Then she took up her doll and went back to the little room over the door. She lay in the bed clasping Angela. Gradually the fire at the windows died away and gave place to the dark. She heard voices going through the hall, she heard the drawing-room door shut. She was alone. No Margaret in the next bed, no Stephen in the next room. She

was in an unfamiliar bed in an unfamiliar room, where no one would come all night. She'd had to give up her place beside her mother to Auntie Vera, who was like a princess and had to have all her own way.

The old stairs creaked under Janet's heavy foot as she came up to turn down the beds. She contemplated the confusion left by Vera, and, setting her mouth, left it as it was. She stood outside Judith's door, and Judith heard her breathing. She lay stone-still, looking towards the door, and by and by a face came round the door, hung there for a moment and withdrew. Janet went downstairs again.

By and by Lucy came up, suspecting that Janet had not tidied away Vera's things.

'Who's that?' said a small voice.

Lucy went in and knelt down by the bed.

'Aren't you asleep, darling?'

'No,' said the child.

'You're not afraid of the dark, are you?' asked Lucy.

'No,' said Judith. 'I'm six,' she added, as if no one could possibly be afraid of the dark at that age.

'Yes, you're a big girl,' said Lucy.

'The curtains have gone out now,' said Judith.

Lucy looked at them. 'Yes, they have, haven't they?' She didn't know what the child meant, but thought it best not to encourage talking.

'Stay a bit longer,' said Judith, nuzzling against Lucy's hand on the pillow.

'Well, just a few minutes,' said Lucy. 'But we won't talk. You shut your eyes and try to go to sleep.'

'Yes,' said Judith. She kept so still that after some time Lucy thought she had gone to sleep and tried gently to disengage her hand. But Judith said at once: 'Don't go.'

'Darling, I must,' said Lucy. 'Auntie Vera and Mummy will be wondering what I'm doing so long upstairs, and Mummy wants you to go to sleep, you know.'

'Can I have the light on then?' asked Judith, sitting up.

'Do you have a light at home?'

'No.'

'Well, I'll put it on and I'll go down and ask Mummy if you can have it this once.' She switched on the light and left Judith, a pathetic little figure, sitting up in bed waiting for the verdict of the grown-ups.

Charlotte, sitting with Vera in the drawing-room, was not inclined to say yes. 'She's never had a light before,' she said. 'Geoffrey has never allowed them one. Why should she want a light now?'

'Because it's probably the first time she's slept in a room alone, isn't it?' asked Lucy.

'Well – yes, it is,' admitted Charlotte. 'Let her have a light then, but it mustn't be inside the room or she'll never go to sleep. Can't you put the bedside lamp outside the door?'

'It will need a longer flex, but William can easily do that,' said Lucy, leaving them.

She went back upstairs with hot milk and William, and Judith drank the milk very slowly, happy to be putting off time and the night.

'Now, darling, you've got a light and I'll tuck you up and you'll be asleep in no time,' said Lucy.

Feeling sure that Judith was now settled, she returned to the drawing-room.

After a time, the household went up to bed. They were all very quiet, remembering the child. There were rustlings backwards and forwards, whispers. Charlotte listened at Judith's door, heard nothing and turned out the light. Immediately Judith called out: 'I want the light on.'

'Oh, Judith, aren't you asleep yet?' said Charlotte. 'It's naughty, darling.'

She went in, kissed her, tucked her up again, left the light on, went into her room and closed the door. Lucy and William went into their room and closed their door too.

After she was in bed, Lucy kept the lamp on beside her, appreciating the fact that she was in bed at last. The room was soothing to look at too, with its white walls, old familiar pieces of furniture, and drawn curtains. The bedside lamp had a pale coral shade and threw a pleasant suffusion over the recumbent figures of William and Lucy in their beds. Lucy had had a busy and not altogether satisfactory day and she wanted to sort things out a little before she went to sleep, though William said that was a bad habit.

It was lovely to have the girls here, she thought, but Charlotte had come more worn and nervous than ever, and Vera harder. She had felt too that she was being kept at arm's length by both of them. She disclosed something of this to William.

'My dear girl,' he said. 'You worry too much about them. Let 'em alone. Charlotte's – how old – thirty-two? Vera's nearly

thirty. If they can't conduct their own lives at that age, when will they?'

'Oh, William,' said Lucy mournfully. 'The conduct of our lives depends so much on the people we live with.'

'With women,' said William firmly, 'it depends far too much. That's what I mean about your sisters. One's husband may not be good enough and the other's may be too good, which is unfortunate for them, but is that any reason why they should jump to the conclusion that life's not worth living? There are other things in life, aren't there? Anyway,' said William, giving them up, 'they must manage. You concern yourself too much about them. You can't run their lives for them, so why try?'

No one, said William, was less inclined to be his brother's keeper than he was.

Lucy, propped on her elbow, considered William's long sardonic cheeks in silence. Then she leaned over him from her bed.

'Now look here,' she charged him. 'That simply isn't true. You concern yourself about what touches you every bit as much as I do about what touches me. You can't bear science to be taught in what you think is the wrong way. You interfere and demonstrate and write and talk and move heaven and earth. You'd go to the stake to get science taught properly. So don't you talk to me about not concerning myself, you fraud.'

William looked startled at being faced with his own inconsistency; then he relapsed into complacency. Science was different.

'Night-night,' he murmured.

'Yes, good night,' said Lucy sternly, kissing him. 'Always end an argument when you're getting the worst of it. Still, I love you. Good night, darling.'

'Good night.' He couldn't say dear or darling to save his life, she thought, but the warm tone of his voice was enough and Lucy turned out the light and lay down contentedly.

A glow came under the door, suffusing the dark. The light on the landing kept vigil for Judith. I'll go out later, thought Lucy, and turn it off. She'll sleep better in the dark.

When she woke and looked at her clock, it was ten-past two. She must be asleep now, she thought, and stole out to the landing. But when her shadow fell across Judith's door, a small voice said: 'Hello.'

'Darling,' said Lucy, going in, shocked. 'D'you mean to say you're not asleep yet?'

'No,' said Judith, chewing the sheet.

Child and woman looked at each other. The endurance of this little pale girl was more than Lucy could bear. She threw aunt-like submission to parental authority to the winds.

'Would you like to come into my bed?' she said.

'Oh, yes,' said Judith fervently.

'Come along then,' said Lucy.

The strange room abandoned, the landing light out, Judith, secure in her aunt's bed, was asleep in five minutes.

Poor little girl, thought Lucy remorsefully, what she must have gone through lying awake while we all went comfortably off to sleep. Why does no one ever remember what it means to be a child? She was afraid of the dark, and too brave to say so. Well, it shan't happen again. Not in this house, anyway.

Cramped and wakeful, but not minding, she passed the night on the edge of the bed. In the morning light that filtered at length through the curtains, she contemplated the face of the sleeping child. She had missed something precious – more, she told herself, something significant – in never having watched, for more than a moment, over a child asleep. We ought to be reminded what we were when we started, she thought. We ought to be able to keep something of this innocence, but how few of us do? I do hope life treats her well, she thought.

Children were so at the mercy of other people, so at the mercy of their parents, and of this child's parents she dismissed the father as hopeless and shied away from criticising the mother with fond evasion. Charlotte, with a different husband, would have been all right, she told herself.

She thought then of Vera's children. Meriel, the younger one, a child with Brian's rather large face, gave no one any trouble, but Sarah was pronounced a problem-child and nurses came and went in quick succession, unable or unwilling to stand her.

Lying in bed, waiting for it to be time to get up, Lucy's thoughts went back to her last visit to Trenton when Sarah came down to the drawing-room when there were visitors. Meriel remained mostly in the nursery, but Sarah, who was amusing, came down.

The nurse, having probably been bitten on the stairs, would open the drawing-room door, lead Sarah in and close the door again. Into the big room with its silvery carpet and pale yellow brocade curtains, with its masses of flowers and the circle of

Vera's friends carelessly disposed in the chairs, the child would advance, an odd-looking little girl of four, with dark hair, a pointed face and strange wild eyes tilted at the outer corners. With these eyes, she considered her mother's friends while they waited to see what she would do or say. They were vastly amused when she brought out their swear-words.

'Take this, damn it,' she would say as a preliminary, plucking an offending ribbon from her hair and handing it to the nearest guest.

When she brought out the word 'bloody' everyone roared with laughter.

Sometimes, Sarah took no notice whatever of the visitors. One afternoon she sat under the grand piano with the score of the latest musical comedy on her knee, a pile of other scores beside her. Vera's admirers kept her supplied with such things; her drawing-room overflowed with flowers, boxes of chocolates, new music. Completely absorbed, Sarah sat under the piano, singing through the score, turning the pages as if she could read the notes and the music, which of course she could not, though she got a good deal surprisingly right. When she had sung through one book at the top of her voice, she reached for another and began on that.

But somebody laughed. Sarah looked up. She remembered the company and saw that they were all laughing or trying not to laugh. Her strange eyes drew together. She almost squinted, Lucy noticed. Suddenly she began to scream like a monkey. She tore the pages of the music across and across, reaching for more to tear, screaming and beating the books like a mad thing.

Lucy started up to go to her, but Vera waved her back imperiously and rang the bell.

'This is beyond a joke,' she said, and waited, cool and lovely, until the nurse appeared.

'Take her away, Nurse,' she said, and the child was borne out, kicking wildly at the woman's starched waist.

It's the parents who are the problem, not the children, reflected Lucy. Then she smiled guiltily and turned to look at William in his bed. If he could overhear her thoughts, he would quote the tag about old maids' children and bachelors' wives.

'Anyway, I'll try to be a good aunt – if they'll let me,' she thought, and dropped a kiss on Judith's incredibly smooth brow.

Light though the kiss was, the child stirred and Lucy shrank to the edge of the bed again.

'Who's this?' asked William, waking later and turning his rumpled head in the other bed.

'It's me,' said Judith, dimpling at him. 'I've been in Auntie Lucy's bed all night and you didn't know, did you? And d'you know what? *You're* going to sleep in that little room with fire at the windows tonight. But you won't mind, will you?' she said persuasively. 'Because you're so old, aren't you?' She considered him with deep interest. 'I expect you're very old, Uncle William. I expect you'll soon be dead, won't you?'

William laughed. 'Oh, don't dispose of me yet,' he begged. 'There's surely plenty of life in the old dog yet.'

Their faces turned towards her, they lay smiling at the child. Her innocent youth laved their adult preoccupations

away and for the moment their lined and battered selves were as smooth and fresh as she was.

But after a sudden thump, the door was flung open and in came Janet with the tea.

'Good morning, Janet,' said Lucy as usual.

''Morning,' replied Janet, hardly moving her lips. She had just had to bring herself to speak to the two in the other room and she wasn't going to do it again. She'd had to say 'This is China,' and such obligingness might be misunderstood as an encouragement to come again. Tomorrow, she determined, she would put a paper in the lid of the teapot so that they could tell for themselves which was which.

She tore the curtains apart and let in the day. Usually she reported, 'It's been raining,' or 'Lovely morning,' but today the sun shone without comment. She cast a sour look at the child. What did she want out of her own bed at this time in the morning, disturbing the mistress? That's what it would be from morning till night, nothing but bother and upset until they went.

Judith's eyes followed Janet gravely all the time she was in the room. When she went out, banging the door, Judith smiled and wriggled lower in her aunt's bed. Lucy saw the smile and thought Judith was amused by Janet's surliness and was glad she didn't mind it. But Judith smiled because she had no need to mind. With Auntie Lucy – and some way behind, Uncle William too – she had no need to mind anything. They gave her what was to this child very rare, a feeling of confidence and security. So she smiled.

CHAPTER THREE

I

The stream of their different lives, their unshared circumstances and experiences, still flowed unbridged between the
sisters. After breakfast, Lucy found herself wondering, like any
anxious hostess with little entertainment to offer, what her
visitors would like to do. She wondered, for a moment, how
she had the temerity to invite them. What was there to do at
Underwood? For her there was always plenty, but for them
what was there? She could not imagine the fashionable Vera,
used to so many excitements, or Charlotte with her harassed
brows, wandering in the lost, lone avenues of the Park. There
was nothing for it but to go into the town; by bus, too, since
William had gone off inspecting in the car.

Calling Janet from her washing-up, which Janet didn't like,
Lucy hurried upstairs to make the beds. Vera and Charlotte,
one with four maids and a nurse whose wages were paid by her
mother-in-law, and the other with two maids, a day-woman,
and a visiting nursery governess, had forgotten what it was to
be in a house where one helped with the beds. So they stood
about in the garden while Lucy did what she had to do.

It was quite like old times, with Lucy throwing on her hat at the last minute, calling out: 'I'll bring the fish back with me,' and rushing out behind them down the lane to the bus.

Luxury coaches with plush seats, two by two, had not reached the village. The bus was a battered, rattling contraption in which the passengers sat facing one another. Usually it was full of friendly talk and laughter, but this morning, when Vera got in, silence fell and remained. Such beauty was an embarrassment, as if everybody were put to shame somehow.

Vera and Charlotte sat on one side, Lucy and Judith on the other. Turning her lovely profile to the window as they travelled along, looking out at the fields of grain, Vera said in her clear voice: 'I wonder what these fields of stuff are. I never know.'

A shock ran round the bus, not missing Lucy. 'Fields of stuff!' The wheat, the oats, the barley – the importance, the necessity of it all, and she didn't know what it was! Why, these people in the bus, in all the villages and farms, and most of the people in the town they were travelling to, lived on, by and through this grain! The character of their stares altered. Beautiful she might be, but surely 'wanting'. Lucy realised suddenly that of course her sisters had never lived in the country; that alone made a gap now between herself and them.

Sitting among the country people, she looked at them from the opposite side of the bus. They had the thin, finished look of town dwellers. They had also the faint conscious superiority and detachment. Of course, you had to be detached

in a town, conceded Lucy. It was all so crowded that if you
didn't wrap yourself in aloofness and silence, you'd have no
peace. In the country there was so much room, so much space
and silence still that it was a pleasure to see and speak to
people.

Her eyes fell to her sisters' feet, their narrow expensively
shod feet among the broad, trodden feet of the country-
women. She looked at her own, and smiled. Brogues again.
Brogues still. It was as if she had remained stationary in
brogues, while they had moved on and away. That wouldn't
matter if they would only come back to her now and again.

Judith turned up her eager little face and asked another
question. Smiling, Lucy bent to answer. 'Don't worry Auntie
Lucy,' said Charlotte from the other side of the bus.

'She's not worrying me,' said Lucy.

They arrived in the town. Farmers stood about in gaiters
and some of the trees dangled wisps of straw. There was a
very small Petty Sessions going on. The shops sold farm
and garden tools, leather goods, excellent pork-pies, cream
cheeses. There were two or three chemists, a lending library,
a tea-shop or two.

'Now where's a flower-shop?' asked Vera.

'A flower-shop?' said Lucy. 'Haven't we plenty of flowers in
the garden?'

'Never mind,' said Vera mysteriously. 'Where's a flower-
shop?'

They went to Bennett's and Vera staggered the proprietor
and her sisters by buying not one dozen hothouse roses in
bud, but three dozen. They were for Lucy. In Vera's world one

gave expensive, sophisticated flowers to one's hostess because there was nothing she needed or could possibly want. One presumed she had everything. One therefore ordered three dozen flowers of some sort. Vera was so far out of touch with her sister as to do the conventional thing by her; also she took a slight satisfaction in showing the others what was done. When she discovered that Bennett's could not send out to Underwood until the next day, she expressed her displeasure and said haughtily that she would take them herself. But Lucy was soon allowed to relieve her of them.

Vera wanted to buy something for Charlotte, for poor Charlotte, her tone implied, to make her happier.

'What can I buy for you, darling? Do tell me.'

'Nothing at all,' said Charlotte, shaking her head. 'There isn't a thing you could buy me, thank you very much.'

They looked at each other across a gap; the one who could still take pleasure in buying and the other who took no pleasure now in being bought for.

'Well, if Charlotte won't have anything,' said Vera lightly, 'it's Judith's turn.'

Judith looked up, her eyes wide, her mouth rounded.

'What is it, child?' asked Vera amused. 'What do you want?'

Judith's head was tilted so far back to look up at her tall aunt that she had to gulp to swallow, which she did before being able to speak.

'Could you . . . could I have a dog?'

'D'you mean a toy dog?' asked Vera indulgently.

'Oh, *no*. . . I mean a real one.'

She stood looking up with breathless hope into the faces

of the grown-ups, but Vera turned away with a laugh and Charlotte was annoyed.

'Judith, why do you bring that up again? You know what Daddy said.'

The hope went out of Judith's face at once. She hung her head with shame at having asked.

'Come along, let's go in here and see what we can find,' said Vera.

They went into Gibson's, where there were bicycles and perambulators downstairs and toys up.

'Now choose anything you like,' said Vera. 'And choose something for Margaret and something for Stephen too.'

'Oh, Vera,' protested Charlotte. 'It will take such a long time.'

'Never mind,' said Vera amiably. 'What else is there to do?'

After the sudden hope of a dog, it was almost impossible for a few moments to contemplate a toy. Judith had to come a long way down from that dizzy height of imagined bliss and at first she could hardly distinguish one toy from another; they seemed just things and undesirable. But soon excitement laid hold upon her and she began to run from one toy to another, calling out: 'Could I have this? Oh, no – that? No, this. . . . '

Lucy followed her about, Vera sauntered, smilingly indifferent, followed by the goggling eyes of the assistant. Charlotte sat at the counter, her chin in her hand.

At last Judith fixed her choice on a washing-set for herself: a tub, a wringer with rubber rollers, a clothes-line, a basket and a bunch of tiny pegs. It was the pegs that decided her;

they were so entrancingly small. For Stephen she chose a water-pistol, because, next to a dog, that was what he had always wanted. For Margaret, a box of pencils and pens. Margaret, at twelve, was getting beyond toys and the range of Judith's imagination. The only thing Margaret wanted that Judith knew of was, again, a dog.

The assistant approached the counter with these purchases and Charlotte came to life.

'Oh, Judith,' she said fretfully. 'Why did you choose things that need water, darling? I don't suppose Daddy will ever let Stephen use that water-pistol and Stephen will be so disappointed. There'll only be trouble, you know.'

Mother and child looked at each other, seeing the trouble.

'Oh, Mummy,' pleaded Judith. 'He does want a water-pistol so badly. Couldn't he squirt over the garden wall sometimes when Daddy's out?'

'Well, do as you like,' said Charlotte, giving up.

Vera and Lucy looked at each other, but looked quickly away again in case Charlotte should see. She saw all the same, and her face closed.

They left the shop, Judith clasping her washing-set, but looking doubtful now. What if she couldn't use it? What if her father withheld the water? She hung behind and confided her anxiety to her Aunt Lucy.

'You can have as many washing-days as you like while you're here,' said Lucy.

'But I want to keep on washing for ever and ever, and I can't with pretend water, can I?'

'Well, I shouldn't worry about it,' said Lucy soothingly.

'Wash as much as possible here and wait and see what happens later.'

Judith's face cleared. She smiled down at her cardboard box.

'The little pegs,' she murmured.

'Are there no more shops? Nowhere else we could go?' asked Vera. 'Is this all there is?' she asked, smiling in amusement.

Her glance belittled the town. I couldn't live here, said her eyes. What a life, how tame.

Nevertheless she made a stir. Vera often made a stir, but was rarely stirred. As she went along the streets now, people stared at her, startled. They stared so that they collided with each other, they missed the kerb and gave themselves a jolt, staring. Old Squire Daley, who always stopped to speak to Lucy in his pompous way, seeing Vera, went past with his mouth open, no eyes for Lucy at all, his pompousness quite shaken out of him by the sight of such beauty in the little town.

When they went into the chemist's for some special soap Vera used, Mr Carson, a pleasant, easy man, became coy and stammered as he sealed up the tablet at each end, deeply apologetic because he hadn't a full box. 'Not much demand for it here,' he said. 'It's too expensive for general use.' And, handing it over the counter, he raised his hitherto shamefaced eyes to Vera with a look that reminded Lucy that chemists were, after all, also men. She saw pleasant Mr Carson in quite another light.

Coming out of Carson's, they met Mrs Bonnington.

'My sisters,' said Lucy, introducing them.

Throughout the short encounter, Mrs Bonnington, whose own face was like one painted on a ping-pong ball, gaped at Vera, and when Lucy made a move to go, she laid her hand on Vera's arm.

'It's a privilege to have seen anyone so beautiful. Thank you,' she said emotionally and hurried, overcome, into the shop.

'Good Lord,' said Vera, smiling.

Lucy noticed that she was more tolerant of the admiration she evoked than she used to be; once she was irritated, now she smilingly accepted it as her due. She breasted the stream of admiration, not looking much at anybody, sure that everybody would look at her.

'What an effect beauty has!' Lucy marvelled, noticing the stares, the behaviour of the women who turned to follow Vera so that they could look at her again. Their faces showed envy or admiration according to their natures; some even sneered strangely. There was a sharpness in the eyes of most of the men. Lucy reached home with a sense of having been in a great crush. People had pressed upon them that morning somehow.

The strangeness persisted between the sisters. Lucy was afraid the visit was going to be a failure. What was the good of their coming together if they remained apart like this? She felt gaieties shut her off from Vera and sorrows from Charlotte.

Vera was restless. 'Ah, me,' she sighed, roaming about.

What does she *expect*, Lucy asked herself. What is it she is always expecting? She is one of those people who feel entitled

to more than other people. But perhaps with a face like that she has a right to, thought Lucy, making the gravy, because Janet always gave up at the gravy when there were visitors. 'There's the gravy yet,' she would say, as if the gravy were the last straw.

Vera, in this mood, could make those round her feel humble, as if they were proving very dull indeed, not worth being with.

At lunch, she talked about the life she led, the races, the meets, the parties, the champagne on Sunday mornings. She and her friends met at one another's houses on Sunday mornings for champagne.

'What a strange time to have champagne,' said Lucy.

'It's just the time you need it,' said Vera.

Charlotte said little. She looked preoccupied with something she could not shake off.

After lunch, Judith retired under the eiderdown of her aunt's bed on condition that the washing-set came too. When Lucy, having covered them both and drawn the curtains, went down to join her sisters before the sitting-room fire, Charlotte had fallen asleep. Keeping quiet so as not to disturb her, the other two grew drowsy. Vera's lashes drooped. Lucy kept her eyes for some time on the sleeping faces of her sisters, until they too closed. The fire burned soft and bright, with comfortable flickerings and fallings. On the side table, Lucy's little Swiss clock ticked time away.

They slept, and in their sleep something worked to restore their old relationship. When they woke, they kept their comfortable positions, smiling drowsily at one another.

'Well, love?' said Lucy as Charlotte opened her eyes.

'Mmm,' murmured Charlotte.

To an outsider it might have sounded meaningless.

'Oh,' said Vera, yawning and stretching her arms. 'It's nice to be here.'

Everything would be all right now, thought Lucy happily.

The door opened and Judith appeared, damp down the front of her frock.

'I've washed all Angela's clothes,' she announced. 'They're pegged out.'

When she saw the three smiling faces turned towards her, she ran forward into the room with a laugh. Everybody was happy together, she felt that. A cloud had lifted; the world was full of light. It was like at home when Daddy was in a good temper and for a time everyone was free, loving, anyone could do anything.

When William came home talk and laughter were flowing out of the sitting-room in the old way. He sat alone in another room trying to read and at the end of a long evening went up to bed, not his own. Janet had retired heavily some time before; she hadn't been able to get a word in about her cousins all day.

II

The visit was now such a success that Vera, one night in the sitting-room, suggested that they should prolong it.

'Instead of going on Monday, let's stay till Thursday, Charlotte. Can you do with us, Lucy?'

'How can you ask?'

'I must be home on Thursday for the Emmersons' dinner, but I could leave Thursday morning. You'll stay, of course, Charlotte?'

'Well, I'd love to,' faltered Charlotte. 'But I don't think I ought to. I said I'd be home on Monday. I don't know what Geoffrey . . . '

'Bother Geoffrey,' said Vera. 'Surely you can please yourself.'

Charlotte looked strained.

'Do stay, Charlotte,' said Lucy. 'It's doing you good. You look quite different.'

'I feel different,' said Charlotte. 'But I don't know if I ought to stay. Geoffrey . . . it all depends . . . ' She didn't say on what, but paused.

'Ring him up and tell him you won't be home till Thursday,' suggested Vera.

Charlotte looked as if she couldn't do that.

'I'll ring him up then,' said Vera.

She got up and moved to the door.

'Oh, I don't know whether . . . ' said Charlotte nervously. But it was so peaceful here, she was sleeping so much better.

'Well, try,' she said.

Vera went out to the telephone in the hall.

'I do hope it will be all right,' said Charlotte.

In a moment they heard Vera's voice.

'Is that you, Geoffrey? This is Vera speaking. Yes,' she called out ringingly. 'Vera.'

You can't bully me, her voice implied over the miles.

'Charlotte won't be home till Thursday. We're staying till Thursday. Yes, Thursday. Goodbye.'

'Vera!' Charlotte sprang up and ran out into the hall. 'That's not the way to do it. You should have asked him . . . '

'Too late,' said Vera. 'It's done.'

'But how did he sound? What did he say?'

'Very little. I did all the talking.'

'But how did he sound?' persisted Charlotte. 'I wish I knew if he minded or not.'

'Why should he mind? What's three days?' said Vera easily. She put her arm round Charlotte and led her back to the sitting-room.

'I wasn't going to say so, but he sounded furious,' she told Lucy afterwards.

'I hope he won't take it out on her for it when she goes home,' said Lucy anxiously.

'If he doesn't take it out on her for that, he'll take it out on her for something else. He doesn't need any excuse or reason. I wish he'd die,' said Vera vehemently. 'But that kind never does. They only destroy those who have to live with them.'

'I'm worried about Charlotte, Lucy,' she went on. 'I think we ought to go there periodically together. Just to show Geoffrey that Charlotte has two sisters who have to be reckoned with. Let's let him know that we know what he is and what he's doing. Let's let him see that we're keeping an eye on him.'

'I'd be only too glad to go with you,' said Lucy.

Vera was so high-handed, so secure in her beauty and her kingdom, that Lucy could leave it to her to get them into the

house uninvited, as uninvited they would be, since Charlotte never invited her sisters. Geoffrey did not like them in the house. Lucy admitted that William didn't like visitors either, but what she excused in William she illogically resented in Geoffrey. So she welcomed the chance of getting past him, as it were, behind her resplendent sister. It warmed her heart, too, that Vera would help her to help Charlotte, though she was vague as to how they were to do it. But when you want so badly to help someone, surely you find the way, she said to herself.

After the decision to pay visits of inspection to Denborough, Vera, and in some measure, Lucy, dealt more briskly and rallyingly with Charlotte, as if everything was going to be much better for her now.

Even before Vera suggested an extension of the visit, Janet felt something was afoot to prevent it coming to an end when it should. Since her bad temper had put a considerable, if temporary, distance between herself and her mistress, she had to seek information from another source. Getting up from her sweeping of the stairs, she went into the bathroom where Judith was engaged on one of her prolonged wash-days, and Lucy, in her bedroom, overheard the conversation.

'When're you going home?' asked Janet sourly.

After a pause, Judith replied: 'When Mummy does.'

'When's that?' asked Janet.

'I don't know,' said Judith, and in a moment added with dignity: 'Auntie Lucy *likes* me to be here.'

'Huh,' said Janet withdrawing.

But she went back.

'Your Auntie Lucy'll be fine and cross with you for slopping all that water over the floor.'

'No,' said Judith calmly. 'She won't. Auntie Lucy will never be cross with me. She loves me too much.'

Lucy, in her bedroom, laughed at this shrewd estimate of herself and could not resist going into the bathroom when Janet had gone downstairs, to kneel on the floor for a few minutes and incidentally assure the busy washerwoman that she mustn't take too much notice of the cross things Janet said because she didn't really mean them.

'You must always be very nice to Janet, won't you?' she said.

'Why?' asked Judith looking up. 'Has she been complaining?'

'Oh, no,' said Lucy tickled.

In spite of the extra days, the visit was soon over.

'Why do I have to go home?' asked Judith. 'Why can't I stay here?'

'I only wish you could, darling,' said Lucy. 'But never mind. Mummy says she'll perhaps let you come for the Christmas holidays.'

'Yes, but will Daddy?' asked Judith, who knew where permission would have to come from.

'I hope so. I shall come and ask him myself,' said Lucy, realising suddenly that it depended on Geoffrey how much she was going to be able to see of this child. It was an uncomfortable thought that she would have to keep on the right side of Geoffrey in order to get Judith to Underwood. How could she combine this with visits of inspection? She didn't know.

71

On Thursday morning the sisters were at the station again. Charlotte's train came in first.

'Now remember, we're coming soon,' said Vera in farewell. It was meant to be a reassurance, but it sounded like a threat.

'Goodbye, my pet,' said Lucy, kissing Judith.

Tears filled her eyes as the train bore them away, but she had to blink them back to see Vera into her compartment. There she sat, her lovely face at the window, a pile of fashionable magazines beside her, a deeply interested young man in the corner opposite.

'Goodbye, darling,' said Vera. 'It's all been so nice. I feel quite different, quite calm and peaceful and as if I shall behave very well, even to Brian's mother, for a very long time.'

Then she, in her turn, was gone.

Lucy went home. William was away, the house was silent. Lucy, looking out at the beauty of the Park in autumn, understood why the old-fashioned artist used to add a group of people to give interest to the picture. The scene seemed empty. She turned to the room behind her; Vera's roses bloomed still in waxy perfection, on the sofa lay one of Judith's drawings, a crooked house with strange two-legged creatures on the crooked path.

Her sisters had gone and their going had torn a hole in her life. It would close over, she knew. Tomorrow, probably, she would get up restored to herself, but today she had to endure the absent melancholy state known as 'missing' them. Her thoughts followed them as they travelled to their own lives, precious, and as it seemed to her, imperilled creatures.

William would have scoffed at that. She looked forward to the end of the day when he would come home, whistling because he had the house to himself, and scoff again.

CHAPTER FOUR

I

In the corner of the carriage, her eyes closed, Charlotte travelled home. She looked, not outwards at the scenes through which the train carried her, but inwards at a private view of her own.

Left to herself, as now on this long journey, or in the middle of the night when she could not sleep, Charlotte went over things, over and over scenes and conversations, always connected with Geoffrey. An endless talking-film with one subject had become a mental habit with her. She was as tired of this private film as if she had been forced, in reality, to sit before a screen for weeks, months, nay years, without relief. But she could not shut it off. She often had the impression that, even when she was thinking and talking of other things, away at the back of her mind it was going on all the time and just the same. Only at Lucy's towards the end of her stay, had the film ceased. But now, nearing home, it was beginning again.

She looked into her own house. It was the contrast with Lucy's that she felt, returning to her own. But her conscious

mind had for so long refused to listen to criticism of Geoffrey that she skimmed over the intimation, coming from somewhere, that she didn't really like any of it.

It was a man's house. She had given in to Geoffrey in everything, even in the furnishing of the house, and she skimmed over the intimation again that there was something hotel-like in Geoffrey's taste, and that the morning-room, his room, the most used room in the house, was very like a bar-parlour with drinks perpetually on the sideboard, quantities of brass, jokes on the poker-work and pottery tobacco-jars, pipe-racks, spill-holders, ash-trays and calendars, jokes of the irate golfer, purple-faced colonel and comic curate variety. Her mental eyes rested dispassionately on the framed hand of bridge over the mantelpiece, but something within her, though disregarded, remarked that there was a dreadful sameness about it. It was not the sort of thing one wished to have before one's eyes for years.

She went in imagination up the stairs. Over the landing was the great glass lantern in the roof. Geoffrey had thought this very handsome when he bought the house in Queen's Walk, but in the winter it was often dark with snow and in the summer dirty with dust.

Wandering about her house, Charlotte considered the nursery. It was obviously a room provided to keep the children out of the way and no more. Charlotte hurried away and went into the servants' quarters, a part of the house she rarely, in reality, went into. Through the kitchen, up a stair, were two bedrooms for the maids. They were thus cut off from the rest of the house and Charlotte was glad of that, because when

Geoffrey made rows in the middle of the night, the maids couldn't hear. Charlotte dreaded and was always on her guard against the watchful eyes and ears of the maids.

She sighed and opened her eyes. There was no one in the carriage but Judith and herself. Judith, her face and hands begrimed, her fair hair hanging in tails, was pointing out of the window and talking to herself. She was naming the shapes the smoke took as it fled from the train and rolled over the fields.

'Oh, an angel. Horses. Oooh – a witch . . . '

She was very good, thought her mother gratefully. All the children were very good. They had to be, said the inner voice.

She closed her eyes and the house appeared again on the screen. In this observed house, the fires burned as clear, the brass, glass and silver shone as bright, the flowers were as fresh, the meals as good, the maids as serviceable as if she herself had been at home. She knew the house was as well run without her as with her.

'The master's the mistress here,' the housemaid had explained to the new cook.

'A house is no place for a man, not all day,' the departing cook had declared. 'Give me a place where the man goes out to business and doesn't stop at home, minding other people's.'

Geoffrey managed the house; Charlotte was merely his anxious subordinate, reprimanded more severely than the maids if things were not kept up to the standard Geoffrey required. Nothing was too small for his notice.

'What's this?' he would ask, picking a spoon from the table

and extending it accusingly at Charlotte. Charlotte, peering into the bowl, located a faint dullness.

'I thought I told you to buy Burton a special table-leather,' said Geoffrey.

'I bought one.'

'Why don't you see that it is used, then?' he said coldly, pinching in his lips. This habit had formed a myriad seams round his mouth. 'I suppose I shall have to speak to her myself.'

'Burton,' he said, when the pretty housemaid came into the room. 'I'm afraid you haven't used your table-leather this morning.'

'Oh, yes, sir, I have, sir,' said Burton, turning in a startled way from the sideboard.

'Well, use it to better purpose, will you? See this spoon?' He took it from Charlotte's hand and pointed minutely into the bowl. 'See that smear?'

'I can't see anything, sir.'

'Look, girl, look,' said Geoffrey with a warning inflexion.

'I think I can see something now, sir.'

'Shouldn't be there, Burton,' said Geoffrey, handing her the spoon. 'Shouldn't be there.'

He patted her shoulder as if she must necessarily be crushed by his rebuke and he wished to assure her that it was not so bad after all, that he was lenient so long as the offence was not repeated. He patted Burton a good deal. She was pretty and he liked women to be pretty, as he often reminded his wife, after remarking that she herself seemed to be ageing. 'Getting rather long in the tooth,' as he put it.

The maids were on Geoffrey's side for the simple reason that if they weren't, they didn't stay. Either they went of their own accord because they couldn't stand him, or were dismissed because he couldn't stand them. The maids who remained for any length of time were of one type: women who liked to have a man like Geoffrey for a master. The scenes he made added interest and excitement to their lives, his standard of perfection kept them on their mettle. He joked with them, noticed them and made them blush and titter, and if he also swore at them, they thought it was only the gentlemanly thing to do.

So far in his married life, Geoffrey had always been able to count on Charlotte's loyalty. She would not complain of him or betray him to anyone, not even to the children or the maids who lived in the house and saw everything. Geoffrey could behave as outrageously as he chose in public, when they went to their friends' houses, when their friends came in, before the maids, before the children, Charlotte said nothing, or merely murmured appeasingly. She bore everything with a faint smile, but it was an enormous cost to her nerves. The state of her nerves frightened her; she felt she might burst into storms of tears at any moment and disgrace herself before everybody, let everything out and bring down on herself Geoffrey's sneering scorn. She was frightened of her nerves nowadays.

The result of having so much to hide, or of thinking she ought to hide it, was that she lived in isolation. She was always fencing, defending the wreck of her intimate life. She kept so much to herself that she was beginning to keep everything.

She was secretive, closed up in herself, and it was this that distressed her sisters.

And the pity of it was that Charlotte's loyalty was wasted; it was the behaviour of an ostrich, because Geoffrey himself gave everything away, almost everybody knew. At parties, or on visits to Queen's Walk, Geoffrey was sometimes thought to be fun, but most women came away thanking their stars that they hadn't to live with him. As for men, he did not appeal to mature men as he had done to the young ones, and he did not appeal to the young ones now because he was no longer young himself. His sort of fun had gone out of fashion.

Charlotte opened her eyes and looked at Judith. Her face was dirtier than ever. In half an hour, thought Charlotte, looking at her watch, I'll wash her. It won't be any good before that, she'll only get dirty again.

Her eyes closed. Staying with Lucy, Charlotte had felt a revival of courage. She felt that when she got home, she would be better able to stand up to Geoffrey and the maids. She felt less afraid of bursting into tears.

'It must be something about me that makes him able to treat me as he does,' thought Charlotte. 'He wouldn't treat Lucy or Vera like that.'

There was something about Lucy you had to respect; no one would shout, swear or throw things at Lucy. At home they had all been given to calling one another fools. 'You fool,' the boys would shout at each other and their younger sisters. Vera and Charlotte had freely called each other fool. But no one had ever been known to tell Lucy she was a fool. Charlotte didn't think even Geoffrey would do it.

As for Vera, she wouldn't stand anything. If Geoffrey had attempted to treat Vera as he treated Charlotte, she would have walked out.

'So there must be something the matter with me,' thought poor Charlotte.

She was still secretly trying to find excuses for Geoffrey. His behaviour was partly her fault, she told herself. She must be calmer, not get into such a state when he began his rows, and she must make the most of his good moods and try to keep him in them.

Then, of course, there was his heart, thought Charlotte, who still believed in Geoffrey's heart. The pains at his heart made him disinclined to take exercise and when he didn't take exercise, when he remained in the house day after day, without so much as putting a foot into the garden, he got very bad-tempered, as was natural, and took it out on them all. She must try and persuade him to lead a more normal life. She must try to get him to see another doctor. Doctor Sands simply did nothing to improve his heart. He kept on saying it was indigestion, even – and how furious Geoffrey was at this! – even flatulence. Flatulence! For so fastidious a person as Geoffrey to be accused of flatulence! So that the last time Doctor Sands came, called in by Charlotte in a frenzy of fear that Geoffrey was going to die, Geoffrey and he had a row. The consequence was that Geoffrey would not now see him at all, and Charlotte, the maids and the children had to get him through his attacks as best they could.

But if she could persuade him to try another doctor, his health and temper might improve and things be better all

round. She was determined to make a fresh start, beginning
with herself. She would keep herself well in hand, be firmer,
not go to pieces the moment she saw one of his scenes coming
on.

But what if she had imperilled the fresh start at the outset
by being three days late in coming home? Geoffrey might
be furious. On the other hand, he might not mind at all.
It depended on what sort of a mood he was in. If this was one
of his good days, he would have filled the house with flowers
for her return, have ordered a special dinner and be at the
station with Margaret and Stephen to meet her. All would be
well, and she could begin on her fresh start at once.

But if it was one of his bad days, he would not be at the
station, and Charlotte's spirit quailed at the thought of all that
would have to be gone through. All depended on whether
Geoffrey was at the station or not. If he was, everything would
be all right; if he was not, she must expect the worst. She
would soon know. It was time now to wash Judith's face and
hands.

When they returned to the carriage, the train was already
running through the outskirts of the city. Buildings were
crowding in, smoke thickened the air, the sky darkened. Out
in the country it was still golden day, here in the city the pall
of smoke made premature dusk. But alighting from the train,
Charlotte did not notice the gloom any more than did the
majority of the passengers, who hurried briskly through it as
if it were their natural element, which indeed it was.

Charlotte let the tide of passengers ebb. She stood, Judith
by the hand, the luggage at her feet, waiting to see if Geoffrey

had come to meet her. In spite of her impulse to hurry about in search of him, she stood where she was so that he should be able to see her and not have to hurry about himself. No one who lived with Geoffrey gave him any inconvenience that could be avoided.

It was not until the platform was entirely cleared that Charlotte gave up hope. He wasn't there.

'Taxi, please,' she said palely to the porter.

'Oh, Mummy,' said Judith, clambering in, 'I do wish Stephen had come to the station.'

'Oh, do be quiet, darling,' said Charlotte wearily. She was already anticipating the row that was sure to come. She didn't know when; it might be as soon as she got into the house, or later at dinner, or tonight, or tomorrow, but come it would. Her nerves would be taut until it was over.

Judith subsided into silence. She took it for granted that at home her mother should be too tired to be bothered with her. At Auntie Lucy's it had been different. You could talk to people there and they would talk to you, even Mummy; but at home it wasn't like that, and Judith accepted it.

She looked out of the windows as the taxi sped away from the thick part of the city, through the great main thorough-fares, climbed the long hill and turned into Queen's Walk, a wide leafy road where once, presumably, a queen had strolled with her ladies. The grassy mound in the public park nearby was all that remained of her castle; nowadays it made a good toboggan run for the children when the snow was on the ground. Queen's Walk was now lined with houses built in the late eighties, with no distinction, but solid, roomy, with many

stone-mullioned bay windows. The gardens were mostly lawns and laurels, with a few beds set for show with things that were planted out and taken up by gardeners with a shortage of ideas, who came by the day, one man having two or three gardens under his care.

'The house by the pillar-box,' Charlotte directed the driver and the taxi drew up. She got out with a sigh. She was reluctant to go in, to begin all over again with the bad humour, reluctant to begin again even with the good.

Stephen and Margaret with Miss Cowley behind them were at the nursery window.

'There's Stephen,' cried Judith, waving excitedly.

'Sh,' said Charlotte, drawing her brows together as if no noise must be made, even in the street. She wanted to creep into the house unheard and unseen. But there was Burton at the door, correct, but unwelcoming.

'Good evening, madam,' said the maid without looking at Charlotte.

Going past her into the hall, Charlotte sensed at once the atmosphere of the house. The morning-room door was closed, Burton wouldn't look at her, the children daren't come downstairs. He must be in one of his worst moods.

'Mummy! Judith!' Stephen was clamouring in hoarse whispers from above. 'Come up! Come quickly.' He kept darting halfway down the stairs but Margaret kept to the landing. If her father had told her not to come down, she wouldn't come.

'Come up, Mummy!'

'I'm coming,' said Charlotte, whispering herself. She

turned to the stairs, but Judith, clambering up before her, kicking the stair-rods in her haste and excitement, suddenly let out at the top of her voice: 'Stephen, what d'you think Auntie Vera's sent you? What d'you think I chose? You'll never guess . . . I've . . . '

The morning-room door opened and there stood Geoffrey in his dressing-gown, the dark red foulard he wore when he didn't mean to go out. The dressing-gown was a bad sign; he was always worse when he had made up his mind not to go out.

'Well, Geoffrey,' said Charlotte faintly, straightening up from the kiss she was about to give Stephen.

He stood there, thin, sallow, his black hair streaked flat over his forehead like the self-portrait of Phil May.

'What the hell is this noise?' he said, through his teeth. 'How d'you expect me to work with this row going on? It's Judith, I suppose.'

His family looked at him in silence. Miss Cowley stepped backwards into the nursery; she avoided trouble.

'No one but that brat would dare to make such a noise,' he said. 'As far as I am concerned, Charlotte, you can take her away again as soon as you like and you can stop away this time. You're both superfluous in this house. Stephen, come away from your mother. All this clinging and kissing is enough to make anybody sick. Stand away. And I thought I told you not to come downstairs,' he said, advancing across the hall with sudden menace. Stephen scuttered upwards.

'Miss Cowley,' called Geoffrey, and Miss Cowley had to come out of the nursery and present herself on the stairs.

'Why the devil can't you keep these children in the nursery? What the hell are you paid for?'

Murmuring shamefacedly, Miss Cowley took Judith by the hand. She restored herself by a glance at the clock on the stairs. Her day was nearly over, she would soon be able to go and Herbert would be waiting for her at the pillar-box. If it had not been for Herbert, she would not have stayed at the Leighs, but having Herbert, it didn't matter where she worked. 'It's only temporary,' she always said when asked about her post. The Leigh children represented so much a week to her, so much a week turning gradually into furnishings for the house where she would eventually live with Herbert. When she had enough of these, she would leave. She would have liked to walk out when Mr Leigh spoke to her as he did, but she wanted some more furnishings yet, so she swallowed her pride and took Judith to get ready for supper.

Charlotte had turned and was going downstairs, supposing that, now Geoffrey had shown himself, she ought to go into the morning-room, but Geoffrey, his lips seamed, said over his shoulder: 'I don't wish to be disturbed,' so she went up again.

When she had taken off her things, she went into the nursery to hear how the children had been getting on. Stephen was eager to show her a crane he had made from his Meccano. It hoisted a box full of nails, he told her, without toppling over.

Margaret leaned on the table, her dark hair hanging over her face. She wasn't happy today; her father was in a bad

temper. Margaret was a sensitive string from which her father could pluck any note he wished. He began early. He used to threaten her when she was no more than a baby that he would go away and get another little girl. Her tears enchanted him. The droop of her mouth was delicious. She used to put her head down on his shoulder and cry, not noisily like a baby, but quietly like an adult. He used to frighten her for the sake of feeling her press closer to him, for the sake of soothing her again. Every morning when she was small she was brought into his bed. He made her do the same tricks over and over again, because he liked to watch her. Long after she was tired, she had to go on. She became an unnaturally patient child.

She was now twelve years old. She went to a small private school farther down Queen's Walk, but her father was playing upon her feelings by saying that she must soon go away to school. When she pleased him, he would say: 'I don't know what I shall do when you go away to school, my pet.' When she displeased him, he would say: 'Well, I shall have to send you away to school, that's all.' In consequence, Margaret lived in dread of going away to school; she had nightmares about it.

Judith burst in, struggling from Miss Cowley's hands, to get it out at last that she had brought Stephen a water-pistol.

Stephen's cheeks flushed, his eyes shone.

'A water-pistol! Phew, Judy! Where is it?'

'In Mummy's trunk. Will you unpack it, please, Mummy?' Judith as the distributor of gifts was important, even imperious. 'And may Margaret have her box? And may I have my washing-set, please? May we all have everything – the books Auntie Lucy sent and Uncle William's sweets, please?'

'Phew!' whistled Stephen again. 'Let's have them.'

But Burton brought up their supper and they had to pull out their chairs and sit down.

'Go and get them, Mummy, please, please,' Stephen and Judith implored. Margaret did not clamour for her pens and pencils; she had plenty already from her father. Her heart contracted to think of him shut up in his room, with no one taking any notice of him, angry and probably hurt because Mummy hadn't wanted to come home to him. She had wanted to stay away three more days and that made it look as if she didn't want to come home to him at all.

Charlotte came back with the children's things, much, she saw, to Miss Cowley's annoyance. This interruption of supper, said Miss Cowley's glance at the clock, is going to make me late for Herbert.

'You'd better keep that out of Daddy's way,' said Charlotte, giving the water-pistol to Stephen.

'Huh,' he said bitterly. 'I shall.'

Margaret sent a deep, unchildish look at her mother and Charlotte saw it. She went out of the nursery. As always when a row was pending, she was restless. She went into the drawing-room, which was on the first floor.

This room had not come under Geoffrey's influence. He took no interest in a drawing-room, having no intention of spending any time there. He had left it to Charlotte and she had made nothing of it, as if she could take no interest if he didn't. The room was melancholy, lifeless, with a closed grand piano like a dark pool in a corner. Net shrouded the windows in case the people in the house across the road should look

in. Books were shut into a bookcase with a glass front. The cushions were uncreased, plump and stiff. The clock did not go.

There were several old photographs, one of the three sisters, Lucy stiff and chubby in a shirt blouse, Charlotte with a youthful, trusting look, Vera eclipsing the other two. There was a single lovely head of Vera in another frame. The photographer in Sefton used to ask permission from time to time to take Vera's portrait, her face so embellished his studio. When new portraits of Vera were exhibited in his window, women came in to have theirs taken, hoping that they too would look like that. They were disappointed, even recriminating, when they came out, in photograph, still looking like themselves.

No one went into the drawing-room, which might have been Charlotte's room. She did not go into it herself, unless Geoffrey barred her from downstairs. It was proof of Geoffrey's power that the life of the house was concentrated in the morning-room, where he spent his time. This room faced south and the garden. They breakfasted there and after breakfast Geoffrey worked there, telephoned from there, interviewed his assistants there. Lunch and dinner were in the dining-room. When she was shut out of the morning-room, Charlotte felt lost and as if she had to stand about until she could get back to it.

She stood about now. She could have seen the children to bed herself and let Miss Cowley go to meet, instead of being met by, Herbert. She could have unpacked for herself instead of leaving it to Burton, but she dismissed the suggestions her

mind made. Someone else could and would do these things; she herself was paralysed, useless, waiting for the storm. It was not only nervous apprehension that paralysed her; it was as if she were waiting for a barrier to be removed, so that she could get *at* Geoffrey, get to him again and then go on with living.

II

Charlotte, changing for dinner, put down her brush and paused. She was seized by one of her old impulses to run down, throw her arms round Geoffrey's neck and implore him to let them be happy, to let them all be open and candid with one another, she and Geoffrey, the children, the maids. They could all be so happy together if only he would let them. But she took up her brush again. The last time she went down like that, he unloosed her arms and said with disgust: 'Don't fawn on me.' Not once had any of these appeals succeeded. He was not a man you could appeal to. His moods lasted as long as he chose; no appeal from outside could shorten them. In fact, he showed his resentment of any such supposition by making them, if implored to end them, last longer than ever. She went on with her dressing.

Miss Cowley saw Stephen and Judith to bed and departed. Margaret, whose bed-time was not until half-past eight, sat at the nursery table, trying to read. During this hour, when he was getting his letters ready for the last post, she was usually running about for her father. He would open his door and call out for her over and over again. 'Where are my paper clips, Margaret?' She tidied his desk and was proud of knowing

where everything was. 'Come and stamp these letters, pet, and then run and put them in the box,' he would shout.

Tonight she listened for the call, though she knew it wouldn't come. If only he would open the door and call 'Margaret,' then everything would come right and this cloud hanging over them all would lift. It was because Mummy was three days late in coming home and she oughtn't to have been. It was really better, Margaret said to herself, when Mummy was away. When she was at home, he was crueller. Margaret formulated the word with an effort. It was a dreadful thing to think, but it was true. Daddy was sometimes cruel, even to her, but it seemed as if it was Mummy who made him so. She let herself speculate what it would be like if her mother were not there, never there. Bowed over the table, her face pinched, she thought: 'Anything, even Mummy not being here, would be better than all these rows.'

The fire was low, the nursery seemed comfortless under the single light, the clock ticked jerkily on the mantelpiece. It was nearly time for her to go to bed. She didn't know whether to go down to say good night to her father or not. He might be cross if she didn't, but he might be much crosser if she did. She spent a long time in nervous indecision. She felt it would be safer not to go, but he might be hurt if she didn't. That decided her. She could not bear him to be hurt. In the innocence of youth, she attributed to him the thoughts and feelings she had herself. So she went down.

'Good night, Daddy,' she said, tiptoeing across the room, a childish figure in school uniform with an unchildish look of anxiety on her face.

'Oh, good night,' said Geoffrey irritably, letting her have his cheek. 'What on earth do you come bothering me for?'

Margaret stole from the room again: it hadn't been so bad after all. . . .

In the night she awoke. They were quarrelling again. She could hear their voices, her father's loud and furious, her mother's high, protesting, imploring. She pulled the blankets over her head, but threw them back again. Judith mustn't hear. She looked at the bed in the corner, but there was no movement from Judith. She sprang out of bed to close the door and keep the dreadful voices out, but she stood there shivering and whimpering, listening in spite of herself. Oh, if only they wouldn't. It was so awful. 'Oh, God, please let them stop, please God.'

'Letting Vera ring me up,' came Geoffrey's voice across the landing. 'As if I want to speak to your damned sisters. You hadn't the guts to ring up yourself. Making out that I'm a bully you daren't speak to. I know you – sitting there with a white face and that smile of yours, letting your sisters pity you.'

'Oh, Geoffrey, stop, stop! I can't stand these scenes. My nerves won't stand much more. . . . '

'*Your* nerves,' shouted Geoffrey. 'What about mine, pray? What did you come home at all for? What good are you? I run this house, don't I? Ach – crying!' he groaned in disgust. 'My God, you should never cry, you look such a sight . . . '

'Oh, God, please let them stop . . . ' whimpered Margaret halfway across the landing. Terrified, she was nevertheless drawn irresistibly to their door.

'Get out of my bed,' Geoffrey burst out again. 'Go on. Get out. What man would want you in his bed? I won't have you in here at all. Get out of the room.'

'Geoffrey, how can I?' wept Charlotte. 'Where can I go? Think of the children.'

'You're getting out, anyway. Get out.'

Margaret fled into her bedroom, but she looked back, sobbing. The landing light went on and she saw her mother come out of the bedroom, her hair dishevelled, a dressing-gown clutched round her shoulders. Charlotte closed the door carefully behind her and turned her piteous face about the landing as if she didn't know where to go. Then she went slowly to the stairs and in a moment the light was turned out again. Margaret, crying wildly, fumbled her way back to her bed. What she had seen and heard was too much for her. She couldn't bear it, she told herself. She couldn't bear it.

Charlotte went into the morning-room and leant her forehead against the edge of the mantelpiece. Without melodrama, without vehemence of any kind, she wished to be dead, to be quiet somewhere, to be out of it all. 'It's no good trying to begin again,' she said to herself. 'I don't want to. I'd rather it ended.'

She trembled so with cold and nausea that she sank to the floor, putting her head down on the low table that always stood beside Geoffrey's chair in the evenings with the whisky on it. She lay there, faint and desperately cold. She must do something for herself, get something, she thought raising her head. There was the whisky. She poured some into Geoffrey's glass and drank it raw. It ran like fire down her throat and

revived her. A blessed warmth crept into her limbs, the nausea receded. She poured out more and put some soda-water to it. She drank that, and in a moment was warmer still, her jangling nerves were quieter. If whisky would help her, she would drink it, she said to herself. She poured out more, and drank again.

She lifted her swollen eyes to the clock. It was five minutes to two. A long night had to be got through. She surveyed the room wondering what to do with herself. She got up and pushed two armchairs seat to seat and went into the hall to get a rug from the chest. The whisky she had drunk was having its effect now. She could hardly think at all. What a relief not to be able to think, she said to herself, climbing into the chairs. 'This is why people drink,' she thought, 'poor people . . . I must wake before Burton comes down in the morning. She mustn't know Geoffrey has turned me out.'

But Burton found her there, the light still on, in the morning. Suppressing an exclamation, she stared in amazement and then went to fetch Cook. From the door, the two women gazed avidly at the defenceless Charlotte.

'Well, upon my word,' whispered Cook.

'There must have been some nice goings-on in the night,' whispered Burton. 'She's never done this before that I know of.'

'The place reeks of whisky,' said Cook sniffing. 'She must have been drinking it.'

'No,' said Burton. 'It always smells like this in a morning. I've never known her to touch whisky, for all there's so much about.'

They looked their fill at Charlotte, dishevelled, pale, sunk low in the chairs.

'It's a nuisance,' complained Burton, now passing beyond the drama of the discovery and thinking of her work. 'I can't get this room done. Shall I wake her?'

'No, let her sleep, poor thing,' said Cook, showing a compassion for Charlotte asleep she did not show for her awake.

When Charlotte awoke and heard the hum of the vacuum-cleaner from the dining-room, she realised that Burton must have been in and seen her. Lying in her makeshift bed, she considered the new situation, or the situation she naïvely imagined to be new. So far she had always been able to persuade herself that the maids didn't know how Geoffrey treated her, but now she could persuade herself of that no longer. Burton knew that she had been turned out of bed to spend the night on the chairs in the morning-room; she must know now that things were pretty bad. Charlotte felt exposed, shamed, made to come out into the open with something she wished to hide. It was the first breach, or the first she admitted, in the privacy, the decency of her married life, and this admission marked a turning-point. For years she had remained in the same state of tortured love, always trying to adapt herself to Geoffrey, always hoping, excusing, and above all, keeping up appearances. It was essential to Charlotte to preserve appearances. Behind the façade of 'appearances' Charlotte had so far kept her self-respect, but the fact that Burton 'knew' made a crack in this façade and through it Charlotte's self-respect began, from this time, imperceptibly to seep.

Burton knew, and if Burton, Cook and Mrs Porter, the

day-woman, already. They knew and it was no good to pretend any longer, at least to them, that there was nothing to know. And in a way, thought Charlotte climbing with a reeling head out of the chairs, it was a relief. It was, at any rate, one thing less, she thought with immense lassitude.

Watched by Burton from behind the dining-room door, Charlotte went through the hall and up the stairs. She was obliged to go into the bedroom for her clothes. She stood outside the door, summoning up courage to enter, but when at length she went in, Geoffrey was sound asleep, in full possession of the bed he had turned her out of. He would sleep halfway through the morning, when he would ring for breakfast to be brought up. He could sleep late and breakfast in bed whenever he chose, but she daren't, unless she were ill, and she was ill as little as possible because Geoffrey hated illness in other people.

At breakfast no one asked where Geoffrey was or what was the matter. Charlotte's white face and swollen lids told them enough. Margaret, pale and heavy-eyed herself, avoided looking at her mother and went off to school with Stephen. Miss Cowley arrived and took charge of Judith. Cook rattled the kitchen range in preparation of the menus Geoffrey always drew up at the beginning of the week. Since he had not enough interests of his own, he usurped what should have been Charlotte's. Mrs Porter and Burton busied themselves in the rooms. The machinery of the day was set in motion. Charlotte was in no way necessary to it. She would go out, she decided, in the hope that fresh air would cure her headache, due, she supposed, to the whisky.

But before she could go out she would have to go into
the bedroom again for her outdoor things. He was having
breakfast now, she knew, and she dreaded having to face him.
He made things so difficult; even such a small thing as going
out of the house. It was as if she always had to be climbing over
something. She was like an ant teased by a child with straws
or stones; no sooner had she climbed over one thing than
another was put in her way. But she went in at last. Geoffrey
was sitting up in bed with the morning paper. She realised at
once that he wasn't going to speak to her and that was a relief.

When Geoffrey appeared at the lunch-table, his mood had
veered. He was now the deeply injured man. His lips were
compressed, his lids lowered half over his eyes, which he kept
dull on purpose. He wished it to be seen that he was bitterly
displeased. He did not speak to Charlotte or the children, but
he spoke in an undertone to Burton about the carving, as if
he and she had the serving of an ungrateful lot.

The children were very quiet. There were days when they
dared not eat celery or apples or biscuits or anything that
made a noise in his presence. But today there was nothing
dangerous on the table and they ate quietly, but heartily.
Margaret glowed secretly. That morning she had been given
twenty lines to speak in a play. She loved speaking lines, and
for the present she had quite forgotten what had happened
in the night. Eating her lunch, she was trying to remember the
lines and determining as soon as lunch was over to rush up
to the nursery and look at them again. Charlotte's head was
much better. She too ate with some appetite. They all looked
as if, though their father had imposed silence on them, they

had forgotten him. His victims were recovering themselves and that Geoffrey would not tolerate.

He reminded them forcibly of his existence by throwing the silver dish-cover violently to the floor, startling the meat off their forks, their lips from the rim of their glasses.

'Damn you all,' he shouted furiously. 'Why can't you behave like civilised beings at the table? Why do you sit dumb, stuffing yourselves with food?'

The colour came slowly back to their cheeks as they stared at him.

'We didn't know you wanted us to talk,' said Charlotte. 'Judith, where did you go for a walk this morning?'

'My goodness,' thought Miss Cowley retrieving her napkin from under the table. 'If Herbert could see him, he wouldn't let me stop here another minute.'

But she would stay until they had paid for the three-piece suite. She was fortified by the feeling that she was suffering for the furnishings.

'Get me a whisky and soda, Burton,' said Geoffrey savagely.

For a moment, Charlotte quailed. Would he notice that the whisky had diminished in the bottle? But he did not look at it. There was always plenty of whisky in the house. It was always offered to the men who called. Geoffrey did business over whisky, and he encouraged his subordinates to do the same. He said a glass of good Scotch had brought him many an order. He wouldn't engage a teetotal traveller; people always felt he was a queer fellow. Whisky, therefore, flowed in his house and he did not notice that one of the many bottles contained less than it had the night before.

He drank the whisky and Charlotte and the children and Miss Cowley went on talking politely because he had told them to. He was angry. He was also, in some secret place, alarmed. He had a fear of being ignored, of being ousted from the centre. His mother and sister – his father died early – had always doted on him, applauded all he did and been tickled to death by his tricks. That had to go on. He sulked throughout lunch and afterwards closed himself into the morning-room whither Charlotte made no attempt to follow him.

It was after tea, as Charlotte sat in the chilly drawing-room and Margaret was happily learning her lines in the nursery, that a strange gasping sound came up from the hall. Margaret raised her head and went pale.

'Charlotte . . . Margaret . . . someone . . . help . . . help me . . .'

Margaret rushed from the room, colliding with her mother who was rushing from the drawing-room. Burton and Cook were already in the hall, bending over Geoffrey on the floor.

'Oh, Geoffrey,' cried Charlotte, all compassion. 'Daddy, Daddy,' wept Margaret.

Stephen, Judith and Miss Cowley, wide-eyed, startled, clustered behind.

'Geoffrey,' Charlotte was on her knees supporting his head. 'Is it your heart again?'

'Yes – yes,' he gasped writhing.

'Miss Cowley, the sal-volatile from the bathroom cupboard, quickly.'

'Undo his collar, mum,' said Cook.

'Oh,' groaned Geoffrey. 'Charlotte, Charlotte . . . the pain . . .'

'It's all right, dear,' Charlotte reassured him. 'We'll get you into the morning-room. Burton, can you . . .? Cook, help on that side. Geoffrey, can you put your arms round my neck?'

With much scuffling they got him into the morning-room and lowered him into his chair. 'Ah – the pain . . . the pain . . .'

'Where, dear, where?' begged the distracted Charlotte.

'At my heart, of course,' he groaned.

'I'm going to send for the doctor,' said Charlotte, getting up from her knees.

'You are not,' said Geoffrey with sudden vigour. 'I forbid it. Oh,' he said, sinking back with another groan. 'You're making me worse.'

'Oh, Cook, what about a hot flannel?' 'Yes, mum, that's a good idea,' said Cook hurrying out.

'Massage over my heart,' gasped Geoffrey.

'Oh, yes, dear, why didn't I think of it?' Charlotte undid his waistcoat and shirt buttons and rubbed round and round, leaning tenderly over him. Margaret rubbed his hands, putting her cheek against them now and again, saying, 'Poor Daddy. Poor, poor Daddy.' Judith hovered behind, getting a look in now and then under people's arms or round their waists. 'Is Daddy going to die this time?' she asked Miss Cowley with interest. 'No, dear, of course he isn't,' said Miss Cowley briskly.

As if to give her the lie, Geoffrey emitted a deep groan. He doubled up with genuine indigestion. His forehead was

bedewed with sweat which Charlotte pitifully wiped away. The beads of sweat convinced everybody that he was seriously ill. Rubbing so that her palm burned, Charlotte was full of remorse. The critical mood induced by the whisky was dispelled as if it had never been. She was back where she had been before, loving, excusing, hoping, and in spite of anxiety about Geoffrey, much happier. She shouldn't have upset him, she told herself. She shouldn't have stayed away those extra days. She blamed Lucy and Vera who had persuaded her to stay. They didn't know what effect anger had on Geoffrey, they didn't know how bad his heart was. If he was ill, everything should be forgiven him. She was entitled to forgive him, she said defensively, in an imaginary conversation with her sisters. She could let herself forgive him and that was a relief, because she wanted to. She stooped and kissed him on the brow and went on rubbing more briskly than before.

'That will do,' said Geoffrey weakly. His head lolling sideways, his thin neck exposed, he looked like a suffering martyr and his household stood round and stared at him.

'Are you feeling better, dear?' asked Charlotte hopefully.

He smiled faintly and gave her his hand. 'Would you like a cup of tea?' she asked.

'I think I would,' he said.

'I'll go and make one,' said Burton and Cook followed her out of the room. Geoffrey rolled his head round, smiling at his family.

'Miss Cowley, take the children back to the nursery, will you?' said Charlotte. 'Mr Leigh needs quiet.'

'Not Margaret,' said Geoffrey.

'Oh, no, Daddy, I'll stay,' said Margaret brightly. The dreadful thing was that now that he was better, she wanted to go back to her lines. But she stifled the unnatural wish at once and sat on the floor at his feet. When Burton brought tea, Charlotte poured it out and tenderly helped him to drink it, and when, since he was so much better, she left him to dress for dinner, he rang for Cook to bring him a dose of bicarbonate of soda.

CHAPTER FIVE

I

The next morning, Geoffrey declared himself well. Quite, quite well, he said rubbing his hands. He was in high good humour and wore the tea-cosy on his head throughout breakfast.

It was Saturday. There was no school and Miss Cowley did not come, so after breakfast, Stephen and Judith withdrew behind the bushes at the bottom of the garden with some much-coveted water drawn surreptitiously from the wash-house. Judith fastened her clothes-line between two twigs of laurel and the sight of it with Angela's vest pegged upon it gave her complete satisfaction. It was all so small and yet it was just like a real clothes-line with real clothes hung out to dry; and the vest was wet and shrinking rapidly too, no pretend about it. Judith returned to her washtub to deal with Angela's ballet skirts. Angela, she reflected, had never been so clean in her life as she had since Auntie Vera had bought the washing-set.

Stephen drew water into his water-pistol and discharged it at different targets, the rhubarb, the gardener's barrow, the

trunk of the maple tree, whistling at the accuracy of his aim. The sun was warm on the children's heads, they were absorbed, contented and fancied themselves doubly safe because it was Saturday morning and their father did not work at the table in the window on Saturday morning, but, with his back to it, sat by the fire reading the papers.

Suddenly, however, the window shot up and the dreaded voice called out: 'Hi! You two!' The children started violently. Stephen threw his pistol into a bush behind him and Judith spilled her washing water. They stood staring at each other.

The trouble in this house was that though some of the alarms were false, they were as alarming as the real ones. This was a false alarm, as they realised after their first fear.

'Come on, you two there,' called their father. 'I'm going to take you all to Merthwaite. I want to be off in ten minutes.'

'Leave the things here,' whispered Stephen. Judith cast an anxious look at Angela's vest. Must it dangle all day? But she scrambled out of the bushes at Stephen's heels and ran into the house. Their father was already springing up the stairs, two at a time, delighted with his own agility. Passing the nursery door, he saw Margaret still leaning over her book, although he had called the news to her from the hall below.

'Here,' he said, going in. 'What are you doing?' A frown threatened his good humour.

'I'm just taking a last look at my part, Daddy, so that I can say it to myself during the day.'

'Well, leave it alone,' he said, snapping the book shut. 'I'm not taking you out so that you can mutter to yourself all day.

I'm taking you out to enjoy yourselves, so remember that. If I can leave my work behind, so can you.'

'But it isn't work,' said Margaret, putting her head on one side conciliatingly.

'Don't answer back and go and get ready. Ten minutes and if you're not ready, you'll be left behind.'

'Hi, you, Stephen,' he shouted going to the landing and throwing a key over the banisters. 'Go and unlock the garage and be quick about it. Where are your eyes, boy? The key's under the radiator. I'm coming down in a minute to get the car out. Then come up and get clean. I expect you're filthy.'

'I'm sure they are,' said Charlotte, hurrying out of her bedroom to secure Judith. Ten minutes was very short notice to make the children as spick and span as they must be to go out with their father. She herself must be spick and span too. Muddy shoes, a hole in a sock, or the wrong hat might ruin the day. When she had seen to the children, she must change the coat and skirt she had put on for the town; she had been on the point of starting for the shops when Geoffrey called out that they were going to Merthwaite. She was worried about the shopping, but would have to wait for the right moment to say so.

The children scurried up and down the stairs with bolting eyes, they knew there would be trouble if they kept their father waiting. Stephen couldn't find his thick shoes. Margaret couldn't find her gloves. 'Mummy, I know I had them in my coat-pocket yesterday,' she came into the bathroom to say in a low voice. 'I know I had . . . '

'What's that?' asked her father, coming in himself. He was

cross with them if they lost things so Margaret said it was nothing really, and went to have another feverish hunt for her gloves. To her great relief she found them and came skipping down the stairs first.

'Come on,' shouted Geoffrey. 'Everybody out. I'm bringing the car round, so I warn you.'

'Geoffrey, dear,' called Charlotte timidly. 'I'm rather worried. I was going to the shops. We need both bacon and cheese. . . . '

'Right you are,' said Geoffrey good-humouredly. 'We'll go to the shops first.'

After an exit that more resembled an escape from fire in the house than a setting out for a day in the country, they scrambled into the car, Margaret in front with her father, Charlotte behind with Stephen and Judith. As she recovered her breath and herself, Charlotte ran an anxious eye over the children. They were all right and she smiled at them for being so.

Geoffrey drove to Watson's, the magnificent grocer's shop. 'Come on,' he said, getting out of the car. 'You can all come in.' They didn't want to, but they got out. Stephen especially disliked to go into a shop with his father, because his father made everybody look at them, and Stephen didn't like that. Neither, he knew, did his mother. She smiled all the time, but Stephen knew she didn't like it. Geoffrey walked into the shop with his family at his heels. He liked occasionally to parade his children. People turned to look at them and at him. The children had sensitive, attractive faces and the state of tension they lived in gave them a responsive manner.

'Morning, Watson,' cried Geoffrey largely to the proprietor,

who was walking about his huge shop while his assistants attended to the many customers.

'Good morning, Mr Leigh, sir,' said the dignified grocer with a bow. He beckoned up Chapple, his chief assistant, narrow as a roll of bacon in a long white apron tied about with tapes, and together they followed Geoffrey as he strode about the shop, inspecting one thing after another, his hands in his hip pockets, displaying his lean waist and the excellent cut of his trousers. His mobile mouth was never still, neither were his feet. He was as conscious of his feet as a male dancer and his shoes always seemed more thinly-soled and supple than other men's.

He wandered about the shop, followed by Mr Watson and Chapple, Charlotte, Margaret and Stephen and the eyes of the other customers. But Judith had gone off to perch herself on a high chair at one of the counters stacked with little bottles. In some were plump cherries like sea-anemones, in others tiny cucumbers, in others little silver fish rolled up tight. She peered into the bottles, humming to herself and waiting for her father to finish. She often eluded her father and removed herself when the others couldn't. From the beginning she had some kind of armour against him, provided perhaps by his indifference to her. Margaret, his first child, had been a novelty and an amusement to Geoffrey; Stephen, his second, he hadn't wanted; of Judith he had thought 'Lord, here's another,' and had really taken no notice of her. He petted Margaret, nagged at Stephen and didn't bother with Judith, so now she could sit alone in a chair and be spared the wear and tear of her father's shopping.

The shop was full of people and Geoffrey strode among them tossing orders over his shoulder to Chapple who took them down. When Charlotte, in the early days, had innocently ordered preserved ginger, cherries in brandy, caviare, jellied chicken, because he liked them, there had been dreadful rows about her extravagance. The housekeeping bills were appalling, he said. Yet he himself always ordered such things. He liked to give a lavish order in a shop and he gave one now.

'What's this – eh?' demanded Geoffrey halting before a tower of biscuit tins arranged against one of the pillars.

'That, Mr Leigh, is a new kind of biscuit, sir,' said Mr Watson. 'I think it's going to be very popular. Will you be so kind as to try one?'

'I bet it's no good,' challenged Geoffrey.

'Indeed it is good, sir,' said Mr Watson gravely. 'Chapple, open a tin and offer the gentleman a biscuit.'

The expert Chapple ripped open a tin in a trice and, taking off the paper shavings, revealed the comb of biscuits. Geoffrey, under the envious eyes of his children, took one, tried it and said offhandedly: 'Not bad. Send me a tin.'

He moved off, followed by his party, but suddenly he broke away at a tangent and crossed the shop in swift strides. Judith still peering into the bottles, still humming, felt herself seized by the shoulder. With one turn of the hand, her father brought her off the high chair.

'You young monkey – taking up the chairs at your age! Let this lady sit down at once. I apologise for my daughter,' he said, bowing to an old lady who had just come to stand beside the counter.

Judith, her hat crooked, stood with startled eyes. The old lady was equally startled.

'She didn't see me. I'd only just arrived,' she protested, flushing. 'The dear little girl! How you made her jump and me too! There was no necessity, none whatever. I have no wish to sit down. I have simply come to leave my order and there it is,' she said laying it down before the assistant. 'And now I am going and you may sit on the chair again, my dear.'

She hurried out, her hat trembling. Geoffrey, collecting glances before he smiled indulgently at the idiosyncrasy of age, turned on his heel and resumed his orders, but Judith hid behind a pillar. She was ashamed. Everybody had seen. She ought to have given the old lady the chair, she knew that. But she hadn't seen her. Blushing, she hung her head and wished she could run out of the shop.

At last the Leigh family left Watson's. But they hadn't finished. They had to go to Prosser's, the fishmonger, for a lobster. Geoffrey was knowledgeable about bacon and cheese; he also knew all the points of a lobster and it took a long time to find one to suit him. But at last, having despaired, the children found themselves on the road to Merthwaite and their spirits began to revive.

The car sped through the beautiful bare country, unencumbered by woods and hedges. Folding one upon the other, fold upon fold, the hills were tawny from the summer, the cloud shadows lying upon them. Their sides trickled thinly with streams, they were traced over by straggling stone walls and the road wound round their feet, winding deeper and deeper into the village of Merthwaite. Here was a stream,

wide and shallow with a stony bed. On each side was a wide green and beyond each green a row of white-washed cottages facing one another widely across the water. There was an old stone church with a square tower, an old stone bridge, and the inn – *The Three Fishes*. Because of the minnows in the pools at the edges and the stepping stones going over, the stream represented all that could be wished for to Stephen and Judith, and they gulped with excitement and apprehension when they got out of the car before the inn and heard the water. What if their father had some plan for spending what was left of the morning? What if they couldn't go down to the stream at once? They waited, looking up at him. But Geoffrey strode off into the inn to be greeted with cries of welcome by fat Mrs Purley, the proprietress.

The children watched their father go as if they could not believe their luck. Then they turned and ran to the water. Charlotte, having greeted Mrs Purley who was by this time serving Geoffrey with a drink, came out and sat down on the bench against the wall. October though it was, the sun was warm and she lifted her face to it. Warmth and light seemed to pass through her closed lids to her very brain. Her blood ran easily in her veins, she was relaxed, happy.

After a perfect hour – one thing that resulted from the uncertainty of life with Geoffrey Leigh was that his family certainly valued to the full the good hours – after a perfect hour, Mrs Purley called them in. They went upstairs to wash for lunch and had a look in at the bedrooms. The old bulging walls were washed pink, the chests of drawers had white china knobs, the quilts were thick white honeycomb, and in each

room there was an oleograph of Queen Victoria. 'If only we could have a holiday here,' breathed Judith.

They went down to lunch. There was ham and eggs, apple-tart and cream, and Mrs Purley kept bringing something extra, scones, lemon curd, currant bread, and when she leaned over to put the plates on the table she almost crushed Judith under the bolster of her vast bosom. After the first time, Judith cowered ready when she saw Mrs Purley coming with a plate.

'After lunch,' said Geoffrey, 'we'll climb the Beacon.'

Judith and Stephen looked at each other. It was goodbye to the stream. But they did not clamour as other children would have done and Charlotte was grateful to them for being so sensible. If somewhere in the recesses of her mind she thought it was unnatural for them to be sensible at that age, she did not admit it. It made it easier that they should be sensible and she would give almost anything to make things easier.

It was a stiff climb up the Beacon and Charlotte, though she smiled steadily, had a pain at her heart and was glad to rest when they reached the top. Geoffrey too sank to the short turf with relief; his knees trembled and his breath came short. 'I'm not so young as I was,' he thought, and didn't like the idea. It made him gloomy. He looked at Charlotte. She was almost as old as he was and looked too cheerful about it. When he felt his age, she should. Charlotte was looking down on the village, smiling spontaneously now. The pain had gone. It had been a good day. The children had behaved well and Geoffrey had been in a good humour all the time, so

she smiled and enjoyed the wind that blew her hair back from her temples.

'Your hair's very grey,' Geoffrey charged her suddenly.

'Oh, I know,' she said startled and put up both hands to hide her grey hairs. She had forgotten them. She wished he hadn't seen them. She got up and followed him down the hill. He could spoil everything for her. She was too much at his mercy, and she knew it. A word from him could change all the current of her thoughts. At night, sometimes, when she was saying her prayers, if he tripped over her feet and said 'Damn it all, why can't you keep your feet out of my way,' she couldn't pray. She got up from her knees, powerless, unable to give her mind to anything but the misery of being spoken to like that by him. It was the same now. She felt she ought not to have grey hairs. They took all the pleasure out of the day.

Geoffrey said they couldn't stay for tea. They must get home. It would soon be dark and he wanted to go to the club. They said goodbye to Mrs Purley and got into the car. Judith rested her chin on the lowered window, listening to the water. She felt as if she was always being hurried away, as if she could never get *enough* of anything. The starting of the engine drowned the sound of the water and the car began to move. But Geoffrey stopped it again at the sight of two people, a man and a woman, coming arm-in-arm across the bridge. With an exclamation, he jumped out of the car, and strode towards them, hand outstretched.

'Well, by George, to think of meeting you here!' he cried heartily.

The man seemed astonished too, but differently; there was

no heartiness in his astonishment. Geoffrey took his hand from him and pumped it up and down. He clapped the man on the back, beaming into his face. 'I'm delighted to see you. I haven't set eyes on you since that weekend we had together. By George, we did have a time – eh? Oh, all right, all right,' he cried, playfully reassuring. 'I won't give you away. I'm just off. Au revoir. Hope I haven't embarrassed you!' Laughing heartily he ran back to the car, jumped in, banged the door and drove off. Charlotte saw the astonished faces of the man and woman turned after them.

'He doesn't seem to remember you,' she said.

'Of course he doesn't,' said Geoffrey delightedly. 'I never saw him before in my life.'

The children peered questioningly back at the pair on the bridge. Used though they were to their father's jokes, they still did not understand them, they still didn't know which were jokes and which were not, until afterwards. All the children had a habit of scanning the faces of adults when they spoke to see if they meant what they said.

Geoffrey suddenly roared with laughter again. 'She looked suspicious, didn't she? I've put a bee in her bonnet all right, haven't I? By George, I have.' It kept him in a high good humour all the way home.

'We had a lovely day in the country,' Charlotte wrote to Lucy. 'Geoffrey took us all to Merthwaite.'

'How *very* kind of him,' said William reading.

II

A blessed period of freedom now set in for the children and Charlotte. One of the Directors of Geoffrey's Firm, one of the actual Family, wrote to say he would shortly pay a visit to Denborough and Geoffrey at once became fully occupied in preparing for him.

And now Geoffrey was to be seen at his best. The minute and critical attention he bestowed on the household, his wife and children, he also bestowed on his business. No traveller ever got the better of him or swindled, under him, the firm out of a penny. Geoffrey knew all they did and how they did it, which was little short of miraculous, considering he rarely left his own house. He was good, tiresomely good, at collecting evidence and putting it together to make a whole.

Alert, interested, confident, he prepared for the visit of the Director and left his family, to their great benefit, alone. He was out most of the day. Margaret and Stephen went to school, Judith was taught and promenaded by Miss Cowley, the maids did their work, Charlotte shopped, sewed, read and sat in the warm morning-room alone. She slept well and looked much better.

Mr Cedric Bancroft arrived at the hotel where rooms had been taken for him by Geoffrey, and Geoffrey was more than ever his best self. Courteous, amusing but restrained, punctilious, well-dressed, he was in constant attendance on his Director. Mr Bancroft came to dinner and the dinner was so excellent he was astonished. Such food in such a small house, he marvelled, with practically no servants. 'These

people live better than I expected,' he thought. 'They even,' he thought, 'live as well as I do.' Geoffrey's knowledge of what was what certainly stood him in good stead. Mr Bancroft was highly satisfied with Geoffrey, as, from his point of view, he had every reason to be.

But the great man went home and the anticlimax followed. Geoffrey flopped. He had done so much that, for the time being, there was nothing left to do. He felt flat and out of sorts, so he kept Margaret at home to amuse him.

He had done this before and the headmistress of the school did not like it. She had protested to Margaret, but with no effect. Margaret said nothing at home; she liked her school and didn't want to be taken away from it. So, on the wet Saturday morning following Margaret's latest absence, when Miss Desmond saw Charlotte in the street, she hurried after her.

Miss Desmond was one of those people who think one really ought to be able to say anything to anybody. She was convinced that, at heart, parents really wanted to do what was best for their children. Put it to them, she always felt, and they will see and agree. She worked on this candid, but clumsy principle. So she hurried after Charlotte and grasped her firmly by the arm, startling her considerably.

'Good morning, Mrs Leigh,' said Miss Desmond briskly. 'Which way are you going? Because I'll walk along with you. I intended to come to see you, but this meeting will save me a journey. I want to speak to you about Margaret.'

A guarded look came into Charlotte's eyes, as always when family subjects were broached.

'I'm sorry Margaret has been away from school again this week,' said Miss Desmond, who was as thin as a rail and took long strides, throwing Charlotte completely out of step. 'The reason she gave for her absence was that Daddy wanted her. These continued absences from school are bad for any child, Mrs Leigh, as I am sure you realise, but they are especially bad for Margaret, who is highly nervous and needs quiet. Regularity. *Stability*,' said Miss Desmond, pleased to have hit on the right word. 'Stability, Mrs Leigh. That is most important to Margaret. She is timid, too. She wants reassurance. She needs to be shown that life is not so dreadful after all, that at any rate, whatever it is, one can and must find the courage to meet it.' Miss Desmond demonstrated with energetic jerks of her umbrella how one must meet life. '"Cast out fear," I say to Margaret, "And ye shall conquer Caesar."'

Miss Desmond's face glowed under her old hat, but Charlotte's face was closed. She resented the way this woman was attempting to crash through Margaret's defences, through hers. She was outraged that a stranger should presume to know so much about Margaret's home life. She wasn't going to discuss timidity and stability with this woman. Miss Desmond's analysis applied to mother as well as to daughter, but Miss Desmond did not know it and blundered on.

'So I appeal to you as Margaret's mother, Mrs Leigh, to see that her education is not ruined by her being kept away from school unnecessarily.'

'Margaret's absences from school,' said Charlotte coldly, when Miss Desmond paused, 'are entirely a matter for her

father to decide. I must go into this shop,' she said. 'Good morning.'

People – Lucy, Vera, Miss Desmond – kept throwing out a life-line to Charlotte, but blindly, trustingly, in the face of all experience, she clung to her straw; she clung to Geoffrey. He had only to be good-tempered, or at least not actively bad-tempered for the space of a few days, for Charlotte to be lulled into false security. Unwilling, or unable, to realise that confidence in one's marriage partner was not for her, she told him things any wife might tell any husband, things she would have been much wiser to keep to herself. She told him now about Miss Desmond.

Coming into the house, she took her dripping umbrella to the cloakroom and went upstairs to take off her things. The house was warm and there was a comfortable smell of cooking, not insistent, but pleasant, the sort of smell it is nice to come in to from cold wet weather in the streets. The children were quiet in the nursery. Charlotte came down again, saw that lunch would not be in for another few moments and went into the morning-room where Geoffrey, in spite of several whiskies and the papers, had spent a dull morning. In the room, with the comforts he had assembled round himself, standing before the fire, his eyes intent, he was like a spider in the centre of his web, waiting for an unwary fly. He was ready to pounce, but Charlotte did not know that and came innocently in.

'It's dreadfully cold and wet outside,' she said, coming to warm her hands at the fire.

He knew. That was why he had let her do the shopping.

He hadn't felt inclined to get the car out and go himself on such a day.

'I saw Miss Desmond at the shops,' she went on. 'And what do you think she said?'

Geoffrey said nothing; he knew she would tell him without his exerting himself to encourage her.

'She said we were spoiling Margaret's chances of education by keeping her at home from school.'

'She said what?'

Charlotte repeated it.

'What the devil does the woman mean by questioning what we do? What I do, because I suppose you told her that it was I who kept Margaret at home?'

The emphasis was dangerous. His temper was rising. Charlotte saw it and began to flounder. 'Of course I didn't, Geoffrey.'

'Why didn't you?'

'Well, I – I didn't want to blame you . . . '

'*Blame* me?' Geoffrey narrowed his eyes at her.

'Well, you know what I mean,' she said.

'Perfectly,' said Geoffrey, balancing himself on his toes. 'You say "blame". You criticise my actions too. You secretly side with Miss Desmond, but you daren't say so. You're the worst funk I ever came across.'

'Geoffrey, I was only telling you what Miss Desmond said. I was angry with her . . . '

'Bah, you're not capable of being angry. It takes guts to be angry. You let that woman say just what she chose. You'd stand anything from anybody.'

His mouth sneered, his eyes were contemptuous. Charlotte's face took on a piteous expression. She felt hopeless, desperate, when he looked at her like this.

'Geoffrey, don't let's quarrel,' she besought him. 'It's been so much better lately, but don't begin again. It makes me feel so ill. My nerves are in a dreadful state. They frighten me.'

'You're always frightened. You're in a chronic state of funk. You're like a spaniel bitch I once had. It went down on its belly and crept over the floor every time I came near it. My God, that dog made me sick. I couldn't cure it, so I got rid of it.'

'I dare say you'd like to get rid of me,' said Charlotte, her tears rising. 'But don't worry. You're killing me all right.'

'Oh, for God's sake,' shouted Geoffrey. 'Don't start blubbering again. I can't stand the sight of you when you cry. Look at yourself. Look!'

'I know,' said Charlotte, biting her trembling lips. 'I know. All I hope is that some day I won't care how you speak or what you do. Some day I won't care . . . I won't care . . .'

The children, coming down in answer to the gong, stood stock-still on the stairs. Burton beckoned to them from the dining-room. 'You come in here,' she said severely, as if it was they who were quarrelling, 'I'll serve you.'

She closed the door on the loud voice from the other room. Margaret, looking sick, said she didn't want any lunch. 'Well, you'd better get on with it,' warned Burton, 'or your father'll notice.'

The morning-room door banged violently, the dining-room door was flung open, flung shut and Geoffrey sat down

with a savage face to the table. His children bent low over their plates without looking at him. As the minutes went by, Stephen began to be terribly concerned because his mother didn't come. He choked down some more beef, but unable to bear her absence any longer, he slipped from his chair and made for the door. 'Did I give you permission to leave the table?' his father shouted. 'Where're you going?'

'To look for Mummy.'

'Get back to your chair,' ordered his father. 'Baby-face,' he added contemptuously. 'You're more like a girl than a boy.'

In the room next door, Charlotte was sobbing in the chair Geoffrey had occupied all the morning. Once she began to cry nowadays, she couldn't stop. She kept telling herself that she must go in to lunch. She must, because of the children. A few weeks ago, she had given herself away to Burton by being found asleep in this room in the morning, now she was breaking down in front of the children. She must control herself, but how she longed to give up and have done. It was all no good. Her life with Geoffrey was nothing but a house of cards; she kept building it up and he kept knocking it down. Her jaw shook as if she had a rigor. She clasped her face in her hands. Lunch would be over if she didn't go in soon. Her eyes fell on the bottle of whisky on the low table and she put out her hand to it. This was the quickest way. Whisky had done it before, it should do it again. She poured out a stiff dose and drank it. The quivering of her jaw lessened. After another drink, it stopped altogether. Some-time she must experiment with herself and find out exactly

how much was enough. But today she was in a hurry. She drank again.

Lunch was nearly over when she went into the dining-room. Geoffrey did not look at her, but the children's startled eyes followed her as she walked up the room and took her place at the end of the table, turning her ravaged face, swollen-lipped, red-eyed, towards them. Burton shot a glance at her from the sideboard and thought, mercy on us. None of them had ever seen her look like this.

Stephen slipped from his chair to go to her, but stood bewildered and in a moment got back again. There was no help or comfort for him in her face; she didn't seem to know he was there. His elbow on the table, he covered his eyes with one hand and tried to go on eating with the other. Judith, her spoon suspended, the pudding she couldn't swallow bulging her cheek, stared from one person to another. Margaret, after a frightened look at her mother, kept her eyes on her father. What would he do, what would he say to Mummy for coming to the table like this? Would there be another row?

But when Geoffrey at length looked at Charlotte, he was startled himself. For the first time, her face silenced him. By God, he thought, she looks awful. He felt something like awe, not of her, but of the effect his anger had on her. Obscurely, he felt a pride in his domination of another human being. In the background of his mind, the line of reasoning he pursued was that he must be important if what he did had such disastrous consequence.

But he felt somehow abashed and when he had finished his biscuits and cheese, he beckoned to Margaret and left

the room. 'Let's go to a cinema, pet,' he whispered conspiratorially and in a few moments, they left the house.

As soon as his father went out of the room, Stephen went to stand beside his mother.

'Was Daddy cross with you?' he got out at last.

'Not really, darling,' said Charlotte, making an effort to answer him. 'It was a misunderstanding,' she said.

Her head throbbed intolerably. She would have to take an aspirin. You had to take whisky to take off the effect of a row and aspirin to take off the effect of the whisky. It couldn't be very good for you; but never mind, she thought. It got you through.

She sent the children to play in the garden and went to lie down on the drawing-room sofa. She did not reappear until dinner-time. When she came down then, there was a letter lying on the hall-table, waiting to be posted. It was addressed to Miss Desmond and Charlotte guessed that it contained Margaret's notice. Her mind, like a creature heavy with sleep, turned away from consideration of the subject. 'I can't help it,' she said to herself. 'What can I do?'

Katherine Mansfield wrote a tale about a fly upon which a man, over and over again, idly dropped a great blot of ink. Over and over again the fly struggled out, dried its wings, worked over itself, recovered, became eager to live, even cheerful, only to be covered by another blot. At last, the fly struggled no more; its resistance was broken. Charlotte was like that fly. Her resistance had been long – thirteen years – but it was at an end. She struggled no more.

Geoffrey's behaviour went in cycles. He made a violent scene and frightened his family off; he then had an attack and drew them all round him again. Then he was violently good-tempered and took them out on a treat. Then he was indifferent for a time, until, bored by inactivity and liverish from lack of exercise, he worked up another row and went through the whole thing again.

It was not long before Geoffrey had another attack and outwardly all was almost as usual. When he called, gasping, from the hall, Charlotte ran to him almost as quickly as before. There was the same struggle to get him back into the morning-room, Cook and Burton helping. But Charlotte found herself thinking it would be much more convenient if he would collapse inside the room instead of out. And though she wiped his brow, took his hand, fussed over him, there was none of the old generous self-blame and warm forgiveness. She admitted suddenly to herself that she no longer believed in his attacks. But she pretended to believe in this one and for a long time in subsequent attacks, because it was easier that way and because he would be furious if he suspected her of seeing through him. She let the farce go on. Charlotte, the slow-grower, the young-so-long, was becoming adult. But at what cost! It doesn't do for some people to see clear; they can't stand it.

Although she did not believe in this attack, it exhausted her just the same. She had a pain at her heart from the effort of lifting Geoffrey and from the running and rubbing she had to do. By dinner-time she was so deadly tired that she asked for wine instead of her customary water.

'Your attack has upset me,' she said to Geoffrey, and ready with sympathy for such a creditable cause, he told Burton to fill her glass again.

You needn't drink whisky, Charlotte noted gratefully; anything would do.

CHAPTER SIX

I

It was Vera's idea, when they were together at Underwood in September, that she and Lucy should, by periodic visits to the house in Queen's Walk, remind Geoffrey that Charlotte had two sisters to be reckoned with, two people who saw and knew what he was doing. So, in December, Lucy wrote to ask Vera when they should go. For some time there was no reply; it was often weeks before Vera wrote. But one night the telephone rang in the hall at Underwood and Lucy put down her book and went to answer it. Lifting the receiver, she heard Vera's voice. 'Oh, hello Vera,' she cried, glowing at once.

Vera was lavish with trunk-calls. Charlotte was not given to telephoning, Lucy did not use trunk-calls unless the need was urgent, but Vera would make a trunk-call to save her the trouble of writing a letter. 'Are you all right, all of you?' cried Lucy.

'Oh, yes,' came Vera's voice from far away, as if they were as right as could be expected. 'About going to Charlotte's, Lucy,' she said.

'Yes?' The telephone at her ear, Lucy's eyes wandered over the wild privet in the white vase, with its narrow leaves and black highly-polished berries.

'I think you'd better go alone this time,' said Vera. 'I can't get away at present. There's too much on at this time of the year – balls, dinners, parties, all sorts of things. Besides,' Vera threw in her trump card, 'there are the children.'

'Yes,' admitted Lucy, who could not deny it. 'But there's no particular hurry. I can wait for you.'

'No, I shouldn't. I don't know when I'll be able to go. You go now. I'll be able to go next time, perhaps.'

'Very well,' said Lucy, distant now in more senses than one. Vera was too fond of backing out of things.

'Well,' resumed Vera briskly, 'what are you doing?'

'Reading.'

Vera laughed affectionately. 'Bookworm. Are you doing anything special for Christmas?'

'No, there will be just William and me.'

'It doesn't sound very festive,' said Vera.

'It will be,' said Lucy.

'What's it like in the country tonight?' asked Vera.

'Very cold, with a bright moon.'

'Ugh,' shuddered Vera. 'What's that noise I can hear? A sort of intermittent screech?'

'It's the owl. He hunts this spot,' said Lucy, becoming more conversational as Vera intended she should. 'He goes on like that all night. Listen, I'll open the window.' Lucy flung open the casement at her hand and held the receiver into the night. The owl screeched. She saw him, dusky, portentous,

legendary, sweep like a shadow in the moonlight. She forgot her annoyance with Vera. The magnificence of the winter night enthralled her. She put the receiver to her ear and closed the window. 'Did you hear him?' she asked.

'I should think I did,' said Vera. 'What a row! How do you sleep?'

'I'm used to it. There's your call finished,' said Lucy, more careful of Vera's money than ever Vera was herself. 'Well, I'll go and see Charlotte soon after Christmas and I'll let you know how things are.'

'All right,' said Vera in a satisfied voice. 'Good night, love.'

'Good night, love,' said Lucy. They used the old north-country endearment for none but one another.

'It was Vera,' said Lucy, going back into the sitting-room and taking up her book.

'What did she want?' asked William, looking over his horn spectacles.

'Just to say she can't go to Charlotte's.'

'I didn't think she would,' said William, returning to his book.

'Well,' said Lucy defendingly, 'it doesn't really matter. I can go by myself.'

'I don't see why you should have to,' said William. 'Or go at all.'

'Never mind,' said Lucy dismissingly, fixing her eyes on Samuel Butler.

'My goodness,' said William after a minute. 'I don't like Geoffrey, but I sympathise with him. I should strongly resent your sisters coming here to see how I behaved myself.'

'You must behave properly,' said Lucy primly. 'Then they won't have to.'

She put her book up before her face and giggled.

William smiled and companionable silence fell. The fire was warm, the lamps glowed softly under their peach-coloured shades. Outside the owl screeched, almost brushing the house in his flights.

II

When Charlotte heard Lucy was coming, she made, for a sister, strange preparations; she laid in whisky and aspirin. There would be trouble during the whole of Lucy's stay. Geoffrey couldn't bear visitors, least of all her sisters. He restrained himself more or less before them, but he took it out on Charlotte in private, and the strain of hiding this fact and of behaving as if nothing was wrong wore her out. The servants knew the worst now, the children knew, but Charlotte was still determined that her sisters should not know; so she took her precautions. She bought whisky and aspirin. Whisky was the only powerful spirit she was acquainted with. It was the first thing she had tried and she kept to it. With a mixture of innocence and deadly deliberation, Charlotte advanced into the dark world of drink and drugs.

It was unthinkable that she should buy whisky for herself from courteous Mr Watson and impossible to buy even aspirin very frequently from Daw, the local chemist, without his wondering what was wrong at home. So Charlotte went down into the city where she was not known. The chemist she hit

upon was a kind man. He gave her a dose of something in the shop because the furtive, guilty feeling occasioned by the expedition had given her wild palpitations and a violent headache. The chemist was so sympathetic that she suddenly told him she couldn't sleep. She slept very badly, she said, standing on the other side of his counter, her blue eyes seeking the help her lips never asked for. He recommended a preparation that had just come out, something to be taken in hot water, sipping it like soup in bed last thing at night. But Charlotte refused it. She couldn't sip anything last thing at night, where Geoffrey was. She must have something inconspicuous. She could not explain this fully to the chemist and had difficulty in avoiding the sleeping soup. But at last he gave her some tablets, with instructions to be careful. 'You don't want to get into the habit of taking this sort of thing,' he said, and Charlotte said oh, no, of course not. She went home and hid tablets and whisky behind the books in the drawing-room bookcase. No one would find them there. Having laid these things in, much as a victim of malaria lays in quinine against the next attack, she felt fortified against Lucy's visit.

After Christmas, Margaret went to the High School, and, Miss Cowley having departed to marry Herbert, Judith went with her. During the last half-term, Margaret had been torn between loyalty to her father and affection for her headmistress and the school. Miss Desmond had been unalterably kind throughout, but that only made it worse for Margaret and she suffered agonies of shame and self-consciousness. It almost broke her heart to leave, and yet it was a relief. But

the move was bad for her. She was lost at the High School; she never did well, never found her feet in the vast flood of four hundred girls. It was different for Judith, who started in the kindergarten, got used to everything and moved easily up the school. There was no doubt that she had a better chance from the first than her sister.

Judith took to school like a duckling to water. Every morning, round-eyed with eagerness and interest, she set off in a heavy domed hat of brown felt and a bunchy, belted coat, also brown. She sat among the schoolgirls in the bus, gazing with awe at these people who knew where to get off and did homework. She went to school in the morning only, returning home at midday, and she had already been doing this for a fortnight when Lucy arrived to stay at the house in Queen's Walk.

III

Lucy was struck anew by the carefulness of Geoffrey's dress. After the creased look of William, she marvelled at Geoffrey's finish. The day she arrived he was a study in brown, dark brown suit, tan silk shirt, dark silk socks and brown shoes without a speck on them. On the little finger of each hand he wore a ring with a blue stone; they matched, noticed Lucy, marvelling. That was something he had added to himself since she last saw him.

Everything about Geoffrey had been thought out, even his gestures. He had a habit of hooking his hands together, waist high, with his elbows out. As soon as his hands hooked, his

right foot advanced in the first position for dancing. It was inevitable. He never missed. It was another of his gestures to dig his hands into his trouser pockets, bow over from the waist and swoop up enquiringly. That was when he asked a question and expected to catch the interrogated out. Lucy's face as she looked on at these posturings would have amused her husband. 'What does he do it for?' her expression mutely, but unmistakably asked. 'Why bother?'

Lucy did not admire Geoffrey at all; she didn't like him; but she understood Charlotte's inferiority-complex, because in his company she almost developed one herself. Not only did she feel that her hair must be coming down and that she was not half so smart as she ought to be, but she felt almost without intelligence. Nothing bloomed in her; the dry, teasing, tiresome wind of Geoffrey blew over her spirit and parched everything up.

At his board, she felt not only unwanted but unentertaining; the one followed upon the other for Lucy. She thought it ridiculous that she, a mature woman, should find herself without enough small talk to get her through the meals, but so it was. Charlotte didn't help much; she sat at her end of the table, replying to Geoffrey, but saying little in between. Geoffrey, however, talked.

'Excellent steak, Burton,' he would say. 'Give Cook my love and tell her she's done it very nicely.'

Burton smiled above him as she removed the dish.

'Although,' Geoffrey amended, drumming his fingers on the table, 'I should have liked a few more mushrooms.'

'I don't think Cook had any more, sir. I think that's what

it was,' said Burton, poised with the dish like the miniature of
Lady Caroline Lamb.

'Good Lord, why not?' said Geoffrey, registering displeasure. 'The woman's only to order, hasn't she?'

'Yes, sir, but I think she forgot, sir.'

'She shouldn't forget. Don't give her my love.'

'Very well, sir.'

'Keep it yourself,' said Geoffrey, looking round the side of
his carving-chair at the handsome red-haired girl.

'Thank you, sir,' said Burton demurely.

Lucy's face was a careful blank. This was all so *silly*, she
thought, glancing at Charlotte. Charlotte sat with a faint
smile; her way of seeming to join in, Lucy surmised.

Both Margaret and Stephen had lunch at school, but
Judith came home and Lucy was glad of her company.
But even with Judith, Lucy found herself, under Geoffrey's
malicious eye, making aunt-like conversation, sententious,
improving. How dreadful is the effect of another person's
opinion, she thought. He expects me to be worthy, so I am
worthy. I won't say anything at table today. Far better not,
since everything sounds wrong.

But whether she made improving conversation or said
nothing, it did not seem to matter to Judith, who, spooning
up potato or pudding, sent smiles of pure friendship across
to her aunt. They got on very well.

During her visit, Lucy went at noon to meet Judith, getting
off the bus at the end of the road. It gave her great pleasure
to see the small figure detach itself from other small figures
and make for her at a rush.

Judith's hand went into her aunt's as a matter of course and as she hopped and skipped over the pavement she told all that had gone on at school.

Modern methods of education left Lucy rather at a loss. When Judith showed a small twig wrapped round with coloured wools and said: 'I've brought my sewing home,' Lucy was puzzled.

'Are you sure it's sewing?' she asked.

'Oh, it's sewing,' Judith gravely assured her.

Instead of the aunt's instructing the niece how to spell, it was the other way round, and Lucy struggled humbly but unsuccessfully with 'Em – er – mer' and other phonetics.

But in the afternoon, when they went for walks while Charlotte rested, Lucy regained adult ascendancy. She told tales, tale after tale, since the world is full of tales, and she saw in Judith's face a rapt interest she had rarely seen in the faces of her sisters. They had not listened like this, they had always been ready to turn off to something more lively than listening. But Judith could lose herself in a tale as Lucy could and it was another bond between them.

Judith announced that she had to learn a 'piece of poetry' to say at school and Lucy hit upon 'The Cow', by Robert Louis Stevenson. Judith chose odd and often inconvenient times for rehearsal and repetition.

'The Cow', she would proclaim, hurling herself into her aunt's bed at seven o'clock in the morning. 'The friendly cow all red and white, I love with all my might,' she would rattle, snuggling in with determination. The cheek, the confidence of the snuggling, the childish roguery in saying it wrong so as

to rouse her conscientious but sleepy aunt, all endeared her more and more to Lucy.

'The Cow' had to be shouted, it had to be whispered, to be chanted. But when Judith burst out with it at lunch, Geoffrey snapped: 'For God's sake, shut up and don't let me hear that damned thing again.'

Margaret would have been crushed, Stephen resentful, but Judith merely sent a conspiratorial glance to her aunt and as soon as they left the house that afternoon, she shouted out 'The Cow' at the top of her voice to make up for having kept it in so long.

'That's the spirit,' thought Lucy, but daren't say so. It was the spirit to set up against Geoffrey, the only spirit that would save anybody from him.

But for Judith, the visit would have been a failure. Lucy could not feel that she was doing anything for Charlotte by being there. Charlotte was as uncommunicative as ever. She seemed to alternate between a highly nervous state and a curious faint dullness, hardly noticeable to anyone who had not known her as she once was.

'Are you well, darling?' asked Lucy anxiously.

'Quite,' said Charlotte dismissingly.

'Have you seen a doctor, lately?'

'We have no doctor since Doctor Sands was so stupid about Geoffrey's heart. But why should I see a doctor? There's nothing wrong with me.'

At first Lucy was admitted to the morning-room and had to sit with Geoffrey in the evenings. She tried to read or talk to Charlotte, but she was acutely conscious of his uncongenial

presence. 'I'm allergic to him,' she wrote to William. 'To me, he's like cats to some people, or pollen to a victim of hay-fever. I'm sure Charlotte is allergic to him too, in a different way. He's a powerful irritant to me, but I'm afraid he is death to her.'

One night as they sat before the morning-room fire, with the day's papers, though Geoffrey was in such a genial mood he wouldn't let anyone read, the telephone rang. Geoffrey reached out and took up the receiver. 'Hello? Hello? Right you are. Wait a moment,' he said, holding out the receiver. 'Lucy.'

'Me?' cried Lucy. Her eyes flew wide, her throat went dry. William must be ill. He must have had an accident. Something must have happened to make somebody ring up at this distance at this time.

'Come on, come on,' said Geoffrey, thrusting the telephone into her hands.

'Hello?' said Lucy. 'Who is it?' A strange voice, a man's, answered 'Hello' and threw Lucy into greater agitation. 'What is it?' she asked. 'What's happened? Is my husband all right?'

'I hope so,' said the voice. 'I haven't the pleasure of knowing him.'

'Who are you?' called Lucy. 'Who is it?'

'Who are *you*?' asked the voice.

'Who am I?' repeated Lucy astonished. 'My name is Moore. I thought you wanted to speak to me. Didn't you?'

'I think this must be one of Leigh's jokes,' said the voice.

Lucy looked round and saw Geoffrey doubled in mirth. 'The fool,' she said vehemently. 'I'm sorry. Goodbye.' She rang off.

'Here,' said Geoffrey in annoyance. 'I wanted to speak to him.'

'You can ring him up then,' said Lucy shortly. She could not forgive him the sharp pang that pierced her when she heard the strange voice about, so she imagined, to tell her that William had been killed in the car.

Displeased with the reception of his joke, Geoffrey evidently gave orders that Lucy was to be admitted no more to the morning-room. A fire was lit in the drawing-room and the sisters sat there. The room was cold from disuse and the wintry weather, and to keep warm the sisters sat close to the fire contemplating nothing but the chimney-piece. But Lucy often had a strange feeling that there was something in the room behind them that Charlotte was acutely conscious of, or that there was something that Charlotte wanted to do that Lucy's presence prevented her from doing. It was an uneasy, puzzling feeling that Lucy could not account for. 'Don't let me interfere with your arrangements, will you?' she said sometimes. But Charlotte only smiled and said she hadn't any. For all that, Lucy wondered if not only Geoffrey, but also Charlotte, waited for her to go.

Now and then, the children came into the room, but soon went back to their own affairs in the nursery. Once, in the hope of keeping them, Lucy jumped up and said: 'Let's play the piano.'

'Oh, don't,' cried Charlotte in alarm. 'Geoffrey's working.'

They never forgot that he was in the house, behind the closed door of the morning-room. Everything was arranged so that he should not be disturbed. All the vacuum-cleaning was done before he began work in the morning. The children always came quietly into the house and stole up and down the stairs. In the hall, everybody spoke in whispers. Geoffrey's business letters, requisitions, telephone calls, required the silence necessary, but probably never obtained, for the composition of a masterpiece of music or literature. Yet, Lucy noticed, though Geoffrey insisted on such silence during the day, in the evening when Margaret and Stephen were doing their homework in the nursery, they could get no quiet at all. Geoffrey called a dozen times an hour from below: 'Margaret! Margaret!'

'It must be very hard for her to do her homework when she keeps being called off like that,' said Lucy in the drawing-room.

Charlotte smiled. 'Margaret doesn't mind. She hates homework.'

'But she won't do well at school if she doesn't keep up with the others.'

'She doesn't do well,' said Charlotte.

'What a pity. What's she going to do when she leaves school?'

'She's going to be Geoffrey's secretary.'

'Oh, dear,' said Lucy, unable to hide her apprehension. 'D'you think that's a good thing?'

Charlotte shrugged her shoulders. 'It's what Geoffrey has decided.'

'I thought young people decided for themselves nowadays,' said Lucy.

'Did you?' said Charlotte.

Though secretly startled, since it was quite unlike the old Charlotte to demolish with two laconic words any generalisation, Lucy admitted that Charlotte was right. The young had no more chance against the old than they had ever had. Adult personality, good or evil, had as much power as ever against the young plastic minds at its mercy in childhood. How could it be otherwise? Even in the apparently small matter of homework, Margaret's powers of perseverance and resistance were being steadily undermined. This was a modern household. The parents were young, prosperous, the children apparently had everything – good schools, friends, toys, treats of all kinds. Yet Geoffrey's influence, in Lucy's opinion, was as disastrous as that of Samuel Butler's father, Mr Barrett of Wimpole Street, or any other old-style parent.

'Can't *you* do anything?' said Lucy. She saw again the dangerous look that had come into Charlotte's eyes that day, long ago, when Vera warned her not to marry Geoffrey. 'I mean,' said Lucy, 'have you no say in Margaret's future? You're her mother.'

'But it's what they both want. Margaret's looking forward tremendously to being Geoffrey's secretary.'

'He's made her want it. You can make the young want anything.'

'Now you're contradicting yourself,' smiled Charlotte. 'A moment ago you said the young decided things for themselves nowadays.'

Lucy blushed faintly. Charlotte was quick against her to defend her own weakness, or powerlessness, or hopelessness, quick to quibble and fence so as not to admit it, whichever it was.

The gong went. Always when they were getting somewhere, drawing near the heart of the matter, the gong went, or Geoffrey called out, or the children came in. Lucy sighed. But going down the stairs, Charlotte put her arm through Lucy's to make up for having caught her out, and Lucy squeezed it with her own. They couldn't speak out, it seemed, but gestures like this now and then reminded them that they were sisters and loved each other, no matter how deeply the circumstances of their lives seemed to divide them.

The last night of Lucy's stay, they all went to the pantomime. On arrival, Lucy had wished to take the children but Geoffrey refused to let them go. He'd heard it was very poor, he said. But now he suddenly announced that he had booked seats for everybody for the night before Lucy's departure. 'By way of celebration,' he said, with malicious ambiguity.

They had seats in the front row of the dress circle, which gave Geoffrey the chance to drop matches and pellets of paper on to the heads of the people below. He did this surreptitiously, inviting the children to be amused. He also stood up unnecessarily several times, collecting notice. At last, however, the curtain went up and he subsided.

The strong light from the stage illuminated the Leighs and Lucy looked at them. The presentation of an ideal family, they must seem, she thought. The children so attractive – the elder girl so prettily fond of her father – the mother so

appealing, the father so cheerful, so bent on being amused and amusing.

Watching Charlotte, Lucy was sad. She had loved Geoffrey with all her heart. Too much. 'You shouldn't love as much as that,' thought Lucy. 'It's a bit abject. You should keep something of your self.' The supposed family recklessness had, in Charlotte, taken the form of love for Geoffrey. It must have been dreadful for her to love such a man so much, and now that she loved him no longer it was equally dreadful for her. 'She can't bear not to love him, any more than she could bear to love him,' thought Lucy. 'My poor girl.'

She looked at Geoffrey. He was biting his nails now, a habit he had. His eyes were on the stage as he bit ferociously, swiftly round each nail. Suddenly he left his nails and looked down at Margaret, flushed and happy beside him. He passed his hand over her hair, dragging her back from her pleasure in the play to remind her of himself. She smiled up at him and he took her hand and drew it through his arm.

'He isn't destroying them of set purpose,' thought Lucy. 'He doesn't mean to. He's just being himself.'

Stephen leaned on the arm of his mother's seat, often turning to share the jokes with her, but often she missed them. She wasn't listening, Lucy could see.

Judith, in a pale pink frock smocked with pale blue, sat on the edge of the seat next to her aunt's. Her fair hair hung forward, her eyes were like stars. You could tell what was happening on the stage by watching Judith. When the fairy queen bowed, Judith bowed. When the cat mewed, Judith's face took on a piteous expression.

What would happen to them all, thought Lucy, love and anxiety in her heart.

The next day, she went home. She spent half the journey yearning backwards over Charlotte and the children, especially Judith. To be able to turn her back on Geoffrey when they couldn't seemed too much discrimination in her favour. She hated to leave them to him; but what else could she do? She couldn't stay; they couldn't go.

Sadly, Lucy was beginning to accept the fact that she could do practically nothing for Charlotte. She understood as never before that God helps those who help themselves. It was not, as she used to interpret it, that God will only, he can only help those who help themselves. It was true of human help too. Charlotte was not open to help; she refused to be. Her attitude baffled and frightened Lucy, who tried to give herself the satisfaction that she was nevertheless doing something by determining to do her best for the children. But what?

To be an aunt is an unenviable thing, she thought. You stand so close, you see mistakes being made, injuries being done, but you daren't say anything. You can only do what the parents allow you to do and that is precious little. In the night when one's thoughts ride high and wild, having cast off the ballast of the day, Lucy made plans for getting Judith away, for adopting her, transplanting her to a soil where she could grow and be happy, but daylight brought her down to the limitations of the practical and all she was able to do was to get Geoffrey's permission that Judith should spend the Easter

holidays at Underwood, and even that might be withdrawn, since he was always changing his mind.

With the other two, she was not accepted as she was by Judith. Margaret was entirely her father's daughter. She knew her aunt did not like her father and she wasn't going to like anyone who didn't like him. That would have been disloyal; so she held off from Lucy. Stephen was a well-mannered little boy, but he wasn't giving himself away to anybody. He and Judith were as good friends as the difference in their ages allowed, but he had no confidence in the grown-ups. He was devoted to his mother, but his attitude towards her was strangely adult, protective rather than confiding.

Altogether, Lucy's chances of helping were limited. It didn't seem as if she were going to be able to do much more than hang about them, fussing in private and doing nothing in public. Just as she did for her sisters. 'It seems to be my lot in life,' she thought. 'It's pitiable.'

Most people scoffed at this notion of helping. Even William thought she shouldn't bother. Even she herself was handicapped by a dislike of interfering and a fear of being thought a prig. The taunt of being like Aunt Phoebe still had power over Lucy.

Her thoughts stretched backwards, caught on the problems of the house she had just left, but the realisation that she was halfway home released them and they sprang forward with pleasure and relief. She was going home! Sitting in the corner with her book, she looked calm, but inwardly she was as excited as a child coming home from boarding-school. She kept smiling at the prospect of seeing William at the station.

He was there. As soon as she got out of the train she saw his tall, lean figure tacking towards her in the windy dark.

'Oh, William,' she said.

'Ah, there you are!' he said in a voice full of satisfaction, and gave her such a hearty kiss that he knocked her hat askew. He dived for her luggage with his usual energy. 'You bring those, porter. I'll take these,' he said and went off so fast she had almost to run to keep up with him.

Cora was in the back of the car, positively yowling with love and excitement. She pawed Lucy's unfortunate hat as she got in with a hard, insistent paw. 'Yes, darling, yes, I know,' said Lucy. 'I'm just as glad as you are, but let me get in and do be a bit quieter.'

When Lucy and William were settled in the front seats and the car began to move, Cora thrust her head between them, her nose on Lucy's shoulder. She was quiet now, she didn't need any more notice. She was as contented as they were; the family was complete again.

'Well, how've you been?' asked Lucy.

'Oh, all right. Bit lonely.'

'Good,' said Lucy complacently. 'I like to be missed. How's Janet? Has she been feeding you properly?'

'Yes. Rather a lot of vivid blancmanges and sawdusty cakes, perhaps.'

'Packets!' pounced Lucy. 'She's always urging me to try those packets from the village shop, but I never will, so she's been seizing the opportunity to try them herself, you poor boy. How're the hens?'

'They're doing their duty as well as the cold allows. Daftie's still laying in the coke.'

'Bother her,' said Lucy.

Daftie was Lucy's special hen. Dull and backward as a chick, or so William had said, Daftie had been reared by Lucy's hand and was now a fine pullet. But she had kept her idiosyncrasies. She would not eat with the others, but came to the kitchen. She would not frequent the public nest-boxes, but when wishful to lay came peeking and picking to the boiler-house, from whence gentle crepitations betrayed the fact that she was climbing the coke. On the cindery summit, she laid her egg and delicately, with more crepitations, descended. But Lucy was not so light-footed; when she climbed up for the egg, the coke rolled upon her, and when she came down again, she brought half of it with her. But though she said 'Bother her' now, she was already looking forward to scrabbling in the coke once more. It was part of home.

'I brought the book you wanted from the library. Letters of Héloïse, is it?' said William.

'Oh, thank you,' said Lucy fervently. A rich glow of satisfaction filled her.

'Mrs Buckle's been up,' said William, continuing the small items of news that mean nothing except to those living under the same roof.

'Oh, dear, is Julia in bed again?'

The village had not at once accepted the Moores when they came to live in it. They thought, at first, that Lucy was a bit queer, walking alone so much in the Park, and stranger still, gathering sticks. 'I don't know whatever she does it for,'

said Mrs Lupton at the shop, defendingly. 'They seem to be quite well off.' The village thought then that Lucy must be mean, but as time disproved it, they came to the conclusion that it was just a harmless fancy of hers to pick up firewood. They now looked on tolerantly; they let her. As for William, the fact that he kept bees and knew a good deal about them opened the gate of every other bee-keeper in the place. Nothing is so uniting as bees.

Gradually, the village had fallen into the habit of coming to Lucy for help. Mrs Buckle had been for it now. Years ago, the village scandalmonger, Mrs Mills, had worked up a quarrel between Julia Buckle and her young man. He flung off to Canada and eventually married there. Julia appeared to take it calmly enough, but suddenly she took to her bed and refused to get up. Nobody could get her up. The Rector failed, the doctor failed, her widowed mother failed, friends and neighbours too. Julia remained in her bed, until, one summer afternoon, the village was electrified by the sight of Julia knitting at the cottage door. Mrs Moore had done it, word went round; persuaded her out of bed and set her to knit. She was to be paid for what she knitted too and Mrs Moore was asking everybody to keep Julia busy. Julia remained, mostly, up, but now and then when the commissions fell off, she retired to bed again. Lucy's friends had almost reached saturation point in the matter of knitted goods and she would be hard put to it now to find something for Julia to knit. But find something she must, she thought, as, passing in the car, she saw the light of Julia's candle glimmering under the thatch and pictured the girl lying there in apathy, her face to the wall.

The car turned into the by-lane and the scene framed now in the windscreen combined the distinction of the wood-cut with the sentiment of the old-fashioned Christmas card. The church tower loomed dark and square, the gaunt trees branched boldly against the starry sky, the Park gates stood sentry to solitude, but the little house, home, lay low and comfortably to the earth, with lights showing through its criss-cross windows exactly in the old tradition. Lucy got out of the car and the country air was sweet after the town and the train. The clock in the church tower struck eight and the sound was like the air and sky and trees, clear, unblurred. She was glad to come home to simplicity and beauty and the things that don't change after the fret and uncertainty of the house in Queen's Walk. She only wished, she thought with a sigh, that she could have brought Judith with her.

The house door was flung open and the warm light from the hall showed Janet's stocky figure. 'I thought I heard the car. Let me take those things, now, and you go in to the fire. You must be starved,' she fussed.

It was good to be home.

Snow fell lightly in the night. In the afternoon, when Lucy took Cora for a walk in the deserted park, she came across, in the spinney, a miniature, bare, bleached snowberry bush holding a little, dry, loose, last-year's nest. When she looked inside, she found it held, not an egg, but a snow-flake. This complete epitome of winter pleased her so much she longed again for Judith. It was just the thing to show to a child. She must get Judith here, she told herself.

At Easter she did. She went to fetch her and aunt and
niece travelled to Underwood in the greatest excitement
and incredulity at having brought it off. Judith was entranced
to make the acquaintance of pussy-willows and lamb's-tails
in the hedges and to gather the first primroses. In summer,
she came again and ran through the fields in tussore frocks
spotted with pink or blue. In the woods, they played hide-
and-seek, Judith always hiding. She instructed Lucy how
to play. 'Say: "I never thought you'd be there." Say: "Where
is she? Where *can* she be?"' One year, at Christmas when
she came, she had measles. When her temperature was high
and Lucy read to her, she would beseech in a hoarse voice:
'Read faster, faster. Read fast.' So Lucy galloped through
Hans Andersen while the hot little girl in bed followed the
words and images, keeping out discomfort with determination.

And so she established her place in the house, and her
aunt and uncle and the house established their place with
her.

By fetching Judith and taking her home again, Lucy told
herself that she was keeping in touch with Charlotte. But
this was not really so. You could no more touch Charlotte
than you could touch a sea-anemone without its closing up
altogether. Vera wrote approvingly of Lucy's frequent visits
to Denborough. She herself had never carried out her plan
of going there from time to time. She could never make
it convenient; there was always too much going on. Since
Charlotte, without making any explanation, entirely gave

up visiting her sisters, and Vera was always too busy to leave home, Lucy felt that, but for her, they would never see one another. She continued, however, to pay determined visits, uninvited, to both of them.

CHAPTER SEVEN

I

The Leigh children had never been allowed animals. Their father had never permitted any kitten, rabbit, guinea-pig or white mouse. The only pet they had ever had was a woolly caterpillar who, though fun at first and kept in a match-box lined with nasturtium leaves, gradually became entirely unresponsive and turned into a cocoon. They could do, and had done, without cats, rabbits, guinea-pigs and mice, but what they could never be happy without, they were sure, was a dog. They had never ceased to long for a dog and to envy passionately the people who had one. Their favourite game, sitting on the rug before the nursery fire in winter, or trailing out on walks in the summer, was to say what sort of a dog they would have if they could have one, what his name would be, who would take him out and in what turn. In his drawer, Stephen had a list of names for a dog that he had made out and added to as time went on.

Lucy was astonished when Judith, on being given sixpence to spend in Woolworth's, bought a dog-collar, a green dog-collar with a medal for the name attached.

'But you haven't a dog, darling,' said Lucy, laughing.

Judith hung her head over the collar.

'I know,' she said.

Lucy was sorry she had laughed; the longing for a dog evidently went deep.

Very rarely, at most only two or three times a year, when their father appeared to be in a very good humour, did the children venture to bring out again their trembling hope. Margaret was, as always, deputised to do it. She always had to ask for everything.

After a day when everything had miraculously gone well, Stephen would suddenly say: 'Let's risk it. Ask him, Margaret.'

Dry-mouthed, they stared at one another, their hearts beating fast with renewed hope and excitement. 'Oh, I daren't,' gulped Margaret, going pale.

'Go on. Try,' urged Stephen compellingly.

'Oh, Margaret, do, do! Think! He might say yes. He might,' cried Judith, jumping up and down.

'Shut up, Ju. Keep quiet,' flashed Stephen. 'You'll give the show away. Go on, Margaret.'

'Oh, if I only dare . . . '

''Course you dare,' encouraged Stephen. 'Go on. He might say yes and then you'd never have to ask again.'

Margaret, silent, taut, would steal to the top of the stairs and hang over, listening. Perhaps her father would hum or whistle below. The atmosphere was still favourable. Perhaps this really was the moment? With a last desperate glance at the others and a nervous swallow, she would go down.

'Damn you, you persistent little beggar,' Geoffrey would

shout, his good humour over. 'Can't you understand the meaning of the word "no"? Once and for all – no! Do you hear? NO. That's what you've been soaping round me all day for, all of you, is it?'

'Oh, Daddy, it isn't,' said Margaret miserably. She could not bear him to think that she pretended to love him to get something out of him.

'Bah, it is. Now get out. I don't want to see you again today.'

It was typical of him, as of all tyrants domestic or otherwise, that he forced people to cringe and then despised them for cringing.

Margaret went slowly back to the others. She had no need to tell them. They had heard their father shout and that was enough. Nobody said anything. Avoiding one another's eyes, they went back to the nursery. But for some time afterwards nobody could find anything to do. The savour had gone out of everything again.

For years, this asking and refusing went on. Then, one Friday evening in spring, when Margaret and Stephen were getting through their homework to have done with it for the weekend and Judith was drawing on the nursery floor, they heard their father come into the house and heard, in addition, a most unaccustomed sound. They lifted their heads, looking at one another. Their mouths fallen open, Stephen slowly paling, they listened. The sounds were yelps, the excited yelps of a very little dog.

The pens fell from the fingers of the two at the table, Judith scrambled up from the floor. They made a rush for the top of the stairs. They leaned over and listened from there.

More yelps. The morning-room door was open and they could see their parents standing together looking down at the floor. Released from the paralysis of incredulity, the children rushed down the stairs.

'Daddy,' shrieked Margaret.

With a gesture he kept them back. There on the green carpet was a little pot-bellied fox-terrier pup, white with brown and black patches.

'Is it . . . ?' Stephen clutched his father's arm and looked up with something like anguish. 'Is it – ours?'

He couldn't bear to look at it if it were not, if it were just a dog that had been brought in and must go out again. But his father nodded and Stephen fell to his knees on the floor, patting the carpet.

'Puppy! Puppy!' he said hoarsely.

The pup responded with ecstasy. It dashed itself at Stephen's hands, at his bare knees, biting at both with its tiny saw-like teeth, yapping madly. It would not be caught, it wriggled like an eel, it dashed to a distance, looked at Stephen out of the corner of an eye and dashed back again.

'Oh, Daddy, let me kiss you,' said Margaret. 'You're so good.'

'Let me kiss you too,' said Judith fervently. She rarely kissed her father, except to say 'good night', but the provider of this longed-for puppy must be thanked, must be rewarded, so she followed him out to the cloakroom, holding up her face ready to bestow the kiss when he should have finished taking off his overcoat. When at last he bent to receive it, she rushed back to the others.

To his annoyance, an important client had presented Geoffrey with the puppy that afternoon. What the hell does the fellow want to saddle me with a dog for, he asked himself. He meant to give it away at once, but in the car one of his sudden changes of mind and mood had come over him. The puppy was a funny, sensible little thing. It lay quietly on the seat beside Geoffrey's, its nose on its paws. Every time Geoffrey looked down at it, it looked up without moving its nose, showing the whites of its eyes. If it had wanted to be kept by Geoffrey, it couldn't have hit on wiser behaviour. He took it home and now he was pleased with the effect of his gift on the children. He felt all the pleasure of the capricious who know the pleasure of giving as well as the pleasure of withholding. He went back into the morning-room and stretched himself out in his chair, watching the children and the pup on the floor.

'Hi,' he said after a moment. 'What about my slippers?'

Margaret got up at once.

'Oh, yes, Daddy,' she said, rushing out and returning with his red morocco slippers. She knelt on the floor and untied his shoe-laces.

Stephen got up from the floor too and came to stand beside his father's chair. Now he forgave his father everything, he loved his father now with all his heart. The father had won the son for ever, if he cared to keep him. Stephen's face, completely candid and happy, beamed on his father. He looked so charming that even Geoffrey noticed and was surprised. He thought his son a morose little blighter as a rule, always hanging round his mother.

Charlotte stood by the fire, looking on; but her reaction to

the scene was not what it would have been once. Once she could have been as happy as the children, not because they had got what they wanted, though she would have been glad of that, but because Geoffrey had shown himself generous and kind. She used to be so happy to be able to think of him as generous and kind, and every time she had so thought of him her hopes rose and she imagined that he would go on being both. But not now. Something would happen before long, she knew, to undo what he had done today. The children wouldn't look like that for long. Here was Stephen forgiving Geoffrey, being grateful to him, loving him as she used to – well, thought Charlotte, he would have to give all that up before long. Geoffrey would make him.

And since they were all absorbed and wouldn't miss her, she thought she would go up to the drawing-room for a while. So, smiling and saying in a bright, conversational way: 'Yes, he certainly is a darling puppy and it's very good of Daddy to give him to you,' she stepped over the arms and legs of the children on the floor and went upstairs.

'What shall we call him, Daddy?' asked Stephen. He wanted to call the puppy by a name his father would like, he wanted to share the puppy with his father.

'Oh, I don't know, old chap,' said Geoffrey. 'What do you think?'

'He's come on a Friday,' said Margaret, looking up from the floor. 'Shall we call him Friday?'

'Like Man Friday in *Robinson Crusoe*,' said Judith with glee, getting a pat in on the puppy's satin coat whenever he kept still enough to allow it.

'Oh,' shouted Stephen with sudden excitement. 'I've got it. What about Crusoe? You know – after the dog Crusoe?'

'Oh, yes,' chorused the girls in fervent agreement. 'Crusoe! Crusoe!'

'Do you like that, Daddy?' asked Stephen.

'Yes, it will do as well as anything,' said Geoffrey. 'Now off you go, all of you. Take him to the nursery.'

'Oooh, yes.' Stephen picked up the puppy, who was easily contained on his haunches, in one hand, his front paws hanging neatly over, his ears cocked, his bright eyes trustfully considering his new world. 'Can we make all arrangements, Daddy? I mean about feeding and sleeping and everything?' asked Stephen.

'Yes, yes,' said Geoffrey, sweeping them away. 'Do as you like. He's yours.'

'Oh, thank you . . . thanks awfully, Daddy . . .'

They rushed out of the room together.

'Hi, Margaret,' called Geoffrey. 'Get me the sherry, pet,' he said when she reappeared, 'and come and tell me what you've been doing today.'

It was some time before she could fly up to the others, who were rushing about getting first one thing, then another: a bowl of water, a plate and some supper, a blanket, a bed. Crusoe rushed with them and every other moment someone had to rescue something from his teeth. They had never been so happy in their lives, and though they had never thought of a dog like this when they used to discuss what kind they would have if they could have one, it was because, said Stephen, they could never have *imagined* a dog so perfect as Crusoe. The

girls agreed with fervour. They all rolled on the floor with laughter when Crusoe growled; his growl was such a miniature affair. They doted on him. 'Oh, look at him!' they kept beseeching one another. 'Look at him now!'

Judith had always been conscious of being the youngest, the least experienced, but through Crusoe now she mysteriously caught up with the other two. Doting on Crusoe, they were at one and Judith was given her equal part and made exquisitely happy when Stephen said: 'You know you'll have to take him out in the afternoons, Ju. You get home earlier than we do.'

'Oh, Stephen,' she said, solemn at the thought of such a trust. 'Shall I really? I'll be very, very careful with him.'

'I shall make him a brace,' said Stephen grandly. 'You know the sort of thing . . . '

They were full of plans. They re-planned their lives which, in future, were to revolve round Crusoe. They did revolve round him. He changed their lives; he was something to love, protect, have fun with, tell things to. Whatever else went wrong in the house, whatever failed to come off, there was always Crusoe. Crusoe was a liberation to the Leigh children.

Judith penned a letter to her Aunt Lucy. It was headed by a drawing of what looked like a tuning-fork topped with a pudding-basin and a rolling-pin on four legs alongside, but was actually, Lucy guessed, a representation of Judith taking Crusoe for a walk.

'Crusoe et Daddy's sliper,' ran the body of the letter. 'We thort Daddy would be cross but Cruso roled on his back wen Daddy came home and loked so funy Daddy only larft so we are biing new slipers for his berthday.'

Geoffrey laughed at the puppy for quite a while, but he laughed less as time went on. The children kept pointing out how funny Crusoe was, but their father gradually ceased to be amused, and by the following winter Stephen, who had found an unexpected ally in Cook, had to deputise her to keep Crusoe out of his father's way in the mornings. Judith could certainly be trusted to keep herself as well as Crusoe out of his way in the afternoons.

It took only one or two kicks to teach Crusoe to keep out of Geoffrey's way himself. To see Crusoe giving his feet a wide berth would have betrayed Geoffrey to any observant caller. He knew when he wasn't wanted all right, thought Stephen proudly. His behaviour showed his extreme intelligence. Although once he made a mistake when Geoffrey's temper blew up suddenly from nowhere. He stormed and shouted and Crusoe, thinking his precious children were going to be hurt, not only barked madly but flew at Geoffrey's trousers. Geoffrey had to stop swearing at his family to swear at the dog. He kicked out at Crusoe, but missed him, which enraged him further. Stephen snatched up Crusoe, and rushed him from the room.

'That was very nice of you, old chap,' he said to him in the nursery. 'But you must never do it again. Never. Do you understand? You'll get yourself and us into the most awful trouble.'

Crusoe never did it again. When Geoffrey began to row, Crusoe went to the door and whined to be let out in case he should give way to temptation.

Geoffrey was annoyed by Crusoe's unalterable distrust of

him. It made no difference that Geoffrey was sometimes very amiable indeed; Crusoe wouldn't trust him. Crusoe's behaviour was an indication to Geoffrey's character. Whatever flattery Geoffrey got from the people who surrounded him, from the dog he got the truth; so he didn't like him. By the time a year and a half had gone, Crusoe had become 'that damned dog of yours.' – 'You'd better keep that dog out of my way,' he threatened. 'Or it will be the worse for it.'

Crusoe liked everybody, except Geoffrey, but he was really Stephen's dog. From the beginning he had recognised Stephen as his natural master, and the girls loved him so much they let him have his preference and were not jealous.

Crusoe slept, officially, in the nursery, but actually he slept on Stephen's bed. It tickled Stephen immensely that Crusoe did not come into his room until after his father had come upstairs and closed his bedroom door. About ten minutes after that, almost to the second, Crusoe, with the lightest possible toe-nail tappings, came into Stephen's room, jumped on to the end of the bed and, puffing out a sigh, turned round twice and lay down. Stephen sometimes stuffed the sheet into his mouth to stifle his mirth and then Crusoe's tail swished against the eiderdown, sharing it. 'Fancy knowing to the minute when to come,' thought Stephen fondly. 'He knows everything. There isn't a thing he doesn't know.' He put out a hand and patted Crusoe and Crusoe licked him and they fell asleep in perfect companionship.

II

Holidays for the Leighs depended upon Geoffrey's caprice. Some summers they had no holiday, others they spent a month at an expensive hotel. This year, since July and August had gone, they had given up expecting a holiday at all. Then their father announced that they were going to the inn at Merthwaite in September for the last fortnight before they went back to school. He himself, he said, would go down for the weekends only.

At this, the children's eyes gleamed with secret joy. To be going away without their father, to have a holiday all to themselves, to be going to Merthwaite where they had always longed to stay, above all to be taking Crusoe to the stream! Even Margaret was glad to be going without her father because Crusoe would have a much better time and they would be freer to enjoy themselves with him. But they kept their joy as secret as they could. They always felt that if they let their hopes be seen, something would happen to ruin them.

Living with Geoffrey was certainly a difficult affair. If the children had shown no pleasure in the holiday he had arranged for them he would have railed at them for ingratitude, but since they did show pleasure, in spite of themselves, he was piqued that they should be glad to go away without him, especially Margaret. Almost unconsciously, he looked about for a way of damping their pleasure.

Everything was arranged. Stephen and Margaret were to ride the eighteen miles to Merthwaite on their bicycles.

Judith, who had only a small share in her sister's bicycle and who rode, anyway, on the pedals, would go with her mother and the luggage by car. Geoffrey would drive them down and come back at once to the town.

The longed-for day of departure drew slowly near; a Tuesday. On Monday, at lunch, since he loved to insist what must and must not be done, Geoffrey reiterated that at two-thirty prompt the next day Charlotte, Judith and the luggage must be in the car.

Judith, with a smile of pure delight, could not forbear to add: 'And Crusoe too.'

'Ah, Crusoe,' said Geoffrey and paused in his delicate carving of the meat. 'Crusoe's not going,' he said. 'He's staying at home with Cook and me.'

He had only just thought of it. He didn't really mean it. It was almost one of his jokes, but unfortunately the children took it seriously. It was Stephen's reaction that brought about the disaster. Stephen flushed and rapped out: 'Of course Crusoe's going.'

Geoffrey narrowed his eyes at his son. He made a long pause.

'Crusoe is not going,' he said.

The food unswallowed in their mouths, their forks suspended, the children stared at their father.

'Why?' Stephen burst out, almost choking. 'Why can't he go?'

Geoffrey raised his eyebrows.

'Don't you ask *me* why,' he said. 'It's enough for you that I say Crusoe's not going.'

'No, it isn't. Why can't he go? Why can't he?'

'Leave the table,' ordered his father. 'Don't you dare to shout at me.'

Stephen plunged away from the table, but stood in the middle of the room, still shouting.

'Why should you take it out on Crusoe? What for? What's he done? He can't bear to stay here without us, he'll be miserable every single day, he'll cry all the time and he won't know why he's been left behind. If he doesn't go, I shan't. I shan't go.'

Geoffrey turned swiftly and seized a book from a table. Clenching his teeth, he hurled it at the angry boy, but Stephen dodged it. Geoffrey seized another and held it ready.

'Get out,' he said furiously. 'Or you'll get this one and I won't miss this time. Get out,' he got up and menaced Stephen out of the door.

'Oh, Geoffrey,' said Charlotte wearily.

'Don't you begin,' he warned, sitting down again, breathing audibly. 'The damned monkey,' he muttered, cutting at his beef. 'Defying me. He wants a damn good hiding, that boy, and by God he'll get it. This is your doing,' he flared accusingly at Charlotte. 'You encourage him. You put him up to it. I'll never do any good with that boy with you about. Judith, don't start blubbering here. God, you make me sick, all of you. All of you. I'm sorry I ever gave you the dog. All this maudlin fussing. The dog's bad for you. It's made you into a set of sloppy babies. Well, you go to Merthwaite tomorrow and the dog does not go with you. That's flat.' He struck the table with the palm of his hand so that the glasses jingled.

A sob escaped Judith.

'Go on,' said Geoffrey, turning on her. 'You go too. Leave the room.'

Judith rushed out, her face convulsed.

'May I go too?' asked Margaret.

Her father looked at her.

'I've finished,' she said.

'You can stay where you are,' said Geoffrey. 'I'm not going to have you joining up with your mother and the others. You stop where you are and get me another whisky and soda. I will not have these rows at meals. They upset my digestion. When a man works as hard as I do he ought to be able to have his meals in peace, but I'm damned if I can get any peace. The only one working in this house and not allowed any peace . . . '

He went on and on. Charlotte sat where she was, afraid to provoke a further outburst by moving, but her nerves jumped and twittered unbearably and her whole being strained towards the moment when she could get away by herself, get some of the new stuff, which was much swifter in effect than the old. Three of those tablets and she would soon be right, let Geoffrey storm as he may. She held on, waiting for the moment to escape.

For the rest of the day, tension persisted. Their father had changed his mind so often before that perhaps he would change it now, the children told one another. He couldn't possibly mean to keep Crusoe at home, they kept saying, getting down on the floor to rub Crusoe's head, or picking him up to hold him against their faces – he was such a clean,

smooth little dog they always loved to do that. But Tuesday came and Geoffrey had not changed his mood or his mind, and though Charlotte tried to persuade him, though Stephen, swallowing his hatred, apologised, though Margaret put her arms round his neck and Judith wept again, he did not change. Crusoe should stay at home and they should be taught a lesson, he told them. And at half-past two he drove off, telling Margaret and Stephen to follow at once on their bicycles.

In the road, Margaret stood with her foot on the pedal.

'We'll have to go,' she kept saying miserably.

Stephen hung over the gate, trying to explain to Crusoe on the other side. Crusoe tried to understand, but he couldn't. He looked very forlorn, sitting on his haunches, his head thrust forward, looking now at the ground, now up imploringly at his master. He whimpered quietly all the time.

'Stephen, come on,' urged Margaret.

Stephen suddenly flung open the gate, snatched up the dog and ran back into the house. Margaret, with her anxious unhappy face, waited. She thought he had gone to fasten Crusoe up, but after a few moments, Stephen reappeared with Cook behind him on the steps. In his arms he carried a plaited straw bag, a fish-bass, and in the bass was Crusoe, looking eagerly out.

'Stephen,' cried Margaret. 'You're not going to take him?'

'I am,' said Stephen, hanging the bass on his handlebars.

'Stephen, you can't. You simply can't. Daddy will go mad.'

'Let him,' said Stephen, compressing his lips. He mounted his bicycle and rode away, wobbling a little.

'Oh, Stephen,' said Margaret, riding after him. 'There'll be such awful trouble.'

Wrinkled, harassed, she rode, her dark hair falling forward. She was fifteen, an age when one's own life seems difficult enough without complications from outside. What would happen, she worried. There would be another terrible row. They might all have to come home again. Not that it would matter, she thought, with an adult renunciation of holidays, if only they could have peace.

They left the town behind and rode out into the country. The hills rose grand and quiet in the clear September sunshine. When they reached the first bridge, a single span of stone over the stream, Stephen dismounted and leaned his bicycle against the wall.

'Crusoe must have a run,' he said. 'It's not very comfortable in there, is it, old chap?'

Boy and dog plunged off the road into the grass and Margaret leaned on the bridge watching them run together. Crusoe was wild with excitement, his fear of being left behind over. They came back by and by and Stephen leaned on the bridge too, letting Crusoe recover from his panting. Crusoe had toughened Stephen. He made himself strong to protect his dog. He was going forward now into certain trouble. Though what he thought he could do against his father, Margaret couldn't imagine.

Stephen gazed at the tawny hills, as if looking for a way beyond them. 'I wish I could get away. With Crusoe,' he said.

'I wish I was old. I wish I had some money. Twelve's such a measly age. You can't do anything at twelve. Nobody would give me work.'

'You couldn't *do* any work,' said Margaret. 'So what's the good of talking. Come on. Let's get on and get it over.'

She rode first this time and Stephen came behind. He was getting more and more frightened. A complete inability to guess what his father would do added to his fear. But he rode on and Merthwaite village came into sight. He saw at once that there was no car in front of the inn. What had happened? For one wild moment, he hoped his father had had an accident and would never get there. Then he remembered that his mother and sister would have to be involved in it too. He pedalled quickly to the inn. Judith came running out, her face streaked with tears she had shed all the way to Merthwaite.

'Oh . . . ' she cried, her expression changing to incredulous joy. 'Oh, Crusoe darling. Darling. Let me get you out. Come and get a drink at the stream. Oh, Stephen.'

'Has Daddy gone?' asked Stephen, looking round as if he couldn't believe his eyes, as if the respite was too much.

'Yes, he went straight back. Oh, Stephen, isn't it lucky he isn't here?' breathed Judith, with Crusoe in her arms.

'No, it isn't lucky,' said Margaret. 'It's only put off.'

She wheeled her bicycle away to the back of the inn.

'Mummy,' said Stephen, going into their sitting-room. 'I've brought Crusoe.'

Charlotte put her hand to her head from which the

strange bursting feeling occasioned by the getting off, by Judith's tears and Geoffrey's savage driving was at last beginning to depart.

'Oh, Stephen,' she said. 'What have you done? Your father's just gone, but he'll come back now. As soon as he finds you've brought Crusoe, he'll come straight back.'

She had just taken her tablets and kind Mrs Purley had just placed an early tea-tray by the open window. Charlotte was hoping to recover in the peace that was closing in after Geoffrey's departure, but now it was shattered again.

'Oh, Stephen,' she said, passing her hands over her face.

'Oh, Mummy,' he said. 'I couldn't leave him behind. I tried, but I couldn't.'

'Well, run away, dear. Go and play while you can. I'm afraid Daddy will soon be back.'

But he wasn't. He didn't come. Their suspense was unrelieved. Mrs Purley wondered what was the matter with her visitors. They didn't seem to be enjoying themselves. They did nothing but hang about; the mother sitting by the window, the children hanging over the bridge, or huddled together on the grass, no life about them. Moping for their Pa, thought Mrs Purley.

'I'm not surprised you don't like taking a holiday without him,' she said bustling in with the supper. 'He's such a lively one, isn't he? But never mind. Saturday'll soon be here.'

When they were going to bed, their spirits lightened to think he couldn't at any rate come in the night. But apprehension returned with the morning. Waking with Crusoe on his bed, Stephen wondered what the load on his mind could

be. Then he remembered. His father would certainly come today.

But he didn't, and every day went by like that, wasted in apprehension and suspense. They had always wanted to spend a holiday at Merthwaite and now here they were, sleeping in the pink-washed bedrooms with the windows looking out to the hills and the sound of the running water coming in all night, here they were spending the holiday they had always wanted with the dog they had always wanted and they could not enjoy any of it. Their father had the power to turn the realisation of their dreams into a nightmare. On Saturday, almost with relief, Stephen shut Crusoe into his room and went down to sit on the wall to wait for his father's certain arrival.

Geoffrey arrived at noon. He merely glanced at his son, who came slowly towards him, his eyes fixed on his father's face. Geoffrey passed him with no more than a glance and went into the bar. During the weekend, he took no notice of Stephen and did not mention the dog. On Monday morning he departed.

As the car disappeared round the bend of the road, Stephen let out a long whistle of relief. His face was radiant. If to be ignored was all! Gosh, he didn't mind that, he told himself. He wouldn't care if his father never spoke to him again as long as he lived. He wouldn't care a straw! His spirits rose to the highest pitch. Calling to Crusoe and Judith, he dashed to the stream and went flying across the stepping-stones in wild irregular jumps. Judith came panting behind him.

'Oh, Stephen, d'you think it's all right? D'you think Daddy's not going to punish you?'

'I expect he thinks he's punishing me by depriving me of his conversation,' said Stephen, grandiloquent with reaction. 'Gosh, he little knows!'

Charlotte was not so sanguine. She knew that Geoffrey was childishly vindictive. She knew with the new clarity that had come upon her, or perhaps she had always known without admitting it, that he treated the children, not as children, but as equals. He worked to get his own back on them as if they had been adults, fair adversaries. But of course they were nothing of the sort. They had no power, thought Charlotte, poor children they had no power at all. Not even the power other children had to wound their father, because he didn't love them; except Margaret.

She hoped, all the same, that he would let Stephen off this time. If he did, it would only be because he was preoccupied with something else, as he certainly was at this time. He had sent them away for his own purposes, but she was too tired to try to find out what those were, too tired even to speculate about them.

In this last week, with the children happy, the weather perfect, beauty all about her and Geoffrey absent, she recovered a little. She tried to take fewer tablets, because she thought they were harming her heart. Her heart flapped like a dying fish, she said to herself, pressing her hand to it when she was alone. At home, before she came away, she had been taking as many as ten tablets a day. It must be too many, she said to herself. She must try to reduce them.

Mrs Purley helped in Charlotte's recuperation, or so she thought, by bringing in a glass of port on a tray now and again.

'Put a bit of life into you,' she said, coming in like a cheerful pig in a flowered overall, little humorous eyes under a curled front, a snout of a nose, short arms and a figure all of a piece from the chin downwards.

'Or a glass of sherry. Me best old brown,' she would say. 'None of your fashionable thin stuff with no body. That's what you want,' she would say watching Charlotte drink it with as much satisfaction as if she were drinking it herself.

Charlotte sipped, trusting to the port and the sherry to make her feel better. Her object nowadays was to get through the moment, just to get along from day to day. Sometime in the future she might be able to do without drinks and tablets, but not yet, she told herself. No one should expect her to. By no one, she meant the remnants of her old self, and Lucy. In spite of herself, she was compelled, sometimes, to measure herself by Lucy's standards. 'It must be because she brought me up,' she thought.

The difference between them, she supposed, was that Lucy took a long view and she took a short one. Lucy said, quoting somebody, that we were here to make our souls, but Charlotte didn't think so. Though eager, questioning, simple once, Charlotte had absorbed Geoffrey's theory that when you were dead you were dead and that was the end of it. So get through this life as best you can, Charlotte said to herself.

There remained her duty to the children. She agreed, sitting at the window looking out at the peaceful hills, that she

had a duty to the children. When she got well, when she was better, she must make a stand against Geoffrey for them. But she was in no fit state to do that at present. With her twittering nerves, her fluttering heart and bursting head and her fear of breaking down, she had no chance against him. She must wait until she felt better.

On Saturday, Geoffrey arrived again. On Monday they were to go home, on Tuesday morning the children would be back at school. With every moment that went by Stephen felt safer. He kept Crusoe out of his father's way and the weekend passed without incident.

On Monday morning, the cases were carried out, the bicycles were propped against the wall, the car was at the door, its engine running. Mrs Purley was at the front to see them go. Stephen with a polite, wary smile on his face, waited with seeming nonchalance to see his father off. Crusoe and the fish-bass were in his bedroom. He would not obtrude either on his father's notice, but as soon as the car was gone, he would bring Crusoe out and set off himself.

But Geoffrey, with a jerk of his head in the direction of Margaret and Stephen, said suddenly: 'Start off, you two. I'll see you off the premises this time.'

Stephen stared for an instant, then darted indoors. In a moment he reappeared with Crusoe in the fish-bass. Moving swiftly, his father took it from him.

'Here's the dog I promised you, Mrs Purley,' he said, handing her the bass.

Stephen sprang forward, but his father's arm thrust him back.

'No, you don't,' he said.

Mrs Purley stood in bewilderment with the bass.

'Eh, when you said you'd give me a dog, I'd no idea you meant this one, Mr Leigh. I couldn't think of taking this one, nice little dog though he is. The children are that attached to him, I couldn't think of depriving them, sir.'

'You will oblige me, Mrs Purley, by keeping the dog,' said Geoffrey coldly. 'Stephen, get on your bicycle. I'll drive behind you this time. So make a start. Did you hear me?'

Stephen, struggling to speak, burst out:

'You can't. Crusoe's our dog. You gave him to us. You can't give a dog to anybody else. He *loves* us. Oh, Daddy,' he said, his lips quivering. 'I'll never disobey you again if you'll let me take him home. Don't give Crusoe away. Let me have him, Daddy, and I'll be different. I promise . . . Please . . . please . . .'

'Get on your bicycle,' ordered his father. 'Mrs Purley, please don't concern yourself with this business. Stephen knows perfectly well why he has lost the dog. If you don't keep the dog, Mrs Purley, you may be sure I shall find other means, perhaps not so pleasant, of getting rid of it. So go in, there's a good soul, and leave family affairs to me.' He turned her round, pushed her into the passage and closed the door.

'Get on your bicycle,' he ordered. 'And don't you dare to make these scenes before outsiders,' he said through his teeth. 'Get on your bicycle.' He stood over Stephen, who was crying in a slow, painful way, his shoulders drawn up to his ears. Judith, in the car, was sobbing into her mother's lap. Margaret jumped on her bicycle and pedalled furiously down the road, her face hidden in her hair.

'Geoffrey, it's too bad,' said Charlotte trembling. 'You shouldn't have given the children a dog if you were going to take it from them in this cold-blooded way. As if nothing mattered,' she said incoherently. 'Our hearts, our nerves . . . torn by you . . . for nothing . . .'

'I'll ask for your opinion when I want it,' said Geoffrey. 'Get on your bicycle, d'you hear?' he said, gripping Stephen's shoulder.

Stephen could do nothing against him. What could he do? He got on his bicycle and rode headlong down the stony road. He passed Margaret. She called after him, but he pedalled wildly on. Geoffrey drove at a deliberate pace behind him. He could see, Charlotte knew, that Stephen was trying insanely to get away from the car, but he kept on his wheel, letting the boy almost burst his heart in his effort to escape.

'Oh, Geoffrey,' Charlotte kept saying in despair. Her hands trembled on Judith's head, still buried in her lap.

'Shut up,' said Geoffrey. 'It's his own fault. Why does he try to pit himself against me? Against the car?'

'He'll be completely knocked up,' said Charlotte.

'Serve him right.'

'You'll not only kill him, you'll kill me,' she said.

'Aw, shut up,' said Geoffrey, maintaining his careful pace, driving his son before him like a sheep. 'You're always talking about being killed or dying an early death. I don't see much evidence of it. I notice you've been doing yourself very well. From the bill, you've been putting away plenty of port and sherry. The young fool! He nearly had me into him then.'

In the traffic of the town, Stephen shook off his father. He got home, flung his bicycle into the garden, stumbled upstairs and locked his bedroom door.

No one saw him again that day. The girls laid food outside his door and whispered: 'Stephen. Stephen.' His mother tried to persuade him to let her in, but he would not.

CHAPTER EIGHT

I

The next morning he would have gone to school without breakfast if Charlotte had not caught him going out and told him his father was having breakfast in bed. He went into the dining-room then with the others and they sat round the table, silent. Spoons worked slowly, porridge stuck in their throats. Charlotte was one with them. Though she was an adult, she was helpless. What could she promise that she could perform? What comfort could she offer them? She tried once, saying that Crusoe would be all right with Mrs Purley, and all they could do now was to try to forget him. But they only looked at her with their swollen eyes, mutely asking how she could say a thing like that, and turned away from her, uncomforted. They went off to school. 'What must people think?' Charlotte wondered, watching the unhappy trio go out of the gate.

They came home again at the end of the afternoon and went up to the nursery. Its emptiness struck their hearts afresh. This was Crusoe's most ecstatic hour and theirs. The moment when they were reunited after a long day and could go mad together.

But now, coming into the quiet nursery, they missed him terribly, though nobody spoke of him. Margaret sat down at the table to try to read, but the other two, trailing round the furniture, reached the window at length, and stood there looking out. There was nothing to look at but the trees across the road and the iron rails of the gate. They stood there, Stephen leaning on the side of the window, Judith with her face pressed against the glass. One moment, they were looking at the square of the gate and there was nothing there. The next moment something was there, something small, low down against the ground. Stephen drew a sharp breath, his eyes riveted. It was a small dog trying to get under the gate, but giving it up and falling back in exhaustion.

'Crusoe!' cried Judith loudly.

'Shut up!' Stephen clutched the chest of her frock as if he would tear the voice out of her.

Margaret jumped up from the table, knocking her chair over.

'He's come back,' whispered Stephen, life and light flaring into his face. 'He's got here. All that way by himself.'

'Think of it,' he said turning his transfigured face on his sisters. 'Finding his way back to us over all those miles – running home.'

'Stay where you are – you two,' he said, making for the door, light, swift. 'Don't let anybody hear. Daddy mustn't know he's come back. I'll fetch him.'

The girls flew to the window. They saw Stephen running to the gate. They saw him stoop down, lift Crusoe tenderly up, cover him with his jacket and run back into the house. In a moment, he was in the nursery.

'Lock the door,' he said, laying Crusoe carefully on the rug.

'Oh, Crusoe . . . ' whispered the girls, hanging over him. 'Crusoe, you clever, clever little boy. . . . '

Crusoe, lying limp, feebly wagged his tail.

'Get some water.'

'Let me, let me,' begged Judith.

Crusoe was too exhausted to drink so they dripped water on to his tongue until he revived sufficiently to drink himself. Having drunk, he lay down again and they mourned over his sore paws. Stephen bathed them gently; the dew-claw of one was broken and had to be cut off and bound up.

'He must have some milk first until he's able to eat his dinner,' said Stephen. 'I must go and tell Cook he's back and get something for him.'

He stood up, resolute, restored. He had to see to everything.

The girls leaned over Crusoe, their hair hanging, making loving murmurs. Judith stroked him all the time, so happy to feel his satin coat under her hand again that she could not stop. She thought of him coming all those miles, led by his love for them. He was a hero, she thought, putting her face down on the rug beside him. He stopped licking his paws for a moment to look into her eyes with his faithful brown ones. His poor little nose was cracked and dry. 'You'll soon be better,' she told him, stroking. She loved him so much that she ached.

Stephen gave all the instructions. Crusoe must be hidden in his bedroom for the time being, he said. Until he had made up his mind what to do. Crusoe must be given time to recover.

'We might have to be on the road again before long,' said Stephen.

'What d'you mean?' asked Margaret, who had no patience with young heroics.

'I may have to run away with him,' said Stephen.

'Don't be so silly,' said Margaret. 'You'd only be brought back. Nowadays with the police and the wireless and everything you wouldn't get ten miles.'

'You could go to Auntie Lucy's, Stephen,' put in Judith. 'She'd adopt you and Crusoe, I know she would.'

'You silly things,' said Margaret in exasperation. They were both so childish.

But she agreed to let Stephen have his way for the present, because she herself did not know what else to do. Crusoe was to be hidden tonight and the next day. When they came home from school tomorrow they would have a conference and really decide what was to be done.

So all night Crusoe lay on Stephen's bed and Stephen, completely happy though too full of wild plans to sleep properly, kept putting out his hand to touch him. Next morning, after careful instructions to Cook who was in the plot, he went to school.

In the afternoon, the girls reached home first. When Stephen rushed into the house twenty minutes later, he came to a dead halt at the sight of Judith on the stairs, her face streaked with grime and tears, her lips trembling.

'Stephen . . . ' she said, gulping piteously. 'Stephen . . . '

'What is it?' he said sharply. 'Quick! What's happened? Crusoe?'

Judith nodded, struggling with her tears.

'He's gone,' she brought out. 'Daddy found him. Cook said he was crying in your room. She thought his paws were hurting him so she went in and Daddy came in behind her. He took him away, but Cook doesn't think he took him back to Mrs Purley because he was only away a little while. He's in there . . . ' Judith nodded towards the morning-room.

Stephen went to the door, flung it open and walked in.

Geoffrey looked up from his desk.

'What the hell do you mean by coming in here like that?' he said.

'Where's Crusoe?' asked Stephen, coming to clutch the front of the desk with both hands. 'Where is he?'

'Get out.'

'Where's Crusoe? Tell me. Tell me where he is.'

'Your dog's gone,' said Geoffrey, leaning forward and speaking with malicious slowness and clarity. 'I took it to the police-station this morning and had it destroyed. So now perhaps you'll understand that I mean to be obeyed, my boy. . . . '

Stephen's face drained slowly and completely of colour, even to his lips. He stared with darkening eyes at his father, taking in the dreadful truth. Crusoe was dead. After all his struggle to get home, his courage, he had been destroyed. The word sank into the boy's very self. Destroyed. Crusoe – so alive, so loving.

'And now go away,' said Geoffrey. 'Don't stand there staring at me. What's a dog, anyway,' he finished lamely. Stephen's face made him, in spite of himself, uneasy.

It must be admitted that Geoffrey did not feel that he had done anything out of the ordinary in getting rid of the dog. A dog was nothing to him. He had no feeling for dogs or any other animal. He had had a dog thrust upon him, he didn't want it. He passed it on to the children, but through the dog, the children had become unmanageable, so he gave it away. The dog came back, provoked deceit and defiance in the children again, so he took it to the police-station and had it painlessly destroyed. He told the man at the station that the dog was vicious and as he had children he couldn't risk keeping it. A lie like that was nothing to Geoffrey. If called upon to explain his action he would have said that he was damned if a dog was going to upset his home.

Charlotte, pale, dishevelled from lying on the drawing-room sofa, appeared at the door. Through a strange swimming haze, induced by the tablets she had taken, she saw Stephen standing with a dreadful look on his face. He seemed such a child standing before his father with his rough hair, scarred knees and crumpled schoolboy clothes, but from his face all childishness was struck away. He had an old, sick look, as if he had become aware of evil and cruelty. It was an appalling look for a child to turn on a father, and Charlotte, struggling against the fog over her mind, went towards him with her arms outstretched.

'Stephen,' she said.

But he put her aside and went up to lock himself in his bedroom.

II

And now Geoffrey had gone too far. He could do no more to them. No more, at any rate, to Charlotte, or Judith or Stephen.

He attempted to bring Margaret round, to jolly her out of it. He played with all he knew for a smile from her. But she was adult, mature, compared with him. She knew he was cruel, callous to other people's suffering, but she also knew he couldn't understand why they should suffer. He didn't suffer; why should they? She did not attempt to make him understand. She didn't attempt to explain what he had done to Stephen; to them all, but most to Stephen. She knew it would be no good.

'Look here,' said Geoffrey one day, when, having pulled her on to his knee, she released herself and got up again. 'Look here, Mouse,' he said, speaking as a fond father ready to indulge the whims of his child. 'I'll tell you what I'll do. I'll get you another dog.'

She shuddered away from him.

'Oh, no, Daddy, don't. Please don't. Never another dog. Never.'

He drew in his lips. He had made a generous offer and she refused it. He was deeply injured.

She forgave him in time. She forgave him as a mother forgives boys who cut off birds' heads and pull off the wings of bees. But their relationship had subtly changed. He was as exacting and capricious as ever, but it was he who tried to please her not she who tried to please him. She did everything

179

he demanded as before, but he tried to please her, always looking to see if he was going too far. And he kept up his heart attacks. They no longer had any effect upon Charlotte, but they brought Margaret to his side as swiftly as ever and kept her there.

Judith and Stephen never forgave him. From this time their father was their enemy. Stephen hated him with a cold scorn that withered him, matured him before his time. He kept out of the way, deliberately biding his time, waiting until he should be old enough, equipped enough to go. Judith avoided her father; but as she had always avoided him, this was scarcely noticeable. She never stayed in the same room with him if she could help it. If he came into a room where she was, after a few moments she left it. She was ten years old and the incident made an impression on her that was never effaced.

Trembling, with a white face and red neck, Charlotte came to speak to Geoffrey. 'What on earth's the matter with your neck?' said Geoffrey as if it were an affront to him. 'You look a perfect fright.'

'Geoffrey, I can't stand any more,' said Charlotte. Even her head trembled, she could feel it, horribly shaking on her neck.

He looked at her.

'I am moving my things into the turret-room. I shall sleep there,' said Charlotte.

He burst into one of his loud laughs. 'What an anticlimax,' he said. 'You can't stand any more so you'll sleep in the turret-room. Sleep where you damn well like. What the hell does it matter to me?'

Cook gave notice. She said she couldn't fancy cooking for a man who would destroy a little dog in cold blood, to say nothing of breaking a boy's heart.

'You're a bigger fool than I took you for,' said Geoffrey blandly, paying her off.

III

Lucy heard the tale from Judith when she came to fetch her for the Christmas holidays. It was still so fresh to Judith that she could do no more than stammer out a few words about it when they sat alone together on the nursery sofa, Lucy about to read from *Tanglewood Tales* because the Greek names were difficult for Judith to read herself. As she listened, the book slid from Lucy's hands and she looked down with incredulous horror into the child's tear-filled eyes. When the tale was over she couldn't say anything. What was there to say that could be said? She could only tighten her arm round Judith and determine, now more than ever, to remove her as much as possible and as long as possible from this man who was not fit to live with. Not fit to live with, she repeated, full of loathing and anger. 'Read,' said Judith, thrusting the book into her aunt's hands. 'Read fast – as fast as anything.' So Lucy plunged into the tale of Persephone, trying to substitute in the child's mind the old magic images for the grief and horror the tale of Crusoe had brought up and would bring up for years to come, Lucy knew.

Her feeling against Geoffrey was so strong that it gave her power; it swept away the minor constraint she used to feel in his critical presence. She no more cared what he thought of

her now than he cared what she thought of him, and she demanded that Stephen should come to Underwood as well as Judith. Geoffrey let them go easily enough; he didn't want them, he was glad to get them out of the house. Lucy tried to persuade Charlotte and Margaret to come too; she would have got them all away if she could. But Charlotte said she would take the opportunity to rest more while the children were away and to Margaret it was unthinkable that her father should be left alone at Christmas. So Lucy returned to Underwood with Judith and Stephen.

After this, Stephen, as well as Judith, spent most holidays at Underwood. Lucy could only hope he enjoyed his visits; she never really knew. He was a mysterious boy and behaved at Underwood much as he did at home; he was always slipping away by himself and when in the house spent most of his time in his bedroom. He seemed more secretive every holiday, Lucy thought. He was at a difficult age, growing long and lanky with a lock of dark hair falling continually over his forehead and as continually being put back. 'Can't he put a pin in that hair?' asked William in exasperation.

'Now, don't be as bad as Geoffrey, please,' begged Lucy.

'He doesn't take an interest in anything,' complained William.

'You mean we don't know what he takes an interest in,' defended Lucy. 'Anyway, don't bother him. He's here to get what he can't get at home. Peace.' But she found Stephen difficult herself and was glad when he formed a friendship with the Rector's son, though they both seemed unnaturally serious for their age.

She didn't know that Stephen was a boy with a purpose. He meant to get away, and he didn't mean, either, to attach himself too much to anyone or anything. His dog had been destroyed and his mother didn't want him. He had worked it out that it was better not to care too much. Moreover, everything felt very temporary to Stephen; he was going, so what did anything matter here? He did well at school. No one had anything to complain of. For the rest he had good manners and careful, wary ways and he worried his aunt considerably.

'Why should you be for ever torn in pieces about people?' exclaimed William.

'Why shouldn't I, you mean,' said Lucy.

All the same, she admitted that her wish to see everybody happy was hopeless of realisation. William made it sound ridiculous too.

'You make yourself unhappy because other people aren't happy, so nobody's happy,' he said.

'Except you, I suppose,' said Lucy.

'No, that's the worst of it,' he said. 'I can't be happy unless you're happy.'

'So you're as bad as I am,' said Lucy.

'Indeed I'm not. You could take Galsworthy's place in Max Beerbohm's cartoon. So full of pity, you feel for the pillar-box for being out in the snow.'

Lucy smiled apologetically and said she couldn't help it. She went on trying to persuade those around her to be happy; but there was always somebody who remained obstinately out. Janet, for instance, when the children were in the house. Janet

was as loud and frequent now in complaint as any modern parent about the length of the holidays. 'They're no sooner out of the house than they're back again,' she declared. 'I haven't time to turn round. All I can say is what with all the treading in and out, I won't answer for the stair-carpet much longer.'

'What do you mean, Janet, when you say you won't answer for the stair-carpet?' asked Judith, who was playing with a scoopful of flour from the bin, smoothing off the top to represent a sixpenny ice, smoothing off more to be a threepenny one, and more still to be a penny one, and then dipping for more to begin all over again.

'What do I mean?' said Janet crossly from the sink. 'How do I know? I mean the same as other people, I suppose. When I say I won't answer for the stair-carpet it's plain enough, isn't it?'

'But has anyone *asked* it anything?' said Judith gravely.

'Oh, good gracious me,' said Janet in exasperation. 'The questions as is asked in this house nowadays. They're enough to drive anybody wild. That flour won't be fit to use if you go on like that with it.'

'Why?' asked Judith with interest.

But with a click of the tongue, Janet would speak no more. Two questions she hadn't been able to answer and there would only be more if she laid herself open to them, so she took her duster and went upstairs, sighing for the day when she would be able to have a bit of a talk in her own kitchen in peace and quiet. Her mistress, she considered, gave in to that child in everything.

Lucy certainly gave in a good deal. She not only allowed, she was definitely glad to hear Judith clattering up and down the stairs, because it was natural to a child to clatter and Judith daren't do it at home. She was glad when she rushed about and sang and shouted. She was thankful to find that, the load of Geoffrey lifted, the child-nature was there unimpaired underneath. Not so with Stephen, or Margaret.

Lucy could not persuade Margaret to come to Underwood. Surface relations between aunt and niece were pleasant, but Margaret always kept at a distance. She knew, not only that Lucy disliked her father, but that she considered he treated her mother badly. That just showed, thought Margaret scornfully, that she knew nothing of what went on in the house. More and more, as she grew older, Margaret resented her mother. She had all youth's intolerance for the failure of adults. They ought to have been able to manage, thinks youth. Why shouldn't they? Youth thinks that to be grown-up is to be master of one's fate. Margaret had no idea that in enslaving herself to Geoffrey she was doing what her mother had done before her.

But Lucy saw it and wrote to Vera about it.

'She has left school and works as her father's secretary now. He can tyrannise over her the whole day, which he does. She is seventeen and he does his best to prevent her from living any life in which he can't take part, and from having any friends of her own. I've heard her at the telephone when she's being asked out. She says: "Wait a minute" and claps her hand over the mouthpiece while she asks him if he will need her on Tuesday, or whatever day it may be. She looks half-afraid he'll

say he doesn't. She's nervous of going out. He's making her like that. But he rarely says he doesn't need her. He says "Tuesday? How do I know what will crop up before Tuesday? Tell them you can't say. Tell them to ring up again." So she can never make arrangements and what's worse she doesn't want to. When she very occasionally has friends in, Geoffrey sits with them all the time, being funny. Something should be done for Margaret before it's too late.'

She urged Vera to ask Margaret to Trenton. Vera had been saying for what now amounted to years that she would have both Margaret and Judith, but now at last she sent a definite invitation for Easter, and as it happened that Geoffrey wanted to take a trip of his own then, he welcomed the prospect of getting Margaret out of the house.

As far as Charlotte was concerned, Geoffrey had no scruples about his affairs with women. He considered they were her fault. He didn't care whether she knew about them or not, but he cared very much that Margaret should not know.

Lucy thought everything ran shallow in Geoffrey, but she was wrong. There were some strange dark pools in his nature where his love for his daughter had collected. The love was complex, made up of his best and his worst. Some of it was tenderness and sheer pleasure in her youth and charming looks. Some of it was jealousy and possessiveness. Some of it was the yearning for an ideal of purity in one who had never had any inclination towards purity for himself. He went very far in his idea of what purity in his daughter should be. She was to be not only pure, but sexless. He could not bear to think

that Margaret should fall in love with and be loved by a man. He winced away from all such ideas. But all this was kept very much underground. Outwardly he petted her. He kept her in a constant state of gratitude; she was always reminding herself how good he was to her. He continually brought surprises for her. He liked to see her well dressed and taught her how to be so. In contrast to Charlotte, who became increasingly careless about her appearance, Margaret appeared better and better dressed and groomed. She must never, her father pointed out, be like her mother.

When Vera invited Margaret to Trenton for Easter, Geoffrey said she must go. With her out of the house, he could get away and stay away without anxiety. He would not have to come straight from the company of his mistress to that of his pure young daughter.

CHAPTER NINE

I

It was all very well for Judith, thought Margaret on the journey. She was only twelve. But she herself as the elder had all the responsibility for the visit. It was she who had to say and do the right thing. It was years since she had been to Trenton, but she vaguely remembered a big house full of maids and people coming to dinner. They would all have to be talked to and the maids would have to be tipped, thought Margaret, growing hot at the idea. Judith would be out of it in the nursery with Sarah and Meriel, but she would be downstairs with the smart women and handsome men. 'Oh, I would so much rather have stayed at home,' she said to herself. She shivered for the shelter of the morning-room and her father's company. But the train bore her relentlessly away from both.

'Judith.'

Judith was reading *What Katy Did*. Lucy, who provided her with all her books, had sent it to her. Frowning, her eyes swiftly followed line after line of print.

'Judith.' This time she heard, and looked up. 'D'you remember Auntie Vera?' It had just struck Margaret that it

would be embarrassing if she could not recognise her aunt, whom she had not seen for so long, at the station. Looking sideways to the flying fields, Judith considered. She had seen her aunt more recently than Margaret had, but it was still years ago and she could not find a picture in her memory.

'I expect we'll know her because she'll be more beautiful than anybody else,' she said. 'Mummy said she always was and I expect she is still.' She returned to her book; it was at the exciting part about the Meeting of the Waters game.

But it was Brian who met them. When he found Vera did not intend to go he said that therefore he must. He said precisely that. 'Therefore I must go,' with grave rebuke. 'My dear Brian,' said Vera derisively. 'Margaret is seventeen years old. She will know quite well to take a taxi.'

Brian did not argue. His face closed. He supposed she was going out with Ward or Stewart or whoever was in favour at the moment. She would have no hesitation in throwing over her two young nieces for one of her men, he knew.

So when the travellers, looking in bewilderment about them, were greeted by a large handsome man with two small girls, it took Judith, at least, some time to readjust herself. Her eyes rose to Brian's face, which seemed at an immense height from the ground. He's like Gulliver, she thought. What huge feet, she thought, her eyes travelling down to them. Still, he needs them, she conceded. Brian was talking to Margaret and directing the porter, so Judith was free to turn her attention to her cousins. The younger one, who had a large face like her father's, stared with no expression whatsoever; the elder one, Sarah, seemed to scowl. Even at ten, even in socks and a

round hat, Sarah looked wild, with her light grey, long-lashed eyes, and brows tilted upwards at the outer corners.

'Hello,' ventured Judith. 'Hello,' her cousins responded and backed behind their father. Judith wondered how she was going to get on with them and for the first time felt uncertain about the visit. Margaret, on the other hand, was relieved to find her uncle so kind. She managed to make quite a few remarks as they went out to the car at the front of the station. Sarah got in beside the chauffeur and took no more notice of anyone, except that once, about halfway home, she turned and had a good stare at Judith.

In the streets the traffic passed in an ever-flowing stream, up one side of the road and down the other. Buses towered among the cars like hippopotami among seals. The side-streets fed the main road, pouring in more cars, more lorries, more bicycles. The car containing the Sargents and the Leighs climbed the long hill out of the city and as it reached the summit, distant lamps showed strung out like necklaces in all directions. The roads were quiet now and flanked on each side by huge walls like ramparts. Beyond these walls, big houses stood high in terraced gardens.

The car swept into the back courtyard of one of these houses; it could not go to the front because the garden fell steeply away there in steps and terraces. Sarah and Meriel got out and rushed at once into the house and up the stairs, presumably to the nursery. Very rude, thought Judith. She followed her uncle into the hall and was awed. It was all so big and there were so many flowers. The hall was like a great room and there was a fire burning on the stone hearth. This was all

very different from the red-carpeted hall at home with the
white-painted doors, blue plates at intervals on a shelf and the
palm in the great brass bowl. A door opened in the distance
and Vera appeared. She was in her riding-habit, and the
young Leighs felt they didn't know her at all.

'Well?' said Vera, bending a cool cheek to Margaret,
then to Judith. Judith shyly, almost imperceptibly kissing,
remembered the faint, enchanting scent of the bedroom at
Underwood. She remembered the washing-set too, now, and
all the laughter. She smiled warmly up at her aunt and Vera
smiled in return.

'It's a good thing I didn't come to meet you at the station,'
she said. 'I should never have known you. You're both so
changed. Come along, let's go up to your room.'

A telephone rang somewhere and a maid appeared.
'Captain Ward on the telephone, madam,' she said.

'Oh, I can't speak to him now,' said Vera carelessly. 'Tell
him to ring up later.' Her hands round the shoulders of the
girls, she led them to the stairs. 'Say in about half an hour,'
she called after the maid.

'So she wasn't with Ward,' thought Brian. 'Who was it
then?'

Left alone in their room, the young Leighs went into
raptures over it. It was very big and the windows looked out
over the deep ravine of the garden. The carpet was almost
white and the glazed chintz blue and pink and yellow. But
what delighted them most were the tiny flowers sprinkled all
over the bedspreads; they were so real they looked as if they
had just been thrown down. And between the beds was a lamp

with a pink shade strewn with silver stars. 'See, I can read all night if I like,' said Judith, turning the light off and on for the pleasure of seeing the stars come out. 'Oh, can you?' said Margaret caustically. 'Well, would you mind getting washed? You have to get ready for nursery supper and I want you out of the way before I dress for dinner.'

'Oh, why?' protested Judith. 'There's plenty of room for both of us. I'd rather be up here until the last minute. Those two look so disagreeable.'

'It can't be helped,' said Margaret. 'I shall have a much worse time than you, facing all the downstairs people. Do stop roaming and get washed.'

'I must put my best dress on,' said Judith. 'This is the sort of house for best dresses.'

'Of course you can't put your best dress on,' said Margaret. 'You must save it. You don't know what will turn up here. Be quick. I want to brush your hair.'

'I'll brush my hair.'

'No, I'll brush your hair, thank you.'

Later, feeling unnaturally clean since Margaret had insisted on washing her after she had washed herself, in her second-best dress and her party slippers, Judith went reluctantly in search of the nursery. Rubbing her way along the passage walls, she came upon an open door through which she saw a bare, bright room with blue paint, drawn blue curtains, a sea of blue cork carpet set with islands in the shape of painted chairs and a table. In one corner, her back turned, her fat thighs exposed, Meriel bent over a doll she was putting to bed. In a chair by the fire sprawled Sarah.

'You have been a time,' she said, as Judith came diffidently in at the door. 'What on earth have you been doing?'

'Oh, washing and things,' said Judith. She went over to Meriel's corner, but Meriel immediately put herself between Judith and the doll's bed.

'Don't touch Eva,' she said.

'Huh, you'd better not,' said Sarah. 'She'll scream like mad if you do.'

Judith went to perch on the high brass-rimmed guard before the fire. A woman in nurse's uniform with a thin nose and a little limp hair lying on each side of her face under her cap, came in with a laden tray.

'Well, here you are, dear,' she said cheerfully. 'I'm sure we're all very pleased to have you in our nursery, aren't we, children?'

No answer from the children.

'I've brought you up a nice poached egg, dear, after your journey. I daren't give you anything heavier at this time of night, but I thought what with that and some stewed apple and cream and your milk . . . '

'It sounds lovely,' said Judith, who was hungry.

'Why can't I have an egg?' said Sarah, coming to look the table over with dissatisfaction.

'You know you can't have an egg at this time of the night, dear. It makes you dream.'

'"Course it doesn't. I want an egg.'

'Now don't begin, dear,' pleaded the nurse. 'Not the first night your cousin's here. Let her see how nicely you can behave when you like.'

'I want an egg,' repeated Sarah. She sat at the table with her pale face and stormy eyes. She had her mother's lovely mouth, but it was sulky. 'Get me an egg,' she said.

'Now dear, how can Nanny stop you from having nightmares if you will eat eggs before going to bed?'

'If you don't get me an egg, I'll go and get one from Cook myself,' threatened Sarah, getting up from her chair.

'All right, I'll get you one,' said Nurse Gill with a sigh. She wasn't going to have it said in the kitchen that she had no authority in the nursery. 'But you're a very naughty girl. You get on with your supper, dear,' she said to Judith. 'Don't wait.'

She went out of the nursery.

'Silly old fool,' said Sarah, kicking the table leg.

Meriel left her doll and went to the nursery door.

'If Sarah has an egg, I want one,' she called out and came back again. Sarah might fight the battles, but Meriel would benefit from the victories.

Judith, eating, didn't know which cousin she disliked most.

After supper, when Nurse Gill had cleared the table and gone out with the tray, Sarah went back to the chair by the fire and Meriel returned to her doll. Judith, perched again on the guard, wished she was at home. Sarah kept firing questions at her and cavilling at the answers. Judith was stiffening; she thought it was cheek of a person two years younger than herself, a mere child of ten, to behave to her like this.

'Have you got a friend?' asked Sarah.

'A friend? Yes, I've got Pamela,' said Judith.

Sarah looked into the fire in silence for a moment. 'I wish I had a friend,' she said wistfully.

'Huh,' thought Judith, 'the way she goes on she'll never get one.'

The door opened and Brian, book in hand, came in. This was the time after their supper and before his dinner that he tried to spend with his children. He thought he ought to see something of them every day, since their mother saw so little. He read aloud to them at this time. Not that they cared for it, but he thought they ought to.

Besides, he liked reading aloud. He used to read to Vera. Night after night when they were first married, he read to her and it was one of his first disillusionments that she burst out laughing one night, in the middle of Goethe's *Conversations* too, and told him that people who read aloud did so for their own and not their listeners' pleasure. He was deeply wounded and it was perhaps from that moment that he began to withdraw.

But it did not stop him from reading aloud. He now read to his children. At the moment, he was reading the *Just So Stories*.

'I make a practice, Judith,' he said, ejecting Sarah from the armchair and taking it himself, 'of reading to my children at this hour. Perhaps you would care to listen too?'

'Yes, I would,' said Judith politely, though she would much rather have read *What Katy Did*, to herself. She sat down on a low stool and clasped her knees, waiting. Sarah took a stool beside her.

'Come along, Meriel,' said her father.

'Well, I shall have to bring Eva,' said Meriel. 'And she's got ammonia.'

'You mean pneumonia,' corrected Brian gravely.

'She oughtn't to be taken out of her cot, really,' said Meriel sulkily.

'I'm waiting,' said Brian.

Meriel wrapped up the doll and fussed over with it to the child's rocking chair beside her sister. As Brian began to boom '"O Best Beloved"', Meriel, tightening shawls with a maternal hand, rocked backwards and forwards, saying 'Sh . . . Sh . . . Sh.' She paid no attention whatever to the reading.

But Judith was soon rapt. She turned on Brian the listening gaze she had turned on Lucy from early childhood and Brian was delighted. All our lives we are seeking for others to share our pleasures and when at times we find them, life takes on a new warmth and we bloom. Brian bloomed now. He forgot to listen to his own voice, which he admired, and tried only to interest this child, over whose face light and shade and question and answer passed as he read. Why haven't I a child like this, he asked himself.

But he hadn't. Before long, Sarah, gazing dreamily into the fire, began to sniff.

'Sarah,' said her father, holding the book aside to look at her. 'Where is your handkerchief?'

'I haven't one.'

'Take mine.' He held out a folded linen handkerchief. She drew the fold across her nose and handed it back.

'Say "Thank you, Daddy."'

'Thank you, Daddy.'

'Now we will continue. Where was I?'

Only Judith could tell him.

'Good girl,' said Brian appreciatively. He settled himself more closely in his chair and continued.

But her father's handkerchief had distracted Sarah from some dream which had at least kept her quiet. Now she began to look about her. She looked at Meriel, still rocking like an automaton and still saying 'Sh,' looking down at her doll with an anxiety that obviously gave her great pleasure. 'Stop it,' hissed Sarah suddenly. Meriel turned her shoulder on her sister and continued to rock and hush. Clenching her teeth, Sarah tweaked the fish-tail of shawl and brought the doll out of her sister's arms. Meriel made a wild snatch, retrieved Eva and burst into a roar.

'She's nearly broken Eva. She's teasing me again! She's teasing me!'

'I'm not teasing, you fool. I mean it and I'll break that horrid doll if you don't stop rocking it.'

Brian dropped the book to his knee.

'They're hopeless,' he said. 'Absolutely hopeless. They can't concentrate on anything. Sarah, how often am I to tell you that you must not use the word "fool"? It is most unsuitable in the mouth of a little girl. And don't you know it is extremely rude to create disturbances when Daddy is reading? Extremely rude not to give him your attention?'

Sarah sighed heavily. She was sick of sitting on the stool, sick of everything. She didn't know what was the matter with her, but something was. Nothing was right, really.

'And Meriel, don't be such a baby,' admonished her father. 'Be quiet both of you. I don't know what your cousin must think of you. Where was I, Judith?'

Judith told him. He went on reading, Meriel went on rocking, Sarah scowling and sighing.

After a few moments, the door opened and Vera, dressed for dinner in the diaphanous black she was fond of, came into the nursery.

'Hello, children. I came in to see if Judith was all right. Quite at home, darling? The other two will be going to bed soon, but you can stay up for another hour and talk to Nanny, can't you?'

She came in, talking in an undiminished voice. Brian would have liked her, when she saw that he was reading, to lay a finger on her lips, smile and steal away. Or better still, sit down quietly, taking one of the children on her knee and listen to him herself. But here she was, behaving as if he were not reading at all. He put a finger in the book, closed it and waited ostentatiously for her to finish. How she annoyed and wounded him, he thought, how she went out of her way to show that she thought nothing of him. But how damnably, unchangingly lovely she was! Looking at her, Brian suffered an unvisible break-up of his stolidity. It was all such a mess, such a mistake, and it might have been so different, but she wouldn't . . . never had loved him, she told him, never could . . . . For one desperate moment, Brian felt he must throw down the book, give it all up and go away; for ever. But he sat where he was, waiting.

'Good night, darlings,' Vera was saying, kissing the children.

'Is anybody coming in tonight, Mummy?' asked Sarah. 'Can I come down? Do let me.'

'Certainly not,' said Vera, going to the door, her dress floating. 'You know what I told you after that last scene.'

A look of shame passed over Sarah's face. She hung her head, and Judith, though she did not really like her, felt anxious and sorry.

A maid appeared at the door through which Vera had not yet passed. 'Mr Hope on the telephone, madam,' she said.

'I'm coming,' said Vera.

Brian resumed his reading. But he had hardly read two pages before Nurse Gill bustled in, looking in a business-like fashion at her watch. It was his mother who paid her wages and she wanted him to report well of her. When he was about, she made a great show of regulating her charges' lives to the minute because she knew that was what he and his mother liked and looked for. She glanced at her watch and stood by respectfully, waiting.

'Well, Nurse,' said Brian closing the book with a sigh. 'I suppose time's up. We haven't got very far. As usual, there were many interruptions.'

'Ah, well, sir, it's always like that where there are children. You can't expect nothink else really.'

Brian winced at these faults of speech, but he could do nothing about them. His mother assured him that this was an excellent woman otherwise and it was extremely difficult to get anybody to remain long in charge of Sarah.

He kissed his children, then saying, 'Shall I kiss Judith too?' he bent to her with a kind, shy look on his face. Judith thought it must be very nice to have such a polite father.

'Thank you for the lovely tale,' she said.

He was charmed. 'That's all right,' he said, patting her on the head and leaving the nursery.

With bribery, persuasion, admonition, the young Sargents were now put on their way to the bathroom.

'You can come and talk to us while we're having our baths,' said Sarah grandly.

'No, thanks,' said Judith. 'I'm going to read.'

'Oh, come on,' said Sarah, quite cordially.

'No,' said Judith. ' I don't want to.'

Staring at her, Sarah went slowly from the room.

When she had gone, Judith sped up to her room for Katy. It was good to come back to an empty nursery and close the door. She had no thought of making herself comfortable, but sat on a wooden chair against the wall and opened her book. Wrapping her legs round the legs of the chair, she read, and strange nurseries, rude cousins were forgotten.

It seemed no time at all before Nurse Gill was back, her hands mauve and wrinkled from the bath-water. She came in looking a different woman, care-free, comfortable, and stood before the fire replacing the starched cuffs she had left one inside the other on the mantelpiece.

'There,' she said cosily.

Nurse Gill had a strong tendency to cosiness, constantly frustrated by her charges who, during the day, would not allow her to be cosy or submit to being made cosy themselves. Fortunately for Nurse Gill, they now attended a small private school, Meriel in the mornings, Sarah until half-past three in the afternoons. All the same, for several hours of every day, Nurse Gill had to do battle with them, and battle it was.

If her employers were afraid that Nurse Gill would give notice as so many nurses had done before her, Nurse Gill also feared that her employers would give notice to her. She wasn't trained as new nurses were, she was no longer young, and worse than all, she couldn't manage the children. She didn't want to leave, they didn't want her to leave, but neither party was sure of this, so each was wary of the other and there was a good deal of tacit putting up with things on both sides. As it happened, each party would have put up with a good deal more without a breach.

Still, during the day, it was a strain disguising the fact that she couldn't manage the children; above all must she keep it from the old lady, old Mrs Sargent, who expected a daily visit from the children and herself, a report on their health and behaviour and as much inside information as possible of her son's household. All this was a strain during the day, but at night, when the children had gone to bed, strain fell away and cosiness closed in. Nurse Gill drew a long breath of relief and came to life, her own life. Her ideal of spending life was to sit by the fire in perfect peace, reading the twopenny women's magazines delivered to the house for her every week. That was another thing in favour of this place: her papers were paid for, also by the old lady. Picture paper every day and two tuppennies on Fridays.

The women's papers gave Nurse Gill her greatest pleasure. She loved the romances, though her day for romance was over, if it had ever dawned. She loved the advice on the rearing of babies, though she would never have a baby, except some other woman's. She loved the recipes, though she never had

the chance of making or partaking of the dishes described. To read, moving her lips over the words as she always did: 'Pour into a small glass or fancy dish, wipe the edges carefully and serve with a little cream,' filled Nurse Gill with cosy happiness. In her imagination there was a home where, exactly as in the twopenny papers, she was loved romantically, she had a baby, a cooking stove and cupboards with rows of glass or fancy dishes, and to this house she returned every night, when her troublesome charges were in bed. Tonight, however, that return must be postponed for an hour.

'Come to the fire, dear,' she said to Judith. 'Whatever are you doing so far off?'

With a constrained smile, holding her book against her knees, Judith came to the stool on the rug. Katy had just had a dreadful accident and she did hope Nurse Gill wouldn't stop her from finding out quickly if everything was going to be all right. She couldn't bear it if Katy was going to die. But Nurse Gill's employer had said talk, so Nurse Gill talked.

'Sarah was a naughty girl tonight, wasn't she?' she said, threading a needle. She might as well get some mending done and have finished with it while she was talking, she thought. 'But she'll have got over it by tomorrow, probably. She's very difficult though. Look at the way she went on about that egg. If I hadn't gone and got her one, like as not she'd have had all the pots on the floor and your egg among them. And you know you can't have scenes like that in your nursery,' explained Nurse Gill in a reasonable way. 'You can't reely.'

'No,' said Judith.

'She teases her sister somethink frightful,' resumed Nurse

Gill, sewing a seam with little clicks. 'They never do get on,' she marvelled. 'Not like sisters at all. Why, you should see me and my sister. Me and Hattie think the world of each other, I'm sure. We were always dressed alike at home.' Needle suspended, Nurse Gill smiled into the fire, thinking of Hattie, and Judith snatched the chance to read a few lines. But Nurse Gill's voice soon demanded her attention again.

'Of course, Sarah's been spoiled,' she said. 'It's not my doing, though it's me as has to put up with her. She's had far too much drawing-room. Living with grown-ups, and such gay ones too, has spoilt her for nursery life, that's what I think. Howsomever,' said Nurse Gill with precision, 'that's all been put a stop to. I don't know what happened,' she said, lowering her voice and raising her eyebrows at the seam. 'It was my afternoon off. But it seems Sarah wanted to go down to the drawing-room when one of her mother's gentlemen friends was calling and her mother said she couldn't, but Sarah got in somehow before he came and hid herself behind the sofa. Then she began to cry and they found her.' Nurse Gill looked dramatically at Judith, but Judith couldn't think why. To her it seemed no more than a babyish game to hide behind the sofa. She gazed uncomprehendingly at Nurse Gill, who, under those candid eyes, bridled a little. 'Well, never mind,' she said dismissingly. 'The top and bottom of it is that she's never been allowed down since, except with her sister at dessert. So she's more awkward than ever at present, though she'll get over it.'

Judith sat, longing to read, but listening politely. She could not contribute much to the conversation, could do no more

than say, 'Yes' or 'No,' 'Did you?' or 'Oh,' and she was very glad when Nurse Gill said, before time, that she could go to bed if she wanted to. She said good night and went out of the nursery with her book.

'Funny little mum thing,' was Nurse Gill's comment, reaching for her papers. But then, in her opinion, all children were difficult.

Judith, relieved to have finished with all strange people for the day, idled down the passage. Now that there was no one about, children withdrawn into bed, the rest of the household drawn down into kitchen and dining-room about the business of dinner, she could really look at the house and take it in. She trailed her hand lightly over closed doors, wondering what was behind them. She looked down at the deep carpet under her feet. She looked at the handsome staircase, broad and of dark shining wood, running up, running down. She looked over into the hall where the fire burning in the great stone chimney-piece sent warm, flower-scented air upwards through the house. Through one open door, below, the firelight lay golden over a silvery carpet. That must be the drawing-room, Judith decided. There were a great many spring flowers, daffodils, mimosa and white lilac. That was where Margaret would sit tonight. The dinner smelled good and the drawing-room looked beautiful, but Judith did not envy Margaret either of them. To have to be with the grown-ups would have spoiled both for Judith. She couldn't think why her cousin Sarah yearned after them.

A maid crossed the hall and went into the drawing-room to see to the fire. Judith saw her fluff up her hair before a

glass, help herself from a box of chocolates. 'Oh,' thought Judith, 'she shouldn't.' She saw the maid start and gulp the chocolate down, as the hall-door opened to admit a very young man, who came in without a hat as if he were used to the house.

'Haven't they finished dinner yet, Birch?' he asked as the maid advanced, smooth-faced, no signs of the chocolate, to meet him.

'No, Mr John, but they won't be long.'

'Right-ho, I'll wait here,' said the young man, taking his stance before the hall-fire and picking up a paper.

The telephone rang in the hall – there were telephones all over the house – and Judith heard the maid say: 'Yes, sir, Mrs Sargent said I was to say that she would be glad to see you this evening.'

'This house is like a hotel,' thought Judith.

Which was precisely what Brian thought when he came out from dinner and found young Watson in the hall, the harbinger of more to come.

'Hello, John,' said Vera cordially. She liked visitors, she liked to surround herself. It was, in fact, essential. 'Margaret, this is John Watson from the next house. He's come to bring the age level down a little, otherwise you might find it rather high. I suppose your father and mother are coming over later, John?'

'They are, yes,' said the boy, wrenching at his tie, forgetting it was a bow and almost bringing it off altogether. He was not shy with the Sargents as a rule, but this girl of his own age, with thin arms and a cloud of dark hair, took away all his

confidence and he looked at her with as much constraint as she at him.

'Come into the drawing-room and have coffee,' said Vera. When the door closed upon them, Judith scuttered up the last flight of stairs. Now for bed and Katy. A lamp with stars and a good book – what bliss! She meant to enjoy them to the full till Margaret came up. But when her sister arrived, towards midnight, she had been asleep for hours.

II

Margaret came to look in a dazed way at her sister. It seemed strange to find anyone belonging to her here. She had been in such a different, exciting world; she had got so far away in such a short time. And everything, after all her fears, had proved so easy. The whole evening had been like the dream of a party where you floated light as air, ate delicious food without knowing what it was and miraculously said the right thing every time. The room was like a dream too, silvery, with yellow brocade and all those heavenly flowers, the freesias and the lilac and the daffodils, and when she caught sight of herself from time to time she looked part of the dream too. She had never spent such an evening, but it had gone so quickly. She couldn't believe it when her aunt said it was almost midnight and she must go to bed. 'I'm not a bit sleepy,' she protested, longing to stay till the end. But Vera, though smiling, was firm, so Margaret with reluctance tore herself away and came upstairs, where she had the excitement of going over it all again.

There was more to come too. On Monday they were all going to the Races, everyone who had been there tonight, except Uncle Brian. He didn't go to Races, it appeared. She had never been to a Race Meeting and her heart leaped at the thought of it. Fancy going to what she had only read of! It sounded so fashionable too. Then one night next week they were going to the theatre. What a lovely time she was having, she thought, as she hung up her dress, and to think she had been so terrified of coming. When she was ready to get into bed, she turned out the lamp and went to the window to see if she could see the house next door, which had taken on interest now since John Watson lived there. Against the night sky, faintly red from the city, she saw the dark bulk of the house towering on its terraces. In one turret there was a light. Perhaps that was his room.

'I oughtn't to be thinking of him,' she thought guiltily. 'Daddy wouldn't like it . . . '

Daddy! She gripped the curtains convulsively. She had promised to send him a card as soon as she arrived, and she had forgotten it. It was still in her bag. She had written it before she came away and there it still was. She turned on the light and got it out. She stood with it in her hand as if it were the most fateful omission. What would he think? What would he say? She knew only too well. He would say that the first time she left him she forgot him. 'Oh, I didn't, I didn't,' she protested. But it was true. She had forgotten him. Throughout the evening she had never once thought of him. But now he was revenged; the thought of him had driven all pleasure in the evening away. She turned out the light at last,

but it was a long time before she could sleep. He would be so hurt.

She worried unnecessarily. By this time, Geoffrey was gone from the house in Queen's Walk, leaving no address. He had exacted the postcard, but he knew he would not be there to receive it.

Downstairs, everyone had gone but Captain Ward. He still stood, one elbow on the mantelpiece, looking down at Vera, who lay in an armchair by the fire. Under the centre lights, his back turned, Brian stood with *The Times*, which he had already read from beginning to end during the evening. He waited for Ward to go. He had left the door wide open as a hint. The other two let it remain open as a hint also, to him. Vera and Ward talked in a desultory way with long pauses. They said nothing but the merest commonplaces. One thing is certain, thought Brian, his eyes on the financial columns, he didn't stay behind for this.

After a time, Vera said: 'You might as well sit down, Johnny.'

Captain Ward sat down. In a few moments, Brian also sat down. Two can play at this game, he thought grimly.

At half-past one Captain Ward departed. Without having spent one moment alone with Vera, thought Brian as, with weary satisfaction, he went up to his room.

'Not only does he bore me to death himself,' thought Vera, climbing the stairs, 'but he does his best to prevent my ever being anything but bored with anyone else.'

Turning on the lights in her own room, she looked at herself in the glass. When people said she was the loveliest

woman in Trenton, she smiled indifferently. It was too easy. What competition was there? If it had been in London or in Europe, it would have been different. She walked about yawning, touching things. She was like an exiled queen living in company that was never quite good enough. Yet she did not know where her kingdom was.

CHAPTER TEN

I

On Easter Sunday morning, as Vera's friends were arriving in cars at the back of the house, Brian, followed by the three little girls, was hastening away down the many steps at the front. When it was Vera's turn to entertain to champagne on Sunday mornings, Brian took his children to visit his mother. Thus he got them out of the way of what he considered a frivolous, extravagant, not to say demoralising spectacle. He also hoped by his marked absence to impress his disapproval upon the guests. But the guests were not impressed by anything. They were delighted to find him out when they called, and said so. He cramped their style, they said.

Margaret, standing with young Watson in the great mullioned window of the drawing-room, waved to Judith and Judith waved mournfully back. She didn't want to visit old Mrs Sargent. Neither did Sarah.

'Grandmother's an old bitch,' said Sarah, going down the steps.

'Oooh,' cried Meriel, clapping her hand to her mouth. 'Now I shall tell. I shall tell Grandmother what you called her.'

'Tell,' said Sarah savagely. 'That's nothing new. You're always telling.'

She made a dive at Eva, but Meriel made a dive forward and caught up with her father. From that safeguard, she tossed her head at her sister. She was going to a place where *she* came first, where everything she did and said was right, where Sarah dared not tease her.

Lawn Cottage was no more than ten minutes' walk away from Southfield, situated in just such another wide tree-shaded road, but this house was old-fashioned, low, cream-coloured, with pagoda-like eaves and verandahs, giving it a mock-Chinese air. Lawns lay about it on every side, there were few flower borders, but many trees.

Coming down the drive to meet them was an old lady in a black hat ornamented with huge bows. Old Mrs Sargent always wore the same sort of hats. She was very particular about them and had several of them at one time. She went to London, taking her daughter Gertrude with her, to have them fitted. Sometimes she went twice and three times about one hat, but always, Vera pointed out, the same hat resulted. No one could tell the difference or had been able to for twenty years; except that, on close observation, the ribbon was sometimes seen to be grosgrain and sometimes taffeta.

Mrs Sargent's snow-white hair was scraped up tightly at the sides, but puffed out to an immense height on top and on this puff the hat was perched like a great bird on an uneasy nest. She had, Judith noticed, white marshmallow cheeks and pale blue eyes.

For an old lady, Mrs Sargent had what Vera considered

unsuitable vanities. Her hats were one; her age another. No one, not even her children, knew how old she was. She had a fear she kept as secret as her age: she was terrified of thunder, but nobody knew.

Old Mrs Sargent bitterly disapproved of Vera and all her works. She should, Vera said, have been grateful for that. Mrs Sargent was a masterful woman and though her husband's fortune was hers to do as she liked with – Brian had been left only his father's business – life had receded from Lawn Cottage when her husband died and her son married. But Vera's shortcomings provided Mrs Sargent with an interest so great as to make up, almost, for what she had lost. She had the never-ending pleasure of fault-finding and interfering and pitying Brian and the children. She had a never-failing source of conversation, and heaven only knew, Vera said, what she and Gertrude would have done without it. Whatever else they disagreed upon, they agreed about Vera. Vera united them. They little knew, Vera said herself, what they owed to her.

'And who is this?' said old Mrs Sargent, stopping in the drive to point her stick at Judith.

'This is Judith Leigh, one of Charlotte's children, and a very nice little girl,' said Brian kindly.

'Really?' said the old lady as if she didn't believe it. She didn't. She thought nothing good could come out of Vera's family. A wild lot, she insisted, forgetting Lucy, forgetting Jack, thinking only of the good-for-nothing boys and that dreadful wedding of the other girl's, this child's mother, she supposed.

'Well, Sarah,' she said. 'And what trouble have you been getting into this week?'

'I haven't been in any trouble,' said Sarah with dignity. 'I haven't been doing anything.'

'Oooh, haven't you? What about – you know what?' said Meriel.

Sarah's eyes drew together, but she daren't fly at her sister as she would have done at home.

'Where's Aunt Gertrude?' asked Meriel.

'In her room, darling. Run and find her,' said her grandmother indulgently, and Meriel ran. Aunt Gertrude always had sweets for her and while she ate them, leaning against Aunt Gertrude's knee, Meriel would say 'D'you know what Sarah called Grandmother? She called her something awful. A dreadful bad word. She called her . . . ' She could already hear Aunt Gertrude's small scream of horror. So she ran.

'Dear, dear,' said old Mrs Sargent watching her go. 'That coat is much too short for the child. Ask Nanny to call round, will you, Brian? We really can't have Meriel going about like that. Now you two children run and play in the garden,' she said dismissingly. 'And you, dear boy, come and have a glass of sherry.'

Brian would drink sherry at his mother's house, but not champagne at his own. There was a difference, he insisted, though when Vera asked what it was he took refuge in a dignified silence.

'I see no difference,' said Vera. 'Except that champagne is sparkling and sherry flat, and the company matches the drinks in both cases.'

'May I remind you, Vera,' said Brian gravely, 'that you are speaking of my mother?'

'And do you know,' said Vera, 'that I could always tell you beforehand what you are going to say?'

Brian sat with his mother in the drawing-room, low-ceilinged and further darkened by the pagoda-verandah over the windows, through which the two long-legged little girls could be seen wandering aimlessly about the lawns. The room, in spite of the fire, had a chilly air, due perhaps to the glitter of the beadwork on chairs, screens and footstools, the glassy lustres, the chalk portraits of children in pale gilt frames on the walls. Among the portraits was one of a little girl with eager blue eyes, blonde ringlets and puff sleeves, a charming child, who had, incredibly, become the stiff, highly conventional old lady by the fire.

'Anything of note at the office this week, dear?' she asked her son.

'No, I don't think so.'

Brian was a careful, if unenterprising business man. He had no need to be enterprising; his father had consolidated the business, with a New York office in which Brian had spent a year or two before his marriage. Brian had nothing to do but to carry on the business on the lines laid down by his father, and this he did. The money, however, was largely in his mother's hands, left, without restriction, to her by her husband. Brian used to remind Vera that she owed much of what she had to his mother's generosity.

'But I don't want to owe her anything,' said Vera. 'Why can't we live on our own money? Why do you keep taking these huge presents of money from your mother?'

'She likes to give them to me. Whom else would she give them to?'

'But it makes so much depend upon her caprice,' objected Vera.

'Mother is never capricious,' said Brian in grave reproof.

But it was a long time since they had discussed this question, or any other. Vera rushed on in the headlong recklessness that had grown upon her. She used to complain that she had no idea how much money she had; a queer complaint, thought Lucy, who had to know almost to a penny. When Vera depleted her bank balance, more always came from somewhere. She had ceased to inquire where. She just didn't bother any more, she told Lucy. She certainly wasn't going to play up to old Mrs Sargent for the sake of what she could get out of her, she said. She was, in fact, rather worse with Mrs Sargent than she would otherwise have been.

Old Mrs Sargent was as regal in her way as Vera in hers. Her attitude was that of the jealous old queen dowager to the reigning queen. Her sharpest pleasure nowadays was in hearing something disparaging about her supplanter, something that would justify her in her bad opinion. But on this Sunday morning she hadn't got hold of anything yet. She always had to deduce for herself, snatch pieces of information here and there and put them together for herself, because Brian was always much too loyal. As if there was any necessity for that sort of thing between mother and son, thought old Mrs Sargent. He should have known he could tell her anything and everything. But he didn't, and she sat moving her hands restlessly on her silken lap, finding the conversation flat and savourless. Faint and far away in the recesses of her mind

something wondered, though never admittedly, if Brian was a little heavy on the hand, just a shade boring, and if Vera found him so.

Old Mrs Sargent was not, however, to be defrauded of some incident to enliven the Sabbath morning. The door opened and Gertrude came in, closing it at once behind her. It was obvious that something had happened, but Gertrude did not omit a proper preface. (The Sargents, Vera said, always listened to themselves speaking, thinking how well it sounded.) Gertrude clasped her hands and leaned over the old lady. 'Mother, I don't want to upset you,' she said. 'And you must not be upset. Remember your heart, dear, and try not to take this too seriously. After all, Sarah is only a child.'

So it was Sarah again. The Sargent family, stiff and stuffy in closed rooms, were always having their windows broken by Vera and Sarah. It made them into enemies. But if these two wild, graceful creatures had consented to come in, eat out of their hands, be petted, suffer themselves to be domesticated, how proud and happy the Sargents would have been! As it was the old lady looked up with an unpleasant gleam in her pale blue eyes.

'What is it, Gertrude?'

'Well, dear – and Brian too – Meriel is only a little girl and she didn't know what she was telling me, I'm sure. But I've just learnt that Sarah, if you please, told her cousin Judith that you were – I hardly like to say it, dear,' said Gertrude. 'She called you – prepare to be shocked both of you – she said you were an old bitch, dear.'

'Brian!' The old lady turned her hat-laden head in such swift outrage in his direction that the hat itself remained pointing at Gertrude.

'Good heavens!' exclaimed Brian, as shocked as his mother could wish.

'And where do you suppose she got that appalling word?' asked Mrs Sargent, while Gertrude solicitously straightened the hat. 'Who has used it of me? Who – but one person? It is just such a word as Vera with her outrageous modern vocabulary would use of her husband's mother.'

'Mother, you're wrong,' protested Brian. 'Sarah picks up all sorts of words from the servants. She doesn't know what she's saying. She hasn't the slightest idea.'

'Call her in, Gertrude,' said Mrs Sargent, pointing her stick at the children wandering in the garden. 'Call her to me.'

Gertrude opened the french windows. 'Sarah . . . Sarah,' she called. 'Grandmother wants you.'

'Oh, blast,' muttered Sarah. 'Something's up, you'll see. Come with me, will you?'

Sarah, making for the window, looked anxious in spite of herself. Her child's nerves were sometimes unequal to a row unless it was of her own making and she was more in awe of her grandmother than she would admit.

'Come here,' said the old lady sternly.

Scowling, the slight cast in her eyes caused by the stress of emotion plainly evident, Sarah approached. Judith remained by the window, her heart beating fast. She hated rows. She hated the baiting of the young by those in authority. It was

nearly as bad here as it was at home, she thought. She was sorry for Sarah, always getting into trouble.

'Sarah,' said old Mrs Sargent, her hat trembling ominously. 'It has just come to my ears that in speaking of me, your grandmother, you have used a word that has shocked me beyond belief.'

Sarah, her eyes on her grandmother, swallowed visibly.

'I see you know what it is and admit it,' said the old lady. 'I am horrified that you should know of the existence of such a word. They may say you are only a child and don't know what such a word means, but it is perfectly clear to me, Sarah,' she said, leaning forward impressively from her chair, 'that it was the worst word you could think of and you used it of me, your grandmother.'

Sarah said nothing.

'I should make no impression on you, I know, if I told you that you are an ungrateful child to speak so of one who has always done her best for you, to whom you owe more than you will ever know, because I don't suppose anyone tells you what I do for you and your mother and your sister, in fact, for the whole household,' said the old lady, pausing for breath. 'But I might make an impression on you if I can make it plain what damage you are doing to yourself. Perhaps you will mind about that if about nothing else.'

Sarah continued to gaze at her grandmother.

'I hear you sometimes complain that you have no friend,' continued Mrs Sargent.

Sarah's eyes fell. The look of humiliation, of minding, that made Judith so uncomfortable showed on her face. 'Oh, why

can't she say this to Sarah somewhere else?' thought Judith shuffling by the window. 'Why does she say it in front of all of us?'

'I hear nobody plays with you,' said the old lady. 'You are shunned, I know. Does it never strike you that it is because of your violent behaviour and your disgusting, unchildlike language? No decent child will play, or be allowed to play with you. No one will ask you to her home. If a nice mother heard you use such a word and about your own grandmother, too, she would never allow her child to go near you again. In fact, she would be justified in complaining to your school and getting you expelled. It would not surprise me at all if that is what happens before long. And then we shall all be disgraced by you. I hope, Brian,' she said, turning stiffly in the direction of her son, 'that you will tell Vera of this incident and try to make her see that the children should not be allowed to hear such language. And now you may take Sarah away,' she finished coldly. 'I don't want to see her for quite some time. Meriel may stay to lunch, Gertrude.'

Sarah stood still, her head low. Brian rose.

'You had better say you are sorry,' he said distantly. He was very angry with her. The affair had thrown too revealing a light on his household.

'I'm sorry,' Sarah muttered.

She went out of the room, Judith following. In the drive, Judith put out a hand and gave Sarah's a squeeze.

'Huh,' said Sarah, blinking away a tear. 'I don't care. She *is* an old bitch.'

II

If Vera had heard only Brian's outraged, but unimaginative version of the morning's incident, she would not have taken much notice. But she also heard Judith's through Margaret, and it roused her amused sympathy for Sarah and indignation with Meriel. When Vera gave herself time to be touched and indignant, she could act. In the afternoon, she went to Lawn Cottage.

Old Mrs Sargent was just waking from her afternoon nap by the fire in the drawing-room. Slowly she opened her eyes and saw Vera coming up the drive. Too beautiful, she thought, not half-awake. Brian would have been better, we should all have been better with somebody plainer. They say beauty is a gift, she thought, but it makes a lot of trouble. It sows dissatisfaction, a kind of yearning all around it. Either we ought all to be beautiful or none of us ought. There's going to be a battle, she thought, waking fully, and I shan't win. Vera's battles were so short and sharp, her mother-in-law never had time to get anything in before they were over. She sat up and strove to straighten the great light puff of hair which had slipped a little sideways.

'Good afternoon, grandmother,' said Vera, sailing in. She bent to kiss the insubstantial cheek. She always thought it was like kissing a doughnut. 'How are you? How is Gertrude? Well, I hope.'

'I don't flatter myself that you have come to ask about my health,' said the old lady grimly.

'No, but it's an opening, isn't it? A soft inquiry sometimes

turneth away wrath. As a matter of fact, I've come to take Meriel home. You were naturally angry with Sarah, but I don't think Meriel should be rewarded for telling tales.'

The old lady flushed.

'Meriel doesn't know what she is repeating when she repeats a word like that.'

'She knows she'll get Sarah into trouble by it, anyway,' said Vera.

'It is a disgrace,' said Mrs Sargent, giving way to anger. 'To *someone*. I won't say who.'

'Do, do,' said Vera lightly. 'Don't hesitate.'

'To your friends then, to the sort of people you associate with and bring into the house, that Sarah should ever have heard such a word.'

'Don't you think you take it too seriously?' asked Vera in a reasonable voice. 'Sarah heard it and liked the sound of it. A lot of words beginning with "b" make good expletives. They relieve one's feelings.'

'But why, I should like to know,' said old Mrs Sargent unwisely. 'Why should Sarah wish to relieve her feelings about her grandmother?'

'Ah,' said Vera. 'That's what you must ask yourself. We only see one side of the medal. We see our opinion of the child, but we don't see the child's opinion of us, except at moments like this. However, I'll go and get Meriel. I suppose she's upstairs with Gertrude. I shouldn't mind too much about that word,' she said, taking the door in her hand and laying her lovely cheek to the edge. 'After all, if you look at it without prejudice, it is rather a compliment. I mean in

the sense in which it is generally used, dear grandmother. Goodbye.'

Before old Mrs Sargent had sufficiently grasped her meaning to be shocked, again, young Mrs Sargent was conducting a bawling daughter down the drive.

Sarah was so happy that her mother had taken her part, had actually gone to Lawn Cottage to do it and to bring Meriel out, that she danced. When Nurse Gill saw her pushing the nursery table to the wall, a look of relief and cosiness came into her face. There had been trouble on all sides, from old Mrs Sargent, young Mrs Sargent, Mr Sargent, Meriel – they all take it out on me, thought Nurse Gill, I'm the one that gets it. She expected the worst trouble of all from Sarah, but if Sarah was going to dance, everything would be all right. 'Now you'll see something,' whispered Nurse Gill to Judith as Sarah got her ballet shoes out of the cupboard.

Sarah put a record on the nursery radiogram and took her place in the middle of the floor. Her feet in the first position, she waited. Her passion for dancing was recognised and encouraged. She had been taught since she was four by the best teachers in a city noted for its dancers; whenever the ballet came to the theatre she was taken every day.

'They say her mother was a lovely dancer,' whispered Nurse Gill. Vera would have resented that 'was'.

'Yes, Mummy told me,' said Judith waiting.

The music of *Les Sylphides* stole enchantingly into the room and gravely Sarah began to dance. She might have been alone.

Judith, who danced herself at school, the Highland Fling, the Hornpipe and other dances that called for nothing but a sound wind and a lively leg, had never seen dancing like this. Her lips parted, she stared at her cousin and her feelings for Sarah underwent an abrupt change. She might be naughty, but what did that matter? She was someone quite extraordinary and wonderful. She was like a tale. Judith felt humble. Never, never could she dance like that herself. She was breathlessly admiring. When the music and the dancer drifted into silence, she said earnestly: 'Oh, Sarah, dance again.'

'Oh, yes,' said Sarah. 'I'm going to.'

Sarah changed the record, then came to stand at Judith's chair. 'This is the "Dance of the Little Swans,"' she said gravely.

'What a lovely name,' said Judith.

'It's from Tchaikovsky's '*Swan Lake*,'' said Sarah.

'*Swan Lake*,' repeated Judith, lingering on the words. What lovely things Sarah knew about. And difficult things too; that name 'Chi . . . something. Judith was sure she couldn't say it and she was two years older, yet Sarah brought it out as if it were quite an ordinary word. 'Swan Lake. The Dance of the Little Swans,' she said, looking into Sarah's eyes as if she could see them there. A swift rapture ran through both children. They caught each other's hands. 'It's coming. The music's coming,' cried Sarah, snatching hers away. 'I must dance.'

'Yes, yes, dance,' said Judith. She leaned forward from her chair. 'Is the lake frozen?' she asked.

'I don't know,' said Sarah dancing.

Though they were already proud of her – they often said it was a pity she had been born rich, the poor ones always go further, take it more seriously, they said – her teachers might have been horrified by the ambitious performances of their pupil; adults might have smiled at its immaturities, but a child understood what another child was trying to do and, to Judith, Sarah's dancing was what Sarah meant it to be, and both were enraptured.

In Judith's heart there began to be born a protective, pardoning, admiring love for her cousin. In her way, she felt for Sarah much as Lucy felt for Sarah's mother. Sarah realised it, because some days later she exclaimed: 'Why, I've got a friend, haven't I? I've got you. What a sell for Grandmother.'

CHAPTER ELEVEN

I

Vera sometimes let the children follow her about the house for a while in the mornings, and passing the nursery door she called out that they could come if they liked. Sarah ran out at once; where her mother was there was always something going on. When Judith and Meriel, with Eva, tracked them down, they were in the garden-room where Vera was preparing to do the flowers.

'There's a dinner-party tonight,' announced Sarah. 'And we're coming down. May I dance, Mummy? Do let me.'

'No, you can't dance tonight,' said Vera absently.

A deep scowl drew Sarah's eyes together and she snipped at a rose with the scissors.

'Oh, don't,' protested Judith.

'I shall. They're not your flowers. You're only staying here,' said Sarah. 'What's it to do with you what I do with our flowers?'

'You'll go back to the nursery if you begin, Sarah,' warned her mother, not recognising the echo.

Sarah, scowling and muttering, rubbed along the edge of the table like a cross cat.

Margaret came in, flushed, her eyes shining.

'Ah, there you are, Auntie – Aunt Vera.'

In her belt, the only place she had to hide anything, she had her first note from a young man. It said:

Can you come out this morning? Will call at 10.30 on the off-chance. JW

She came to her aunt at the table and putting her hair back with nervous fingers almost whispered: 'Would you mind if I went out with John Watson, Auntie Vera – Aunt Vera? Would it be all right? Are you *sure* you don't want me to do anything for you?'

'There's nothing for you to do, so run along and enjoy yourself,' said Vera.

'Oh, thank you most awfully, Aunt Vera. Thank you so much.' She ran, but at the door she turned. 'I *am* having a lovely time,' she said fervently. How she loved her aunt when she was kind like this and how she shrank when she incurred her displeasure. Last night, for instance, when she had said before all those people, 'for heaven's sake don't call me "auntie". Auntie!' she mocked, sitting there in a dress of palest grey with spreading skirts and a cherry-coloured sash. She was right, thought the assembled company; she shouldn't be called 'auntie'. – 'Say Aunt Vera if you must say anything,' she finished testily.

Margaret blushed so hard the tears came to her eyes, and for the rest of the evening she daren't address her aunt at all in case she should forget the new injunction. She had

impressed on Judith in their bedroom that she must not say 'auntie' any more, but Judith couldn't see why. 'Auntie Lucy wouldn't mind whether we called her aunt or auntie,' she said sturdily. 'I expect Auntie – well Aunt Vera then – doesn't really like being an aunt. That's what it is,' she said.

But having remembered to say aunt and having permission to go out with John Watson, Margaret ran lightly up the stairs, her hair flying. Every day here the world seemed brighter, lighter, more exciting, and there was nothing to be anxious about. Margaret was amazed at that. But alas, it was all going so fast. This was Thursday and on Monday they must go. But she wouldn't think about it. She was going out with John and tonight he was coming to the dinner-party. Life was so thrilling that she could hardly bear it. Reaching her bedroom she suddenly hugged her dressing-gown hanging behind the door, squeezed it so hard that she went red and the tears came to her eyes. Then she hid the note in the pocket of her suitcase and rushing to the dressing-table, began furiously to brush her hair.

In the garden-room Vera was piling flowers on a trestle-table near the door. 'Those are to be thrown away,' she said.

'But they're not dead,' said Judith.

'Oh, yes they are,' said Vera, turning to the fresh ones.

Judith fingered the discarded flowers. It seemed to her that Auntie Vera was always throwing things away. She didn't seem to value anything, but threw away and turned to the more that was always coming in. Now to Auntie Lucy, thought Judith, comparing, everything seemed to matter. She seemed closer to things. She didn't have masses of flowers sent in from

the shops; she picked them from the garden and arranged them in her mixed bunches, where every flower seemed to have its special place. Auntie Vera would never have spent hours taking sheep-ticks off the hedgehog, reflected Judith. Fifty-seven horrible blood-sucking ticks had she counted as Auntie Lucy took them off with Uncle William's dissecting forceps. The poor little hedgehog was dying of them; it was so weak it couldn't curl itself up. But Auntie Lucy fed it with milk from the palm of her hand for three days, and then after frisking about the lawn in the dusk like a little dog, it went back to its life in the fields, restored. Judith was glad Auntie Lucy did things like that; you could always count on her to help anything. Auntie Vera, Judith thought, would probably have said 'Ugh' and let the hedgehog die.

She turned from the discarded flowers and sat rather disconsolately on the edge of a chair. Sarah approached, holding out a sweet which gave every evidence of having been long sat upon. 'You can have this if you like,' she said.

'I don't want it, thanks,' said Judith.

'Yes, do have it,' urged Sarah, pressing it upon her. 'Do, please.'

It had given her a fright when she found herself speaking rudely to Judith; she was terrified of losing her friend, so she offered the sweet and made an anxious, loving smile at her cousin. Judith relented, accepted the sweet, made room on the chair and Sarah sat down beside her with relief.

There was a clicking of high heels across the hall and a figure appeared, startling Judith who had not seen Mrs Clarey before. She gave the effect of a gallows with a black garment

fluttering therefrom, and her sallow face was so seamed with
wrinkles that Judith stared at it in astonishment. How had she
got like that? wondered Judith, who was given to naïve wonder
as to how people got so thin, so fat, so old-looking or, otherwise, so battered by time and care. It never crossed her mind
that she must some day share one of these fates.

'They told me where you were, Vera, so I came right
in. How heavenly,' said Mrs Clarey, leaning over the flowers.
'But my God, the cost! That's the worst of being poor,
you keep calculating the cost of this sort of thing. Not that
I didn't spend as much as you on entertaining, my dear,
don't think I'm blaming you,' said Mrs Clarey, waving her
black-gloved hand. 'Only I wish to God I hadn't. What was
the good of it all? It's cutlet for cutlet in our world, my
dear. I can't entertain now, so no one entertains me, except
you. You should take note of me sometimes, my dear. I'm a
warning.'

'Cassandra,' said Vera lightly, putting blue hyacinths
among the pink. 'Cassandra Clarey. A good name for you.'

'What does that mean?' Sarah asked Judith.

'She lived in Greece. She foretold evil. No one believed
her, but she was right,' explained Judith.

'Dear me, children know so much nowadays,' said Vera.
'But run along. You can all go back to the nursery now.'

'Oh, I don't want to,' said Sarah, flinging herself back in
the chair.

'Come on,' said Judith, laughing, and plucking her up by
the front of her frock. Sarah's face cleared and she went.

'Well, who's coming tonight?' asked Mrs Clarey briskly.

'The party is really for the bride – Brenda Spencer – Crawford now.'

'What's the husband like? I haven't seen him yet.'

'Oh, nice-looking,' said Vera.

'She's got good value for her money, has she?'

'I can't say. He's been made director of the colliery, I hear, but I don't suppose he'll do much but hunt.'

'How do they seem? Do they love each other?'

'Well, I don't suppose he has much chance against the dogs, you know.'

'No, he won't have. They'll be sleeping on the bed still, if I know her.'

'A bad beginning, if they are,' said Vera. 'Napoleon was bitten by Josephine's dog when he tried to get into her bed, and look how that marriage turned out.'

'You ought to tell them about it,' said Mrs Clarey. 'What's his name?'

'Brenda calls him Terry.'

'Irish?'

'Originally, I think, but he comes from South Africa. He's of good family, I believe, but poor.'

'Ah, I'm in good company,' said Mrs Clarey. 'And more will join me. There's a conspiracy against the upper and middle classes. No one sticks up for us. We don't stick up for ourselves. We're like a lot of sheep submitting to the shears without a baa. Not that it should matter to me. I've no wool left. Ah well, my dear, I'll be with you tonight in the same old dress with a constellation from Woolworth's in my hair. Goodbye. Amuse yourself while you can.'

'What do you think of the flowers?' asked Vera when Brian came home at the end of the afternoon. She waved an airy hand at them but did not stay for an answer, and he looked after her with resentment. He had been going to compliment her on them and that in spite of his bad day and prospect of a worse evening. She had sent him to his mother's for lunch because the maids had so much to do. His mother, throughout lunch, had pointed out that Vera entertained far too lavishly and too often. Though he agreed, he would not say so, and that had not pleased the old lady. He knew he was going to be ill at ease the whole evening. He hated these parties where no one was asked for him. They were all Vera's friends, all people he disapproved of, giddy-pated creatures who never spoke a serious word. Vera never considered him or his tastes, he reflected. Well, he at any rate would do his duty. He would go up and read to his children. It would calm his mind and improve theirs.

He went upstairs only to find the nursery empty and Nurse Gill reading a paper which she popped behind a cushion as guiltily as if it had been *La Vie Parisienne* instead of *Home*. The children, it appeared, were resting because they were to come down after dinner. He disapproved of this too. They should be kept out of such worldly company. Meriel would be all right, she took after him, but his mother said Sarah was too fond of notice and would soon have her head turned.

The house was quiet, the occupants withdrawn so that they should be the more ready to rush out on the evening's entertainment when the time came. Disregarded, unlistened-to, uncatered-for, Brian went into his dressing-room and

locked the door. He sat down on the bed, which splayed its legs alarmingly under his weight. This was the bed he slept in. It was hardly more than camp, it had been meant to be temporary, but it had become permanent. Night after night now, he extended his large frame on this bed. His feet stuck out at the end, but did anyone mind? Looking at the bed, tears filled his eyes and he began to cry.

From childhood Brian had cried easily. When on their marriage night Brian wept for happiness, Vera, though startled, was touched. But she found he often cried, for self-pity, for disappointment, for obscure reasons and she was alienated by his tears. He cried on her shoulder and at first she held him, looking over his head with incredulous amazement. For a man to cry – nay, to blubber! She couldn't get over it. And by and by she began to feel that her married life was going to turn out to be one long holding of a large wet baby of somebody else's. That was the worst of it: somebody else's. Nothing to do with her. Mentally, she returned him to his mother.

His tears were probably the outcome of some deep emotional disturbance or repression, but Vera had no patience to go into that.

Though she herself would not have chosen Brian in the first instance, preferring someone drier, terser, Lucy felt that having drawn him in the lottery of marriage, she would have tried to be more tolerant with him. After all, he was fundamentally sound and kind, so why not let him, she felt, let him write careful letters, read aloud, turn a phrase? She didn't see why people shouldn't play at things if they wanted to. But Vera couldn't bear that. She went about pricking

pretence and pretension whenever she met it, and most savagely of all in her own husband.

Brian was unfortunate. He would not have been any happier with a wife who admired him, than with one he whole-heartedly, in spite of everything, admired. He seemed to have no luck with anything he admired. He admired modern poetry, but he couldn't understand it. The reviewers hailed the poets, Brian, impressed, eager, bought their works, earnestly sought, but could not find what he knew must be there. In the same way, he was baffled by Vera. Comprehension of poetry was just beyond his range, Vera was just out of his reach. This ache without satisfaction seemed to be his lot in life. He felt it as he sat on his bed, weeping.

'I'll go to America,' he thought. 'Mother's right. I ought to have gone long ago.'

His mother had implied at lunch that he was neglecting the New York end of the business and leaving it far too much to his partners because he daren't turn his back on his home. It was true. Vera would probably go off with Ward or one of them if he left her. He wondered, for a moment, if she would go to America with him if he asked her. But if she refused, he would be committed to going by himself. She would despise him if he didn't go because she wouldn't. He sat on in a miserable state of indecision. 'I'll leave it a bit longer,' he thought in the end, drying his eyes. He got up from the bed and walked about the room, sniffing, taking the small change from his waistcoat pocket, getting ready for the party. He sniffed, and slowly his eyes cleared, his nose lost its flush and he looked himself again, stolid and handsome.

In the room overhead, the young Leighs were also getting ready for the party, though Judith's preparations were for the time being suspended. Her best dress must be preserved from crease, and she would not put it on until the last moment, so she lay across the bed, reading, in her petticoat.

Margaret was brushing her hair at the dressing-table. Pausing, she leaned to look into the glass. Her own face looked back at her, lips parted, cheeks flushed, eyes darkly blue. Her heart gave one of its ecstatic leaps and she went on brushing her hair.

Margaret, at Vera's, was like a creature just emerged from the chrysalis and finding its wings. She was making a dazzled, uncertain, highly excited flight in what she felt must be a most brilliant world. Compared with this world, the morning-room at home was as mud at the bottom of the pond to the winged creature. With the difference that the insect did not remember the mud it had left and Margaret, with guilt, did remember the morning-room. She kept dismissing both room and guilt from her mind. After all, this was only Thursday. She had until Monday, and anything might happen before then, since every day was packed with incident and excitement.

She was soon ready; her toilet was so simple. The older one gets the longer it takes to present a good face to the world, but Margaret was so young she had nothing to do to make herself prettier than she was. She brushed her hair until it shone and tied a ribbon round it. She lifted her diaphanous dress over her head and whirling round to Judith said 'Hi!'

Judith was startled. She was frequently startled in this

room by her sister's liveliness. Margaret never called out 'Hi'
at home.

'Do me up, please,' said Margaret, presenting her back.

Judith applied herself to hooks and eyes so minute that
she had to fumble for them between her sister's thin shoulder
blades.

'Ow – your hands are cold!' protested Margaret, wriggling
and giggling.

Judith began to laugh too. Every time she approached
the hooks, they both laughed harder. They threatened, with
the absurdity of youth, to become helpless, until Margaret's
eyes fell on the clock and she sobered. 'Quick. I must bear it.
Plunge at them and get them done,' she said. John was
coming early and she must go down.

II

From the landing, the children looked over the banisters at
the guests drinking sherry in the hall. Judith had been sure,
in the bedroom, that Margaret would be the prettiest at the
party, but now that she was down there, Judith could see that
she wasn't. She wasn't anything like Auntie Vera, who stood
slim and proud in a golden dress. But Margaret was having a
lovely time, laughing and talking to John Watson.

Uncle Brian didn't seem to be enjoying himself, she
observed. He stood by the fire drinking gloomily out of his
little glass. 'That's the one who's just got married,' said Sarah
pointing. 'That's Brenda Spencer.'

'Has she brought a dog?' asked Meriel.

'No, of course not, silly. People don't bring dogs to dinner-parties.

'She did once, because Mummy said so. She said she was sure nobody would mind, but everybody minded, Mummy said.'

'Well, she's brought a man this time,' said Sarah.

In the hall, the bride, a dumpy young person with her hair scraped back into a bun, handed her sherry-glass to her new husband as she might have handed it to a servant. 'Put that down,' she said. Her bad manners were due to shyness and lack of correction on the part of doting aunts, by whom she had been surrounded since her mother died soon after her birth.

Her tall husband gravely complied. Terry Crawford was an extremely personable young man, thought Vera, receiving him. But there was something elusive about him, as if he did not wish to give himself up to his company, as if, thought Vera recognising the same thing in herself, he wished to be somewhere else, unspecified.

Terry Crawford, born of Irish parents in South Africa, had been sent to an English public school at fourteen, too late for him to forget the old life or adapt himself entirely to the new. He felt at a disadvantage because he was unlike the other boys. He set out to make himself as like them as possible, and succeeded so well that when, at eighteen, he went home, his father said bitterly that no one would have thought he'd been anywhere near South Africa before. He couldn't settle in Rhodesia and after a few years returned to England, where, after trying one thing after another, and getting hopelessly

into debt, he became agent to John Spencer's brother in Devonshire. He hadn't been able to manage his own affairs, so it was hardly surprising that he could not manage anyone else's, and a crisis was approaching when he became engaged to his employer's niece.

He thought he had met, in Brenda, another rebel against convention but he hadn't; only another misfit. Brenda shunned society because, the only young person in an elderly home circle, she didn't seem to be able to get on with anybody under sixty. She wouldn't have got on with Terry if she hadn't met him in the intimacy of her uncle's house. There was no one else there and she was, as at home, the indulged darling of the house. She liked dogs, she didn't like parties, she was rich, she was a way out. What he needed, Terry told himself, was a stake in the country, a wife, a home, work he liked, children; then he would settle at last. So they were married and now found themselves launched on a succession of congratulatory parties. He looked as if he were enduring, not enjoying this one, thought Vera, piqued, and was relieved when dinner was announced.

As the youngest guests, Margaret and John Watson made up the tail of the procession moving to the dining-room, and as they went, John's hand found and held Margaret's. They went forward in a rapturous daze, breathlessly aware of each other, but finding themselves up against the dining-table, had to loose hands and sit down, fortunately side by side.

From the landing Sarah kept calling down in a loud whisper to any maid that crossed the hall, 'Is it time yet? Is it time?' At last Birch came out of the dining-room and looking

up, said, 'You can come now, Miss Sarah.' They ran down the stairs, Judith with them, as eager as anybody. But though her cousins ran forward to claim their promised sweets, she came to a dead halt at the door. At the sight of the table with the candlelight shining on the strange faces, so many people laughing and talking, she daren't go any farther. It was dark by the door and there she stood in an agony of shyness. Nobody noticed her. The guests were occupied with each other, her cousins bent their heads over the dishes of sweets. It seemed to her that she was standing there for hours. At last she advanced slowly into the circle of light.

Terry Crawford, the only one to see her come, was startled. She was like an apparition of a child. He looked at the fair, pale little girl with curiosity, until it dawned upon him that she was extremely shy. Then he pushed his chair back from the table to make room for her and held out an arm. 'Come along,' he said, with the first warm note his voice had held that evening. 'You're missing all the best sweets. The other two are mopping them up at a fearful rate.'

He drew her in with his arm, but she was stiff with shyness and leaned away from him. 'The lady resists,' said Mrs Clarey, and everybody laughed. Why did they, what had she done? wondered Judith. Her lashes felt stuck to her cheeks, she couldn't look up. Terry Crawford reached for sweets and laid them on the table before her. She managed to look at them and then at him. He was kind and smiling, perhaps she had hurt him or been rude leaning away from him like that. She turned towards him in compunction and in turning laid her hand lightly at the back of his collar. 'Ah, she's warming up,'

said Mrs Clarey again, and again everybody laughed. Judith looked at them, the look of a child bewildered in an adult world. What was it? What had she done wrong again?

Terry Crawford tightened his arm. 'Don't mind them,' he said and reaching over to a dish, he took up a tiny marzipan apple displaying its rosy cheek in a paper case. 'Isn't that neat?' he said. A feeling of coolness and lightness came over Judith. The shyness was gone as suddenly as it had come. She smiled at the apple on her open palm and at him. 'I shan't eat it,' she said. 'It's too pretty.'

Her eyes, as she stood beside him, were on a level with his and child and man considered each other with an interest that was both serious and smiling. Judith accepted him as a friend and hero, one who had saved her from miserable shyness, one who could put everything right. As for Terry, he was touched to a tenderness and simplicity he had not suspected in himself. He marvelled at the purity of her forehead and her clear, child's gaze. Why do they ever grow up, or why do they grow up as they do, he thought, like his hostess, beautiful but dissatisfied, like Brenda, spoilt, plain and mad on dogs?

Odd young man, thought Vera, on his other side. He must be a mass of contradictions. He looked like a musical-comedy hero, he almost certainly married for money, and yet a child is the only one who has induced him to show any interest this evening.

She felt an irritable wish to put an end to this *tête-à-tête* between Terry and the child and tried to catch the eye of the guest of honour, the bride. But Brenda – how like an Indian squaw with that broad face and hair parted in the middle!

– Brenda was never any help to a hostess in these matters. Her elbows on the table, she talked to Brian about her dogs. Giving her up, Vera rose from the table.

III

After the party, Margaret must, Vera had said, breakfast in bed and Margaret was glad. Not that she was tired – who could be tired from such a heavenly party? – but it was so lovely to lie, after Judith had gone down, and go over it all again. That ecstatic moment when John had held her hand prolonged itself through the night; even when she was asleep she lived in it, she was living in it still. Youth can draw out such a moment indefinitely without thinning out the first ecstasy. Margaret smiled radiantly to herself on her pillow and when the maid came in, she smiled radiantly at her. She would have smiled at anybody, life seemed so warm and easy. She sat up to receive her tray and saw that there was a letter on it; from her father.

Vera was also breakfasting in bed. She leaned against her pillows, stirring China tea. The party in retrospect seemed very dull. 'I'm getting worse,' she thought. 'I don't care about anything. Lucy's right. To live without effort is the dullest thing in the world. But what could I begin to make an effort about now?' She reviewed her existence and all effort seemed unnecessary. Too much money, she thought, yet shuddered at the idea of having less. 'No,' she thought, pressing closer into her luxurious pillows. 'I couldn't live in any other way now.'

There was a knock at the door. 'Come in,' she said, hoping it wasn't Brian.

Margaret hurried in, hair and dressing-gown flying, a letter in her hand. 'Oh, Aunt Vera,' she burst out. 'Daddy says we have to go home today!' Vera received this with calm. 'Today? Why?'

'He says he wants me home for the weekend. He says I've been away long enough. See . . .' She thrust the letter into Vera's hands and kept her eyes anxiously on her aunt as she read. Vera had once rung up to say her mother was staying longer, surely she would do the same now? Margaret had thought she ought not to have done it then, it made her father so angry, but surely this was different? She simply couldn't go home today. To be torn away – surely Aunt Vera wouldn't let that happen?

Vera handed back the letter. 'Well, it looks as if you'll have to go, doesn't it? But after all, you were going on Monday, weren't you?' She smiled consolingly at Margaret, but she wasn't sorry she was going. She was in such a state of boredom that the prospect of any change, however slight, seemed a relief. She had had Margaret continually with her for some time; the prospect of not having her with her was welcome. Besides, it was rather a strain having a young girl about. Young girls were so enthusiastic, and you had to be careful what you said and what other people said. 'Brian will look up a train for you and send a wire,' she said. Brian always looked up trains and saw to everything. He was what the French call *serviable*. – 'Can you pack?' she asked. 'Or shall Birch help you?'

'I can pack, thank you,' said Margaret, turning away.

'You can always come again, you know,' said Vera kindly.

On the landing, Margaret hesitated. In the little study there was a telephone. But would anybody hear if she telephoned to John? Their secret was so new, it was hardly anything, but she couldn't bear anyone to know of it, or think what she vaguely termed 'things'. But she must let him know she had to go home. Emboldened by this necessity, she stole into the dead little room where Brian had meant to study, even to write, poetry, but where neither he nor anyone else ever came. She held the telephone to her ear, her eyes dilated as she waited.

'Hello?' said a voice. But not his. A maid's.

'Hello,' breathed Margaret. 'May I speak to Mr John Watson, please?'

'I can't hear. I'm sorry.'

'May I speak to Mr John Watson, please?' said Margaret a little louder.

'Mr John has just gone out,' said the voice cheerfully.

'Oh,' said Margaret. 'Thank you,' she said, after a pause and put the telephone down.

CHAPTER TWELVE

I

The bustle of the return had died down and Judith sat in the nursery with her mother and Stephen, both reading now, before going to bed. She had a book on her knee, but she did not read. She was considering things. This house seemed very dull and quiet after Auntie Vera's, and how shabby this nursery was after Sarah's. There wasn't a single nice, fresh thing in it. The carpet was so worn you couldn't see the pattern, the table legs were kicked white, the wicker chair was so old it creaked and sagged every time her mother moved in it. And how different her mother was from her Aunt Vera! How dreadfully different, thought Judith, appalled by this comparison. Auntie Vera would never have worn that shabby velvet coatee. As she looked, Judith saw how her mother fumbled to put her handkerchief into the pocket of the coatee. Her hand missed the pocket over and over again, until at last leaning over to hold the pocket open with the other hand, she put the handkerchief away. Judith felt a strange pang of fear.

What were they doing, the three of them, sitting up here in this shabby nursery while her father and Margaret sat

downstairs in the comfortable morning-room? The three of
them had been sitting up here for years, while the other two
sat downstairs, but for the first time it struck Judith as strange.
Why was it like this? How had her mother got separated from
her father, and how had Margaret taken her place? And why?
Why were they all so separate in this house? At Auntie Vera's,
she had felt quite close to Margaret, but the moment they
arrived home, all that had changed and they were back to
what they had been before. As soon as they were in their own
room at home, unpacking, and she said 'This isn't much like
our room at Auntie Vera's, is it?' Margaret said in a cold way:
'Don't talk about it, please.' Shutting her up and making it so
that she couldn't say any more.

Judith looked at her mother, reading without interest.
She looked at her brother. He was reading, too, but from time
to time, he looked sideways from his book as if he were
thinking deeply about something. She didn't know what it
was. Everyone is alone in this house, she thought forlornly.
She wished for her Aunt Lucy. Only to her could she have
told these new thoughts that frightened her. Auntie Lucy
might have been able to explain them away, or make her feel
safe in spite of them. Auntie Lucy always made her feel safe,
somehow, or brave enough not to mind whether she were safe
or not.

Downstairs in the morning-room, Geoffrey had pulled
Margaret down to the arm of his chair. 'You won't have to go
away again if you come back looking like this, my pet,' he said.
'Though I daresay you were homesick, weren't you? Never
mind. I won't make you go away for ages. We've got heaps of

work to do together and you're going to take up golf. Then you can play with me. I shall always have a partner on hand then. Those bf's at the club take the game so damned seriously. They can't see a joke for the life of them. So we'll leave 'em alone. I've arranged with Walker to give you lessons and I'm going to buy your clubs tomorrow. You see how Daddy thinks of his girl while she's away?'

But her smile was wan and Geoffrey's face changed.

'It wasn't that you didn't want to come home, was it?' he asked suspiciously.

'Oh, no, Daddy,' she said flushing. 'Of course we had planned things until Monday, but if you wanted me, it didn't matter,' she finished, looking down at her fingers.

Indeed it didn't, Geoffrey felt. 'Damn it all, you'd been away a fortnight. You made enough fuss about going. I thought you'd be delighted when I said you could come back.'

He hadn't said could. He said must; and at once. But she agreed that she must seem unreasonable. He didn't know what had happened between her going and her coming back. And he mustn't know. She made a cheerful smile and said: 'Let's play double-dummy. I don't suppose you've had a game while I've been away.'

Geoffrey was appeased for the time being, but not thrown off the scent. Something was wrong, something had happened to take her from him. A few days later he knew what it was. Margaret was taking her first golf lesson and while she swung her club without interest at nothing, the post arriving at Queen's Walk was delivered directly into Geoffrey's hands, as usual. There was a letter for Margaret in a masculine hand,

postmarked Trenton. 'Ah,' said Geoffrey. 'Here it is.' He opened the letter. He opened all the letters that came to the house, except the maids'. So far he had done it out of idle curiosity. No letter of secrecy or importance had ever arrived for a member of his family since he had a family. Until now. This was a letter he really must see.

'Damned pup!' he exclaimed, reading. Telling her what a blow it had been to find her gone, wanting to come to see her, wanting her to write to him. 'I think of you all the time . . . ' Ach, he would read no more. It disgusted him. He crushed the letter into a ball and threw it into the fire. He glared at the ashen flag it made, waving in the flame, as if he would have liked to do worse to it than that. Margaret had deceived him. She hadn't told him; she never would have told him. Child though she was, she could play a woman's game. He felt so sick, angry, and to tell the truth, alarmed at the thought of losing her, that he went to the sideboard and poured himself a drink. Glass in hand, he loped about the room, ranging from window to door in his agitation. To play these games at seventeen. It was time enough in ten years. Ten years, he vowed; not a day before. It was for her good he had destroyed the letter, and he'd destroy the next that came, if it came; though this boy was evidently very young, it was such a fool of a letter, humble, childish. If he didn't get any encouragement he would be easily put off, thought Geoffrey. But if he did write again, he should hear, not from his lady-love, but from his lady-love's father. The thought of the boy's discomfiture put Geoffrey in a better temper. He poured himself another drink. She would be in soon and he mustn't give an inkling of

what had happened. He must be his usual genial self, he determined, and not show the slightest resentment. After all, she was only a child; and he must keep her so, he told himself sternly, not allow her to make these dangerous, disgusting excursions into womanhood. She should never go to stay with Vera again; he ought to have known better, knowing Vera, than to let her go at all. It was just the sort of thing that would happen in Vera's house, and she had evidently connived at the affair because the young cub said he got Margaret's address from her aunt.

The front door opened and closed. Margaret began to climb the stairs. 'Hi!' he called, bringing her to heel. She always used to come straight to him as soon as she came in; it showed the difference in her that she didn't do it now. She came into the room, looking pale and tired; womanish, he thought. He stood on the hearthrug looking at her with the bright, hard gaze of one who knows something. Anyone with a scrap of experience seeing that expression would have said: 'Well – what is it?' But Margaret had no experience, and merely wondered why he looked at her like that.

'Aren't you going to tell me how you got on?' he said angrily. He could not help being angry about something, after that letter.

'I was coming in later, Daddy,' she said apologetically. After all, he thought he was doing something she liked by arranging for golf lessons. 'I didn't get on very well, I'm afraid, but Walker's a nice man, isn't he? And my clubs are beautiful.'

'Well, let's have tea at once, leave the letters till tomorrow and go off to the cinema, shall we?' he said. He had only just

thought of it, but he needed his ideas changed as much as she did.

Her face brightened a little. She had dreaded the prospect of an evening in that hot room, trying to keep her thoughts from John so as to be ready to respond as quickly as was always necessary to her father.

To write to John Watson was beyond what Margaret considered possible. It had been a great effort to telephone, she could not go so far as writing. Besides, there was nothing to warrant a letter. Simply a pressure of the hand, which had seemed so much at the time, but which might not have been anything – to him. She knew girls who would have shrieked with laughter at the idea of attaching any significance to a mere hand-holding. They would have thought her a simple creature. Perhaps he did. She felt she was. It was his part to write, if he wanted to. But would he? She asked that all day and most of the night. She would be glad to go to the cinema where she could ask it still, without the nervous strain of being suspected by her father. So her face brightened and Geoffrey was encouraged. He'd soon make her forget that fellow, he vowed.

'We'll have tea now,' he said pressing the bell. 'Just you and I.' The sight of Charlotte would only irritate him; she could have tea upstairs with the other two. 'Go and take your hat off, pet, but come and give me a kiss first.'

She kissed him obediently.

'You're my girl, aren't you?' he said. 'Eh?' he asked sharply, when she didn't answer immediately.

'Yes, Daddy,' she said hastily. 'Of course I am.'

II

The weeks went on and the hope of a letter from John Watson waned until there was nothing left of it. But another hope – youth is so hopeful – came to take its place. As the summer holiday approached, Margaret began to hope that Vera would invite her to Trenton. She began to feel sure she would. That was what Aunt Vera meant, Margaret told herself, when she said: 'You can always come again, you know.' She must have meant all the time to invite her for part of the summer holiday, otherwise she would not have let her go so easily before the visit was up. That was it, thought Margaret, cheering herself. And if she could only see him again, everything would come right, she knew. After all, it was too much to expect him to write. He had held her hand for a moment; that was all. She had magnified it too much. It wasn't that it had been anything, really; it was only that it was *going to be something*. She was sure of that, and if she could see him again, this lovely thing would continue.

So she pinned her hopes to Vera and began to look for a letter by every post. When she came back to the house after any absence, she enquired: 'Have you had any letters, Mummy?' She became more explicit in her enquiry. 'Have you had a letter from Auntie Vera?'

'No. She doesn't often write,' said Charlotte.

'Have you written to her lately?' asked Margaret.

'No,' said Charlotte, 'I can't say that I have.'

'Don't you think you ought to?'

'No,' said Charlotte, showing the irritation she felt

nowadays when anyone tried to make her do something she didn't want to do.

In the end, Margaret wrote herself. She felt very uncomfortable about it, writing to her aunt to get something out of her. Without saying straight out what it was, too. But she wrote. She surreptitiously took a sheet of the heavily embossed notepaper used only by her father and wrote: 'My dear Aunt Vera, I thought it was a long time since we had heard from you, so I thought I would write. . . . ' Were they all well, she asked, Uncle Brian and Sarah and Meriel and everybody? She bit the end of her pen, adding small items of news at long intervals. Then she threw out her hint, making it as strong as she dared: 'Judith is going to Auntie Lucy's for the holidays, but Stephen isn't going this time, he says. I don't think I am going anywhere. Daddy says he can't arrange anything for us this year. I often think of the lovely time I had with you at Easter. It was the loveliest time I ever had in my life.' She signed herself, 'your loving niece, Margaret', and posted the letter.

Now the invitation would come. She had made it so that it would come. With her hopes rising to meet every post, sinking when each post had gone, rising again before the next, rising, in spite of bitter disappointment, at the end of every day, sure that the letter would come tomorrow, she waited.

Vera saw through the letter. She saw that Margaret wanted to be invited again, but the summer was booked up. Still, she meant to write to the child, she meant to say that she must come again sometime. But she didn't do it.

CHAPTER THIRTEEN

I

No letter came from Vera, but there was one from Lucy. Lucy
had some time ago received a mysterious letter from Stephen
telling her that he didn't want to come to Underwood these
holidays. Not at the beginning, anyway, so would she please
not press it, or even invite him, though she might say, if she
would, that he could come later if he wanted to. Puzzled
though she was, Lucy wrote asking Charlotte to bring Judith
herself and stay for a week or two. Stephen could come later
if he wished, she said. But Charlotte wrote back to say she
wouldn't come. She was better at home. She was able to have
a good rest when the children were away, she said, forgetting
that only Judith would be absent. Since Charlotte had never,
since her marriage, given the true reason for anything, Lucy
supplied the reason for herself. It was Geoffrey. Every time
Lucy went to the house in Queen's Walk, she found Charlotte
a little worse. People attribute the sad changes they find in
others to time, age, worry, illness, but Lucy did not look
beyond Geoffrey for the cause of the change in Charlotte. He
was enough to ruin anybody's health and happiness. So she

sighed and thought Charlotte did not leave home because Geoffrey wouldn't let her; and she wrote to say she would fetch Judith herself.

She made the long, hot journey to Denborough and found Charlotte wan and listless, Margaret looking desperate about something, Stephen evasive, Geoffrey his usual tiresome self, and only Judith welcoming. Judith's welcome was warm enough to make up for any lack in the others. She greeted Lucy as if she were especially her own, capered round her like a young dog, said she had all her things packed and could they please go straight back to Underwood the next day? Lucy waited for a protest from Charlotte, but as none came, she said they might as well.

That night, when she was on her way to her room, she saw a line of light under Stephen's door. She had not been able to be alone with him during the evening to tell him that she had done as he wished. So she knocked and when he said 'Who's there?' would have gone in, but found the door locked. When she said who she was, he unlocked it. Lucy had not been into his room for years, not since he was a little boy, and she saw with dismay that Crusoe's collar still hung on a nail above the chest of drawers. Why did he keep such a painful reminder before him, she wondered? All the time she was talking to him she was thinking what a strange remote boy he was.

'I haven't said anything about your coming to Underwood, Stephen, since you asked me not to, but you know you can come later. Just come whenever you want to.'

He smiled at her. He had a charming smile, she thought, as often before. 'Thanks awfully, Auntie Lucy,' he said, putting

his hair back. 'I'll – er – I'll remember that. It's just that – well – I have something else on at the moment.'

'Yes, dear. You just do as you like.' She didn't know what to say to him. She blamed herself for not knowing how to get in touch with him. 'Good night, then.' She had to reach up to kiss him. He was taller now than she was. He stood there smiling strangely as she went out of the room. A queer boy, she thought.

The next day, she and Judith had a hot journey, but they arrived at Underwood in the cool of the evening and both sighed with pleasure when they got out of the car before the little house. Janet appeared, to give her mistress a restrained welcome. If Lucy had returned alone, Janet would have been all fuss, but since the child had come, Janet had to show her displeasure. But Judith said good evening in a polite way and went stepping up the stairs, two at a time, unperturbed. She had grown up in a house where people were difficult and unaccountable; her father, her mother, Burton were difficult – even Margaret, even Stephen now. It would have been no good trying to bring them round; so Judith didn't try. In Janet she recognised another difficult adult, so she did not try to ingratiate herself with Janet either. William approved of this. 'That's the spirit,' he said to Lucy. 'More women like that and there'd be less bad temper shown in the world.' But Lucy, though she found this childish dignity endearing, thought Judith had acquired it at too great a cost.

Night fell, bringing freshness to Underwood but none to Denborough. The heat was stifling. Charlotte, after taking her tablets, slept only until two o'clock nowadays. She got through

an hour by having a drink or two, by reading something that did not require much concentration; she couldn't concentrate now. At three or half-past she took more tablets and slept until after six.

The heat continued. Charlotte spent most of her time sitting by the open nursery window. It was quiet there. No one came into the room but Stephen and when he was in it, he sat at the table, reading. 'Why didn't you go to Underwood, dear?' Charlotte asked one day. She had brought her evasive mind round to consideration of the subject. 'Wouldn't you like to go now? It's so hot here. You'd be better there. I'll give you the money.'

Charlotte, like her sisters, had a little money from her father. Without it, she would have had to account to Geoffrey for what she spent and that would have been awkward. She used to spend it on clothes, hair-dressing, manicure, face-massage, scent, soaps, powders, anything and everything to keep her attractive to Geoffrey. But that was all over. The money went on things to arm her against him now. But she had always given Stephen his pocket-money, since his father never seemed to think he needed any, and she said now she would give him the money to go to Underwood if he liked.

Stephen considered for a moment in silence. 'All right, Mother,' he said, getting up from the table. Imperceptibly he had dropped the 'Mummy' and 'Daddy' of his childish days. 'Thanks very much. It's a good idea.'

A curious alertness came into his eyes, as if some moment he had been waiting for had come. Charlotte did not notice;

her own eyes watered a good deal and she did not see clearly to the other side of the room.

'Would you like to give me the money now?' said Stephen. 'Shall I go for your bag?'

'I have my bag, dear,' said Charlotte, fishing for it down the side of the chair. She never parted from her bag nowadays. 'I'll give you three pounds. No, I'll give you four.' She felt an impulse to give him all the notes in her case, but held back remembering how much her purchases cost. She was sure the man at the place behind the Central Station cheated her. He was a dreadful, leering creature; she felt he might blackmail her. She ought to go to a new place, but she had a nervous dread of new places. 'Yes, I'll give you four pounds,' she said, holding out the notes with tremulous, slightly dirty fingers.

He came to take them and to thank her. He stood looking down at her. This was his once fresh, sweet, anxious, sensitive mother. Now she was all blurred; her mind slow, her hair dull, a little net of red veins flung over each pale cheek and she smelled strongly of something – sherry, he supposed, since sherry was the only thing he saw her drink.

'Oh, Mother,' he knelt down and put one arm behind her chair. 'I wish I could take you out of all this. I wish I could take you away, Mother.'

'You've been saying that ever since you were a little boy, dear,' she said, with a wavering smile.

'When I've made enough money I'll come back for you,' he said.

'Oh, well, dear,' said Charlotte. 'I don't know that I want

to go, really. Once I might have gone. But while you've been growing up, I've been growing older, you know. I'm only fit for here now.'

'Oh, Mother, you make me wretched.'

'Well, I can't help it,' said Charlotte, with one of her swift changes of mood. Now he'd upset her. Now she'd have to go and take another tablet. She pushed him aside and went out of the room. Stephen stood by the table, staring down at the notes in his hand.

II

September came in. William resumed inspection. The willows began to drop their narrow leaves into the stream at the bottom of the meadow. It was time for Judith to go home and with regret they prepared for the journey. Lucy had written two or three times to give Charlotte news of Judith, but Charlotte had not replied. She said she hated writing letters. The day before they were due at the house in Queen's Walk, Lucy sent a postcard. 'Arriving 4.45 as usual.' As usual no one met them, and as usual they entered the house without causing any stir. They crept as usual up the stairs so as not to disturb the business being transacted in the morning-room. They went to greet Charlotte in the nursery. She turned her head from her place at the window as they came in. Slowly astonishment overspread her face. 'Why, it's you, Lucy!'

'Of course,' said Lucy, kissing her. 'How else could Judith get home?'

'But where's Stephen?' asked Charlotte.

'Stephen?' echoed Lucy, staring at her.

'Well, isn't he with you?' said Charlotte.

'Stephen with us?' said Lucy. 'We haven't seen him these holidays.'

'Where is he then?' asked Charlotte, gripping the arms of the wicker chair. She felt dreaded emotion fluttering her heart, a tide of fear rising to engulf her. 'Where's Stephen? Judith! D'you know? Did he say anything to you? Where has he gone?'

Lucy and Judith stared at her, unable to grasp the situation, but Charlotte, knocking against the table, hurried to Stephen's room. They went after her. They all stared at the empty room with Crusoe's collar hanging on the wall. His room had been dusted and swept as usual, but suspecting nothing, no one had gone through the drawers. Charlotte began to pull these out one after the other. 'He's left a letter – here it is,' she said bringing out a sealed envelope. They looked at it. It was addressed to his father. Any other mother could have torn it open, but old habit was too strong for Charlotte. Trembling and weeping, she went down the stairs, the others behind her. She burst into the morning-room where Geoffrey was dictating letters to Margaret.

'Damn it all,' he said. 'What's the meaning of this?'

'Open this, open it,' stammered Charlotte, thrusting the letter into his hands. 'Stephen's gone. He went long ago. He never went to Lucy's. Open it.'

Geoffrey ran his finger under the flap of the envelope and brought out the sheet of paper. Amid silence, he read:

Father,

I am going. I might have changed things in this house if I'd been older. I might even have killed you. I'd have knocked you out, anyway. But as it is, I'm going because I can't do anything by staying. You've destroyed Mother, there's no hope for Margaret. There's only Judith left, and Auntie Lucy will see that nothing happens to her. I am going to sea, because that seems to be the best way of losing myself. You'll never get me back. Not that you'll try, except to save your face with the firm, but I've calculated that by the time you get this letter, I'll have had seven weeks' start, perhaps more. I don't care how tough a life I have to lead if it will make me strong enough to come back one day and give you a thrashing. There's never been anybody in this house strong enough to stand up to you, but I'll do it one day, believe me. So all these next years you can be expecting me. It would be a farce to sign myself your loving son, as other sons do, I've heard, to their fathers. I wish I hadn't to sign myself your son at all. In fact, I won't.

Stephen

Under the intent eyes of the others, Geoffrey paled with rage. 'What does he say? Where is he?' asked Charlotte urgently. Lucy had put out her hand for the letter, but Geoffrey with a savage face tore it, pulling it apart with both hands. He threw the pieces into the fire and rammed them into the coals with the poker. 'That's the end of him,' he said.

'But where is he?' asked Charlotte, twisting her hands together. 'Where's he gone?'

'To sea, the fool,' said Geoffrey, his lips seamed. 'As a ship's boy, I suppose. He doesn't know what he's in for. I hope they give him hell. He'll whine to be bought out before long. You'll see. But he won't get out. He's made his own bed and by God he can lie on it. I never want to set eyes on him again.'

'Oh, Geoffrey, Geoffrey,' cried Charlotte, putting her hands over her face. She sobbed, tears bursting through her fingers. The room was filled with the awful sound of her sobbing.

'Oh, for God's sake, take her away,' said Geoffrey. 'The young fool's gone. What d'you expect me to do about it? Go on – go away, all of you and let me have some peace. Margaret, finish these letters.'

Lucy took Charlotte upstairs to her room. 'Oh, Lucy,' wept Charlotte. 'Stephen – the only one who understood – driven away to sea. He'll never come home. I'll never see him again. He's only sixteen, Lucy. Sixteen.'

'Hush, darling, hush now. Lie down and let me cover you up. Try to be quiet. You're doing yourself harm and you're frightening the girls. Hush now.'

'I can't hush. I can't. I feel I shall scream and never be able to stop.' She rose on her elbow, her eyes wild, her teeth chattering.

'Now, listen, darling, you must take a hold on yourself,' said Lucy, putting her hands over Charlotte's.

'Where's my bag? Oh, where's my bag? I've left it in the nursery.' Charlotte scrambled off the bed.

'I'll get it,' said Lucy, but Charlotte thrust her back. 'Leave me alone. Don't touch my bag. I'll get it.'

She came back with it and took a box from it. 'Get me some water, will you, Lucy?' she asked, taking three or four tablets. She lay down on the bed again and pulled up the eiderdown. 'I'll be all right soon,' she said. 'Go away, will you? Just leave me, please.'

'I'll come back to look at you soon,' said Lucy.

'No, don't. Don't,' said Charlotte. 'I might go to sleep now.'

Sighing, Lucy left her. Judith was coming up the stairs, crying in a child's way with her knuckles to her eyes. Lucy went with her to the nursery and took her on to her lap. 'Stephen will be all right, darling,' she comforted. 'He'll grow into a man able to face anything and he'll certainly come back to see us all one day.'

'Oh, Auntie Lucy,' wept Judith. 'Don't leave me. Don't go back tomorrow.'

'I won't, darling. I'll stay as long as I can,' promised Lucy.

The next morning, she bearded Geoffrey in his den. It was a mistake. Geoffrey had had what was for him a bad night. That is, he wakened in the small hours and found himself assailed with thoughts he would have dismissed with a drink in the daytime. Stephen's letter rankled. Geoffrey did not tolerate adverse criticism. Not that he believed it, but he didn't tolerate it. Approbation he took as his due, but if he met with adverse criticism, the critic was always a damn fool who didn't know anything. All the same, it annoyed him, and it somehow increased the ominous silence Geoffrey was creating round himself as time went on.

Once, young himself, he had been sure of the admiring laughter of the young men in bars, offices, streets, theatres, wherever he went. But one by one his audience, through the years, had melted away, like spectators bored with a play that had gone on too long. After his performances now there was only a clap or two. Soon there would not be a sound. Vaguely, uneasily, Geoffrey was becoming aware of this.

And Stephen made another who had gone out.

Also, Stephen had put his father in an awkward position with his firm. Human beings are full of incongruities and Geoffrey was no exception. He liked his solid, old, decent-dealing firm and served it with honesty and devotion. His firm and his daughter embodied for Geoffrey two different ideals; his firm conformed already to his ideal; his daughter would have to.

Sir Cedric Bancroft, who, as Mr Bancroft, had many years ago come to dinner, had lately written to Geoffrey to say that when his son had finished his education, the firm would gladly welcome him into its employment for the sake of his father. It was like a Royal Command to Geoffrey; he accepted the proposal with gratitude and enthusiasm, and from that day, he had actually begun to take some belated notice of Stephen, to see him with the firm's eye and to note with satisfaction that he was intelligent and presentable. Then for the boy to run away to sea, and to leave this letter! It was a bitter pill for Geoffrey to swallow. Also, it was very awkward to explain away. He was at his worst, therefore, when Lucy went into the morning-room after breakfast.

'May I speak to you for a moment?' she said.

'Good Lord, what is it?' he said petulantly. 'This is my busiest time.' He rattled the newspaper he was reading as he stood with his back to the fire.

'I thought you mightn't have started yet,' said Lucy. 'And I see you haven't.'

'Go on, then,' he said ungraciously. 'You can speak in front of Margaret.'

'I'd rather not,' said Lucy. It was not what she would say, but what he might, that she didn't want Margaret to hear. 'I'm sure she won't mind if I speak to you alone, will you, Margaret?'

Margaret got up from the desk and went out of the room. Her eyelids were red and swollen; she had wept in the night for her brother.

'Well?' said Geoffrey with hostility. 'I warn you, don't speak to me about Stephen. I won't lift a finger to get him back.'

'It's not about Stephen,' said Lucy. 'It's about Judith. Will you let me take Judith back to Underwood for a time? For one or two years, or for several, or for good? Charlotte isn't well enough to do much for her. Margaret's very busy with you and now Stephen's gone, I feel it will be lonely for her. And the strain at present is too much for a little girl.'

'What the devil do you mean?' said Geoffrey. 'The strain, let me tell you, is caused by your precious sister. She's the one that ought to be looking after Judith and isn't. I hardly ever see the kid.'

'You wouldn't miss her then. I do earnestly ask you to let me have her for a time. I'll undertake all responsibility and expense.'

'The hell you will,' said Geoffrey. 'You damn well won't. I know your little game. You've been trying for years to get hold of Judith. You've no children of your own, you and William – too clever, or too virtuous, or just too damn dry to breed, aren't you? – so you try to get one of ours. But I tell you once and for all, you'll never get Judith, never. And you'd better watch your step, too, or I'll not even let you have her for the holidays. God, I'm sick and tired of sisters-in-law. You try to get hold of Judith, and Vera encourages Margaret to be as fast as she is herself. . . . ' He stopped suddenly, realising that he was on the point of giving himself away. He strode to the door and flung it open. 'Margaret!' he shouted. 'Margaret! Come back and let's start work. I've had enough of this nonsense,' he said with a contemptuous glance in the direction of Lucy's feet.

Her face cold with dislike, Lucy went out of the room. He held the whip-hand; he could stop her from seeing Judith, so she said nothing. She must keep what she had, though she had damaged her chances of more for ever, she told herself.

She waited until she saw that Judith was settled at school and that Charlotte had regained some measure of stability. Then she went home.

When she came back to fetch her at Christmas, Judith was touchingly glad to see her. She had been lonelier since Stephen went, the more so because she had been separated from Margaret and put into Stephen's room where everything remained the same, even to Crusoe's collar hanging on the nail.

Margaret had the room the sisters had so far shared. It was

entirely refurnished and redecorated. Margaret had chosen everything herself, and, though Geoffrey did not know it, it was as close a replica as possible of the room she had occupied at Vera's. Geoffrey congratulated Margaret on her taste and said he would probably let her do the whole house over in time. He was trying to teach her to console herself for the loss of the big things by the substitution of the small. But though her new room pleased Margaret for a time, she soon grew used to it and it made no more difference then to her state of mind than the old one had done.

Geoffrey kept her fully occupied. Once, with a wife, he had appeared in public a great deal. His wife became unpresentable; she shamed him, he considered, so he almost retired from view, since he was not a man who could go out by himself. But now he re-emerged with a very presentable daughter. He basked again in public notice, though he was less exuberant in his efforts to attract it. His object now was to get notice for Margaret as well as for himself; he was showing altruism at last.

He had Margaret taught, not only to play golf, but to drive the car, and when they had finished work they drove to the links or into the country to tea. Not to Merthwaite. The gift of Crusoe had turned fat Mrs Purley against Geoffrey for ever. Dislike triumphed over a wish for custom and Mrs Purley treated Geoffrey, making a call, with such coolness that he left, damning her impertinence and never went again.

He taught Margaret how to run the house. He took her to the shops and while showing off himself, instructed her in the buying of bacon, meat, fish, game and poultry. Margaret could

not feel that these things were important enough for all this time and attention. It didn't really matter to her whether the chicken had hung too long or the pheasants not long enough. But the easiest course to take with Geoffrey was to do as he wished at once. It saved much wear and tear, and so, long trained in patience, she bent dutifully over the counters.

With golf, country excursions, the stimulation of public appearances and the constant company of his daughter, Geoffrey took on a new lease of life. He gained in health and spirits at the expense of hers. But he so constantly chivvied her to be cheerful that she began to cultivate a brittle liveliness in self-protection. It didn't suit her, and people said that they thought Margaret Leigh was turning out to be a rather insincere, affected sort of girl.

CHAPTER FOURTEEN

I

During the Christmas holidays a Charity Matinée was always held at the Theatre Royal in Trenton. It was a social function to which everybody looked forward. This year Sarah Sargent was to dance solo in a Children's Ballet. The theatre was crowded. Vera had taken seats for her friends and sat between Mrs Clarey and Terry Crawford. Terry's wife had cried off at the last moment and the only person Vera dared to offer the ticket to was Mrs Clarey, who had no false pride and would accept a free ticket to anything.

Meriel and Nurse Gill were with old Mrs Sargent and Gertrude in a stage-box. Mrs Sargent had taken a box, Vera explained, because she would not remove her hat and no one would have allowed her to keep it on in the stalls. In the obscurity of the box, Mrs Sargent's hat, said Vera, was like an eagle's nest with the eagle on it, and she and Terry laughed about it together. She was glad his wife hadn't come.

The Duchess, who had organised the Matinée, in passing the stage-box laid her hand on the edge to have a word with Mrs Sargent. The old lady had subscribed heavily to the

Matinée – she always subscribed heavily to the Duchess's charities – and the Duchess wanted her to feel she was getting good value for her money. Mrs Sargent's quivering hat bent over the edge of the box and together they looked over the crowded auditorium. 'You've done splendidly, Duchess,' said Mrs Sargent.

'Ah, well, I can always trust 'em to support me, bless 'em,' said the Duchess, beaming about her. 'Lord,' she said, her eyes falling to her wrists. 'I've not done up my cuffs. I was in such a rush.' Busily buttoning, her eyes on the stalls, nodding here, nodding there, she threw out: 'Oh, by the way, at the dress rehearsal yesterday I noticed a child dancing beautifully and was told it was your granddaughter. If she dances as well today, I'm giving her a box of chocolates.'

Old Mrs Sargent momentarily recoiled. She did not approve of Sarah's passion for dancing and thought it ought to be eradicated. But she recovered herself. 'That is charming of you, Duchess,' she said. 'We shall all be very proud. This is Sarah's sister. This is Meriel,' she said, anxious to secure notice for her favourite. But the Duchess was moving off. 'The curtain will go up in a moment. I'm going round to the back now,' she said.

The matinée was an arrangement for mutual benefit. The performers, all amateur, did the Duchess a service by appearing without payment, thereby enabling her to hand over all the money raised to charity. The Duchess did the performers a service by giving them the chance to appear at all. If the performances that afternoon were not up to professional standard, nobody seemed to mind. There was a great

deal of animation in the audience if not upon the stage, much conversation was exchanged and there was a constant coming and going of nurses leading children out and in. The verdict on the afternoon, when people were saying goodbye in the foyer, was that it had been so nice to see everybody.

But among the inadequacies of performance that afternoon there was one success: the Children's Ballet put on by Madame Fouquet. Madame Fouquet had her reputation to think of. She had trained many famous dancers. She knew neither fear nor favour. She included in the Ballet no tiny tots to make sentimental weight with the audience, nor any children merely to please their mothers. Only good dancers appeared, and though they were children, they could dance. She prepared a ballet adapted to their limitations and worked over it as if it had been a Command Performance. Sarah danced solo, not because she was a rich pupil, but because she could dance. Old Mrs Sargent remarked afterwards that she didn't know why such a fuss had been made about Sarah. The dance was nothing but flittering and fluttering, she said, and she was sure Meriel could have done it. Flittering and fluttering it may have been, but Sarah's lightness and grace, her gravity and complete absorption in her dancing exacted the tribute of the audience's full attention as nothing else that afternoon had been able to do.

The Ballet ended to vigorous applause and the Duchess herself appeared on the stage to give Sarah the box of chocolates and thank the audience. The curtain came down. The orchestra played 'God Save the King'. Terry went to fetch his car, Vera went behind for Sarah. When she appeared in the

vestibule, with Sarah by the hand, old Mrs Sargent, who walked very slowly, had just arrived there with Gertrude and Meriel.

'Well, Sarah,' she said. 'I suppose you're very pleased with yourself, but you mustn't get foolish ideas into your head, you know. You ought to take her home, Vera, and put her to bed. All this excitement,' she said.

'Grandmother says I could have done your dance,' said Meriel. She had had her fingers in a box of sweets all afternoon and was still chewing.

''Course you couldn't,' said Sarah with scorn. 'You're much too fat.'

'Sarah, don't speak like that to Meriel,' said Gertrude.

'I'm afraid it's true,' said Vera. 'Meriel is too fat and she'll be fatter still if she doesn't stop eating sweets. Where's Nanny?'

'I sent her home,' said Mrs Sargent in a regal way. Since it was she who paid Nurse Gill, she supposed she could give an order? 'Sarah is getting all the attention today. Meriel is bound to feel a little out of the picture. I will take her home with me for the night, unless you want her.'

'No, I don't want her,' said Vera carelessly.

Terry Crawford appeared to say he had brought the car round. 'Another man in attendance,' thought old Mrs Sargent. 'Is your wife here, Mr Crawford?' she asked pointedly.

'No, she's out with the dogs,' said Terry cheerfully.

'And Brian is attending to his business, of course, Vera?' She meant to discomfit them, but unperturbed, smiling, they

said goodbye and left her. They left her standing on the black and white chequerboard of the theatre entrance, now empty, like a queen nobody had troubled to take.

Her chauffeur was waiting. Meriel skipped on in front and got into the car. 'Do you notice, Mother,' said Gertrude, 'that Vera never shows the slightest affection for darling Meriel?'

'I notice everything, my dear Gertrude,' said old Mrs Sargent. 'Nothing escapes me. You may be sure I shall protect Meriel from her mother's indifference.'

She handed her stick to the chauffeur and prepared to climb into the car. It was a great effort and it humiliated her to make it. She grasped each side of the door and hauled herself up, knocking her hat askew. A woman going past over the dirty snow laughed to another. 'See what it is to be rich,' she said. 'If y'ave a car, you get too fat to get into it.'

Old Mrs Sargent sank breathless to the padded seat. She was putting on too much weight, but she could not avoid it. Her bad heart prevented her from taking exercise, lack of exercise made her fat, fat made her heart worse. She could not break the vicious circle. Pride rose to compensate her for these humiliations of the flesh.

'I may be old and ill,' she thought. 'But Vera is unwise to disregard me. I have power.' She took up the speaking tube. 'Hurry home, Bradley,' she said.

Lawn Cottage was sunk into the winter night, huddled among its trees, its lawns faintly discernible with snow. Meriel ran forward into the lighted house. Servants appeared to help their mistress in. It was soothing to be waited on, to have people at her beck and call. That night after dinner she had

her jewel-case brought down to the drawing-room. It was a marquetry table on legs and Meriel sat under it, hanging herself with necklaces, pinning on large brooches, putting rings on every finger. 'May I have this, Grandmother?' she kept saying.

'Someday, dear,' replied old Mrs Sargent.

She put aside a collection of rubies in claw-settings so fierce that it looked as if the jewels had been grabbed up and held in the face of all resistance. She spent a pleasant evening sorting things out. Her way of meeting her death was to contemplate the disappointments and satisfactions it would cause to the living.

'I think I shall turn this room into my bedroom,' she said to Gertrude that night. 'I don't think I shall climb the stairs any more.'

So she had her large brass bedstead put up in the drawing-room. She sat during the day in the morning-room and at night the rest of the household went upstairs and left her below among the chilly lustres, the chalk drawings spotted with mould, the must of the old velvet curtains. She meant, by saving herself the stairs, to last as long as possible.

But that summer she died. She died alone one hot night during a thunderstorm. No one knew she was afraid of thunder. No one came to see if she was all right. When they found her in the morning, they were shocked by the fear in her face. The servants whispered that she 'must have seen something'. She had evidently tried to reach the bell and the exertion had been too much for her heart.

She left a curious will. Calculated malevolence, Vera said.

The money went largely to Gertrude and Meriel. Sarah had a small legacy, Vera nothing but the rubies, which she smilingly declined. Brian had nothing but the business, until the age of fifty when he would come into a considerable sum of money. His mother had judged that by that time Vera would either have left him, or be too old to cause any more trouble. His mother meant Brian to work, and now he would have to.

Her age, old Mrs Sargent stipulated, was not to appear in the papers or on her tombstone. Her vanity extended beyond the grave. Oddly enough, she was younger by several years than people had thought.

Her will began at once to make itself felt. Nurse Gill had to go. She was an expense Brian could no longer afford. The chauffeur went; in future Brian would drive his own car and Vera hers. After a while, he said the parlour-maid must go too and entertaining be considerably reduced. No more champagne on Sunday mornings, he decreed. He was surprised that Vera took these changes with equanimity. The truth was that she hadn't cared much about the things she had to part with. Brian began to hope that now she was without the irritation of his mother's presence and without, also, the softening effect of too much luxury, Vera would be happier and incidentally kinder to him. For his part, he felt brisker, busier, less depressed by his relations with Vera. He felt more capable of decision and action.

His sister Gertrude was now a rich woman and her own mistress. For several months Lawn Cottage was conducted exactly as it had been in her mother's lifetime and Gertrude occupied herself in going through her mother's things. There

was a wearisome collection of old papers, old furs, old music, letters, books, photographs. The drawers, chests, cupboards, were full of old, old things. It was like a spring-cleaning that would not end and suddenly Gertrude threw it all up. One Sunday morning, she slammed a drawer shut, sat on her heels for some time and decided to go round to see her brother in the afternoon.

It was a wet day and for once there were no visitors in the drawing-room at Southfield. Brian and Vera were alone, waiting for tea. When Gertrude arrived, it suddenly occurred to Brian that this was the moment he had been waiting for. He too had reached a decision and Gertrude's presence made it easier for him to speak to Vera about it.

II

'Vera,' said Brian, taking tea from her hand, 'I must go to America this spring. I suggest that we leave the children in Gertrude's charge – I'm sure you won't mind that, will you Gertrude? – and that you should come with me. Will you come, Vera?' He held his breath, waiting. He felt she would be less likely to refuse if Gertrude were there, for what excuse could she openly give?

But Vera needed no excuses; she never made excuses. She had been twice to America with Brian. She didn't want to go again and that was enough for her. 'No, thank you, Brian,' she said yawning. It had been a long stuffy afternoon somehow. 'I don't want to go. I don't suppose you'll be away for long. I'll stay here.'

'That is fortunate,' said Gertrude stiffly. 'Because I should have told you, if Brian had given me the chance, that I cannot take charge of the children. I've decided to sell Lawn Cottage and everything in it.'

They looked at her in amazement. Vera recovered first. 'I think you're very wise,' she said.

'I shall take a long holiday,' said Gertrude. 'I need a complete change.' If she had said that in the old days of her bondage, no one would have taken any notice, or helped her to get it. It is doubtful if she would ever have said it. But now she could say it and it wouldn't matter whether anyone took notice or not, she could get the holiday for herself. A sudden exhilaration seized Gertrude, her horizon expanded enormously. She wouldn't go to Brighton or Bournemouth as she had intended. Why should she, when the world was before her?

'Brian,' she said. 'Shall *I* go to America with you?'

Brian turned swiftly from the window whither he had gone to hide his chagrin at Vera's careless refusal. A look of warm pleasure came into his face, he crossed the room and sat down by his sister on the sofa. 'What a splendid idea, Gertrude! Excellent, my dear.' He clapped his hand on hers. 'I shall be very, very glad of your company. Now when shall we go? I must put Lawn Cottage into the agents' hands tomorrow.'

Vera left them. She felt slightly piqued somehow. She went round to Mrs Clarey's house, the only place she could be sure of a welcome at the dead hour between tea and cold supper on a Sunday.

When she came back, Brian and Gertrude were still talking. Their plans had broadened. They had now decided to engage a governess and take Meriel with them.

'Mother wanted Meriel to have every advantage,' said Gertrude, emotional with excitement.

'But what about Sarah?' asked Vera indignantly.

'Meriel will pay for herself,' said Brian. 'I can't afford to take Sarah.'

'You would have taken me,' said Vera.

Brian was silent. He couldn't say that Vera's company would have been a pleasure whereas Sarah's would only be a worry. But Gertrude said it for him.

'Sarah and Meriel never get on. They would quarrel the whole time. Frankly, Vera, I can't manage Sarah on a holiday and I don't particularly want to try.'

'Very well,' said Vera grimly.

CHAPTER FIFTEEN

I

It looked as if it would be April before the travellers got off and Vera grew heartily tired of their preparations. After Lawn Cottage was sold, Gertrude moved to Southfield, and in her own house now Vera was like a queen, deposed or otherwise set aside by people who had hitherto listened while she talked, or had at least taken their subjects of conversation from her. Now, disregarding her, they babbled of their own affairs from morning till night. She wasn't used to it and looked forward to the time when they should take themselves and their enthusiasm to America.

Brian had been chafing at the delay. The longer he was in getting off, the longer it would be before he could come back. But suddenly he wondered why he should worry. He and his partners were auditors for firms with factories in England and offices in America, and vice versa. He could control his affairs from either end. Why should he hurry home to someone who didn't want him? The prospect of his being away for several months didn't seem to worry Vera in the least. He was wounded, but he was not so easily hurt by her as once he was,

he reflected; and the reflection afforded him some pride and much relief.

If he had to remain in America over the summer, he would go to a lake he knew in the foothills of the Adirondacks with Gertrude, Meriel and her new governess, Miss Evans. They would enjoy that and so would he, thought Brian, remembering the fields sloping down to the lake, the pine-trees crowding to the water's edge and the sandy coves where it was so pleasant to bathe. Brian was discovering that he liked being with people who enjoyed things. Vera was so cool and critical that when he was with her, he was anxious in case things should not be good enough for her. They rarely were. It was a change to be in charge of a party so enthusiastic and excited as that made up of Gertrude, Meriel and Miss Evans, a pleasant girl with a round childish brow, auburn hair and a powdering of freckles over her pale skin. Vera thought her unattractive but at any rate, reflected Brian, she showed proper sense of her good fortune in accompanying her charge to America, and she did know how to listen, and to make Meriel listen, when he read aloud. He decided to pack a few books suitable for reading aloud. He liked a domestic atmos-phere and this time he was taking it with him.

Vera and Sarah saw the party off from Trenton station and though Vera waved two or three times, once she began to walk away, she did not turn again, though Brian leaned from the window to the last. With pain he watched her go, he knew that if she had been parting from him for ever it would have made no difference, she would have shown no more regret.

Going down the platform, Sarah reached up to take her

mother's arm. 'Now it's just us, isn't it?' she said happily. Now she was going to be with her mother all the time. No more nursery with stupid Meriel. She was going to have meals with her mother in the little morning-room, she was going to do her homework there. It was going to be *their* room. The family had shrunk to a very cosy size, Sarah considered.

Vera, for her part, felt as if a grand clearance had been made. Several sources of irritation had been removed at one swoop: old Mrs Sargent, Brian, Gertrude and in a lesser degree, Meriel. Things should be much better now thought Vera, and in anticipation of increased enjoyment, bought many new clothes and had the drawing-room done up.

But the changes that set in were not all for the better. For one thing, she began to feel short of money. The allowance Brian had left her seemed entirely inadequate. True, when he had begun to explain why it could not be larger, it had all seemed so lengthy and wearisome that she had cut him short, saying carelessly that she would be all right. But now that she came to manage on it, it was very different. However, she would not ask for more. She had intended to give some good parties, but they must wait. She would always rather give a party than go to one, but now she must give up entertaining – she had always done more than her share anyway – and be content to be entertained.

But invitations were not so numerous as she had expected. The superficial society cultivated by Vera was loosely held together by but one common aim: to have a good time. They had had a good time at Vera's house. When that was no longer available, they went to have a good time at somebody else's,

but Vera was less frequently included. For one thing, it is awkward to fit in an odd woman at a dinner-table; there are so many odd women. For another, it is not safe to flout the susceptibilities of the society you live in; that is, if you want anything from it. If you don't, you may flout all you like. For years, Vera had annexed the men, attached and unattached, had wounded many women in doing it and had been indifferent to resentment or censure. But her mother-in-law's will suddenly gave point to the undercurrent of disapproval. The old lady hadn't liked her behaviour and it reminded other people that they didn't like it either. They began to say so to one another. A chill set in. Vera had had everything her own way far too long, they felt. Now that her husband was away, it was a good excuse not to invite her to everything, and when one heard another hadn't invited her, one didn't invite her either. Outwardly they were still very pleasant: 'You mustn't be lonely,' they said. 'Do drop in to tea any afternoon.'

Vera, from early girlhood, had always had some man, or men, since there were often several of them at the same time, in love with her. It had been Brian's painful lot to stand by and watch these successive affairs. He tortured himself to know how far they went. He could never tell. Was she faithful to him or not, he agonised? Technically, she was, though she wouldn't have called it being faithful. She would have said she wasn't tempted. Undisturbed herself, she disturbed others. But she pointed out that the remedy was in their own hands. They must keep away. Some did, but others replaced them. Men were constantly changing places beside the lovely creature.

For years the three most stubborn in attendance had been Dudley Hope, Gerald Stewart and Captain Ward. Stewart had recently left the city. Some months previously Dudley Hope had paid a desperate visit to Vera to tell her he could stand the situation no longer. He was determined to rid himself of this hopeless love and get married. 'Whom have you in view?' Vera asked him. He had nobody it appeared, but he was determined to find someone. He withdrew and his engagement to a distant cousin had just been announced. There remained Captain Ward. But he, hitherto looked upon by Vera and everybody else as a permanent attachment, now astonished her by announcing that while Brian was away, he dared not come too often to the house. His Colonel was strict and would not permit a breath of scandal. This from a man who had been at the house almost every day for the last three years was nothing short of ridiculous, Vera considered, but after an amazed silence she said she quite agreed with him. 'Yes,' she said. 'To have reached the age of forty without a single breach of the conventions is such a marvellous achievement that you mustn't spoil it now by calling without a chaperone. Goodbye,' she said, pressing his hand. 'It's been so nice knowing you.'

Bewildered and hurt, he went away and wondered why he never saw her alone after that. 'I say,' he said angrily, ringing up. 'This is overdoing it. I didn't say I could never come when Brian was away. I only said I mustn't come too often. I'm coming tonight.'

'My dear Johnny,' said Vera. 'If you have now become so reckless that you will no longer consider your reputation, you must please think of mine. I shall be out tonight.'

She dismissed him and for the first time since she could remember, found herself without a man in ardent attendance. It felt strange.

So, with the absence of men and invitations, Vera, after Sarah had gone to bed, actually found herself quite often alone. She did not enjoy the new experience. When she was alone, she was more acutely aware of the dissatisfaction that lay at the bottom of her soul like a stone. And the summer evenings were melancholy, she thought, sitting at the drawing-room windows high over the terraced garden. Early in the evening it was warm still, with a thrush singing and a star bright silver in the primrose sky. But it was melancholy even then, because you felt you ought to be doing something, you ought to be out enjoying it all until the last minute with someone; and there was no one. When the sun sank and the birds were quiet, the melancholy deepened. She sat alone with the dusk of the ravine on one hand and the empty room on the other. The mirrors showed ghostly on the walls. She understood now why a maid in the old days at home used to cover her looking-glass at night. Sitting there between the outer and the inner, deeper dusk, the pressure of her soul was too much. It is at such times that the soul asks its insistent questions. But Vera escaped from them by taking a novel to bed, or going round to see Mrs Clarey.

Mrs Clarey lived in what Vera considered a horrible little house, one of a row, from the windows of which Mrs Clarey could see the chimneys of the great house she had lived in when her husband was alive. Mr Clarey had not wished to survive his failure in the lace trade and had thrown himself in

front of a train. So selfish, said Mrs Clarey, who thought he ought to have lived to share the discomfort he had brought her to. But observing Mrs Clarey's housekeeping without the help of maids, people often thought that Mr Clarey had chosen the better part. Gloom and confusion reigned in the house; gloom because all windows were shrouded in grey net, confusion because the rooms were crammed with the things nobody had wanted to buy at the sale. After ten years, the house still looked as if Mrs Clarey had moved in yesterday. A woman came in once a week and got through the worst of the work. For the rest Mrs Clarey lived amongst her relics on boiled eggs and endless cigarettes. When Vera arrived, she was usually playing patience or doing crossword puzzles.

'I hope I never come to that,' said Vera.

'You will, my dear, you will,' Mrs Clarey assured her, laying out the cards.

Watching Mrs Clarey, with her sallow hands on which the last diamonds still twinkled, with her hair more like cinders after each successive cheap permanent wave, with her seamed, cynical face, Vera had a grim foreboding that she might be watching herself twenty-five years hence. She had escaped from solitude to Mrs Clarey; now she felt she must escape from Mrs Clarey. She wanted different company, fresher, more hopeful company and her thoughts turned to Lucy. Lucy would do her good. She and Sarah would go to Underwood. It would be a solution of the holiday problem too. Vera had Sarah on her hands and she was so little used to it that she hadn't known how to arrange a holiday agreeable

to both of them. But Judith would be at Underwood for Sarah and she herself would have Lucy. She telephoned to ask Lucy to urge Charlotte to come too, so that they could all, like old times, be together.

Lucy wrote to Charlotte, but it was Judith who replied. It was taken for granted now that someone should answer Charlotte's letters for her. Judith wrote that her mother couldn't come, but she herself would arrive in due course. She was fourteen now and travelled by herself.

Since Charlotte was not coming and there would be room for Margaret, Lucy invited her. She thought the girl would like to be with Vera. She had been full of admiration and affection for her, Lucy remembered, after the visit to Trenton. But Margaret wrote back at once to say she couldn't come. Margaret's inner life, the one subject to such strange fluctuations and developments, had taken another turn. She was persuaded now that on that visit to Trenton she had offered something that had been refused. She felt everybody must be aware of the humiliation she had suffered. She must have been mad, she told herself, to expect so much from so little. She shrank from all thought of John Watson and Vera, from whom she had too plainly besought an invitation. Nothing would have induced her to present herself at Trenton again. Her one desire was to make herself into a sophisticated young woman who didn't feel anything. She modelled herself on Vera, but she didn't want to see her again.

'Why must Vera come when I'm taking my holiday?' asked William.

'Oh, William, she must come when she likes,' said Lucy in

a shocked voice. 'She doesn't often want to come. When she does, she must be able to.'

'No need to wonder why Vera expects to have her own way,' said William. 'Everybody conspires to hide the fact that there is any other.'

'Darling, be nice,' begged Lucy. 'No one in this house seems to realise that it gives me pleasure to have my family here. I've Janet to deal with yet.'

'So she's coming again, is she?' said Janet with a sniff.

'Janet, it must be six years since Mrs Sargent was here,' said Lucy sternly.

'Seems like yesterday,' said Janet. 'I've only just got that dressing-table right from that powder. Now it'll all be to do again.'

II

It was a hot summer. The lawns were hard as iron and rusty from the drought. The annuals, complained Lucy, were all in flower at once instead of spreading themselves out as she intended. Sarah and Judith wandered far afield, two leggy girls in cotton frocks and sandals.

Judith was much the taller. Her hair had a tendency to part on the back of her neck and hang forward on each side of her face. To Lucy, she was touching in her adolescence. The protective resistance of childhood was leaving her, she was more vulnerable now. Inexperienced though she had been, Lucy had to smooth the path from childhood to adolescence for her sisters; she did it for Judith now and no one else could

284

have done it in the same way. Margaret was too harassed and bitter herself to help her sister and no one expected help or advice from Charlotte now.

In the heat of the day, Lucy and Vera lay in chairs under the deep shade of the beech tree at the bottom of the garden. It was a long time since they had been so much together and in the fitful talks they had in between dozing and reading, they rediscovered each other. Lucy was the more aware of and concerned with Vera, but Vera was more interested in Lucy than ever before. She wanted to find out why Lucy was happy when she herself wasn't. Why should she, so much better-looking, with much more money, with two children, have missed happiness and Lucy found it? Of course, she probably expects less, thought Vera, justifying her own dissatisfaction. But she observed her sister, hoping to learn something. All she could find out, though, was that Lucy took an absorbed interest in things she herself could take no interest in at all; endless books for instance, tame solitary pursuits like gardening and walking, domestic drudgery like cooking and working in the house, in silly things like hens, and in going to the help of tiresome people in the village who were always appealing to her about something. Lucy also took an open, and in Vera's opinion, eccentric interest in God. She wanted to know more and more about God, she said. She said life was discovery and that was why you didn't need to mind about growing old, because the older you got the farther you went down the road of life and the more you found out. She thought that after death you went on learning. She really believed it, you could see it in her face, glowing with an

interest which merely surprised Vera who felt nothing of it at all. 'But I would like to,' she said wistfully. 'It seems to me that there's nothing much else. The prospect of growing old appals me, Lucy. D'you realise that I shall be an old hag one day?' she said, clapping her hands to her lovely face and looking between them with horrified eyes at her sister.

'You won't,' said Lucy staunchly. 'You'll always be lovely.'

'That may be,' said Vera. 'But when I'm forty-five, say, it won't matter how good-looking I am. Any man would choose any plain little piece of seventeen to fall in love with in preference.'

'I don't know why that worries you,' said Lucy. 'You've never valued the admiration you've aroused, so far as I've seen.'

'Ah – but you know that the more you have of anything the less you want it. I'm afraid the opposite holds true, too. I'll probably be going about looking anxiously for it when I can't get it.'

'Of course you won't,' said Lucy. 'You'll be too proud.'

'I don't know what I'll be when old age starts undermining my defences,' said Vera.

It may have been this talk of age that made Lucy turn and look for signs of it in Vera's face as she lay with closed eyes in the chair beside hers. She felt a chill when she saw that they were there. She had never noticed before that line under Vera's chin or that faint fan-shaped set of lines at the corner of each eye. And were those grey hairs or very fair ones at her temples? It was true that Vera was nearly thirty-eight. This lovely face was subject to time like any other, and must change.

But Lucy who bore her own middle-age with equanimity felt a sense of loss and dread at the thought of it for Vera. She felt an impulse to lean over and kiss her sister, but repressed it because Vera would wonder why. Vera turned her head on the cushion and the look of age disappeared. Lucy was relieved. But having seen it once, she saw it again, and every time she felt a pang.

III

The holiday ended and Vera went home. The house seemed empty and far too big. If Brian had come home now, Vera might have welcomed him. Alternatively, if she had remained alone she might have found herself.

But one September evening as she sat alone at the drawing-room windows, Terry Crawford came up the steps to the terrace. A warm flush of surprise and welcome rose to Vera's cheeks.

'Terry,' she cried, running out with as much animation as a girl. 'I'm delighted to see you, but I thought you were all in Scotland.'

'I came home,' said Terry, holding her hand gloomily. 'I left them. I couldn't stand it any longer. The aunts and uncles are there, of course. It's a shooting party that never was on land or sea. If you put it on the films, no one would believe it. In the house you have to sit with the aunts, all bristling with knitting needles. When you go out you have to go with the uncles and they're such ghastly shots they don't kill the birds, they only wound them. I have to spend my time searching for

them to put them out of their pain. I won't shoot with such people and I've told the old man so, and now he's furious. Wherever Brenda goes,' he said, 'she takes the family party. She can't live without it and I can't live with it, so there we are. I've come back and I find it a relief to have the house here to myself. What about you? When's Brian coming home?'

'I don't know.'

'So you're rather at a loose end too?' said Terry. 'Good. Let's join forces, shall we? I say, you look lovely. Nice dress. You look like what's it? That flower – love-in-a-mist,' he achieved. His wife wore tweed skirts usually covered with dog-hairs.

Terry Crawford was not like Captain Ward. Gossip didn't bother him. In England you couldn't escape it, he said. People were too much on top of one another; if they didn't talk about one person, they'd talk about another, he said, so let 'em.

So they went about together. It was not the sort of association Vera was used to. Men usually sat at her feet, humbly adoring, while she queened it above. But she had to hurry about with Terry. He was at least five years younger than she was, she feared, and very active. She found herself wishing quite often that she was a different sort of person. She had never been good at tennis, but now she wished she could play with him. She didn't attempt to, being too wise to appear at a disadvantage on the court at Holly Lodge where, as he said, they could have played all day long if she had been able to. The Spencers had a model farm twenty miles out from Trenton and there was a lake there where Terry liked to swim. He wanted her to swim with him, but she recoiled at the

thought of entering that cold, reedy water, looking blue and getting her hair wet. She sat on a seat by the lake, watching him. All this was a new and chastening experience for Vera, but one in which she took a strange pleasure.

CHAPTER SIXTEEN

I

Brian's letters had always bored Vera. He wrote to himself, she said, not to her, turning phrases with conscious pleasure and writing in a stiff, neat hand. But for three weeks now there had been no letter from America and she began to look for one with something like annoyance. She had written every week as usual. It was as if she had rung a bell and nobody answered, which was unheard of in her existence.

One afternoon, however, when she came hurrying into the house because Terry was coming to tea, there was a letter in the familiar hand on the hall-table. She took it with her into the drawing-room, and looking round to see that everything was all right for tea, ran her eyes carelessly over the first few lines. Now that the letter had come, she didn't feel much interest in it.

My Dear Vera, [she read]
I haven't written by the last few mails as you may or may not have noticed because I have been turning over a good many matters in my mind. I have now come to

a conclusion and I hope you will believe that I have not come to it carelessly or with haste. I have given your side of the affair every consideration. . . .

The careless look left her face and she read on:

'There will be serious trouble in Europe. England will be plunged into war and she isn't ready. I see disaster ahead for England and so do all outside our country. Our prestige is unbelievably low. It has been a shock to me to realise how low . . .'

What's this to do with me, wondered Vera, skipping half a page.

'I will come to the point,' he wrote, and Vera said thank goodness.

'I propose to develop the American end of the business myself, since that is what we shall depend on in the event of war. I propose to remain here for several years, perhaps for the rest of my business life and I ask you to join me here with Sarah.'

Vera's eyes flew under her frowning brows. Was he mad?

'I am not thinking of the business alone when I ask you to come out here to me. I am thinking of you and of myself. I cannot return to the old conditions. They were insupportable and humiliating, and you must have known that I was very unhappy. I have been happier in America these last months than I have been for years in Trenton. Your life there does not really suit you either, whatever you may say to the contrary. Come and start again with me in this country. Sell the house and all that's in it and bring Sarah and let's try

again. Meriel is very happy here and has much improved under Miss Evans's tuition. We have indeed been fortunate in Miss Evans. Gertrude too wishes to remain here. It certainly is a wonderful country. I feel a different man . . . '

He writes like one too, thought Vera grimly.

'I repeat I am willing to start again here, but not there, and I want a considered answer, Vera, because much depends upon it. Think well. Take several days over it. Then cable me. . . . '

The door opened and Terry came in.

'Terry,' she said, raising her bemused eyes. 'Brian wants me to go and *live* in America.'

'Live in America?' he echoed in stupefaction. 'What on earth for?'

Denham brought in tea and Vera threw Brian's letter down on the sofa. 'Do sit down,' she said, pouring out tea.

'But what's the idea of living in America?' asked Terry when the maid had gone. 'What's the matter with England?'

'A great deal according to Brian. He says there's going to be a war and England's going to find herself in trouble.'

'There'll be no war,' said Terry. 'And if there were England would fight as she's always fought – to win. But suppose England did go to war, what's the idea of going to live in America?'

'To get out, I suppose. To be safe and keep the business going.'

'What a horrible idea,' said Terry, biting into his toast.

'It is and I shall tell Brian so,' said Vera preparing her case. 'If there's not going to be a war, there's no need to go, and if there is going to be a war, it's a disgrace to go. People would

say we were running away. He wouldn't like that. That'll bring him home.'

'I should hate you to go,' said Terry reaching for more toast. 'My God, what should I do?'

'Don't worry,' said Vera. 'I'm not going.'

Terry did not stay long. Vera was so indignant and, in spite of herself, disturbed by Brian's letter that she could not leave it alone, and Terry never liked it when a woman went on and on about a thing. Besides, he had annoyances of his own. Brenda was sulking heavily because he had come away from Scotland and of course all the household, down to the least important maid, was on her side. He had his own difficulties; he felt he couldn't cope with anyone else's, so he made an excuse to leave and went to the club.

When he had gone, Vera read Brian's letter again. She knew he had been pleased with it. A good letter, he would think, reading it over and putting commas in. He prided himself on good letters. In the old days when they used to discuss his business affairs, he would often say, gravely: 'I wrote him a good letter,' or: 'I wrote him a very nice letter, really. I'm surprised he should have replied in such a tone.' He took himself and his letters very seriously and was hurt that she didn't.

As if she would ever consent to start again in a strange place with him, she thought, reading. Here where she had plenty of people about her to mitigate him, she could manage. But not anywhere else. No, she thought grimly, heaven forbid. Here she had got everything as she wanted it; she reigned. She saw herself coming down the staircase dressed

for a party, receiving people in the hall, presiding at the dinner-table. Many a time it had not seemed much, but at any rate it was better than it would be in America. It would be years before they reached the same social pitch in a strange country where they would be without background. And for all those years she would be thrown back upon Brian's unrelieved company. No, thank you, she thought.

'"Sell the house and all that's in it,"' she read again. 'My home,' she thought indignantly. 'All my lovely things.' She looked round at the silvery carpet, at the fluted folds of the yellow brocade curtains, the wide chairs, the grand piano, the banked flowers. 'As if I would,' she thought.

The door opened. 'Mrs Clarey,' Denham announced, and Vera hurriedly thrust Brian's letter behind a cushion.

'All alone?' asked Mrs Clarey, entering in customary black. Her eyes fell on the tea-table and brightened for two reasons. One, it gave her a chance of tea. Two, it gave her a piece of information. Mrs Clarey liked information, especially when it had been withheld. 'Ah – you've had company. Terry Crawford again?'

Vera did not answer and Mrs Clarey sat down in Terry's chair and threw back her worn furs.

'Is there any tea left? I know I'm late, but if there is a cup I may as well have it.'

'This is cold,' said Vera. 'I'll ring for more.'

She didn't feel gracious. When you were comfortable and contented, Mrs Clarey didn't matter, but when you were on edge Mrs Clarey seemed like a bird of ill omen. It was time Brian came back, thought Vera with seeming inconsequence.

She felt the need of presenting an ordered home life to the sharp eyes of Mrs Clarey and the world in general. She resented these frequent implications that Brian was staying away too long and Terry Crawford coming too often.

'Have you heard from Brian yet?' asked Mrs Clarey.

'I had a letter today.'

'Oh, really. At last. Anything new?'

Denham appeared in answer to the bell. Vera was able to busy herself with instructions about tea.

'Does he say anything about coming home?' persisted Mrs Clarey.

A cutting reply rose to Vera's lips, but the door opened again and Sarah came in.

'Come along, darling,' said Vera holding out an arm from her corner of the couch. 'Mrs Clarey's going to have some fresh tea and you can have some with her.'

Dragging her feet, Sarah came to sit down. She was untidy, pale and dirty. She leaned her face against her mother's arm and stared, mournful with fatigue, across at Mrs Clarey.

Mrs Clarey was hurt that Vera would not tell her anything about Brian's letter and the reason for his silence. That was the worst of Vera. You never knew where you were with her. One time she would tell you anything and everything, but another time, if you approached the subjects she had freely discussed before, she would look at you as if you were presuming altogether too much and close up like an oyster. Mrs Clarey tried to get back to a more comfortable footing.

'That child looks tired out,' she said. 'Isn't dancing rather too much for her after school?'

'It's school that's too much,' said Sarah from her mother's arm. 'If I hadn't to go to school first I shouldn't be a bit tired.'

'Ah – but you must go to school,' said Mrs Clarey. 'School's more important than dancing at your age.'

'It's not,' said Sarah sitting up indignantly, fire in her eyes. 'I'm going to be a dancer. I don't need to know arithmetic to dance. Anyway,' she said sinking back against her mother's arm and scowling at Mrs Clarey, 'I'm only going till I'm fifteen and then I'm going to do dancing all the time.'

Mrs Clarey felt she had not been any more fortunate with the daughter than with the mother.

'I'm thirteen now,' said Sarah. 'It won't be long.'

'Darling, you're very dirty,' said Vera, looking with distaste at the hands lying slackly in Sarah's lap. 'You ought to have washed, and brushed your hair, when you came in from school.'

'I'm too tired to wash,' said Sarah crossly.

Yes, it was time Brian and Meriel came home, thought Vera again, as Denham came in with the tea. Time Sarah was taken in hand again by someone. Miss Evans presumably. Miss Evans could take charge of Sarah as well as Meriel surely? And do the mending. What a relief to have someone to do the mending again. As it was, it wasn't done. Sarah's drawer was full of unmended stockings and things with buttons off. Vera's imagination presented her with a comforting picture of Miss Evans's neat auburn head bent over Sarah's stockings in the nursery. With Sarah upstairs again, kept in order by Miss Evans, and Brian at home managing the money – what a bore that had been – her life would return to normal.

Vera doesn't want much, her brothers used to say long ago

at home; she only wants everything. She wanted now to keep what she had, with Terry in addition. That was all she asked.

The next morning, she went into the town to send off her cable:

'Cannot agree to your preposterous proposal. Please come home.'

Her feeling was chiefly one of complete amazement that he should ever have made it. She was as astonished as if a horse she had driven for years had suddenly turned and told her it would like to drive in future. In the afternoon, she wrote a letter to him and thereafter dismissed the matter from her mind. That is, she didn't need to dismiss it; it went. She was so taken up with Terry who, though his wife had returned from Scotland, still contrived to spend a great deal of time at Vera's house, that when a cable arrived from Brian she had to reflect for a moment to gather what it referred to. He cabled, after getting her letter:

'Your decision received. On your own head be it.'

What did that mean, she wondered irritably. When his letter came, she knew.

II

At the end of a November afternoon, soon after William had come in, the telephone rang in the hall at Underwood. Lucy answered it. It was a trunk-call from Trenton and she called out to William to pour out tea for himself.

'Hello, Lucy?' came Vera's voice.

'Hello, darling, how are you?' called Lucy.

'I'm well enough, but I've just had rather a shock,' Vera's voice was muffled by distance. 'Brian wants to marry Miss Evans.'

Lucy thought she hadn't heard correctly. 'What? I can't hear properly.'

'He wants to marry Miss Evans,' repeated Vera slowly and distinctly.

'Miss Evans? Who's Miss Evans?' asked Lucy in stupefaction.

'The governess. The girl they took out with them,' said Vera impatiently.

'Marry her!' exclaimed Lucy. 'How can he?'

'Oh, he can all right. He's going to divorce me and marry her, and then I'm to claim a divorce at this end.'

There was a long pause. 'Brian . . . !' exclaimed Lucy incredulously. 'What for . . . ? Is this the first you've heard of it?'

'Yes,' said Vera. 'But he's never forgiven me for not going out to America with him. And he wrote a little while ago asking me to sell the house and everything and go out there to live. Of course I refused. I'd no idea there was this behind it, though I'd have refused even if I had known. Why should he be able to divorce me because I won't go out to him when I can't divorce him because he won't come home to me? There's no justice in it. But that's what he's going to do,' she finished, her voice tailing off with a forlorn effect.

'Oh, Vera,' said Lucy.

There was another pause. 'A little plain red-headed creature,' said Vera bitterly.

'But, darling, what are you going to do?' asked Lucy anxiously.

'What can I do? He's quite determined.'

'But what about Meriel?'

'He's to keep her. I'm to have Sarah.'

Lucy was silent, appalled. That a family – that precious unit – should be broken up so casually. 'It's incredible,' she said. 'Are you sure he can do it – I mean divorce you and marry her?'

'You may be sure he can,' said Vera. 'Or he wouldn't say so. He'll have gone into it with his usual thoroughness.'

'It's all so cold-blooded,' said Lucy despairingly. Another pause. 'Would you like to come here for a bit?' she asked.

'I can't leave Sarah,' said Vera. 'No, I'd better stay where I am and see it through. I'll ring off now, Lucy. I've lost count of my calls. Perhaps you'll come here later?'

'Oh, I will. I'll come now if you like.'

'No, not now. I'll let you know when. Goodbye, Lucy.'

'Goodbye, darling, I'm so dreadfully sorry . . . ' The telephone clicked in her ear. Vera was gone.

'So the worm has turned?' said William who had come out, during the conversation, to the hall.

'William, I can't believe it,' said Lucy appalled. 'Solid, stolid Brian, to break everything up and marry the governess. What an awful situation for Vera.'

'She's asked for it, you know,' said William. 'She's been asking for it for years. Damn it all, a man has a right to expect something for his money.'

'Don't joke,' said Lucy frowning.

'I'm not joking,' said William.

'But can he do it?' asked Lucy bewildered. 'Can he really divorce her for what looks like nothing at all?'

'He can. There was a case in the paper only the other day. I read it carefully because I was surprised myself. An Englishman got a divorce in Idaho from his wife living in England for mental cruelty. The divorce is effective in Britain if admitted by the law of the country where the parties are domiciled. Brian can marry out there. Vera gets her divorce here as a matter of course.'

'I think it's appalling,' said Lucy.

CHAPTER SEVENTEEN

It was not until after Christmas that Vera signified to Lucy that she could come if she liked, and then Lucy arrived to find the situation not at all what she had expected. Not for the first time had she come full of anxious sympathy to one or the other of her sisters, only to find it wasn't needed. Either she took things too seriously or the other members of her family took them too lightly. It certainly seemed as if her concern was exaggerated and unnecessary. After all, as William said, if they didn't mind, why should she?

She had expected Vera, the victim of this domestic drama, to be both angry and wounded. After all, if she hadn't cared much about Brian, surely she cared about Meriel? Lucy could not believe that you could bring a child into the world and not care about it. And looked at materially, a heavy blow had been struck at Vera's pride and position. There must have been a lot of talk, disagreeable curiosity and publicity – paragraphs in the paper, and all that sort of thing – yet Vera arrived at the station in radiant health and spirits and drove her sister to Southfield, blithely remarking on the way that she wasn't sorry it had happened, really. 'Not that I don't think it was a very shabby trick,' she said. 'I don't think he'll show his face

in Trenton again. He's taking out naturalisation papers, I
hear. So he's deserting not only me, but his country. Amazing
turn of events, isn't it?' she said with amused interest. When
Lucy ventured to mention Meriel, Vera said, 'Oh, well, she's
always been much more Brian's child than mine. It's right he
should have her. They weaned her from me very early, you
know. She spent most of her time with that venomous old
woman and Gertrude.'

She drove into the back courtyard of Southfield as she
spoke and Lucy had another shock. Over the wall reared a
white-painted board on which was posted a single word in red
letters: SOLD!

'Oh,' cried Lucy. 'Is the house sold?'

'Oh, yes,' said Vera calmly. 'Didn't I tell you? I've got
another.'

'Oh, Vera, you're leaving your lovely house,' grieved Lucy,
looking up at it.

'Go in, go in,' said Vera, 'while I put the car away. You
didn't think I could possibly keep up a place like this, did you?
I'm to have seven hundred a year, which isn't bad I suppose,
but I certainly couldn't live here on it.'

Lucy went into the house and was met by Sarah, who, now
that she was out of the nursery, seemed always to have a dirty
face and inky fingers.

'You'll have to excuse everything,' said Vera, taking Lucy
to her room. 'Cook and Denham are leaving, you know.
Beatrice, the kitchen-maid, is going with me. She's the best of
the bunch, so it'll be all right.'

Passing the open door, Lucy saw that Brian's dressing-

room was emptied. Every fresh evidence that he had really gone, that the marriage was really over, gave Lucy a shock.

'You're going to stay in Trenton then?' she said.

'Oh, yes, I shall stay,' said Vera.

'And where is your new house?' asked Lucy.

'Right at the other side of the city.'

'Is it nice?'

'Well, it'll do,' said Vera. 'I'm going there tomorrow afternoon and you can see it then, if you like.'

Lucy became more puzzled as the evening wore on. There was something so airy about Vera's behaviour, as if what was happening, the break-up, removal, re-establishment, was a side-issue to something else, but what that something was Lucy had no idea. The family irresponsibility, she felt anxiously, was manifesting itself in Vera now. Not that it had not often appeared before, but never so palpably as this. Vera seemed to be in full career down some private road of her own.

As they sat together in the little morning-room after Sarah had gone to bed, Lucy felt that Vera wasn't really with her, she was absent. She was restless too. She, who used to sit so beautifully still, commanding admiration, could not keep quiet now. She bit her fingers, kept touching her hair and her pearls and lost the thread of Lucy's conversation. She kept trying to pick it up again. 'What were you saying, Lucy?' she had to ask over and over again. Her restlessness began to affect her sister.

'Is there any mending I can be doing for you?' she asked. She knew Vera never mended anything if she could help it,

and there was no one now to mend for her or for Sarah. Her offer brought Vera back to the moment as nothing else had been able to do.

'What an inspiration!' she said gratefully. 'Sarah's buttons are mostly off and the holes in her stockings are simply beyond me. I'll go and fetch you some, bless you!'

The evening went better after that. Lucy darned, Vera sewed on buttons. 'There is a certain satisfaction in getting these things done,' she admitted, looking at her handiwork. 'But I'd never do it if you weren't here to keep me company. You should have brought me up differently. You or Charlotte always did my mending, you know.'

The next morning, she announced that she had an appointment for a face-massage. 'But I shan't be long,' she said, and Lucy knew at once that Vera didn't want her to go into town with her. Lucy made it easy for her.

'It's very wet,' she said. 'I'll stay in, write to William, read the papers, do some more mending and be quite all right by myself.'

So Vera drove away in her car. Sarah had gone to school. Lucy went up through the silent house, with doors standing open on empty rooms, and sorted out more mending from the jumble of Sarah's clothes. The maids were going about in a careless way, flicking at furniture with their dusters. The house was going, they were going, they seemed to imply, so why bother? Lucy didn't like the atmosphere of restlessness and impending change. She never had liked to be unsettled. That was her weakness, she considered. The caution and anxiety that should have been distributed over the whole

family had been concentrated in her and Jack, she told herself. The others seemed to be entirely without it. They were reckless, maybe, but she wasn't reckless enough, and she was always oppressed when the people and things she cared about were threatened by change.

Sitting by the fire in the morning-room, with the rain on the windows, it seemed part of the general disintegration going on in the world that Vera's home life should be disintegrating too. Another thing gone in a world where so much was going. As if there were not enough families being forcibly torn apart by persecution or preparation for war, Vera had to let hers fall apart too and for no unavoidable reason. And Charlotte too, thought Lucy, making no stand at all against Geoffrey to keep hers together.

As she was coming down the stairs, towards lunch-time, with more of Sarah's undarned stockings in her hands, Vera, with Terry behind her, came into the hall. 'Oh, Lucy,' she cried, turning a radiant face upwards. 'This is Terry Crawford. Terry, you know all about Lucy. Go into the drawing-room both of you and I'll bring the sherry.'

Something very pleasant must have happened to Vera while she was out, thought Lucy, and naïvely wondered if Brian were coming home and everything going to be all right after all. She stood by the fire with the young man; very handsome, very attractive, she thought with indulgent indifference, until she remembered all at once that it must have been him who had been nice to Judith at the dinner-party. She looked at him with warmer interest then. 'I think I've heard about you from Judith,' she said.

'Oh, that charming little girl?' he said. 'How is she?'

'She's a big girl now, you know. Nearly as tall as I am. She's fifteen.'

'Pity they have to grow up,' said Terry. 'I think she was the most attractive little girl I've ever seen.'

'She hasn't changed,' said Lucy fondly.

Vera came in with the sherry and Lucy wondered again what could have happened. She was so gay and lovely, laughing and talking to them both. She ought always to be like this, thought Lucy. This is how she was meant to be. 'You'll see him again today,' said Vera to Lucy, taking Terry out to his car in spite of the rain. 'He's going to drive us to the house. It's on his way to the colliery.'

The sisters lunched together. Sarah stayed at school for lunch, which Vera spoke of as a great relief. Lucy could feel the undercurrent of excitement in Vera, but whatever it was that had happened, she was keeping it to herself. For lunch, Vera had merely taken off her hat; she remained in her black coat and skirt, slender, very finished, hair, face and hands groomed to perfection. 'It's very nice to look at, but it takes such a *time*,' thought Lucy. Vera kept recurring to the subject of Terry Crawford. 'Poor darling, he has such a dull wife. You've never seen Brenda, have you? A stodgy, podgy little person, surrounded by dogs and elderly relatives. Pots of money, of course. She's what you'd call non-adult. She's not really grown-up, you know.'

Lucy thought that Terry Crawford was possibly not entirely grown-up either, but since Vera seemed so concerned for him, she didn't say so.

After lunch Vera wandered about the room, her hands spread fanwise at the back of her slender waist, or stood at the mantelpiece, fingering her pearls. 'Can't you sit down, darling?' suggested Lucy.

'You shouldn't sit after meals,' said Vera severely, and Lucy thought Vera was taking much more care of her beauty than she used to. I suppose you have to when it's beginning to go, she thought, sad for her sister.

At three o'clock Terry Crawford again presented himself, and during the drive across the city Lucy felt relegated to her old part of gooseberry. But it must be mere association of ideas, she told herself, due to sitting in the back of a car with Vera in front with a young man, neither taking much notice of her. Not that it mattered, she liked to be free to look about her. What a huge place Trenton was, and what a different world they were now in! This district had seen better days, it had obviously come down. The houses were still big, but they had a faintly seedy air, as if they would soon be given over, if they weren't already, to theatrical lodgings. This road was gloomy; on one side of it there was an old cemetery crowded with crooked stones, full up long ago. Each pavement was planted at the edge with trees. They had grown far too big, so their tops had been cut off. In winter now they presented a sad, truncated appearance. But as if to get their own back for the outrage perpetrated upon them above, they had pursued such furious activity below that their roots upheaved the pavements; so that from one end of the long road to the other it looked as if the dead from the adjacent cemetery were trying to rise.

'Here we are,' said Vera and the car drew up at the pavement. Lucy was incredulous. 'Here?' she asked. But the others got out and she had to follow them. She stood on the pavement looking in amazement at the grim façade of a pair of tall houses standing on a flight of dark stone steps, but Vera had gone in and Terry Crawford was holding the battered gate open for her. She climbed the steps and went, bemused, into the empty house. Why, she asked, why come here when you didn't have to? Why choose a place like this? 'Terry,' called Vera from upstairs. 'Come up, will you? The bath's come. Lucy, you be having a look round.' But Lucy was most disinclined to. She stood at the top of the three steps down into the kitchen and, her coat gathered about her in case it should touch anything, she peered into the gloom. It was the sort of kitchen where there would be black-beetles at night. And silverfish in all the cupboards, she whispered to herself. Damp had drawn maps on the walls, and the dark red tiles of the floor were cracked. The dining-room was dark; the back and side of the house looked out on to a high brick wall. The sitting-room was a good room, large and lofty, with a good white marble mantelpiece. Stumbling upstairs – she had never been in such a dark house – she discovered that Vera's bedroom was a good room too, but the rest of the house was impossible, and Lucy was aghast at the thought of Vera and Sarah living in such a place. But when she went into the bathroom where Vera and Terry were examining a new primrose-yellow bath Vera didn't ask her what she thought of the house. Either Vera didn't want to know or she didn't care. Her manner, as many a time in the old days at home, implied:

'It doesn't matter what you think, I shall do as I like.' So Lucy did not say anything. Vera had taken the house. It was like a hat that didn't suit the purchaser. No good saying anything now: it was too late. But she wouldn't say a word in praise of it either. She felt her way down the stairs again and went out to the car. What possessed Vera, what was the matter with her that she could contemplate living in a place like this? Vera and Terry came out behind her, and suddenly from a look that Vera threw upwards at Terry as she locked the door, Lucy knew the truth. Vera was in love with this young man, in love as she had never been before. She knew too, in a flash, that he was not in love with her, though he might be having what was for him a mild affair. He was years younger than Vera, he was unsatisfactorily married, he was irresponsible, unreliable – what happiness could there possibly be for Vera in this? Deeply perturbed, Lucy took her seat in the back of the car as before. She saw it all now. Vera would not leave Trenton because Terry was there, but by choosing a house in this district, she had hidden herself as effectively as if she had left the city. And she had let drop that he passed the house on his way to the colliery offices, whither he went every day, keeping up, supposed Lucy caustically, some pretence of work. Driving back, Lucy kept her face turned away, unwilling to look on while her infatuated, reckless, but dearly-loved sister courted disaster in the shape of Terry Crawford.

CHAPTER EIGHTEEN

That night when the sisters were alone together after dinner
they were constrained with each other. Lucy went on with the
mending, but Vera lay idle in her chair. They were mostly
silent, and if they spoke, what they said had no relation to
what they were thinking of. Lucy was wondering how best
to say what she must say. She had to be very careful how
she did it. One false step and Vera with an icy word would
close the subject; and there would be no reopening it. Lucy
knew her Vera. So she sat, mending a blouse of Sarah's,
considering her approach and Vera sat opposite, mutely
fending it off. She was exasperated that Lucy would make
it, as she knew she eventually would. She'd get her words of
wisdom in somehow, trust her for that. 'Interfering,' thought
Vera furiously. 'As if I can't do as I like at my age. As if it's
anything to do with her what I do. Terry and I might be out-
and-out lovers, the way she disapproves, and we're nothing
of the kind. If she says anything I'll tell her so. The *word* alone
would give her a shock. She's shocked at everything. As if
she knows anything about love. As if she knows anything
about the torture of loving Terry,' thought Vera, turning her
head away. 'I didn't want to fall in love. Why should I have

kept out of love all these years and then fall in love at my age with a man years younger than myself? Is it a thing I should choose? Why should I have to keep bothering about my looks, fussing about my hair and my face and my figure, I, who have never had to do it until now? Why should I keep listening for the telephone now, when I used to tell them to take the receivers off so that I shouldn't be annoyed? Why should I torture myself wondering if he loves me, and knowing he doesn't – not yet, anyway. Let Lucy begin about there being no happiness to be got out of it, let her begin, that's all. As if I don't know.' She bit her fingers, her eyes again on her sister.

Something in the expression of Lucy's face, bent over the child's blouse, touched Vera unexpectedly. Poor Lucy, she thought, the guardian of the family. Standing guard over a door that had been broken down long ago. Why couldn't she realise that? When you married you left your family and made one for yourself. The old bond was broken. But it wasn't, she admitted suddenly. This mysterious bond still held, or why did she care what Lucy thought of her? Why was Lucy her conscience still? Why had she any need to defend herself to Lucy, if there was nothing in family feeling? And why was the old bond stronger than any in Vera's own family? Simply because of Lucy. No matter how you choked her off, how rude or resisting you were, she went quietly on looking after you, caring what happened to you. Steadfast, good, she kept the sisters together. If it had not been for Lucy, they would have drifted apart years ago. Exasperation and affection warred together in Vera, as in sisters they often do, and for the

moment affection had the upper hand. 'You're very quiet,' she said to Lucy with one of her lovely smiles.

'I was thinking of Judith just then,' said Lucy.

'Judith?' This was unexpected.

'Yes. I was thinking someone will soon have to struggle with Geoffrey for Judith's future. Left to him, either it won't occur to him that she's got one, or if it did, he'd think it was nothing but a nuisance.'

'Can't Charlotte tackle him?'

'Oh, no, Charlotte's completely given up. She takes no part in anything now. He's cured her of that,' said Lucy bitterly.

'Why does she give in to him so? I can't understand it,' said Vera, who could easily see where other people went wrong.

'She can't struggle against him any longer,' said Lucy. 'I haven't seen her for nearly twelve months, you know. Judith travels backwards and forwards from Underwood by herself now, but I must go back with her after Easter. She's taking School Certificate this year and something must be settled for her. What's Sarah going to do when she leaves school?'

'No need to consider that. She's only thirteen. She says she's going to be a dancer, and if so, she's as well with Madame Fouquet as anywhere.'

'Don't you think she'd be better away at school?' said Lucy.

'Ah, here it is,' thought Vera. 'I thought you didn't approve of boarding-schools?' she said aloud.

Lucy blushed slightly. It was true. She had always said parents were the proper persons to bring up their own

children, but only if the parents were suitable for the task. 'In the case of only children . . . ' she hedged. 'And Sarah is an only child now. She doesn't seem to like her school here. She makes any excuse not to go, doesn't she?' You'd only to look at Sarah to know she didn't like the school and wasn't doing any good there. But Vera wouldn't have that.

'Oh, nonsense,' she said tersely. 'The school's all right. It's Sarah who's wrong. She wouldn't like any school, but she likes being with me. It's all she cares about. It would be cruel to send her away from me. Besides, we're very well as we are for the present.'

For the present. No looking ahead, because Vera didn't know what to look to. She had an almost superstitious feeling that she must keep things in a state of flux, not determine anything. Everything was merely temporary, the move to the house in Burnham Road, the chaos in her affairs and her outlook – it was just for the time being until – what? But to send Sarah away to school and be alone would be too plain a move; it might startle him. Besides, she didn't want to send Sarah away. She liked her to be there.

'I wish you'd consider sending Sarah away to school, all the same,' said Lucy.

'Why do you harp on it?' said Vera coldly. 'I've said I won't.'

'She's going to have a bad time then,' said Lucy. 'She's devoted to you, and that's pathetic because she isn't devoted to anyone else. If you let her down, she'll suffer. If you're not prepared to put yourself aside and devote yourself to her, you'd far better send her away to a good school where other people will look after her, and keep her out of emotional

conflicts until she's old enough to face them. You're making yourself Sarah's only companion and it's a great responsibility.'

'I wish you'd mind your own business,' said Vera.

Lucy flushed and picked up the blouse again. The part of the interferer wasn't pleasant, but it sometimes had to be played. Vera was not as impervious to suggestion as she liked to make out. Many a time she had known her repulse an idea with scorn and act upon it later. Lucy hoped that would happen now. 'I know you think I'm like Aunt Phoebe,' she said, raising her eyes to her sister, 'but I just want to say for the last time: remember Sarah.'

The telephone rang in the hall and Vera hurried out. It was Terry. She switched the telephone through to her bedroom and went to have a long conversation with him from there.

A few days later Lucy went home. She had wanted to help with the removal, but Vera airily said there would be nothing to help with. Lucy had found her own removals exhausting, but perhaps Vera was right, she admitted. Vera would leave everything to the men and that was probably the most sensible thing to do.

So Lucy went home. She felt she was always taking ineffectual journeys to her sisters' houses, casting a look at their lives, sighing and coming away again. It was ridiculous in its uselessness. She was like an anxious cat that had to keep going to look at its kittens. And she must make another journey soon. She must go back with Judith after Easter and have a surreptitious interview with Judith's headmistress

and alas! an interview with Geoffrey. She dreaded that. You
never knew which way he would jump and when so much was
at stake you had to be so careful. To think of Charlotte having
to make these cautious approaches all these years, she
thought. No wonder her nerves were ruined.

Lucy wanted Judith to have what she herself had missed,
a university training, and she wanted to propose to Geoffrey
that she and William should pay her fees. All Geoffrey had
to give was his consent. It sounded easy and reasonable
enough, but Lucy knew it wouldn't be. There was nothing easy
or reasonable about Geoffrey. She did not tell Judith what
her plan was, in case it shouldn't come off, but walking in
the lanes or sitting by the fire in the Easter holidays, they
often discussed Judith's career, which after all lay beyond the
years she might spend at a university. Judith gaily envisaged
any and every possibility and impossibility from starting an
orphanage where the children should be really happy and
have cake for tea every day, to being frightfully rich and
travelling about the world in search of Stephen. Her plans,
Lucy was touched to find, invariably included her. 'Wherever
I am and whatever I do, I can always come here for the
holidays, can't I? After I'm twenty-one, can this be my real
home? Daddy can't make me go home any more after I'm
twenty-one, can he?'

By tacit consent they did not discuss Judith's home
conditions. Judith thought her aunt knew everything; Lucy
couldn't discuss the child's father with her because she
disliked him so much. She always tried to foster Judith's
affection for her mother by telling her about Charlotte in her

childhood. Judith listened, looked thoughtful and said nothing. She sometimes looked as if she didn't understand what her aunt was getting at. There was something slightly baffling to each in the attitude of the other towards Charlotte.

Aunt and niece travelled to Denborough, Lucy full of plans for Judith and affectionate anticipation of seeing Charlotte again after so long. She came into the house as she had so often done before, into the square red-carpeted hall with the white doors closed all round it, the blue plates at intervals on the shelf above, the giant palm, rather rusty at the edges, in the great brass bowl. The hall was empty as the travellers entered, but hearing a sound, Lucy looked up at a figure coming round the bend of the stairs, and stood stock-still, shocked to the heart. It was Charlotte, but mortally changed. She was fat, she was infirm, leaning heavily on the rail. She was shabby in an old tweed skirt and sagging cardigan. What was the matter with her? Why did she walk like that?

'Charlotte,' she cried in distress. 'Are you lame?'

'Oh, no,' said Charlotte, reaching her and offering a puffy cheek to her kiss. 'No, dear. My feet and ankles are very swollen these days, that's all.'

'But why?' asked Lucy.

'Oh, I don't know,' said Charlotte. 'It's nothing. How are you? And how is William?' she asked, without pausing for an answer. 'Well, Judith. Have you had a nice time? Yes, I suppose you have. Come upstairs, Lucy, tea's in the nursery. I generally have tea in the nursery now, you know.'

She turned and laboriously climbed the stairs she had just come down. Lucy, dread and foreboding in her heart,

followed in silence. Judith cast an anxious look at her aunt and looked away again.

'Charlotte,' said Lucy when they reached her room. 'You look so strange, darling. You look ill.'

'Well, I'm not ill,' said Charlotte in mild exasperation. 'You said exactly the same last time you came.'

'But you look worse,' said Lucy, her voice sharp with apprehension.

'Of course I don't,' said Charlotte. 'Don't begin that again, Lucy, please. Come and have tea. Did you say Vera had gone into a new house? And is it true that Brian's never coming home any more?'

With every word she spoke, Lucy's heart sank lower. Was the deterioration mental as well as physical? She had told Charlotte about Vera's divorce long ago, but she didn't seem to have grasped it. They sat down to tea in the shabby nursery and Charlotte rambled on, but Lucy hardly heard her. Charlotte's hand on the teapot was enough to shock her into silence. It was puffy and fumbling. It wasn't like Charlotte's hand at all, cried Lucy to herself. What were they all doing in this house that they couldn't see something terrible had happened to Charlotte? Why hadn't they done something about it? Why had they let her get like this?

After dinner, she caught first at Geoffrey, then at Margaret. They were on their way out somewhere. 'Charlotte looks very ill,' she said to Geoffrey. He gave a bark of a laugh and went out. 'Your mother ought to see a doctor,' she said to Margaret, but Margaret remarked that she didn't think a doctor would do much good and followed her father. Lucy was left standing

in the hall, looking after them. She trembled with anger. Cruel and indifferent, both of them. Geoffrey was unnatural, less than human, but how dared he turn Margaret from her mother when she was ill? Burning with indignation and protective love she went upstairs to Charlotte.

'Are they going out?' asked Charlotte.

'They've gone,' said Lucy shortly.

'Well, then, we can go down and sit in the morning-room,' said Charlotte as gleefully as a child. 'It's so nice down there. It's the nicest room in the house, you know, that's why Geoffrey has it for himself.'

Judith stayed behind to read *Pride and Prejudice* in the nursery, but the sisters ensconced themselves on each side of Geoffrey's fire. It was not long, however, before Charlotte fell asleep and Lucy was left to contemplate the changed face of her sister. Sitting in that bright hot room with the whisky on the table and the tiresome hand of bridge still above the mantelpiece, Lucy wept.

'I shall get a doctor myself, tomorrow,' she said.

She had arranged, by letter, an interview with Miss Porteous, Judith's headmistress, for the following morning, and soon after breakfast she hurried away to keep her appointment. Geoffrey and Margaret, she gathered, were going off somewhere in the car. When she came back, she would see about getting a doctor. The one from the end of the road would do.

She liked Miss Porteous at once. 'I'm very glad to know someone takes an interest in Judith's education,' said Miss Porteous. 'Her parents, if you will excuse my saying so, have never shown any at all.'

'Her mother isn't well. She hasn't been well for years,' said Lucy defendingly, looking so distressed that Miss Porteous murmured reassuringly:

'I understand. I have heard . . . one does hear things, somehow.'

'But her father,' said Lucy, suddenly laying the cards on the table before this frank, capable woman, 'will be an obstacle and I've come to see if we can circumvent him.'

'We'll try, anyway,' said Miss Porteous, smiling.

The interview was a success. 'I've great hopes for a scholarship for Judith next year, but even if she gets one, she'll only be seventeen and there'll have to be a postponement of holding,' said Miss Porteous. 'We shouldn't want her to hang about at home for a year until she can be admitted to a university, should we?' Lucy fervently agreed that they would not. The thing to do, then, the conspirators agreed, was to lie low, not to rouse Geoffrey in any way and to keep Judith at school as long as possible. They parted with mutual liking and Lucy was relieved to know that she was not alone in trying to save Judith from the ruin Geoffrey was bringing on his household. She felt as if a load had been lifted from her mind. Now she would get Charlotte put right.

She walked briskly along Queen's Walk, noting the name on the doctor's plate at the corner. She would go to the house, make sure that Charlotte was there and then ring up this Doctor Salter. It was a lovely day, the daffodils were out in the gardens, the birds twittered; they didn't sing as they did in the country, but they twittered pleasantly, Lucy admitted. It was at once obvious on entering the house that Geoffrey was

out. The doors were wide open, there was the sound of the vacuum cleaner and an air of constrained bustle. Judith, it appeared, was out too. Lucy went up through the house in search of Charlotte. She was not in the nursery, where Lucy had expected to find her. She must be in her bedroom, thought Lucy, opening the door.

Charlotte was sitting on a chair beside the bed, holding a flask of whisky on her knee and as Lucy stood, rooted, she lifted it to her mouth and drank from it with satisfaction. Then she turned her head and saw Lucy. She slowly lowered the flask and put it behind her back, her face crumpling like a child caught in the wrong. Her eyes fixed on her sister she began, in piteous admission of weakness, to cry. 'Oh, Charlotte,' said Lucy, her heart wrung.

She went to her and took the flask. She screwed it up and put it on the table. Charlotte clambered on to the bed and lay down with her face turned to the wall, weeping noisily. Sick at heart, Lucy covered her over and sat down beside her.

So this was it.

Charlotte fell asleep within a few moments, but Lucy sat there, numb.

When the gong sounded, she went down. The others had come in and were at the table.

'Charlotte's asleep,' she said with stiff pale lips to Geoffrey. He went on carving without concern; only Judith looked up anxiously at her aunt. Lucy got through lunch somehow, but when Geoffrey left the table she followed him to the morning-room.

'There's a fire in the nursery, I understand,' he said, intimating that her presence was not required.

But she closed the door and came towards him.

'Geoffrey,' she said. 'I'm afraid Charlotte is drinking too much.'

His reception of this was startling. He burst into loud laughter. 'Ha! Ha! Ha!' he laughed, throwing his head back and showing all his teeth. Lucy stared speechlessly. 'It's taken you all this time to discover that, has it? Where are your wits or your eyes? Your sister not only drinks, my dear Lucy, but is more or less permanently sozzled.'

Still speechless, Lucy's face hardened with anger.

'Your sister has been drinking for years,' said Geoffrey, narrowing his eyes at her and speaking with precision.

'You've known that, and still you've had all this stuff about?' Lucy pointed to the whisky standing as usual on his table.

Geoffrey shrugged his shoulders. 'Once women start to drink there's no doing anything with them. They're not like men. There's hope for a man who drinks, but never for a woman.'

'No, because a woman has given up hope before she starts to drink. It's the end before she begins. A woman doesn't drink for fun, like a man, she drinks in despair. When you found out that Charlotte was drinking you ought to have cleared every bottle of whisky out of the house and never allowed another in. You ought to have stopped drinking yourself.'

'Thank you,' said Geoffrey with a bow. 'Telling me what to

do now. The incorrigible reformer, as usual. It might interest
you to know that your beloved sister has already been brought
home drunk from the town. It's a miracle she didn't land in a
police-station. There was an envelope with her address on in
her pocket and a man who happened to know me brought her
home in a taxi. Nice situation for me, isn't it? She's completely
disgracing me. I'm seriously thinking of leaving the place. I
can't carry on where everybody knows I've got a dipsomaniac
for a wife. But drink is in your family. I should have been more
careful.'

'In my family?' blazed Lucy. 'Do I drink, does Vera, does
Jack?'

'Harry and Aubrey drank,' said Geoffrey.

'Who led them to it? Who drank with them? You were the
ruin of the boys and you've been the ruin of Charlotte,' said
Lucy now brilliant with anger. 'You've ruined her health
and her nerves. She was loyal until the last minute, until she
broke under the strain. She loved you with all her heart and
you knew it and you destroyed her. You've driven your son
out of the house and destroyed Charlotte and you'll destroy
Margaret too before you've finished. You're fatal. No one
could live near you.'

'Thank you very much,' said Geoffrey going to the door
and throwing it open. 'And now will you kindly leave my
house? Yes, at once. You can spend the night in a hotel or
where you damn well please. You're not staying here, nor are
you coming back again.' He strode to the bell and Burton
appeared with suspicious alacrity. 'Burton, pack Mrs Moore's
things. She's leaving at once.'

'I don't need your help, thank you,' said Lucy, passing her.

Shaken, she climbed the stairs. He'd won. What she had feared for so long had happened at last. She had lost her temper and he'd forbidden her the house. And she had only meant to ask him to let her take Charlotte home and try to nurse her back to health. Now she had cut herself off from Charlotte altogether, and Judith too. 'What a fool I was, what a fool,' she said bitterly. She had just played into his hands. He had done what he'd wanted to do for years.

She went into Charlotte's room and stood by the bed. But Charlotte was still sleeping heavily and Burton appeared at the door. 'The taxi will be here in half an hour, madam,' she said.

Lucy went into the nursery where Judith was getting her books ready for school the following day. The girl looked up and saw her aunt's white face and trembling lips. 'Oh, what is it? What's happened?' she cried, dropping her books and running to Lucy.

'Judith, I've quarrelled with your father at last. I always felt I should some day. I've to leave at once and he's forbidden me to come again.'

'Oh, he can't,' cried Judith, darting for the door. Lucy caught her back. 'It's no good, darling, we can't do anything against him yet. But I shall find some way of seeing you, never fear. He won't let you come to Underwood. Yes,' she said, seeing Judith's distress, 'that's the worst of it. I should have kept quiet and let him say what he liked, but I didn't and we have to pay. But the time will come when you can be with me

as much as you like, love, and we must think of that. Your father opens all the letters that come to the house I know, so I shan't write here. I shall write through Miss Porteous and have no scruple in doing it either. You must write and tell me what you want, and everything. Don't cry, darling. I shall think out something very soon.' She smoothed Judith's hair back. 'Finish your School Certificate and do well, because a lot depends on it. Miss Porteous and I have splendid plans for you. The future's all right, but the present will be hard. Just set your teeth and get through it.'

Judith pressed childishly close, her arms round her aunt's neck.

'Don't turn against your mother, will you, darling? It seems dreadful and even frightening to you, I know, but it's mostly been brought about by bad nerves and bad health and unhappiness. Help her as much as you can. Don't leave her alone when you're in the house. Try to interest her. And beg Margaret to send for a doctor. Margaret is the only one who can do anything with your father. I'm going to write to Auntie Vera. She'll come, I know. I'm not allowed here, but she can still get in. Now I must go and pack. Come and help me, and dry those tears. I'll be back before you know where you are,' said Lucy bracingly. 'I'll come and stay in the town and meet you coming out of school.'

'Oh, will you?' said Judith eagerly. 'I will,' said Lucy firmly. 'I've just thought of it. I'll come in a few weeks' time.'

It was monstrous that such a man as Geoffrey should have such power, Lucy kept saying to herself, but there was no appeal against it. In half an hour she was out of the house. She

went to the station, found there was a train at four o'clock, rang up Underwood to ask that she should be met and as she still had more than an hour to wait, she went again to see Miss Porteous.

CHAPTER NINETEEN

I

Lucy's letter lay on the hall-table of the house in Burnham Road. Vera, coming in with the cakes she had rushed to buy when Terry telephoned to say he would come for tea, bent over it, saw it was from her sister and left it where it was. She hadn't time to read it now.

'Here are the cakes, Beatrice.' She stood at the top of the three steps down to the kitchen and held out the cardboard box. 'But in future tell me in the morning when we have no cake. I can't rush out like this just before Mr Crawford arrives,' she said with displeasure, and went upstairs.

Beatrice flopped to her rubber kneeler again and went on scrubbing the floor. It was a bit too much of a good thing, she told herself. He came pretty well every day now. She had this floor to scrub, had to wash and change herself and take tea in at four. The mistress expected things to be done in the same style where there was only one pair of hands as where there had been three, and never thought of lifting a finger herself. 'I was soft to come,' thought Beatrice, slapping the tiles with the floorcloth.

Beatrice had been one of Vera's humble adorers. At the other house she had always wanted to wait on her, because when she smiled at you, Beatrice said, you felt you could do anything for her. But being prepared to do anything was different from having everything to do, and Beatrice was beginning to flag from sheer fatigue. But only privately. That very afternoon she'd given the girl next door what-for because the cheeky piece had dared to suggest that there was something not so nice about that car always being at the door.

'It's your nasty mind, Clarice,' said Beatrice over the backyard wall. 'It's the neighbourhood. You're all ignorant. Where we come from, nobody thinks twice about a gentleman visiting a lady . . . ' Still, she wished Mr Crawford would leave his car somewhere else. It drew attention, that car always standing outside.

'Looks no better for scrubbing,' she said, getting up with disgust from the floor. 'My goodness, I wonder what Cook and Denham'ud think to this kitchen.'

She went to empty her bucket and the girl next door was only just pegging out her tea-cloths. 'Haven't you done yet?' said Beatrice pityingly. 'I'm just going up to change me.'

'Well, you see I don't have to push,' said Clarice, cheeky as ever. 'We haven't got a gentleman calling.'

In her bedroom, Vera couldn't see well enough to do her face. The sun was shining outside, but the room was darkened by the trees in the road and Vera had darkened it still further by veiling the windows in triple ninon. She didn't like the view of Burnham Road, so she shut it out. The

sitting-room below was similarly shrouded. It was almost symbolic. Vera wanted to shut the world out and herself in, with Terry.

She switched on the lights, sat down at her dressing-table and with nervous, hurried fingers began to apply cream to her face. She needed plenty of time to do her face nowadays and today she hadn't got it. Because she had rushed out for cake. Why couldn't Beatrice *think*? All these petty annoyances, she thought furiously.

The truth was that Vera, the aloof beauty, had stepped down into the life of the ordinary housekeeping woman and didn't like it. She didn't like coping with meals, bills, mending, and the hundred lilliputian jobs that bind the average woman to her average day. Vera liked them so little that she refused mostly to do them, but they intruded themselves upon her notice all the same, and roused her to anger and disgust.

She wiped the cream from her face and leaned anxiously into the glass. 'You're beginning to go just here,' the masseuse had said last week, touching her jaw on each side of her chin. This doleful knell sounded again and again nowadays. 'You must remember,' said the doctor when she spoke of not being able to throw off a cold, 'that you're not as young as you were.' That anyone should say that to *me*, she thought in sad astonishment. She was feverishly impatient that Terry should love her now, soon, while she was still beautiful. Because, though the masseuse said the line of her chin was going, she didn't think anyone else would notice it yet, she said to herself, leaning into the glass.

Now for skin-tonic, now complexion milk, now rouge, eye-

shadow, powder, mascara, lipstick; her fingers moved swiftly and with skill. Her face was done.

Meanwhile Terry was ostentatiously leaving Holly Lodge. He did it by way of protest. The aunts were arriving as usual for tea, like tabbies coming to purr round the fire. His father-in-law had come to live with him too, since the summer. Brenda, who had not forgiven him for leaving them in Scotland, had not so much as consulted her husband. Old John Spencer's house was closed. He moved back into Holly Lodge with relief and all was as it had been before Terry came on the scene. He would leave 'em to it, Terry implied, striding out to his car.

The house in Burnham Road was an escape for him. He liked to go there. Nobody about, no fuss or convention; freedom to arrive when he liked, stay as long as he liked and leave when he wanted to. But for the last few visits he had approached the house with a mixture of excitement and apprehension. He didn't want to get out of his depth, he told himself. He didn't really want an affair. He didn't want to entangle himself. He was quite tangled up enough with his marriage. At the back of his mind, he wanted to feel that he could always clear off to South Africa if things at Holly Lodge got too intolerable. But Vera was a very beautiful woman, though a trifle older than he liked 'em. He couldn't go on playing with fire for ever without getting burnt. He felt a crisis was coming up. He felt he was asking for it, for instance, by going today.

'Hello, Terry,' said Vera, turning from the fire as he came into her sitting-room.

'By Jove, she's lovely,' he thought. 'I'm afraid I'm sunk.'

II

Far down the road Sarah, coming home from school, turned the corner. Her eyes went at once to the car and her pace slackened. A lanky, leggy figure, her hair untidy under her school hat, she dawdled along the railings, frequently coming to a stop altogether, her eyes on the car. Two or three doors away from home, she leaned against the wall, propping her back against her school-bag, her legs stiffly out in front of her, a look of sulky resentment on her face. A girl called Gwen, who went to the same dancing-class and lived in the road, paused in passing. She knew all about the car in the road, or fancied she did. 'D'you have to stop out till he's gone?' she asked with sympathy. But it was ill received. Sarah glared at her.

'No, I don't,' she said. 'And don't speak to me about it. You don't know me well enough.' A haughty expression on her pale, smudged face, she went in at her own gate and into the house.

Her mother did not like her to go into the sitting-room when he was there. She no longer thought of him as Uncle Terry, but always as 'he', the enemy. She went into the kitchen, threw her hat and coat on the dresser and slumped into Beatrice's chair. She sat in silence while Beatrice bustled backwards and forwards. 'I'm taking your tea into the dining-room,' said Beatrice.

'You don't need to,' said Sarah. 'I'll have it here.'

'Well, you can have a tray on the corner of my table then,' conceded Beatrice, feeling that thus the proprieties would be observed.

'No, take the things off and put them with yours,' directed Sarah.

She sat at the table with her back curved and her hair hanging forward. 'Oh, Miss Sarah,' said Beatrice, shocked. 'What dirty hands! They're worse nor mine when I've been doing the range. You ought to have washed them. You should see our Daphne. She's not as old as you and she never needs to be told anything. Keeps herself as clean as a new pin, Daff does.'

Sarah took no notice. She could not be made to do things by being told what other people did. She was not suggestible, except by people she loved or admired. 'Is there no jam?' she asked. And Beatrice had to get up to get it.

After tea, she threw herself again into Beatrice's chair. She didn't know what to do with herself. She wasn't going to do her homework, anyway. There would be another row at school tomorrow, but what did it matter?

Sarah had left her first small private school and gone to another, larger one, where she drifted along, giving the maximum amount of trouble and the minimum of satisfaction. An aura of disapproval was about poor Sarah. She was too unimpressionable. When youth is not impressed, it is very difficult to deal with. Sarah Sargent's home conditions were very unsatisfactory, the mistresses said to one another, as if that explained everything, their inability to manage her included.

It was the custom for a mistress called out of form to put the girls on their honour not to speak. But if Sarah was in a mood to talk, she talked. Swinging on her chair, she

made rude remarks about the others, knowing they would not answer back. 'You know you're on your honour,' said the prefect sternly at last. 'I'm not,' said Sarah. 'I didn't agree, did I?' The form groaned. She kept letting them down. It was almost impossible to win any inter-form prizes or competitions with Sarah Sargent on their side. She had no team spirit. She played a lone game, her hand against the rest. She scorned them, but they hurt her. She knew they talked about her mother. She knew they thought Burnham Road a dreadful place to live in. She was the only one who lived outside the radius of Overton Park and she felt it when they all turned in one direction and she alone turned in the other. They went off laughing and talking, easy with one another as she could never be. They were together not only in school but outside it, going to each other's houses to tea and helping each other with homework; they lived the same kind of life and she no longer did. One or two of the meek ones, outcasts themselves, would have made up to her, but she wouldn't have those. If no one else wanted them, she didn't.

At lessons she made no attempt to shine, but even her dancing was discredited. It was too much like the real thing. Proficiency in the ballroom was to be encouraged; it was a social asset. But the pupils of such a select school would never be called upon to dance as Sarah Sargent danced. She was never chosen to dance at the school concerts, where a well-bred amateurishness was all that was expected.

She sat on in the kitchen chair, idly watching Beatrice wash and put the tea-things away. 'Now,' said that busy young

woman, 'I must go and tidy your mother's bedroom or there'll be ruptions. Like to come and help me?'

'No,' said Sarah.

When Beatrice had gone, the kitchen was very quiet. The house was quiet. What were they doing, shut up in that room for such hours? He'd been there for hours already, she thought, and how many more would he stay? Probably till nearly eight o'clock. Why did they shut her out now, when they used to let her sit on the rug and listen and laugh with them? When they came to live in this house, she'd thought she was going to be with her mother all the time and now she was hardly ever with her, and it was all his fault.

Suddenly she got up and went out of the kitchen. She stood in the dark hall, listening. She could only hear murmurs of talk, punctuated by laughter; an intimate sound she couldn't bear. She flung the door open and walked in.

On the hearth, Vera and Terry started apart. A moment before Terry had, for the first time, kissed Vera and his arm was still round her. Vera, startled from rapture, turned to confront her daughter. Had Sarah seen? – That was her first horror-stricken reaction. Frozen, the two adults watched the child approach. Sullen, defiant, not looking at them, Sarah walked to an armchair and sat down. One dirty hand lay along the yellow brocade, she bit the nails of the other, glowering at the fire.

'Well,' said Vera, recovering herself. Sarah hadn't seen, she persuaded herself. 'What do you want?'

'Nothing,' said Sarah.

Terry laughed, rather too heartily. 'How are you getting on at school?' he asked.

'I'm not getting on,' said Sarah.

He laughed again, but she did not smile. She sat stubbornly. Just being there, thought Vera and was reminded of Brian. He used to impose himself like this when she didn't want him. Anger was rising in her now that the shock was passing. Sarah had ruined everything. Vera wished for the days when she could ring the bell for a nurse and have her taken away. But Sarah was older now and could make a nuisance of herself. How tiresome the young were! You were so apt to forget them, not to take them into account, but they were coming on all the time. Like new, seemingly tender growths pushing up the pavements. No sooner had you got everything laid down as you wanted it than up came the young!

'Don't bite your nails, Sarah,' she said coldly. 'And go and wash your hands and face and do your hair. You're not fit to be in here. Have you done your homework?'

'No,' said Sarah. Her mother never bothered about her homework. Why should she now?

'Then go and do it,' said Vera.

'I can't do it,' said Sarah.

'Bring it here and let me have a shot at it,' said Terry, wishing somehow to appease this small accusing person.

Sarah gave him a strange look from her long-lashed eyes, and levering herself up with her dirty hands on the arms of the chair, she got up and went slowly from the room.

When the door closed, Vera turned swiftly to Terry. 'What on earth made her come in just then? D'you think she saw?'

'Oh, no,' said Terry firmly. He didn't know whether she had seen or not, but it was easier to say no. Saved a lot of bother.

Vera was only too eager to be reassured. She didn't want to be disturbed by the thought of Sarah. She didn't want to think of her at all. This was the supreme moment of her life. She had never been so happy as now. She lifted her face and Terry kissed her again. The relief of being able to touch him, to kiss and be kissed at last, intoxicated her. She stretched her arms up and laughed. She was so radiant that Terry was swept into a depth of emotion he had not expected. He must actually love her, he thought, or he couldn't feel like this. And he was glad if he did, because otherwise everything got a bit sordid. After all, he said to himself, love *is* the only justification.

So he told her he loved her and happiness showed another dazzling facet. It was perfect now, and innocent in its relief and satisfaction. It was perfect to sit with her hand in his and to take him, when he had to go, to the sitting-room door with her arm in his, kiss him again and beg him to come tomorrow. It was perfect as it was, she told herself, and she didn't want any more than this.

When she had at last closed the front door after him and turned back into the hall, she saw Lucy's letter lying still unopened on the hall-table. She took it back into the sitting-room with her and read it, frowning at having to read it at all when her heart was still throbbing from Terry's last kiss. What on earth was it all about, she thought, rustling through the pages, reading here and there. Geoffrey had turned Lucy out

and forbidden her the house? But what nonsense. What had Lucy done? Ah – interfering or disapproving there as here. Vera knew how annoying that was. Charlotte drinking. But that was impossible. Charlotte? Never, thought Vera. That must be what had made Geoffrey so angry. Lucy was apt to think people drank too much if they had three or four cocktails before dinner. If only Lucy would leave her sisters alone, thought Vera with exasperation, accept them as they were and let them live their own lives. She wanted Vera to go to Charlotte at once. Well, that was impossible. She couldn't go. At any rate, she wasn't going. What on earth could she do if she went? She skimmed through the letter again. She would answer it in a day or two. In the meantime, it was not a letter that should be left about for Beatrice or Sarah to see. She tore it up and threw it into the fire. That gave her the illusion that she had dealt with the situation.

As she looked up from the flames licking over Lucy's writing, she saw in the white radiance of the lamp beside the mirror that she was as lovely tonight as she had ever been. Leaning on the mantelshelf she was lost in contemplation of the face he had kissed, seeing herself as he must have seen her.

CHAPTER TWENTY

It was May and in the world of nature everything was fresh, lovely and full of hope, but the world of man was reeling into catastrophe. Underwood was embowered in blossom, the church tower rose serene against the blue of the sky. The avenues were delicately veiled in new leaf, but in the papers there were pictures of Jews being hurried away with placards round their necks, of aged Jews scrubbing pavements while plump Gestapo looked on. The tide of public and private disaster seemed to be rising all the time. To Lucy, the thought of Charlotte recurred like a pain. When she was gardening the trowel would hang from her hand as her thoughts went to her sister. Waking in the morning she wondered for a moment what the cloud was that already hung over the day, and remembered Charlotte. In the night, she woke and prayed for her. Vera couldn't, or wouldn't go to Denborough, so Lucy said she must go herself. 'But you've only just come back,' objected William. 'And what can you do if you go?'

'I can at least see Judith and hear at first hand how Charlotte is,' said Lucy.

So she travelled again to Denborough and again on the familiar journey there was the contrast between the world of

nature and the world of man. Long stretches of fields and woods, exquisitely green, quiet rivers, ponds starred with white-flowered weed, lambs, rather fat now, but still gambolling, a patient mare standing over its foal having its afternoon nap on the grass, these alternated with towns like blots on the landscape, with serried rows of slate-roofed houses, with backyards where grey washing fluttered, with glimpses into dreadful back bedrooms when the train stopped. Man made such a mess of everything, thought Lucy. God must almost despair waiting for man to be as strong to do good as he was to do evil. Immense forces of evil were at work in the world, but the well-disposed, those who wished for good were passive. Everybody kept saying how awful all this persecution, childish cruelty and preparation for war was, but no one did anything about it. What could be done? people asked. The answer seemed to be, individually, nothing. That was her situation with regard to Charlotte. Public and private helplessness reigned, thought Lucy.

She went to Denborough and came away again having achieved precisely nothing as far as Charlotte was concerned, although she had the satisfaction of seeing that Judith was well and working hard and happily. She met her every day after school and since no one in the house in Queen's Walk occupied themselves with Judith, aunt and niece saw a good deal of each other. So long as Judith put in an appearance at meals, no questions were asked.

On the last morning of her stay Lucy felt that, Geoffrey or no Geoffrey, she could not leave without seeing Charlotte. She determined to walk straight into the house. He couldn't

kill her, she told herself. She took the bus to Queen's Walk and hurried along the road in the sunshine but suddenly, when she came into sight of the house, it occurred to her that if she went in, if Geoffrey or anyone saw her, he would question Judith. He would ask if she knew Lucy was in the city, if she had seen her. He would get it out of Judith that Lucy was in league with her headmistress and that would be the end of Judith's attendance at the school. Her education and career might be ruined; most certainly would. Horrified at the thought of the disaster she had almost precipitated, Lucy turned and hurried back the way she had come and in the afternoon she travelled back to Underwood, sad to leave Judith, who, for the first time for nine years, would not be coming for the summer holidays.

They were not, however, to be alone at Underwood. Vera rang up to ask if Sarah could come for a fortnight. 'She can come for the whole of the holiday,' said Lucy, who was sure Sarah needed a change from Burnham Road. But Vera said a fortnight would be quite enough. 'For you,' she said. 'She's very difficult, you know. She gets worse. I don't know what I'm going to do with her. Perhaps you'll do her good. Beatrice will take her holiday at the same time, so I shall close the house.' She didn't say what she was going to do herself. 'I'll bring Sarah,' she said. 'But I can only stay for one night.'

They arrived at the end of one hot afternoon, Vera irritable, Sarah sulky. Lucy noticed at once that Vera had done something to her hair. It didn't suit her, it was hard and bright and cheapened her lovely face. All the way home, Lucy carefully did not look at Vera's hair. She must have done it to keep

up with the young man, thought Lucy. Vera's brightened hair told her as plainly as possible that Vera was still in love with Terry Crawford.

'What's she done to her hair?' asked William cheerfully, when they were alone.

'Oh, don't, William,' begged Lucy. She couldn't bear it to be spoken of. William only saw the dye, he didn't understand the anxiety.

Upstairs, Vera was staring in horror at the hair in question. In Lucy's glass it suddenly looked like a wig. It was that stuff, she thought in a panic. They had sworn it would be all right and it wasn't. The light in Burnham Road was bad, she hadn't seen it in strong sunlight until now. 'I shall have to go to London first thing in the morning. I'll have to go to those people in South Molton Street and have it toned down before Terry comes up.'

But she groaned. She saw how it would be; she would always have to be slipping away to have her hair and face done. Fate had played a particularly malicious trick in making her, who had once been so confident and careless of her beauty, so anxious now. 'I shall have to leave first thing in the morning,' she said as Lucy came into the room.

'Very well, dear. Just go when you like,' said Lucy, wondering why Vera should speak with such bitterness and despair about catching the early train.

After breakfast next morning, Sarah disappeared. No one noticed until it was time for Vera to go, and then they couldn't find her. But she was not far away. She was sitting on the low wall on the other side of the church, kicking her heels against

the stone, deliberately spoiling her shoes. Occasionally she examined the scratches and gouges in the brown leather and continued to kick. Before her lay the Park, with the house dreaming far away, silent, beautiful. The little deer moved slowly, grazing. But Sarah's attention was not on what she could see; she strained her ears to hear what was going on in the house behind her. She heard the car brought round, she heard them calling for her. Her mother was going. Let her go. When she told Auntie Lucy she was going to Brittany with friends it wasn't true. She was going with him. Sarah had listened at the door at home. It was the only way she could find things out. She had to know what they were doing and what they were talking about, shut up for hours like that. Grown-up people should never tell lies; mothers should never tell lies, she thought sternly. Her mother kept letting her down. It was no good trusting her any more. Sometimes it seemed as if things were all right, but it didn't last long. It never would. There was something ugly going on, something she didn't understand about, but which made her feel sick. She felt sick a lot of the time now; not in her stomach, but in her head. Sort of sick, she said to herself. And she thought Beatrice felt sick about it too, though she didn't say anything.

She sat on the wall, kicking. She wore a red and white gingham frock with two red celluloid bows in her hair that she had bought when she was out with Beatrice once. Her mother had forbidden her to wear them, so she wore them today in defiance; and her mother had not noticed. The car doors banged, the engine started. Her mother was going. She had said she would take Sarah away, just the two of them together,

but she had left Sarah behind and was going away with him. Tears filled Sarah's eyes. Her heart swelled to have to let her mother go like this, to have to punish her. She had wanted to kiss her, but she couldn't. It was too bad, what her mother had done to her. She had done bad things too often. She listened to the diminishing sound of the car until she could hear it no more. Silence flowed back over the peaceful scene.

After some time, she dropped over the wall into the churchyard. No need to hide now. She wandered about among the crooked gravestones. They were very old, so old you couldn't read what was on them. She tried, crouching by one stone with scrolls and a cherub's head, tracing the obliterated inscription with her finger. Then she got up and went to look under the trees for a twig. She came back with one and began to gouge the moss out of the lettering.

Lucy paused at the landing window of the house to watch her. So that was where she was! Lucy wished, as she wished many a time a day, that Judith was at Underwood. Judith would have kept Sarah happy during her stay. Sarah needed the right sort of companionship of her own age, or near it. Lucy was diffident of her own ability to win Sarah's affection. She knew the child was deeply attached to her mother and as deeply disappointed in her. Well, she wasn't the first of Vera's victims, thought Lucy, but she was the saddest. She was the one Vera could damage most. Her heart yearned over the industrious little figure working at the gravestone with a twig, the celluloid bows flashing in her hair. 'I don't know what to do for her,' thought Lucy. 'I think I'd better just take everything as it comes, without fuss.'

Sarah had meant to be a nuisance on this visit. Her mother had pushed her on to Auntie Lucy. It was Judith who was the favourite in this house; they probably all wished Judith had come instead of her. Judith had just done frightfully well in her exams, too – Auntie Lucy was very proud of her. Sarah decided she wouldn't try to compete with Judith. On the contrary, she'd make herself so unpleasant that when Auntie Lucy was asked to have her another time, she would say no, and then her mother wouldn't know what to do with her.

Sarah had formed no opinion herself of her aunt; she took her mother's, which was confusing. Sometimes her mother said there was no one like Auntie Lucy, no one so kind or loving, no one who understood so well or minded so much what happened to you. Another time, her mother would say that Auntie Lucy didn't understand at all and that she was always interfering. She had heard her mother say to Uncle Terry that Auntie Lucy was narrow-minded and behind the times. About Uncle William, her mother's opinion had never changed: she had always said that he was an odd, rude, untidy man and she didn't know how Auntie Lucy put up with him. As for Janet, her mother said she was a bad-tempered, badly-trained maid who didn't know her place. She wouldn't have kept her five minutes, her mother said. With these second-hand opinions of the people in the house, Sarah came to stay.

When the church clock chimed tranquilly, Sarah looked up. Quarter to one. She supposed she'd have to go in and now she would get into trouble about not saying goodbye to her mother and about the backs of her shoes. She began to scowl as she went out of the churchyard. But Lucy made no

reference to her mother and managed to stifle an exclamation at the sight of the shoes.

But later when Sarah saw the trouble her aunt went to to restore them, taking hold of each small piece of leather with Uncle William's dissecting forceps and laying it back against the shoe, darkening each scratch with stain and rubbing polish in with her fingers, Sarah felt uncomfortable.

'I did that on purpose,' she said suddenly and waited for an explosion. None came.

'It's a pity,' said Lucy gravely. There was a silence.

'I won't do it again,' said Sarah.

Lucy smiled at her, and Sarah, with sudden relief and lightening of her spirits, smiled back. Released from watching the operation on the shoes, she rushed out of the house and began to dance on the lawn.

It soothed Sarah to watch her aunt sew; especially if it was something for her. She liked someone to be occupied with her. Lucy lengthened Sarah's frocks, let gathers out, did some very necessary repairs, and made a new dress from some flowered stuff she had bought for herself. Sarah was delighted and flashed about the lanes and fields in it.

'Do you like these red bow things I wear in my hair?' she asked Lucy suddenly one day.

'No,' said Lucy.

'I don't think I do either,' said Sarah, and snatching them out threw them into the kitchen fire by which she was standing to watch Lucy bake.

'Tch, tch,' said Janet disapprovingly. 'That's waste. They would have done for someone in the village.'

'Oh, no,' said Sarah. 'What's ugly for one to wear is ugly for another, isn't it, Auntie Lucy?'

'Yes, it is, really,' said Lucy. Janet cast an indignant glance and went out of the kitchen.

Lucy was having as much trouble with Janet about Sarah as she had had about Judith. But Janet had almost come to accept Judith, and she would accept Sarah too, in time, Lucy hoped, though Sarah made much more work for Janet than Judith had ever done. 'Never picks a thing up after herself,' complained Janet. 'Can't even put her shoes out to be cleaned.'

By asking Sarah to help her here and there in the house, Lucy tried to teach her to be tidy, but she didn't know whether or not she was succeeding. Sometimes Sarah flew about tidying everything; other times, she could hardly be got out of the chair she was lolling in, and as soon as she had done the minimum of work, she went back to loll again. Her looks matched her moods to an extraordinary degree, so that Lucy could not tell whether she looked tired because she was sulky, or sulky because she was tired. Her astonishing lashes shadowed her eyes, her mouth drooped, her very hair seemed to flag in these moods. She would sit on the wall or loll in a chair for half the day if Lucy would let her. But Lucy wouldn't. She asked her to collect the eggs, which Sarah liked to do, or to feed the hens, or to go with her to the village, or to play over some records on the gramophone. There was nothing like activity, or music, she found, to dispel Sarah's black moods. There were many ways of approach to Sarah, but a fortnight was so short and Vera wrote from France and

said that Beatrice would come for Sarah, arriving on one train and going home on the next. Would Lucy please take Sarah to the station? Lucy liked the look of Beatrice. A kind, reliable girl, she thought her, and much relieved, saw Sarah go away in her charge.

But before Sarah could come to Underwood at Easter – she had influenza in the Christmas holidays – Beatrice was gone.

Beatrice belonged to a family of girls ruled by a purposeful, strong-willed mother. Their home was in the country outside Trenton and Alice, the eldest sister, who was in service in Overton Park, carried tales about Beatrice's mistress. The mother, who had been in service, prided herself on knowing a place when she saw it, and came to investigate. One Wednesday afternoon, market day, she arrived unheralded in Burnham Road. Her lips tightened as soon as she saw the road. Going downhill fast, was her verdict. Her lips tightened still more when she saw the gentleman's car at the gate. The gentleman was shut up in the sitting-room with the mistress, she soon got out of Beatrice when she got inside. During all the time Beatrice's mother sat in strong disapproval in the kitchen, the mistress did not stir out of the sitting-room. And the kitchen was nothing but a hole, she pointed out. Dark, damp, unhealthy. There was a cross-looking untidy girl with no manners, wandering about like a lost dog, and Beatrice herself seemed to be in a proper muddle, with her hair coming down and safety-pins at the back of her apron. 'You'll get yourself another place, Trissy,' said her mother. Beatrice wept and said the place mightn't be much good, but she didn't

know what Sarah would do without her. 'No concern of yours,' said the mother firmly. 'You've to think of number one in this world, for nobody else will. Alice knows of a good place for you to go as housemaid. In a classy district with nice people. It's time you bettered yourself. Now give your notice today, and see that you get a week at home before you've to go out again. You can have a bit of a rest and I'll put your clothes to rights. You're letting yourself go. Like the place. Funny, you can always tell, soon as you put your foot in a house, what sort of a mistress it's got. Give your notice.'

And Beatrice had to.

It was a calamity for Sarah when Beatrice went. After a fashion, Beatrice had looked after her, had tea ready for her when she came in, made her change wet shoes and stockings, washed and ironed a school blouse overnight, kept her company in the kitchen and felt as she did about the one who spoilt everything, Terry Crawford. For Beatrice, Vera and Sarah still trailed the glory of their former days, but the girl who succeeded her knew nothing of these. Sarah hated this girl, who called herself Evverlin, from the beginning, and went no more into the kitchen. After Evverlin's arrival Sarah acquired a hauteur that was a childish copy of her mother's. She sat in her bedroom while 'he' was in the house and then went silently down to the sitting-room to read in the chair he had vacated.

Evverlin was not like Beatrice. She would never leave a place because it wasn't respectable. Let's all have a good time, was her motto. Her mistress could do as she liked so long as she didn't try to stop Evverlin doing as she liked,

and she surely wouldn't have the face to do that, was Evverlin's argument to Clarice over the wall.

Evverlin was sluttish in the mornings, with dirty stockings, and her hair in grips, but in the afternoon, with lipstick, rouge, mascara, a short black satin dress, minute apron and a frilled cap like a halo she rivalled any maid in a film. She never did any work in the afternoons but take tea in. The rest of the time was spent standing on the rainwater pump in the yard, talking to Clarice over the wall. This might have gone on longer than it did, if Vera from the open bathroom window above, had not overheard a conversation.

'I looked through the key-hole but I couldn't see anything,' Evverlin was saying. 'But I think I 'eard 'im come back last night about twelve. Not that I blame 'er. I could do with 'im myself. 'E's lovely. 'Ave you never seen him? 'E gave me such a look when I went in this afternoon. 'Course, she's years too old for him. Men like somebody young, don't they? She must be twenty years older than me. Twenty years! Think of that. Not that she 'asn't been beautiful,' conceded Evverlin. 'Granted. Sometimes when you go into that front room where the light's bad, she takes your breath away. 'Course, she tries very hard to keep it up. You should see the pots and bottles she's got for her face. Some lovely stuff. Suits my skin a treat. You must come in and try some one day when she's out. And next time you're going out with Jack, give me a call and I'll give you a splash of her scent. You'll have more than Jack after you!'

So Evverlin went and a girl called Daisy came in her place. But Daisy was apathetic and listless and had such a terrible

cough that after two or three months without improvement, Vera had her examined and was told that she was consumptive. So Daisy, in her turn, went and no suitable maid could be found to succeed her. Vera engaged a day-woman, a Mrs Parsons, a small woman, as grey as the dust and ashes she was so constantly cleaning up for other people.

Mrs Parsons, arriving with a rough apron in a paper-carrier, let herself into number twenty-six at seven-thirty in the morning. She put the kettle on to boil while she lit the kitchen fire.

When the kettle boiled, she took up Vera's early tea, slopping milk, tea and hot water over the tray as she stumbled up and down the steps laid about the landing to trap the unwary. She drew Vera's curtains with dirty hands, marvelled afresh at the luxury of the room, knocked fit to wake the dead on Sarah's door and went down again. Standing by the struggling fire, she sipped her own tea reflectively. Her cup emptied twice over, she went to stand at the foot of the stairs. If she couldn't hear Sarah, she went up to knock again, not from anxiety that Sarah should be in time for school but from a wish to get the breakfast out of the way. When she was sure Sarah was up, she set a corner of the dining-room table, put the kettle on again, and prepared Vera's tray. Vera had always had breakfast in bed and saw no reason to give up the habit now. There was far less to get up for nowadays than there had been at Southfield, she said to herself.

Mrs Parsons fried bacon and made more tea. Sarah, always at the last minute, dashed down the stairs and ate, putting on her shoes, usually uncleaned, and collecting her undone

homework as she swallowed. Then she rushed from the house, leaving Mrs Parsons to make a leisurely breakfast with bread fried with the bacon and sometimes an egg popped in, and more tea. She then took up Vera's tea and toast and came down to turn her attention to the sitting-room, another room that filled Mrs Parsons with awe and admiration. She was not allowed to do much in here but light the fire and vacuum the carpet, but somehow she managed to thumb round the walls very effectively. The mistress did this room herself later, wearing gloves. This room and her bedroom and what Mrs Parsons called 'a bit of dab washing', silk stockings and such, with a hurried visit to the nearest shops perhaps, took up the mistress's morning. Mrs Parsons herself 'went through' the house, but from dirty floorcloths, dirty dusters, dirty wash-leathers, the whole gradually became more dingy every day. Mrs Parsons cooked a meal for the two of them, the child stayed at school for hers, and while the mistress was resting, Mrs Parsons washed up, got the coal in, mended the fires and at three o'clock, went home.

Then Vera got up and began to get ready for Terry. She did her face, smoothing cream in, wiping it off again. One afternoon in early summer just as she had reached this stage, sitting at her table in a chintz house-gown, her hair bound up in white gauze, there was a ring at the front-door bell. 'Bother,' said Vera, her fingers pausing. There was no one to answer the bell but her. She sat at her table in indecision. She thought she wouldn't go down. It couldn't be anything special; it never was. She had discouraged callers very effectively and no one came now. The bell rang again. There is something

about a summons from door or telephone that few can resist. Vera took the gauze off, combed her hair up, zipped up her chintz gown and ran down the stairs. As she did so, the bell rang again. 'One moment, please,' said Vera in annoyance, opening the door, and there on the step outside stood Brenda Crawford and her father, old John Spencer. Beyond them in the road was their great car, with several dogs looking anxiously out of the windows behind the imperturbable chauffeur. 'My daughter would like to speak to you,' said old Spencer firmly, stepping into the house.

Vera had never been at such a loss in her life. They were the last people she wanted or had expected to see. And to be caught by them in this state of undress, no make-up on, her hair pinned up and a chintz house-gown on in the middle of the afternoon put her, she felt, at an acute disadvantage. That she, of all people, should find herself in this vulgar situation, galled her so much that she could not speak. She stood there awkwardly, the hot blood surging over her neck and face.

'In here?' said old Mr Spencer coldly, indicating the open sitting-room door with his stick.

They stood inside the room. Vera did not ask them to sit down; they might have refused. Brenda, a dumpy figure in brown, her chest under her chin, looked about her, then brought her large, liquid brown eyes to bear on Vera with hostility and contempt.

'I've come to make this situation quite clear,' she said. 'You'll never get Terry for a husband because I'll never divorce him.'

'Has he asked for a divorce?' said Vera, her heart leaping. Perhaps he had. Perhaps he wanted to marry her.

'No,' said Brenda sulkily. 'But it wouldn't be any good if he did, I wouldn't divorce him.'

'If he doesn't ask for a divorce then you won't have the pleasure of refusing him,' said Vera.

Brenda didn't seem to know what else to say. She looked at her father as if she expected him to take up the cudgels for her.

'You're doing my girl a great wrong, Vera,' he said heavily.

'I don't think so,' said Vera. 'I'm taking nothing from her that she had before. Everything was over between her and Terry long before he began to come here.'

Under the shadow of her brown felt hat Brenda flushed painfully. They must have talked about her, these two. Terry must have told her everything.

'You're doing her a wrong all the same,' said old John Spencer. 'You're making her talked about. Two good old Trenton names, Spencer and Sargent, dragged in the mud by two outsiders. It was a bad day for poor young Sargent when he met you, and a bad day for my girl when she met Crawford. Look what we've done for him! He was on his beam ends. We've given him everything. He could have had and done whatever he liked. But this is how he repays us. And what do you want with a young fellow like Terry? A woman of your age? You ought to be ashamed of yourself. And a daughter growing up with this going on. Why don't you think about her?'

'That's enough,' said Vera. 'You must go. I don't know what you came for.'

They didn't really know either. The situation was beyond them all; they couldn't deal with it. Vera opened the door and

the Spencers escaped with relief. The chauffeur got out of the car and a great yapping and barking of dogs proclaimed the re-entry of father and daughter into the Rolls-Royce. In a moment the street was empty.

Vera went back upstairs. The incident had been futile, even, she supposed, funny, but it had shaken her badly.

She sat down at her table and leaned into the glass to finish her face. The hand that held the lipstick trembled and her lips were white under the red she was trying to apply. What presumption, she kept saying to herself. What presumption of those two to come pushing into the house! What presumption to remind her of her duty to Sarah! What presumption of maids and neighbours to talk about her – her! But underneath, all the time, one part of her felt like some poor, small creature that couldn't bear the light of the day a rough hand had pulled it into. It cried, it struggled to be let go, to burrow deeper out of sight. Its behaviour humiliated her, it made her feel sick with shame.

She did her hair. It was a better colour this time, but she had seen Brenda staring at it and wondered painfully if she had noticed 'anything'.

To have to dye her hair at all, to have to wonder whether such a plain, dull, dumpy person as Brenda Spencer knew that she dyed it, stung her beyond bearing. 'Why do I put myself into such a situation?' she asked herself. 'All for him . . .' She seemed always to be outraging herself, to be doing what she most hated and despised nowadays. It was madness, she told herself, putting on her dress, nothing but madness.

He came into the house just as she was ready. He whistled for her and she went slowly down. She felt as if something slimy and furtive had got between them since the Spencers' visit. But when she kissed him, she knew it had not. She sighed with relief and happiness. In a world where nothing else had come up to her expectations, this alone had far exceeded them. She loved him; it didn't matter if he was someone else's husband, it didn't matter what faults he had, what other people thought or said, it didn't matter if she would have to suffer when he left her, nothing mattered but the fact that she loved him, and that she had him now. The familiar sense of well-being invaded her. She felt almost drowsy with happiness. When she was with him, nothing worried her. Madness it might be, but not for anything would she forego it. She could not even bring herself to disturb her happiness by telling him his wife·had been. 'Let's go and make tea,' she said, drawing his arm round her neck to go into the kitchen.

CHAPTER TWENTY-ONE

I

The night was so beautiful that William and Lucy were reluctant to go into the house and leave it. They strolled about the green, arm-in-arm, old Cora stalking with them. The great yellow August moon seemed to balance on the tips of the Rectory trees, the air smelled of hay and roses, it was deliciously cool after the hot day. Slowly making the circle of the green, they turned towards the house again and saw that a white patch had come to glimmer at the door; it was Janet's apron. 'D'you want me, Janet?' called Lucy.

'Oh, yes, I couldn't see you,' said Janet, hurrying to the gate. 'You're wanted on the telephone, 'm. A trunk-call from Denborough, they said.' Lucy's heart gave an uncomfortable leap as she ran. Denborough. There must be something wrong.

It was Margaret speaking. 'Oh, Auntie Lucy,' she sounded frightened. 'Will you please come? Mummy's very ill and Daddy says will you come and Auntie Vera too?'

'I'll come. First thing tomorrow, Margaret. What is it? Is it bad, darling?'

'Yes, it is. She's had a stroke, they say. She's not conscious – she just lies there.'

'Have you got a doctor?' asked Lucy.

'Oh, yes, and two nurses,' said Margaret.

So Charlotte had a doctor at last, but too late, thought Lucy bitterly. 'I'll come as soon as possible tomorrow, and I'll let Vera know. Goodbye till then, dear.'

'Goodbye,' said Margaret.

'Bad news?' said William beside her. 'She's dying, I can tell,' said Lucy turning her stricken face. 'She's had a stroke. I've never heard of anyone having a stroke at forty-two.'

'Come and sit down,' said William, putting his arm round her. Why did they ring up at this time of the night, he thought angrily. What could Lucy do? Morning would have been soon enough and she would at least have had some sleep.

'I shan't ring up Vera until morning,' said Lucy, who thought of her sister as swiftly as he had thought of his wife. 'I wish I was with Judith. She'll be frightened. I know how frightened I was when Mother died. I wish I could get there tonight, William.'

'Well, you can't,' said William firmly. 'You must go to bed and try to sleep. You'll have enough to face tomorrow. I'm going to get some hot milk for you from Janet. You go upstairs.'

Lucy went. She was vividly conscious of Charlotte, of Charlotte at all stages of her life, as a child, as a young girl, as she stood in the sitting-room at home with reddened eyelids the day Geoffrey proposed. She had been so young, trusting and child-like, and so loyal to Geoffrey, who had beaten her

spirit down through the years and brought her to this early death. She had brought herself to it, perhaps, but it was his fault. His fault, thought Lucy bitterly, throwing herself down by her bed in tears. Nothing could have saved Charlotte but faith in God. Weak herself, she could have found strength in God. Timidly, too timidly, Lucy had said this to her, but since Geoffrey didn't believe in God, Charlotte couldn't. 'Oh, God, help her now,' prayed Lucy. 'Be with her. Let her know that you love her. Receive her, help her, she's had such a bad deal . . . '

She heard William coming up the stairs and got up from her knees. She didn't want to worry him with her distress. She took the glass of milk from his hand and drank it quickly to be rid of it, unsuspecting that it contained two dissolved aspirin tablets that William had taken from the medicine cupboard. He meant her to sleep.

She did sleep and woke just before dawn. The curtains were drawn far back because of the heat, the windows were wide open, only the faintly-lit sky was visible. The room was like a ship riding into the harbour of the morning. Lucy lay still, borne forward into a day Charlotte would not see. She knew her sister was dead.

She got out of her bed and went to the windows. The land was dark, but the sky was growing lighter, it was colourless like water. It was very still, until a breath of wind came from far off, travelling audibly, tapping the leaves of the trees and bushes as it came. Lucy felt it on her face at the window. It passed and went on up the avenue, visible in the double ruffling of the trees on either hand. The birds were making a toneless

sound, as colourless as the light, a pattering like summer rain. Lucy stood quiet and aware.

There was no easy assumption to be made about death, or if there were she could not make it. All she could do was to pin her faith to what Jesus said. He was right in everything he said and did, intrinsically, undeniably right. For years she had held this firm conviction. He must be right about death. Death was not the end.

Charlotte had not cared what became of her, she had almost deliberately destroyed herself, or at least taken the easy way out, but if her sister could love and understand, how much more could God? Standing at the window, Lucy felt a quiet assurance that her anxiety need follow her sister no further. She knew she would feel, again and again, grief, fear, strangeness, all the natural reaction of a living being to the death of a beloved body, but she told herself that she must remember too the comfort of this moment, which would recur too, she must remember Jesus 'who also hath taught us . . . not to be sorry, as men without hope.'

The single note of a blackbird pierced the rustling under-tones of birdsong. He began to sing loud and clear in the garden below. A flood of gold began to pour through the water-light. Like a burst of trumpets the sun sent his splendid beams up before him in the east, and rose. Lucy turned from the window. The trial of the day had begun.

II

The telephone rang beside Vera's bed. She paid an extra rate to have this telephone in her bedroom. She had had one beside her bed at Southfield and had not been able to imagine a life where people would not ring her up incessantly. But in this house the telephone was mostly silent; hardly anyone rang up now.

She woke with a start, and putting out her hand to the receiver, looked at her clock. It was barely half-past seven. Was it Terry with some plan for the day? But it was a trunk-call, so it must be Lucy, going to ask her again to take Sarah to Underwood. She had already refused and was preparing to refuse again. 'Oh, Lucy,' she said half-crossly. 'What is it? I was asleep.' But listening, her face changed. Charlotte was ill. She was dying. It sounded as though Lucy thought she was already dead. Charlotte! Vera, the telephone to her ear, looked sharply round. She felt Charlotte had come into the room as she used to in the old days when they slept together. The tears rushed to her eyes.

But listening still, a guarded look came into her face. 'Have we to go?' she said. She didn't want to, she was afraid to go. 'Lucy, why should we go? What can we do? They'll want you no doubt, but what can I do? Besides, it's so difficult to leave Sarah,' she said, thrashing about for excuses. 'I do go away at times, certainly, but Mrs Parsons has to sleep in and she doesn't like it. She can't always manage it, either.'

'Don't go, if you'd rather not,' said Lucy. 'It would be very sad for you. Far better remember Charlotte as she was . . . '

But, suddenly moved by Lucy's willingness to spare her, and to shoulder the whole burden herself, Vera called out: 'I'll come, Lucy. I'll come. Wait a moment – here's Mrs Parsons with my tea. Mrs Parsons,' she said, turning her tear-streaked face, 'could you stay for two or three nights with Sarah? I have to go to my sister. She's very ill.'

'Well, I think I can manage to. Just to oblige. Yes, I think it'll be all right,' said Mrs Parsons.

'Thank you,' said Vera. 'Lucy, I'll take the twelve-o'clock train. I arrive about six o'clock, I think, don't I? Goodbye then . . . goodbye.'

III

It was very hot in the train; no one ought to have to travel in August. And it was frightfully expensive, thought Vera, who could not bring herself to travel anything but first-class. The morning impulse to share with Lucy had gone. She now felt she was being dragged from Trenton to Denborough against her will, made to witness something from which she recoiled with fear. She was glad to think that Lucy had been at the house for several hours. It made it much easier for her to arrive. She'd had to come away without seeing Terry, she thought resentfully. She hadn't been able to leave him a message. She rang up the colliery offices, but he wasn't there and she could not ring him up at his house. This worried her out of all proportion. She was restless, as if she had left part of herself behind. Throughout the journey she thought more of her lover than of her sister.

360

When she got out of the taxi and looked up at the house, she knew Charlotte was dead. Someone had pulled the blinds half-down here and there. Vera felt a strong instinct to protect herself from grief. She went into the house and was met by Lucy, white-faced and red-eyed. It was Lucy who clung to Vera, not Vera to Lucy. Vera stood stiffly in Lucy's embrace and said: 'I'm not going to see Charlotte, you know. I hate all the morbid things you're expected to do when anybody dies. I don't want to see Charlotte dead. I want to remember her alive.'

'Yes,' said Lucy, wiping her eyes again. 'Think of her as she was.'

She was even more anxious to protect Vera than Vera was to protect herself, she was glad that Vera should know nothing and feel as little as possible. She was glad Vera had not been there to hear what the nurse, the last to leave, had told Lucy. 'It was hopeless from the start,' the nurse said. 'She was unconscious when they brought her home and she never recovered consciousness.'

'Brought her home?' faltered Lucy.

'Oh, yes, they brought her home in the police ambulance, you know. She'd been picked up in the street and taken to the police-station. Oh, am I telling you something I oughtn't to?' said the woman, seeing Lucy's distress.

'No, no, tell me,' said Lucy.

'Poor lady, it wasn't her fault,' said the nurse compassionately. 'The doctor was very stern about the case. He said she ought to have had care and treatment long ago. Her heart was in a fearful state. Well, anybody could have told that

from the swelling of her legs. Her blood pressure was fearfully high. What was she doing wandering about the streets in that state? She ought to have been in bed months ago. But don't distress yourself, dear,' said the woman laying her hand on poor Lucy's arm. 'You couldn't have saved her. It had all gone on too long. It's my belief the poor lady felt so ill she took whatever she could get to help her along. Those drugs, you know, they were the very worst things she could have taken.'

'Did she take drugs too?' Lucy faltered.

'Drugs! My goodness, yes. She had a hypodermic. Didn't you know? Her arms are full of punctures. I've had hard work to hide them today.'

'Oh, it's dreadful,' cried Lucy, covering her face. 'Oh, Charlotte, Charlotte . . . ' She turned from the stranger and rushed away to weep for her sister alone. She didn't want Vera to know, or to be torn with pity as she was. She was very ready to help Vera to avoid the stark reality of death.

So Vera was able to remain dry-eyed and unwrung though Lucy was wan and exhausted.

'Where are we staying? Not here, I hope,' said Vera.

'Yes, we are. Now the nurses have gone, we're to stay here.'

'I'd far rather go to a hotel, Lucy. Can't we possibly?'

'I don't want to leave Judith,' said Lucy.

'This is no place for Judith,' said Vera firmly. 'It's the trappings of death that are so awful, Lucy. Children should have nothing to do with them.'

'Judith's not exactly a child. She's seventeen. But I agree that it would be better for her not to be here.'

'I wish she'd go and stay with Sarah,' said Vera, struck with

the idea. 'I'll ask Geoffrey if she can go tomorrow. I hated leaving Sarah with Mrs Parsons. Judith would do her all the good in the world, and it would do Judith good to get away too.'

She was brisk in her arrangements; Lucy was too tired and sad to think. 'Come upstairs and take off your things,' she said, leading the way.

Vera went up reluctantly, glancing at the closed door of the turret-room. She daren't tell her sister or anyone the horror she felt at having to sleep in this house tonight. 'Jack's coming tomorrow,' said Lucy.

'Oh, is he?' said Vera flatly. She felt a strange reluctance to meet her brother, whom she had not seen for so long.

Vera exclaimed in astonishment at the sight of Judith who came out of the nursery to greet her. 'I should never have known you. You've grown so.' She was amazed at the way these girls came on. For so many years they had been children, whom you could more or less ignore; but suddenly they appeared as equals, as supplanters. Suddenly you realised that as they waxed, you had waned, without noticing, until they brought it home to you. Vera took Judith back into the nursery, as if they must not speak on the landing in case it should disturb Charlotte.

'Judith's just been offered a scholarship,' said Lucy proudly. 'But don't say a word. She's got to put in a year somehow, but we can't fix anything yet, can we, darling?'

'That's excellent,' said Vera, who hardly knew what a scholarship was. 'But listen, Judith, I have a plan. I do hope you'll fall in with it. I've had to leave Sarah at home with an

old day-woman. I'd very much like you to go and stay with
her until I come home, and as much longer as you would like
to, of course. We'd like you to go tomorrow, wouldn't we,
Lucy? If I can get your father's permission, will you go?'

Judith looked enquiringly at Lucy. She didn't know
whether she wanted to go or not. She wanted to stay with Lucy,
but she also had a youthful instinct to get away from the house
where so many terrible things had happened within the last
few days. 'I should go, darling, if your father will let you,'
prompted Lucy. So Judith thanked Vera, and her face cleared
a little now that she had something different to think of.

'Where is Geoffrey?' asked Vera.

'He's shut up in the morning-room with Margaret.
I've only seen him for a moment.' Lucy had been on the point
of saying that he was more taken up with the disgrace of
Charlotte's being brought home from the police-station than
with the pity of her death. But she checked herself in time.

Geoffrey was terrified of the presence of death in the
house, Lucy knew. In the night, when the nurses had called
him, he dared not go. He had a prolonged shuddering fit and
Margaret had held brandy to his chattering teeth, while
Judith stood crying and shivering on the landing.

'I'll go down and see him,' said Vera.

Geoffrey, in his dressing-gown, had his chair, with Margaret
on the arm, drawn up to the open windows. He frowned when
the door opened, but his face cleared when he saw it was Vera.
'Ah, Vera,' he said, prepared to be amiable with her because
she wasn't Lucy. He got up and came towards her with outstretched hand, and both of them suffered the shock of those

who have not met for years. The once lovely girl, the once gay young man, met now as a woman of forty, 'with dyed hair, good Lord, and almost a double chin,' thought Geoffrey, and a middle-aged man as shrivelled and dry, thought Vera, as an old kid glove. They had diminished in physical beauty without adding to their spiritual stature and somehow they were ashamed of the change in themselves and in consequence more diffident with each other than they used to be.

While Geoffrey and Vera were greeting each other, Margaret stood by, looking deeply at her aunt. To think she had once thought her the most beautiful, the most enchanting person in the world, holding the keys to power and love! No doubt her aunt was a handsome woman still, but she wasn't what she had been, a *princesse lointaine*. With the vanishing of that princess a world had somehow vanished too. One doesn't often feel that at Margaret's age. It is a middle-aged discovery. Some music that had lingered in Margaret's ears for six years now died quite away. She didn't know why, she didn't reason it out, but it was gone.

She kissed her aunt without warmth. 'You could have done so much for me once,' she thought. 'But you didn't do it.'

'I shouldn't have known you, Margaret,' said Vera, as she had said to Judith. 'How old are you now?' When Margaret said twenty-two, Vera thought that she looked much older. She was very finished in appearance, but quite spoilt, Vera considered, by her expression. She compressed her lips just as Geoffrey did and above them her dark eyes were harassed. She looked as if she had all the cares of the world on her shoulders.

'Come and sit here, Vera,' said Geoffrey, drawing a chair round to the windows. He sat down in his own and Margaret perched on the arm again.

'Dreadful affair this, isn't it?' said Geoffrey, passing a narrow hand over his eyes. 'I've had such an awful day. People coming and going all the time. The doctor about the death certificate. How old was Charlotte? I said forty-three. Forty-two, was she? And then the nurses to get off, with all their talk. And then the undertaker. Asking me questions about the coffin and the number of cars and everything. And the grave,' Geoffrey's voice rose in outraged horror. 'Asking me if I wanted to go in it later. Asking how many I wanted room for. Have you ever heard of anything so ghastly? And yet it's funny, isn't it?' He laughed grimly and then shuddered. 'I'm not going to be put in the ground. Cremation for me. Remember that, Margaret.'

Margaret put an arm round his shoulders.

'I don't know what I should have done,' said Geoffrey, very sorry for himself, 'if it hadn't been for Patterson, my second-in-command. He's seen to everything. And Margaret,' he took her hand and smiled up at her, 'she's been splendid, as usual. I've never had much of a home life, with apologies to the dead and all that, but I've had one pearl of great price, my daughter. Bless you, pet,' he said, giving her hand a squeeze and releasing it.

Vera's old dislike of Geoffrey was beginning to revive. She thought she had better make her request and leave him as soon as possible, or she might spoil everything. But Geoffrey gave her no chance at the moment. He was glad of her

company. The more people, the more of life there was in this house the less there seemed of death.

'Of course, this affair has absolutely cooked my goose here,' he said. 'Taken to the police-station for drunk. Brought home in the police ambulance. It's been in all the papers, you know. I don't know what sort of a letter I can write to the firm. They're sure to have heard of it. As a matter of fact they take press-cuttings of all their employees. Nice for me, isn't it?'

Vera didn't know what he was talking about. She didn't want to know. She let him talk.

'I can't afford to stay in a place where there's been a scandal. I'll have to put in for somewhere else and it's a shame. I've been very comfortable here and worked up a splendid connection. Anyway, the firm's grateful, I know. They once asked me to go on a mission to Canada. The offer may still be open. If so, I may take it.' It might be a good idea to go to Canada for another reason. Stephen must be twenty now. He might be thinking of coming home. It would be as well not to be there. Not that the young fool would do anything, but he didn't mean to let him try.

'Geoffrey,' said Vera, snatching at the first pause in the conversation. 'Don't you think it would be a good idea to get Judith out of the house? She's so young to face all this.'

Geoffrey looked at her, his amiability fading. So this was her game, was it? Making herself agreeable only to get permission for Lucy to take Judith to Underwood.

'I wondered if you'd let her go to Trenton to keep Sarah

company for a while – at least until I go back? It would do Judith good and help me out of a difficulty with Sarah.'

Geoffrey's face cleared again. Again he was ready to do something simply because it wasn't for Lucy, or what Lucy would like. 'Certainly,' he said. 'Send her off tomorrow. As a matter of fact, it would be a convenience to me to have her out of the way. Margaret and I must have a change after this packet, and so must the maids. I shall close the house, so you can keep Judith until you hear from me, if you like. It's not as if she has to hurry back to school. I took the precaution of giving her notice at half-term. I don't know what to do with her. But I'm not going to bother about that now. I've too much to worry me as it is,' he finished petulantly.

Burton came in to put up a small table in readiness for the dinner he had said he and Margaret would have in this room. 'Don't put that up, Burton,' he said. 'I'll dine in the other room after all.' He felt better for talking to Vera. She was, at any rate, a change, and she didn't look at him as if he'd murdered Charlotte, as her sister did. There would be more company in the dining-room and that was what he wanted, a lot of people moving about and distracting his attention.

Vera seized her opportunity. 'I'll see you at dinner then,' she said and left him. She went up to the nursery to tell Judith she was to go, and could stay, evidently, quite a long time. 'So pack all you need,' she said. Lucy's face fell. 'You can have her later, Lucy, but do let her stay with Sarah for a while. Sarah needs company.'

'But I'd willingly have them both,' said Lucy.

'I don't think Geoffrey would let Judith go to you in the

mood he's in at present,' said Vera, and Lucy sighed. He wouldn't, she knew.

After dinner, Lucy went up with Judith to help her pack. They found comfort in being together. They packed and talked and once, Judith, kneeling by her aunt on the floor before her trunk, pressed her face against Lucy's shoulder for a moment. Lucy nearly wept again. She loved this child, but she wasn't allowed to take her home and make a secure place for her and send her forward into life. Judith was still to be tossed about, not really wanted at home, not allowed to stay permanently anywhere else.

Lucy was uneasy, too. She didn't want Judith to go to Trenton and come upon Vera's affair with Terry Crawford. This might not have gone far, it might be over. She didn't know, but she ought to find out. The young are fierce idealists, but their idealism is so tender, it turns to cynicism at the first breath of disillusion. Knowledge of the world of men and women had to come, Lucy admitted, but she shrank from the thought that it should come to Judith through Vera. Judith had seen too much ugliness. She should be protected from more, at least for the present. Lucy decided, nervously, that she must, somehow, say something to Vera.

Was that Vera coming upstairs now, she wondered, thinking she heard the rustle of a dress? But Vera did not appear and they went on with the packing.

'Stay with me till I'm in bed,' begged Judith, and Lucy stayed, putting off the inevitable moment when she must abandon her to the night. She used to feel this reluctance when Judith was a child, she remembered, but tonight she was

more unwilling than ever before to leave her to the lonely fears that follow youth's first experience of death. But at last, she kissed her good night and went.

Crossing the landing she saw that the door of the turret-room was slightly open and with the realisation coming fully home to her again that Charlotte was really dead, she went in to look at her once more while she could, and there was Vera kneeling by the bed, her sister's dead hand in hers. Lucy went to her, but she couldn't speak. They knelt side by side, weeping.

'Come away, darling,' said Lucy at last. She didn't know how long Vera had been there. She thought it must have been ever since she heard that rustle on the stairs. 'Come along, Vera. We've no need to cry for her. Whatever she's suffered, it's over now. Let's leave her to God.'

She took Vera out of the room and into their own, but Vera threw herself down by the bed, her face still in her hands. She was suffering not only from the shock of seeing the change illness and death had made in Charlotte, but from the sense of guilt the dead bring home to the living, the consciousness of things left undone, of chances wasted. Lucy sat on the bed beside her, and Vera knelt there. When she stopped crying, she kept her face turned away. She spoke now and again, condemning herself.

'I never did anything for her. You told me and I knew I ought to, but I never did anything.'

'Neither did I,' Lucy told her. 'I didn't know what to do. She wouldn't let me do anything.'

But Vera would not spare herself or Lucy's feelings either.

'I was closer to her than you were. I knew better how to get at her and I never tried.

'I never do anything for anybody,' she said in a moment. 'Geoffrey's destroyed Charlotte just as much as if he'd killed her with a knife, and I hate him. But I'm not much better myself. Look what I did to Brian. I could have made him happy and I made him wretched. But I didn't love him, so I couldn't be bothered. Well, perhaps he's happy with Miss Evans. It was a good thing he got away from me. But I've lost Meriel. And I don't do anything for Sarah.

'But I will,' she said, turning her swollen eyes to Lucy. 'I'll be different before it's too late.'

Lucy's face was as wan as her own, but it seemed to Vera that something shone behind it. 'What makes you so comforting?' she asked, putting her head against Lucy's knee.

'I only wish I was comforting,' said Lucy. 'I don't feel *without* comfort, but I don't seem to be able to pass it on. Death is as much a mystery to me as it is to you and everybody else. It frightens me, just as it frightens you. I haven't got to the stage when I'm not frightened to die, but I hope I shall have when the time comes. I hope I'll be able to commit myself to God and go out with confidence. Jesus came out on the other side of death . . . '

'Oh, Lucy, do you really believe it?'

'I do,' said Lucy. 'The people with him believed it. You read the Gospels. They believed it all right. They were changed creatures because they believed it. They seemed to be poor timid followers before that, but afterwards they could face persecution and death rather than falter. Of course I believe it.'

'Why don't other people then? It always seems as if no one with intelligence believes it.'

'Oh, darling, how can you say such a thing? Although I used almost to think the same myself,' confessed Lucy naïvely. 'Yes, I remember thinking like that too in my youth. As if all the accumulated human intelligence had done any more than scratch the surface of knowledge! Every day reveals a little more. Think of all there must be to know! Oh – it all goes so slowly and I'm in a fever, sometimes, to find out – especially about God. I'm so *interested*,' she said.

'Yes, you are, aren't you?' said Vera wonderingly. 'But I haven't been so happy in my life,' she said in a moment, 'that I want to go on with it. I mean I don't think I want to believe in eternity.'

'That won't make any difference to eternity,' said Lucy.

Vera looked startled. She didn't like the idea of having to go on whether she wanted to or not.

'So you think it matters what we do while we're here?' she said.

'I do,' said Lucy. 'It matters to ourselves, of course, but it matters terribly to other people. Moral failure or spiritual failure or whatever you call it, makes such a vicious circle. Look at poor Charlotte. She loved Geoffrey and he failed her. It seems as if when we love people and they fall short, we retaliate by falling shorter ourselves. Children are like that. Adults have a fearful responsibility. When they fail to live up to what children expect of them, the children give up themselves. So each generation keeps failing the next.'

Humble, sad, Vera sat on the floor her head against Lucy's

knee. That night, death had illuminated life and in the relentless light, she saw what a poor thing she had made of her own. As long as she could remember, she had been absolutely selfish, she told herself, and she wanted to be different. The stumbling-block was Terry. Their association might not be doing them much harm, though it was doing them no good, but it was certainly harming Sarah. It was no good thinking she had a right to live her own life, she hadn't; any more than anyone else had. She knew it in this stern moment. She must give Terry up, and facing the truth as she had never faced it before, she knew he wouldn't really mind. Selfish in this as in everything else it was she, she told herself, who wanted to keep him. Well, hers would be the pain of giving him up and she must face it.

Lucy, silent, her hand on her sister's, knew what was going on in Vera's heart and waited for the outcome. She knew, she had always known, that Vera could never be happy until she tried to live up to her own standards. She couldn't go on repressing the best in herself without being unhappy. The disgust Vera felt for life and other people was largely self-disgust and until she allowed herself to aspire, as she secretly wanted to, to goodness and truth, she would never be rid of it.

Raising her head, Vera smiled at her sister as if her mind was made up. Cramped and exhausted, she got up from the floor.

CHAPTER TWENTY-TWO

I

Judith, in the train, kept trying not to be relieved to get away from home. Relief was not what she ought to feel. She ought to be stricken with grief like her aunts. But her mother had been something to them that Judith had not known or could not remember. Lucy said that her mother had not been herself for years, but though Judith tried to picture her, she could only see the strange, remote person you could never get near to, or get any response from. She was oppressed with sadness that her mother should have been like that, but she could not help being relieved that it was over. They had known at school. They were sorry about it, she knew. No one was jealous because she had been taken so much notice of by the Head; they allowed it to her because her mother drank, they whispered, and her father didn't care much about her or something. They had all been very kind, but Judith would rather there had been no necessity for kindness. Except from Miss Porteous; to her she was unreservedly grateful. Dear Porty, she thought affectionately. I wonder if I shall ever go back. She hoped so, thinking of the sixth-form room with

flowers on the broad window-sills, the pleasant atmosphere – the atmosphere that suited her so well – of books and friendly competition. Judith liked to do well. She liked to get to the top and stay there, holding her own against all comers. She'd had a lot of fun and excitement at school, she thought, and she hoped even if it meant living at home again, that she could go back when she came away from Auntie Vera's. She hadn't dared to ask her father what was going to happen to her. It was always safer not to. This morning he had surprised her by telling her that he was making over her mother's allowance to her. Margaret didn't need it, he said, so she could have it. 'So see that you don't put your aunt to any expense,' he had said. 'And don't make a nuisance of yourself,' he added, as if she had never done anything else since she was born. Judith though grateful and astonished to be provided with some money, had a feeling nevertheless that he was wiping his hands of her altogether. Not that she minded, she said to herself, but she wondered what it meant exactly. Perhaps Auntie Vera would be able to throw some light on it later.

How awful, she thought, Vera had looked that morning. As if she had cried all the night through. Judith was secretly astonished. She hadn't known her aunt loved her mother so much. They hadn't seen anything of each other for years. But there was something strange and deep about being sisters, Judith reflected. Take herself and Margaret this morning. They had lived in the same house together all their lives, they had grown farther apart with every year, they were as unlike each other as possible. Margaret was so irritable that Judith, wrapped up in her books, had almost given up speaking to

her lately. But when the time came to part, they felt an almost painful tenderness for each other. Margaret had insisted on giving Judith the navy blue dress she wore at this moment. It was one of her best. The navy blue cap, the silk stockings too, and the leather case Judith held carefully on her knee had been Margaret's. Judith was overwhelmed. They had clung together at the last moment almost as if, Judith thought, she were going away for ever. She did not know, as Margaret knew, that she probably was.

Sitting in the train, Judith took a surreptitious look down at her dress and silk stockings. She had never felt so elegant and grown-up in her life and could not suppress a secret satisfaction, although she thought she ought not to be thinking of such things today.

Grown-up she might feel but she looked very young and appealing with her eyes wide open on the world from which, in spite of experience, she still expected nothing but good. Her expectation had, on the journey at any rate, been justified, for strangers smiled at her, people made room for her to sit beside them, men lifted her things from the rack, raised their hats and plunged away, lest, if they lingered, they should be suspected of making advances to this young and innocent creature. Nevertheless, when she walked about the platform they looked at her over the tops of their newspapers. On the journey to Trenton, she had three changes to make, with long waits, and so had plenty of opportunity to attract the attention of fellow-travellers. She didn't attach any importance to it; she only thought that people were kind, as, anywhere but at home, they mostly seemed to be.

They must be getting near Trenton now, she thought. She hoped her trunk would prove to be in the luggage-van. It had successfully made the three changes with her and she had seen it safely into the van at the third, but that did not mean that she would see it safely out again. She must look out for Sarah on the platform. She had heard Vera tell Sarah to meet her when she telephoned to Trenton that morning. It was three years since she had seen her cousin and she wondered if she had changed much. 'People do change a good deal between twelve and fifteen,' she thought maturely, little realising how much she had changed herself.

The train was running through the flat marshy country lying about the city of Trenton. There was the river, thought Judith, looking out. She hadn't been to Trenton since she was twelve and now she was seventeen and a great deal had happened in between. Uncle Brian and Meriel had gone to America and never come back. Stephen had run away from home. Her mother was dead. Auntie Vera had left her big house and was somehow not so important as she used to be. Judith couldn't think why, but somehow the spell was broken. Only Auntie Lucy remained the same. 'Dear, dear Auntie Lucy. I do hope I can go to Underwood soon,' thought Judith.

The train was coming into the station now. Judith stood up, and a young man got ready to open the door for her. She thanked him with a smile and without noticing his gratified blush. She got out of the train and caught at a passing porter. First her trunk and then her cousin. She identified the former with relief and looked about for the latter. Far down the platform a forlorn figure in an old school blazer, a panama hat

on the back of her head, stood watching the people go by. Judith saw at once and even from a distance that Sarah had changed a good deal. This was not the self-confident, arrogant child who might begin to dance at any moment. This was an untidy, over-grown, unhappy-looking girl, who stooped as she stood, her hair parted on the back of her neck and hanging limply forward over each shoulder. Judith felt a quick sympathy about that hair; hers used to do the same.

'Hello, Sarah,' she said coming up from behind and taking her cousin by the arm.

Sarah turned an astonished face and looked at her for a moment, taking her in. 'Why, you're grown up,' she said indignantly.

'I can't help that,' said Judith laughing. 'D'you mean I'm not welcome? I've always been two years older than you, you know. We can't change that now.'

II

Judith wasn't so grown up after all, Sarah found, or if she was, it hadn't changed her. The old sense of companionship at once began to come back. Sarah had shut herself up into a stubborn misery, sure that there was nobody she cared about, and nobody who cared about her. But there was; there was Judith. She couldn't think how it was she had forgotten that there was Judith. Now it was as if something precious had been restored to her, something that altered everything. Life began to flow in Sarah, and in the house as well.

The house had hitherto dominated, dark, brooding, silent, with her mother shut into the sitting-room with him, and Mrs Parsons creeping about with her dusters. But now the house was negligible, it was nothing but a place to rush about in, a background for two young figures flashing up and down the stairs and through the rooms. Sarah moved down into the second bed in Judith's room and loneliness was over. By the second day of Judith's stay, Sarah looked a different person, with her hair washed and tied up with one of Judith's ribbons, like Madame Vigée-Lebrun's in the portrait painted by herself. 'To be so pretty and paint so well, wasn't it marvellous?' Judith demanded.

Laughter rang on the stairs and in the garden and people looked through the hedge in surprise, wondering what was happening in the mystery house, and where the car was that used to stand outside.

Vera rang up from Underwood to ask if they were all right and Sarah assured her with enthusiasm that they were. 'Can Judith manage?' asked Vera. 'She's simply splendid at managing. She can cook too. Much better than you can, Mummy,' said Sarah with brutal candour.

In that case, Vera said, she would stay another day or two at Underwood. Vera was still shaken. She could not forget how her sister had looked in death. The impact of solemn death had been too much for her unready soul. She felt she must stay with Lucy; she wasn't ready to move away from this comfort yet. So she said, over the telephone, that if the girls were all right, she would stay a little longer, and Sarah agreed with unflattering pleasure, put the telephone down

and rushed to tell Judith that they were to have the house to themselves for another few days.

It was an adventure to them both to have a house to themselves; for Sarah to have no Terry Crawford calling, for Judith to have no father to be everlastingly aware of. Sarah had imperiously sent Mrs Parsons home at her usual time. 'There's no need for you to sleep here now my cousin has come,' she said, and Mrs Parsons said that suited her all right.

'No bed like me own,' she said, and Judith, looking at the dirty little woman, said afterwards that there probably wasn't, and they giggled.

Keeping house was a game. It was all fun; going out with a basket to buy whatever they liked, cooking all sorts of things, some successful, some not, going to bed when they chose, talking late into the night, sleeping together at last, Judith's smooth fair head on one pillow, Sarah's ruffled dark one on the other.

Sarah told Judith about school, which she hated, about the dancing-class in which she took no interest now, because Madame Fouquet was too old to teach and Élise, her daughter, couldn't dance for nuts, said Sarah with scorn. 'I need to go somewhere else now,' she said. 'But there isn't anywhere here, so I suppose I'll just give it up.' She told Judith a good deal, but she never spoke of her mother or Terry Crawford. She seemed candid enough, but she never disclosed the secret shame and fear she felt. With Judith there, it was almost buried. She almost forgot it, she kept noticing. But sometimes when she woke in the night and heard Judith's quiet breathing in the bed next to hers, she wished her mother need never

come home so that he would never come again. She wished she could be left to go on with Judith, just like this.

The weather was hot. In the Burnham Road, the leaves lay curled, brown and brittle under the trees. 'Like brandy-snaps,' said Judith, picking one up to fribble it to dust between her fingers. 'Let's go and look at Southfield,' she said, emerging with Sarah from the house in the afternoon. They had come out to buy bread, but the idea of going to look at Southfield struck her suddenly.

'Yes, let's,' said Sarah. 'I've never been back since we left.' So they went along the uneven pavements in their shady hats and summer frocks, with the basket to carry the bread in when they got it, and the key to let themselves into the house with, because Mrs Parsons would be gone when they returned. 'Phew, isn't it hot?' said Sarah.

They looked up at the sky, leaden between the trees. 'I think there'll be a thunder-storm later,' said Judith.

They came to Lawn Cottage and looked over the gate. Judith remembered the old lady with puffed white hair coming down the drive that Sunday morning when Sarah got into trouble. They walked on and here were the great walls again, like ramparts. Here was the Watsons' house perched on its terraces. 'What became of that boy – was his name John?'

'They went to live in Overton Park and I never saw him again,' said Sarah. 'I think he must have been keen on Margaret, because he used to stop me in the road and ask if she was coming to stay again. But she never came, did she?'

'No, she never came again,' said Judith. 'I have some kind of idea myself that she was keen on him. I didn't know at the time, but looking back, I feel there was something.'

They sauntered on, unconscious of the missed chance of happiness the incident had contained.

Here in the wall now was the garden-door with 'Southfield' painted on it in white letters. Judith laid her hand on the wood, hot from the sun. 'Isn't it queer that we used to go in and out of here and now we don't any more? Isn't it queer how the scenes keep shifting behind us?' she said.

Sarah put her thumb to the latch and opened the door. The girls peered upwards at the face of the house showing through the trees and bushes of the steep garden. 'Other people have no right to live here,' said Sarah, resentfully.

'I wish we could see ourselves as we were then,' said Judith. 'You and I and Meriel would be coming down these steps with Uncle Brian on our way to your grandmother's that Sunday morning. And Margaret would be standing at the window with John Watson, waving her hand. Auntie Vera would be looking lovely and the drawing-room would be full of pale yellow flowers and there'd be pale yellow champagne in the glasses. And it's all gone,' she finished.

She was amazed at the changes in all those lives since that morning, and she saw, all at once, that it was Vera who had brought the changes about. As if she had been the keystone, when she fell out, too careless to keep her place, the rest was loosened and fell away too. Everything had depended upon Vera. Judith felt as if she had taken this walk and reached this house to make this discovery. It was one of those flashes that

illuminate past stretches of the years behind. Closing the door, the girls turned away.

On the way back, it was hotter than ever. The sky was indigo over the Burnham Road. Sudden, short gusts of hot wind stirred up little snakes of dust on the pavement; they writhed briefly and disappeared. 'The storm's coming now,' said Judith. 'And, oh, Sarah, we haven't been for the bread.'

'Give me the basket,' said Sarah, who was very obliging these days. 'I'll run for it. You've got your best hat on. You go on to the house and put the kettle on for tea.'

'Right you are,' said Judith, speeding off. 'But be sure to shelter if you get caught.'

'Yes, I will,' called Sarah, running lightly down the side-street.

As she reached the house, Judith heard the first low rumble of thunder. It was almost dark. She liked it; it was full of drama. She left the door open so that Sarah could dash in from the rain which was now beginning to fall in large slow drops. She went through to the kitchen and put the kettle on the stove. As she went up to take off her hat, lightning flashed over the stairs, thunder shook the house and rain fell in a solid weight of water from the swollen skies. Judith rushed from room to room closing the windows. Curtains streamed inwards to wrap round her, water-drops splashed on her face and arms as she reached for the window-sashes. She was wholly taken up with the business of getting the windows shut. From Vera's bedroom, she pelted down the stairs to do the sitting-room. She rushed into the room and came to a dead halt.

'It's all right. I've closed these,' said a man's voice. All she could see of the speaker was his dark figure against the lurid light at the windows. She was very startled.

'Who are you? How did you get in?' she asked and turning swiftly, switched on the lights. Then she smiled. 'Oh, I know you now,' she said. 'But you gave me a bad fright.'

Who could she be, thought Terry Crawford, so young, fair and totally unexpected? 'You may know me,' he said, with his attractive smile. 'But I don't know you. Unfortunately.'

'I'm Judith,' she said, the colour running up into her clear cheek in the way she deplored. 'Judith Leigh. But perhaps you don't remember . . . '

'You're Judith!' he cried, striding towards her to take her hands. 'Little Judith grown-up – or almost. Well, Judith,' he kept saying her name in delighted astonishment. 'I've thought of you many a time. You were the nicest little girl I ever met. And you haven't changed either. Here, let's turn the lights off. The sky's clearing. Where's Vera? Isn't she home yet? Oh, I say,' he said, remembering what Mrs Parsons had told him when he called. 'Wasn't your mother ill? How is she?'

'She's dead,' said Judith, raising her eyes to him like a child.

'I'm sorry,' said Terry. He took her hand and stood looking down at her, marvelling at her dazzling youth. 'Look, let's sit down and talk. So Vera isn't back then?'

'No, she's coming back tomorrow,' said Judith, letting him lead her to the sofa, where they sat down side by side.

'How long are you staying?'

'Quite a fortnight,' said Judith.

'Oh, good,' said Terry. 'Any hope of tennis?'

'Oh, rather. I've brought my racket. I'd love to play.'

'Right you are. I'll take you on. You must come to my house and we'll have some singles. My wife and her father have just gone to Scotland, but you won't mind that, will you? Is there anything else you like to do? D'you like to go swimming?'

'I love it.'

'This is going to be fun,' said Terry. 'We'll go to the farm and swim in the lake. It's a bit cold and weedy, but it's the best bathing there is in this god-forsaken place.'

Judith wondered briefly why he spoke as if he hated it.

The sun was shining now. The rain abruptly ceased. Water ran merrily in the gutters, the trees dripped, diamond drops twinkled in the privet hedges, there was the delicious smell of gardens after rain. Sarah, leaving the shelter of the baker's shop, sped up the street in a series of the lightest possible leaps. Now for tea with Judith. 'I hed to sheltah because of my het,' she was rehearsing to say. They had been in the middle of being extremely genteel and she would go on where they had left off.

But when she turned the corner, she saw the car. She stood in the road, staring at it.

She went slowly to the house and round to the back-door so that she should not pass the sitting-room window. In the kitchen the kettle had boiled all over the floor. She turned off the gas, but did not mop up the water. 'Let Judith do it, it's her fault,' she thought sullenly, and threw herself into the chair to wait. Waiting again for the same person to go.

The pendulum of the clock on the wall swung backwards and forwards, backwards and forwards. What on earth were they talking about? Judith had forgotten all about her. Forgotten, and they'd been having such a lovely time. She'd thought Judith was enjoying it as much as she was, but she couldn't have been if she could forget that Sarah had been caught in the storm and hadn't, for all she knew, come back yet.

Suddenly Judith came flying: 'Oh, the kettle! The kettle!'

'I've turned it off,' said Sarah flatly, from the chair.

Judith looked at her in surprise. What was the matter with her? Behind Judith at the top of the steps, Terry Crawford appeared. 'Hello, Sarah,' he said briefly. He had long given up trying to conciliate Sarah.

'Am I going to be asked to stay to tea?' he said, looking down at Judith.

'Oh, yes, do stay if you'd like to,' said Judith politely. 'But we've nothing nice to eat. We were going to have new bread and butter and jam, weren't we, Sarah? But I don't suppose you'd like that,' she said, turning to him with anxiety. She thought he was probably too old for new bread; nobody seemed to eat new bread after about thirty.

'I dote on new bread,' he said. 'Though I never get it now. In South Africa I used to eat it hot from the oven.'

'Have you been to South Africa?' asked Judith.

'Been to South Africa?' he said with a laugh. 'I was born there. I am a South African.'

He was very fond of telling people he was a South African nowadays; once he hardly ever mentioned it.

'I'll get the tray ready. The kettle will boil again in a few minutes,' said Judith.

'Let me help,' he said, stepping down into the kitchen.

Sarah did not offer to help. She would not look at them, but gazed out of the window and bit her nails.

'You didn't get wet, did you, Sarah?' asked Judith. 'You sheltered, didn't you?'

'Yes, I sheltered,' said Sarah.

'D'you want me to cut bread-and-butter?' asked Judith anxiously of Terry. The bread was so new and the knife so blunt she shrank from attempting it, and was relieved when he said they would take the loaf and the butter into the sitting-room.

'This is fun,' he said.

'For you perhaps,' thought Sarah grimly. 'But you've spoilt mine.'

'Let me take that in,' he said, lifting the heavy silver tray.

Judith followed him up the steps and Sarah looked bitterly after her. She wasn't going in, so they needn't think so. She sat on in the empty kitchen, done out of her tea. In a moment, Judith reappeared, flushed from the anxiety of pouring out tea. 'Sarah, do come,' she whispered urgently. 'What's the matter? You're not sick are you?'

'No, but I'm not coming while he's there,' said Sarah.

'But why?' asked Judith astonished.

'I don't like him.'

'But why don't you like him? You used to.'

'I don't like him,' repeated Sarah. 'And I'm not coming.'

'But he knows I've come to fetch you,' whispered Judith in agitation. 'It looks awful for me to go back without you.'

'He's much more used to me than you are,' said Sarah maturely. 'He knows I won't come.'

'I shall have to go back. I can't leave him any longer,' said Judith.

'Yes, go,' said Sarah, with a strange glance. 'Go on. Go back.'

Bewildered, Judith went.

It was a new experience for Judith to have the entire responsibility of entertaining a man to tea, and one who had remained in her memory as a romantic hero, rescuing her from a paralysing situation as Perseus Andromeda from the rock. Now that she saw him again, she suffered no disillusionment either, which was pretty wonderful, considering what usually happened when you hadn't seen people for years. He was as handsome as she remembered him, and just as kind. Somehow, too, though she had grown older, he seemed to have remained the same, so that she was almost level with him now. It was all strange and exciting, and everything seemed to have become very vivid and noticeable in the sitting-room. A diffused golden glow filled the room, repeated again by the yellow brocade of the chairs and curtains, as if the sun threw light at them and they threw it back. The ninon curtains were rather soiled, but it didn't matter. Even their faint greyness was somehow right – like part of the atmosphere built up before the play began. The piano was open and it seemed wonderful that if the right person came in, he could strike glorious music from those keys. The strong excitement of youth that comes for no apparent reason, leaped in Judith's veins and she smiled at Terry. She bit into the new bread with

great pleasure and wished Sarah wouldn't be so silly, but would come and have tea too, instead of sulking in the kitchen.

'What about tennis tomorrow?' Terry asked.

'I'm sorry, I can't play tomorrow. I don't want to leave Sarah.'

If Sarah wouldn't come in to tea, she certainly wouldn't go to tennis.

'Are you going to be tied to Sarah the whole time you're here?' asked Terry.

'Oh, no,' said Judith. 'When Auntie Vera comes home, I shall be able to play quite often, I expect.'

Terry looked put out. It was precisely because Vera was away that he wanted to play with Judith tomorrow. He didn't know how Vera would react, he said to himself.

To Terry Crawford, women were creatures to be managed, to be deceived, if necessary. He had one code of behaviour for men, another for women. He rarely lied to men, but lies to women didn't count. They asked for them, he considered. Women had pursued him a good deal and he had had to be wary, or so he imagined, to rescue himself from their machinations. He was quite afraid of the fusses women made. A hunted look came into his eyes when one began. He never tried to defend himself, but agreed with whatever was said, because that seemed the quickest way to get it over.

But a young girl was different, he said to himself, watching Judith. She wasn't up to the tricks of a grown woman. He found the diffidence and inexperience of youth both charming and touching, and he didn't want Vera to make any silly

fuss about his taking Judith about. Tomorrow – and Terry did not often look beyond – would have been a good opportunity to take her out without bother from Vera. So he looked glum now. He hated to be crossed.

Although it occurred to him in a moment that if she wouldn't play with him, it might be good policy to meet Vera in his car. She would expect it and it might save bother later on.

'What time does Vera arrive tomorrow?' he asked.

'Five fifty-five,' said Judith.

'I'll meet her with the car,' said Terry.

'Oh, thank you very much,' said Judith politely, as if he were an outsider doing a kindness to one of her family. 'That would be very good of you. Sarah and I won't go to the station in that case.'

She knew Sarah wouldn't, if he were going to be there. How awkward all this was, she reflected. And it became more and more awkward, because he stayed on and on. Excitement, novelty, faded and Judith grew restive and absent, thinking of poor Sarah, tealess, supperless, in the kitchen. At last, he rose. He didn't want to go. He had nothing particular to do and he thought of his great empty house and of the club, stuffy on a summer evening, with distaste. He would much rather have stayed with this charming young girl. But she was worrying, about Sarah – she wasn't giving him her attention any more, so, piqued, he rose. At the top of the steps, he turned and gave her a wistful smile she couldn't interpret at all, and finally went.

Judith rushed to the kitchen. 'Oh, Sarah, you should have

come in,' she said reproachfully. 'You shouldn't have left him to me all that time. Not that he isn't awfully nice. Why don't you like him?'

'I don't,' said Sarah, setting her lips. 'And you never need think I'll come in when he's here, because I won't.'

One of her difficult moods, decided Judith and did not pursue the subject. She began to get supper as quickly as possible to make up to Sarah for having missed tea, and Sarah, coming to the conclusion that it was not Judith's fault he had stayed so long, recovered her spirits.

CHAPTER TWENTY-THREE

I

Vera was recovering. Travelling home, though she was still
subdued and exhausted, she felt what she thought of as
'much better'. Each day was removing her farther from the
soul-searing experience of the hours she had spent beside
her dead sister. The impression was daily fainter. It was not
gone, but Vera, recovering, was compromising with herself.
In the first violence of renunciation, she had seen plainly
that she must give up her lover. But now she asked herself why
she should not keep him as a friend. It would be needlessly
unkind to him and too stern to herself never to see him again.
Besides, she had come to the conclusion that she couldn't
do it. Far better attempt the possible, she told herself, than
attempt the impossible and fail. She had read in a psychology
book once that that was awfully bad for you; it discouraged
you from ever trying again. Perhaps Terry would help her, if
she appealed to him. With Terry's co-operation, how happy
they could all be! Vera thought with loving kindness even of
Brenda. It pleased her, reckoning without Terry, to think she
was going to restore him to his wife. She made these rosy

pictures going home. Everything was going to be all right now. Everything was working out very well, for the betterment of everybody. Judith's presence in the house, for instance, made it all easier. Under cover of Judith she could make the transition from love to friendship, and with Judith there, she could win Sarah back without seeming to.

The train was running into Trenton now and Vera raised her eyes to her dressing-case in the luggage-rack. The only other occupant of the first-class carriage, a young man, taking the hint, rose and lifted it down for her. But with none of the old *empressement*, Vera noticed. She always noticed these things now. Ah, well, she thought, all that is over and I must accept it.

She was touched when she saw Terry's tall and somehow always lonely figure waiting for her on the platform. Terry, for his part, had a shock as she came towards him, the signs of grief and sleeplessness in her face. 'By George, she looks her age,' he thought, and solemn with discomfort took her dressing-case. He felt self-conscious when he got it; he didn't like carrying anything, especially women's gear, but he didn't know how to avoid it, seeing she had lost her sister and was obviously very cut up. He walked beside her to the car with his long, loping step and wished he hadn't come. When embarrassed he became extremely conventional and when Vera, sitting by him as they drove away, said 'Oh, Terry, it's been so sad,' all he could reply was: 'Mm – bad show.'

'Terry, I'm so glad you came to meet me,' said Vera, hurriedly plunging. 'There's something I want to say before we get to the house. I've been doing a lot of thinking these last

few days. I had to. Charlotte's death made me. I love you as much as ever, and I always shall, but let's stop this furtive love-making, shall we? I don't want to have anything to hide. I must think of Sarah now, and I've got Judith, too, in my charge. I'm not free to do as I like. I thought I was, but I'm not. Let's be friends always, you must come as much as you want to, because I couldn't bear not to see you. But – no more, Terry darling.'

She was tired and tears came easily. She looked at him with wet eyes, but he kept his on the road. He was relieved, but he didn't want her to see it. He wanted to say the right thing, but didn't know what it was. He almost spoke the truth. He almost said: 'That suits me all right.' But he managed not to. After a pause, he said: 'Just as you say, Vera.'

But it did suit him. It would have to come to an end in time and it was better for her to break it off than for him. There would have been a painful scene if he'd said what she had just said to him. Men took these things much better than women, he reflected. He simply said quietly: 'Just as you say.' He felt that must have sounded admirably well.

It suited him too, that she should break off at this precise moment, because though he had no sense of wrong-doing – few men of his kind have – he wouldn't have liked a young girl, Judith, for instance, to know about the affair. He felt squeamish about that. Vera was right that in a house where there were two young girls there should be nothing to hide. So after a moment, he gave Vera's hand a squeeze and said gratefully and affectionately, 'Bless you.'

They reached the house and as the car drew up, Vera said:

'Don't come in, Terry dear, do you mind?' He looked at her in surprise. This was going a bit too far. Not come in? He had nowhere he wanted to go. He was absolutely at a loose end. Besides, he wanted to fix up some tennis with Judith. 'I want to give my whole attention to the girls,' said Vera. 'I've a good deal to explain to Judith. And I'm very tired. I shouldn't be good company, so you'll lose nothing by not coming in.'

'Very well,' he said gloomily. 'I suppose I can come tomorrow?'

Vera smiled. It was sweet of him to be so disappointed about not being allowed in. 'Yes, come tomorrow. I shall be more myself after some sleep, I hope. Goodbye, Terry dear, and thank you so much for meeting me.'

'Yes, and poor reward I got,' he thought resentfully, driving away.

It was Judith who welcomed Vera. Her aunt's pale looks were a reproach to her; she felt Vera had borne grief in her place. She kissed her with compunction and took her dressing-case upstairs. But Vera had to force a welcome from Sarah. She laid her cheek against her daughter's and said: 'Kiss me, darling. I'm tired and sad and very glad to get home to you.' Sarah obediently kissed her mother's cheek, but without warmth. It was no good beginning all this again; it would only come to an end before long. She never began again nowadays. Her hopes had been dashed too often. Vera was hurt by her lack of response, but reminded herself that it would take time to win her back. She went upstairs with a feeling of revulsion. Life was going to be empty, savourless without Terry. This house, taken so that she could be with him,

appeared now for what it was, hideous, depressing, not the
sort of place she need have been in at all. As soon as she had
the strength of mind to leave it, she would.

'Judith,' she said at supper, 'I'm afraid you're going to have
to stay here longer than the fortnight we first thought of.
I hope you won't mind.'

'No, of course not,' said Judith politely. 'But why?'

'Your father has asked me to keep you until he makes up
his mind what he's going to do. He talks of going on a mission
to Canada.'

'A mission!' exclaimed Judith, who naïvely thought there
was only one kind, and what could her father have to do with
the spread of the gospel?

'A trade mission for his firm, of course,' said Vera. 'In that
case he says he would sell the house and everything in it. He
would be away for several years.'

'Should I have to go with him?' asked Judith, with
apprehension in her eyes.

'It doesn't sound as if you would,' said Vera, trying to break
it gently that Geoffrey proposed to leave Judith behind.

'I don't want to go. He's sure to take Margaret, but I do
hope he won't take me. But what can I do if I'm left behind?'

'You can stay with us, can't she, Sarah?'

'Oh, Judith, yes!' cried Sarah, flaming into life. 'Oh, how
heavenly!' She rushed round the table to hug her cousin, but
Judith put out a hand to keep her off for a moment.

'What about Auntie Lucy?' she asked. 'Can't I – can't I go
to Underwood?'

'That's the awkward part,' said Vera. 'Your father won't

agree. He and Lucy have never been able to get on. I haven't seen as much of him as she has, so he hasn't worked up the same strong dislike of me. He's using me because there's no one else, of course. We can't mention your going to Underwood yet, but once he's out of the way I shall have no scruple in letting you go as often as you want to.'

Judith submitted then to Sarah's hug and hugged her in return. But she had more questions to ask still. 'What am I going to do? I must work.'

'I've talked about that with Lucy. You're not old enough to take up your scholarship, you have to wait another year. I thought you might just help me in the house, but Lucy wants you to attend classes here. I'm sure there are some,' said Vera, who was vague on the subject. 'Yes, I'm sure I've seen notices up. But we'll look into all that later. Your father hasn't decided to go yet, but I thought I'd better warn you.'

Judith was silent, trying to adjust herself. It was very kind of Vera, but she would rather have been at Underwood. It seemed so queer not to be able to go to her natural place. Underwood was really her home; it had been that since she was about six years old. It was appalling that her father should carry spite against her aunt to this length. No one ought to have such power and be able to abuse it as he did, she thought angrily. 'I'm glad he's going away and I hope I never see him again,' she thought. Her heart swelled. Not only did she want to live with Lucy, but she knew Lucy wanted her to. Vera, seeing her wistful look, said: 'It will be lovely for us to have you here, but we'll try to make you very happy too, won't we, Sarah?'

'We will,' said Sarah fervently. 'I say, will you meet me every day out of school? Will you come to the concert next term?'

The thought of having someone to show off at school, and someone so pretty and clever as her cousin, made Sarah radiant. She sat on the floor, her bony elbows digging affectionately into Judith's knees, her eyes turned up to Judith, beaming with happiness. 'Will you play tennis with me *sometimes?*' she begged. 'I'm not awfully good, but perhaps I should improve with you. And can we go to the Swimming Baths every week, even in winter?'

Judith smiled down at her. It touched her that Sarah should be so glad she was staying. She must swallow her disappointment about Underwood and keep Sarah happy. Sarah had had a bad time; now it should all be different. And it was very good of Vera to offer her a home. At one time she would have been full of misgivings at the thought of living with her, but she had been very kind and understanding lately. Judith felt she must have misjudged her before.

'Thank you very much for taking me in,' she said shyly. She sprang up and began to clear the table. She must make herself useful, she must show she was grateful. Sarah sprang up to help her; she would do anything so long as Judith was doing it too.

Vera went into the sitting-room; it seemed melancholy, slightly stale, the yellow brocade soiled, grey dust in the crevices of the white marble chimney-piece. She sat down in an armchair set in the curve of the grand piano, thinking of Terry. What was he doing now? Probably nothing, and suffering agonies of boredom in consequence. It was going to

be hard, she said to herself. Her thoughts had centred on him so long, she had to keep tearing them away. Not that he wouldn't often be in this room, but she wouldn't shut the girls out. They must all be together. A different note must be struck now. She meant to persevere in what she had decided was the right course, and if she did, perhaps some of Lucy's steadfastness would become hers. Anyway, something had to be tried for, she told herself.

The girls came in and sat down side by side on the sofa. They talked for a little while to each other and to Vera, who was too tired to make much response. Judith opened the paper, remarking that she must keep up with *The Times*. Miss Porteous had taught her to read the daily paper and if she missed it, she felt something was wrong. So she read, while Sarah hung over her arm, reading pieces for herself and asking a question now and again.

Vera watched them. It had been an inspiration to get Judith here. Everything was going to be all right, she thought, her lids drooping. By and by she slept. The curtains at the open windows breathed gently in and out. Footsteps passed occasionally in the street. The summer dusk thickened. The girls whispered on the sofa.

II

Vera, refreshed by sleep, woke next morning to the sounds of laughter and running water. Who would have thought that the addition of one girl to the household would make such a difference? The water stopped, but the laughter rose

to squealing pitch. Vera jumped from her bed and went to see what the commotion was. In the bathroom, with the window wide open, the morning sun striking the bright water and their naked bodies, the girls were urging each other into a cold bath. 'You're the eldest, you go first,' cried Sarah, her hair pinned up on the top of her head.

'Not I! You're the youngest. It's your duty to warm it up for me.' Judith tried to push Sarah in, then suddenly thrust her aside and jumped in, thrashed wildly and scrambled out again, gasping and protesting. 'Now get in,' she cried. 'Go on, coward.'

Sarah cautiously inserted one toe, and lost her breath. 'It's perfectly frightful,' she said. 'I daren't.'

'I know you daren't,' taunted Judith, dripping all over the floor.

'Oh, daren't I?' said Sarah and flung herself in with such abandon that a great wave of cold water heaved up the sides of the bath and slapped down on Vera's bedroom slippers. She was wetter still when Sarah got out, shaking herself like a dog.

'Now watch me,' said Judith stalking to the bath. 'I'll get in without a sound, without a catch of the breath.' With unnatural calm, she stepped into the water, lay down, got up again and stepped out – looking to Sarah for admiration.

'Huh, I can do it if you can,' said Sarah, and did it.

'Jolly good,' said Judith. 'It takes some doing, doesn't it? Here's your towel. I'm as warm as toast already. In fact, I'm too warm. I think I'll have to get back in again. No, I don't think I will.'

'No, I don't think I should,' said Vera. 'There's as much water on the floor as in the bath already. I should think it's dripping through on Mrs Parsons in the kitchen.'

'If it is, it'll be the only bath-water that's ever touched her,' said Judith, and Sarah giggled. With complete absence of self-consciousness they went on drying their slender bodies, and Vera went back to her bedroom.

She was vicariously invigorated by their radiant freshness when they came down to breakfast. She felt she wanted to do something brisk. So she harnessed the energy of the girls to a grand turning-out of the sitting-room, a better one than it had ever had before. Sarah protested at first, but when Judith said they would soon get through it and go out, she set to with a will. It was quite fun rushing everything out of the room into the passage.

'What about these curtains?' asked Judith, holding up the triple ninon between finger and thumb.

'They must come down,' said Vera, so Judith ran up to the top of the steps and dropped the grey veils from the windows.

'Don't you think it looks better without them?' she asked tentatively.

'Heaps better,' said Sarah emphatically.

'Well, they needn't go up again, really,' said Vera. No need for them now. The fall of the ninon curtains was the end of something; it was symbolic. Let the windows, like her life, be unshaded, let anyone who chose look in.

In the middle of the activity, the telephone rang in the room. The girls paused, duster in hand, and looked towards it enquiringly. Vera picked up the receiver. 'Hello?' she said,

and turned her back on the girls so that they should not see the warm colour that ran up into her face. It was Terry. But what was he saying? That he wanted Judith to play tennis in the evening. Tennis? With Judith? What made him think of it, Vera wondered. It sounded as if they had made some arrangement about it. But how? She realised that she hadn't heard what Terry was saying and had to ask him to repeat it. It was too hot to play before six, he said, but he would call for her then and bring her back at eight, if that was all right. Vera felt an unreasonable impulse to say Judith couldn't go, but forced it back. 'I'll ask Judith,' she said. 'She's here in the room. Judith, Terry wants you to play tennis at six. Would you like to?'

'Don't go,' said Sarah sharply. Judith looked at her in surprise.

'But, Sarah, I want to go,' she said. 'I love tennis.'

'She'll be ready at six then, Terry. Thank you so much. It is kind of you to help us to amuse her,' said Vera, conventionally. 'Yes, I'm much better today, thank you. Goodbye.' She replaced the receiver and smiled rather mechanically. Her heart was beating in a queer way.

Sarah had gone from the room and in a moment Judith threw down her duster and went to look for her. She found her sitting on her bed.

'Now, look here, Miss Sargent,' said Judith, sitting down beside her. 'If I'm going to live here for good, one thing must be understood. I must be free to do as I like sometimes. I shan't complain when you go out with your friends.'

'I haven't any,' said Sarah.

'But, Sarah, perhaps this is why,' said Judith, taking her hand. 'People can't stand being held down tight and not allowed to look at anybody else.'

Sarah gave a peculiar half-laugh, as if Judith didn't know what she was talking about, and got up from the bed. 'Come on,' she said, as if it was no good going on with the conversation. 'Let's go back and finish that room.'

But interest in the sitting-room had somehow evaporated. It had been fun moving the things out, but it was tedious getting them back again. Sarah put them into their wrong places, but Vera did not redirect her. Mother and daughter moved about looking very alike, with the same air of being preoccupied with some anxiety which they kept trying to dismiss and make light of. Their behaviour fluctuated all day and puzzled Judith. She felt a slight weariness too. Other people's dark moods affected her and she had had so much of them in her life. She had hoped that here it was going to be different, but it hardly looked like it today. She felt, not homesick, because she had no home she could be sick for, but she felt a longing for Lucy. 'I wish I could have gone to Underwood instead of coming here,' she thought wistfully.

III

Towards six o'clock, while Judith was changing for tennis, Vera sat by the open window in the sitting-room. The worst of it was that the less she saw of Terry, the more she wanted to see him. A longing to see him had been gathering force all day and now it possessed her entirely. He was coming, it was true, but

not for her. Her ears strained, as so many times before, for the sound of his car. At last she heard it. It came swiftly nearer, it stopped at the gate. He sprang up the steps. He was in the hall, calling out not to her but to Judith. Then he came into the room.

'Well, Terry,' she said, smiling up at him.

'Ah, you're better today,' he said, bending to take both her hands, press them lightly and return them to her lap. 'You gave me a fright when I saw you yesterday. You did really,' he assured her, lifting his eyebrows. 'I say, what's different about this room? Something, but I don't know what.'

'The curtains,' said Vera. 'They're gone.'

'Oh, yes. It looks much better, doesn't it? I wonder you didn't think of it before. I say, d'you mind if I help myself to cigarettes?' He strode over to the box beside the telephone. 'I've run out.'

'Fill your case, of course,' said Vera, watching him. No other man had ever pleased her eyes so much. Surely he was the most graceful of male creatures. She was smiling as she watched him, when, suddenly, Judith was in the room. They both turned to look at her and neither, for the moment, spoke. Judith, in white shorts and a shirt, looked like the youngest of the goddesses. Her hair was bound up on the top of her head with a blue ribbon, which added to the inno-cent candour of her appearance. Vera felt a piercing and unexpected pang of envy, admiration, and regret for her own lost youth. She could have looked like this once, but never did, because no girl wore this scanty dress in her day. Another, uglier emotion overtook her and she had to smother an

impulse to tell Judith to go back upstairs and put some more clothes on.

Judith advanced, looking enquiringly from one to the other. Wouldn't she do? Was there something wrong? her eyes asked. She had a white coat on her arm and when she put her racket between her knees to put it on, Terry strode forward. 'Let me,' he said and Vera heard the change in his voice. He was as struck by Judith's lovely youth as she was. For the first time in her life, Vera knew herself eclipsed.

'You'll bring her back at eight, won't you, Terry? Supper will be ready,' she said, swallowing her bitterness.

'Eight prompt,' said Terry briskly, ready to promise anything so long as he was getting what he wanted. 'And you rest, Vera, till we come back. You look better, but still far too tired. Ready, Judith?'

'Goodbye, Auntie Vera,' said Judith, smiling radiantly over her shoulder. She was looking forward to the tennis.

From the window, Vera watched them go out of the gate together. They got into the car, the doors banged, they moved off, the sound of the engine diminishing down the Burnham Road.

An extraordinary sense of desolation overcame Vera.

She sat unmoving at the window. She sat there for what seemed an age. Then she turned her head inwards to the room and listened. The house was very quiet. Nothing moved. Vera had a sudden sharp fear that she had been left in alone. 'Sarah?' she called. Then more urgently: 'Sarah!'

There was no immediate response. Then a reluctant voice from upstairs said, 'Yes?'

'Come and sit with me, darling. Come and cheer me up.'
Vera was imploring Sarah's company where Sarah had once
implored hers.

After a pause, Sarah stirred in her bedroom and came
slowly down, her fingers in a book.

'What are you doing, darling?' asked Vera, with simulated
brightness.

'Reading,' said Sarah, throwing herself into a chair.

Vera took up the paper, but to read of the world unrest
increased her own and she threw it down again. Mother and
daughter sat together, their thoughts absent, but in the same
place. They were with the tennis players at Holly Lodge.

'Would you like me to play to you?' said Vera, getting up.

'If you like,' mumbled Sarah, but when Vera began, she put
her fingers in her ears under her hair to keep the sound out.
Vera played in a desultory way for a while, then she got up and
closed the piano. She couldn't settle to anything. A dreadful
restlessness possessed her. 'Come along, let's go and get
supper. Judith will soon be back and she'll be hungry.'

Sarah closed her book with an ill grace. 'If only she'd
leave me alone,' she thought, 'I might get interested.' She
followed her mother to the kitchen and did as she was told
about setting the table. Vera felt better now that she was doing
something and she admonished Sarah and at the same
time herself. 'We mustn't mope every time Judith goes out,
darling,' she said, mincing parsley for the omelette. 'We must
let her enjoy herself, or she won't want to stay with us. You and
I will have to amuse ourselves. We'll go to the pictures, shall
we, sometimes? And on these nice evenings, I think we ought

to go for a walk. We might go across the park and see Mrs Clarey.'

'That *will* be fun,' said Sarah with sarcasm.

'If you can think of anything better to do, I'll do it,' said Vera with determined patience. But she thought: 'Oh, the young, the young! They're no company for us, nor we for them.'

CHAPTER TWENTY-FOUR

I

It became a daily occurrence for Terry to arrange something for himself and Judith; tennis, mostly; if not tennis, swimming; if not swimming, then something that at any rate took them away for two or three hours from the house in Burnham Road. Vera did not know how to object. It was her own fault, she told herself. He was only taking her at her word. She had dismissed him herself. It was what she had wanted. But she had not thought it would be like this. She had imagined a noble renunciation on both sides, but the renunciation had been all hers. And it had been so abrupt, so unflattering. Just those few words in the car coming up from the station and he had accepted the situation. He had never tried to be alone with her since; in fact, she thought he tried not to be alone with her. He was gay, considerate – very considerate, always telling her to rest – and friendly, but as slippery as a fish. She couldn't hold him for five minutes in serious conversation.

It was hard that Vera should immediately have been put to so severe a test. Her frail new intentions had hardly come up before they were swept over by a consuming fire of jealousy.

They had no chance against it. They shrivelled. But if only she could deal with this situation and dissolve it, she could start again, she told herself. At the moment she was obsessed and could think of nothing but keeping Judith and Terry apart. It was not that she suspected that they were falling in love – how could he fall in love with such a child? – but she could not bear them to be together. She could not bear it that Judith should be with him when she wasn't.

When Geoffrey first disclosed the fact that he might be going to Canada, Vera had begged him to let her have Judith. She would be only too happy, she assured him, to keep Judith for years. But by the time his letter appeared on the breakfast-table – Vera got up to breakfast now, being too restless to stay in bed – the position had reversed itself. Vera now wanted Judith to go; Judith, on the other hand, wanted to stay. Vera opened the letter and Judith watched her read it with anxious eyes. Sarah watched Judith.

Nothing was to be gathered from Vera's face and when she had finished reading, she held out the letter between the tips of two fingers with a wounding absence of comment. Judith blushed, murmured 'thank you', and began to read. Her father was going to Canada. He and Margaret would be away for at least three years, he wrote. Vera had been appointed Judith's guardian, and in default of Vera, Lucy. A sum of money had been paid into Judith's account to be drawn upon for her maintenance. The house was already sold and the furniture was going. They expected to sail in ten days' time. It was all cut and dried. She was disposed of, thought Judith with a moment's bitterness.

Then she realised the silence at the table. This was all very different from the time her aunt had said she might make her home with them. Even Sarah showed no pleasure now. Judith blushed again. How awful if they didn't really want her! She busied herself with folding the letter with care and when it was done she offered it back to her aunt across the table.

'I don't want it,' said Vera coldly.

Judith put the letter down and began to butter a piece of toast.

'Now it's decided that you're to stay, Judith,' said Vera, in a moment, 'you must find out about classes at the university. You can't hang about the house indefinitely, you know. Doing nothing.'

Judith's colour deepened. 'No,' she said in a low voice.

Bowed over her plate, she struggled with painful embarrassment. She tried to stay in her place, but it was no good, she couldn't. Murmuring an excuse, she got up and hurried out of the room.

She sped noiselessly up the stairs and shut herself into the bedroom. She sat on her unmade bed before the open window with its view over the old graves. The sunlight of the September morning lay over the peaceful, melancholy scene, the crooked stones, the weeping willows, the drifts of leaves and a solitary old woman wandering up and down the paths, looking for someone buried a long time ago. Judith forgot herself in the contemplation of it. Her blushes cooled, her chagrin receded. She sat surrounded by the things that used to be in the top guest-room at Southfield. They had delighted her and Margaret in those days, but they were too crowded

together here to appear to any advantage. Even the lamp with stars was still here, between her bed and Sarah's, but the shade was faded and the stars showed but dimly when the light was on.

Recovering from her aunt's wounding implication that she was no longer wanted in the house, Judith was conscious of an undercurrent of fierce joy. She was staying, she was staying, her pulses began to sing. They didn't want her, it may be, but *he* did. He would be glad. She would still be with him, for some part of every day she would be with him. He had promised that. Whatever unpleasantness there might be in the house, she had always got Terry.

He was so handsome, he was so wonderful, she said to herself, clasping her hands. And so kind! Who else would spend so much time giving her practice on her back-hand stroke? Why – she had improved so much that if she went back to play for the Girls now, they'd beat the Mistresses hollow! In her inexperienced heart, schoolgirl fervour, hero-worship and a strong physical attraction towards Terry Crawford were inextricably, bewilderingly mixed.

Last night, after tennis, when they had gone in for drinks, lemonade for her, gin, lime and soda-water for him, he had taken her over the house. She looked at everything with eager interest. Finding out more about him was like reading an absorbing book and coming, page by page, to some terribly exciting crisis. She didn't know what the crisis was, but it caught her breath and made her heart race with anticipation.

Last night, lemonade in hand, she had wandered over the house, followed by Terry. The beams of the evening sun

struck across the silent rooms, all very richly furnished and to Judith's mind, very stuffy. There was evidence everywhere of the dog-lover; in every room a drinking bowl and a dog-chair covered with an old rug. The pictures were mostly of dogs. There were framed photographs of Brenda with her dogs from childhood upwards. Judith, looking at them, thought the absent mistress of the house astonishingly plain. 'I never remember that you have a wife,' she said naïvely.

Terry laughed. 'As a matter of fact,' he said. 'I hardly ever remember myself.'

'This is Brenda's room,' he said, opening a door. Judith looked at the narrow single bed, so low it was almost on the floor. Brenda had slept in it as a child and had gone back to it. Judith looked at all the arrangements for the dogs, the Mabel Lucie Attwell pictures on the walls, the girlish collection of books on a white-painted shelf, and marvelling, went out again. A strange sort of wife for Terry, she thought. She was sorry for him now, and that made him more attractive than ever. It was sad for such a dear person as Terry not to have a more interesting wife, a wife he could love, and who would enjoy camping with him in South Africa, she thought compassionately. He was always talking about camping in South Africa and made it sound splendid. She thought, if she hadn't been a girl, how marvellous it would have been to go camping with him. Or if she'd been older, and if he were not married . . . that of course, would have been more marvellous still. But she mustn't think of things like that.

In his house, when she encountered any of the ancient maids, they looked at her sourly, their caps, in the shape of

starched water-lilies with streamers, trembling with indignation. She did not overhear their conversations.

'Is this her?' asked Byland of Masters, the parlour-maid.

'No, go on, of course it isn't,' said Masters. 'She's years
older than this one. This is probably the daughter.'

'Well, if it is, he ought to be ashamed of himself,' said
Byland. 'Bringing her here. He didn't ought to bring any
woman, young or old, to this house while Miss Brenda's away.'

They continued to look with deep disapproval on Judith,
but Judith, accustomed to Burton and Janet, had never
expected amiability from maids and did not look for it now.

She sat on her bed, remembering everything, remembering things he said. He actually thought she was pretty. He
was the first person to tell her so and it made intoxicating
hearing. He went farther; he said 'lovely', but she didn't dare
to think that was true. Auntie Vera had been lovely, she
pointed out to him, and she could never come up to her. She
told him tales Lucy had told her about Vera's dazzling beauty
when she was young.

She heard Vera coming upstairs now and sprang to her
feet. Her aunt said she musn't hang about doing nothing, and
she had been doing nothing for quite a long time. Guiltily, she
began to make her bed.

II

Vera was always on the point of 'speaking' to Terry. 'I shall
speak to him today. I shall say something,' she promised
herself. But for some reason it seemed to need more courage

than she could muster. It was incredible, she thought, that she, who had never in her life hesitated to speak her mind, couldn't pluck up courage to speak now. Why should she falter and tremble before this man who was nothing but good-looking, who was a third-rate person really, with nothing in him she admired, who was shifty and selfish, she went on, trying to goad herself out of love? She sometimes thought he had crossed her path simply to humiliate her and put her through the gamut of searing emotions she had never known before. She had been immune from them before she knew him, and now she was jealous and frightened of showing it. She daren't speak to him in case she should give herself away and yet he wasn't so perspicacious as all that, she thought bitterly. She had no great opinion of his brain, she said to herself. Love was an illness, a poison. Titania's passion for Bottom with the ass's head was as reasonable as hers for Terry Crawford, she said to herself.

At last, suddenly, as they were crossing the sitting-room on their way out of it, she moved forward swiftly and closed the door, leaning her back against it as if she meant to keep him where he was until she had finished what she had to say.

'Terry,' she said, trembling ridiculously. 'I'm afraid I must ask you not to take Judith out any more. She's in my charge and I can't allow her to be seen about with you all the time.'

Terry registered amazement, though he felt none at all. He had expected this for some time; that was why he had avoided being alone with her.

'Not be seen with me? Why on earth not?'

'You're married. Your wife's away.'

Terry laughed. 'What has that to do with it?'

'You don't imagine there hasn't been a lot of talk about us – about you and me, do you?' said Vera.

'I don't care what talk there's been. Why should I?' asked Terry. 'Men don't care about talk, you know.'

'No, but it's I who've been seen about with you until now,' said Vera, conscious that she was floundering. 'But now you're always with a girl young enough to be your daughter. It doesn't look right. It looks . . . well, she's far too young for you, Terry. There's something slightly nauseating about it.'

He laughed again. 'To you, possibly. But not to anyone else. It's because Judith is so young that no one will think anything of it. And I'm surprised that you, of all people,' he raised his eyebrows at her, 'should suspect me of baby-snatching. Don't, for heaven's sake, say to Judith what you've just said to me. Don't put ideas like that into her head. It would spoil everything.'

Vera looked at him closely.

'But if it would make you any happier about the conventions,' he said indulgently, 'we'll knock off a bit . . . I'll come for her tomorrow, because we've fixed it and she'd wonder what was the matter if I didn't turn up. But I'll space things out a bit after that. I'll say I'm busy at the colliery or something. Do it gradually. And of course, Brenda will be home soon and that will be the end of tennis. So you'll have nothing to worry about by and by,' he said, taking her by the arm and drawing her gently from the door so that he could get out. 'And don't play the heavy aunt, Vera dear. It doesn't suit you. You're not old enough for the part yet, good Lord.'

'We shall have to be careful,' he said to Judith, driving her to Holly Lodge the following afternoon. Dusk fell too soon to allow much tennis in the evenings now. 'Vera's beginning to object to my taking you out.'

'Oh, dear,' said Judith alarmed. 'Is she? Though, I think, for some reason or other, she's objected all the time really. Oh, I do hope she won't stop me from seeing you.'

'You mustn't let her,' said Terry firmly. 'Both Vera and Sarah are as jealous and possessive as hell. Your life will be a perfect misery if you allow them to dictate to you.'

'But what can I do?' said Judith, in distress. 'I've got to do what Auntie Vera says. I'm in her house.'

'You can get out of the house sometimes, can't you?' said Terry. 'You don't have to ask permission every time you go out, do you?'

'Of course not.'

'That's all right then,' said Terry easily. 'We'll meet as usual, but you don't need to say anything about it.'

'Oh, I don't think I ought to do anything like that,' said Judith, breathlessly.

'My dear innocent,' he said indulgently, taking one hand from the wheel to lay it over hers in her lap. 'Why ever not? You're not at school any more. Why should you run to tell someone where you've been every time you go back to the house? Vera's the sort of person you simply can't tell things to. She takes advantage of them if you do. If we're going to keep our friendship intact, we've got to be secretive about it. After all, it's worth it, isn't it?'

She was silent.

'Isn't it worth it, darling?' he said tenderly. He turned to look at her. With difficulty she raised her eyes to his.

'Yes,' she said in a low voice. 'It's worth it.'

A strange, painful excitement set her pulses leaping. She didn't like what she was going to have to do: meet him on the sly, hide everything, tell lies or at least act them. She didn't like it, she was frightened and yet she knew she would do it. She must see him.

'Don't think I like hiding things any better than you do,' he said in a moment. 'But it's forced on us in this country. People are so close on top of one another that you've got to hide things if you're going to have any life of your own at all. Lord, when I'm driving down the street sometimes, with houses packed like sardines on every side, with all these windows, somebody looking through the curtains in every one, I'll bet, I could swear like a trooper, or go mad. I have an awful longing, Judith, to get back to the veldt where there's not a soul in sight. We could meet there all right, couldn't we, my pet? Wouldn't it be heavenly. Wouldn't it, Judith?'

'Mmm,' said Judith.

III

In the house now it was like living in a bad dream, Judith thought. Each one seemed to want to avoid, yet to watch the other two. Vera would have them all together in the sitting-room and there they sat, silent, with their books, their eyes sliding often from the pages to look under their lashes at one another. The clock seemed to tick very loudly; footsteps

sounded ominous in the street, as if someone was coming with bad news. Judith thought the others must hear her heart beating, it sounded so loud too. She was conscious that she was being watched all the time by her aunt and cousin. And they were justified in watching her, she thought wretchedly, because she was deceiving them now. She kept slipping out to meet Terry. Her days and nights alternated between peaks of happiness and excitement and depths of misery. She did not thrive in her world of intrigue; it made her feel ill, it took her appetite away, it took her sleep.

And Sarah seemed no better, she thought unhappily. She had relapsed into sullen silence. In the bedroom she hardly spoke, or if she did, it was to say something disagreeable. She always pretended to be asleep when Judith came to bed. She was careless about everything, throwing her clothes down anyhow, neglecting her hair. Judith hadn't tried to bring her round. She didn't want to bring up the subject of Terry. It wasn't safe now.

Sitting through the evenings, Judith's eyes wandered without looking up. You had to be careful to keep your eyes low, so that the others couldn't see what you were thinking. So Judith's eyes – she couldn't keep them on her book, she who used to read with such absorption – her eyes wandered over the grey carpet and the lower reaches of the yellow chairs, over Sarah's long legs and Vera's slender restless foot, swinging, swinging, never still.

One evening, in this room of silence and lowered lids, the telephone rang sharply, making them start and look up at last. Vera put out her hand. 'Yes?' she said.

It was Lucy. Judith, although she could not hear her, sat up and began involuntarily to smile. Her lips parted, her eyes eager, she waited. The mere thought of Lucy's voice cleared the atmosphere.

'I expect you want to speak to Judith,' said Vera, whose face had not changed much as she listened. 'Judith,' she said coldly, and left the chair by the telephone.

'Judith, what d'you think? I've had a letter from Stephen,' came Lucy's warm, animated voice.

'From Stephen!' cried Judith. 'Oh, Auntie Lucy! Where is he? Is he safe? Is he all right? Is he in England?'

'No, darling, he's in Australia, on a fruit farm. He's well. He seems to be doing well. He's saving up to come home and see us. He wants news of us all. But I'll send the letter on. It only came by the afternoon post. Isn't it splendid, Judith? I'm so relieved. Isn't it wonderful to get word of him after all these years? I'm so relieved,' she said again.

'Oh, so am I,' said Judith fervently. 'Oh, Stephen . . . It's simply marvellous.'

'He's sent some snapshots,' went on Lucy. 'He looks splendid. Such a man. He's so tall and strong. You'll be amazed, darling. Of course, he's nearly twenty-one now, isn't he? He says he's waited to write until it didn't matter who knows where he is. He's his own master now, he says, and he looks it. But I'll send the letter and the photographs on, and you'll write, won't you? I'm going to write tonight, before I part with the letter. And are you all right, pet? Are you happy?'

'Oh, well . . . ' faltered Judith, taken aback. 'I'm all right, yes. I'm all right, thank you, Auntie Lucy. Are you? And is

Uncle William? Sarah's all right. She's here, in the room. Do you want to speak to Auntie Vera again?'

Judith gave up the chair and the telephone and Vera continued to speak about nothing in particular for a moment or two before ringing off.

Lucy replaced the telephone in the hall at Underwood. What was wrong? Something certainly was. She had not missed the tone of Vera's voice when she called Judith to the telephone, or the evasion in Judith's when she asked if she was happy. Lucy's quick ears could not be deceived. It sounded as if they were not getting on well together. She knew that voice of Vera's. What had happened to Vera's good resolutions? She went slowly back to the sitting-room. The old anxiety had raised its head again.

CHAPTER TWENTY-FIVE

Sarah had gone to bed. She always went to bed first so that she could pretend to be asleep when Judith came up. In the sitting-room under the light from the lamp with the fluted white shade, Vera sat with a book. On the other side of the empty hearth Judith turned the pages of *The Times*, unaware that she had been turning them thus for the last hour or so. She couldn't really see to read because the light from the lamp did not reach quite so far as her chair. Vera knew it; but she let her pretend, and Judith did not like to ask for permission to turn on the other lamp.

The night was warm, the windows were wide open, but the brocade curtains drawn across them hung unstirred by any breath of air. In the silence, the clock ticked audibly on the mantelpiece. Outside the street lamps threw a greenish-yellow effulgence into the trees on which the last leaves still hung.

Judith felt hollow, she felt like a shell with nothing in it but a heavily beating heart. She kept glancing at the clock. Terry had set her a nerve-racking task tonight. He said he would be passing down the road towards ten o'clock. He would sound one note on his horn, there were so many like it no one would notice, he said. When she heard it she must steal

out and run round the corner to say good night to him. In vain Judith protested that she couldn't, that she daren't. He pleaded and persuaded and finally left it that he would expect her, and she had, in consequence, spent the evening in extreme tension, her ears straining for the sound of the horn, which she both dreaded and longed to hear.

It did not occur to Judith that he should not subject her to these strains. Whatever he did must be right. He was so much older than she was, he must know, and he was so kind, he would never do anything purposely unkind. It was she who hadn't the courage he expected her to have. It seemed a little thing to him to go out of the house for a few moments to say good night to one's friend, and it was a little thing, really, but it seemed to bring so many dark bewildering other things in its train. It didn't feel right. But why not? They weren't harming anybody else, as he said. He could argue all her doubts and scruples away. It was all right as soon as she reached him. But she had to get out, and she had to get in again.

She looked at the clock. Five minutes to ten. Involuntarily, she drew a long breath. Vera heard it. If this silly child only knew how she gave herself away, she thought.

In the street now there was the faint, far-away sound of a car. Judith listened, her lips parted, her eyes sliding fearfully to the window. The car approached, passed the house, receded and then, just as Judith was beginning to breathe again, there came the cautious signal. A desperate look came into Judith's face. She must go. If she didn't, he might wait all night, as she would have waited for him. But she didn't

know how to get out, she didn't know how, she said to herself, turning the pages of *The Times* again to cover her panic. Vera decided to help her to go.

'You've been rustling that paper for the last hour, Judith,' she said coldly. 'I think it's about time you stopped.'

'Oh, I beg your pardon,' said Judith hurriedly. 'I didn't realise . . . I'll put it down.'

She folded the paper and got up from her chair. She stood for a moment, fiddling with her belt.

'Well,' said Vera, raising her head and looking fully at her. 'Are you going to bed?'

'Er –' Judith swallowed visibly. She was a bad liar and hated having to lie. 'I might as well,' she said.

She still stood, uncertain, tense.

'Go along then,' said Vera, impatiently.

'Yes,' said Judith. 'Good night.'

'Good night,' said Vera.

Judith went out of the room and closed the door. Like a flash she was down the stairs, had opened the front door without a sound and was out through the gate into the street.

Vera, leaving the lamp on and the doors open, followed. She saw Judith's light dress appear and reappear under the lamps, she saw her turn the corner fifty yards away. Without a sound, close under the wall, Vera went after her. She got so near she saw Terry draw the girl under the heavy shadow of a tree and heard Judith saying breathlessly: 'I must go back at once and I must never come again. I can't do this sort of thing, Terry. I can't, I can't. It feels so awful . . . ' Vera could

not hear what Terry said, but Judith's voice was higher and in a moment she heard her again. 'Oh, don't kiss me please. Yes, I do love you. I do, but I mustn't. And I never kiss anybody. I must go . . .'

Vera turned and fled back to the house. Stumbling, breathless, she reached the sitting-room and stood with her hands pressed to her side, trying to quieten the wild beating of her heart. Her breath came in great gasps. She wanted to listen, but she couldn't hear anything but herself, the pounding of her own blood deafened her. But it grew quieter, and she waited. In a few moments, there was a stealthy step on the stairs.

'Judith,' she called.

After a pause Judith, her face white, her eyes dilated appeared in the doorway.

'Come here,' said Vera, compelling her to advance.

A door opened upstairs, but they didn't hear it.

'You're – how old? Seventeen?' said Vera harshly. 'You've just left school. Your mother has just died. I took you into this house to be as I thought – fool that I was – an example to Sarah. You've been here five weeks, or at most six, and you sneak out of the house to stand under a wall like a servant with my dearest friend, *my* friend, mark you.'

Judith hung her head. It was true. She deserved it.

'And does it occur to you that everyone round here will think it is I? It's *my* reputation that will suffer by your behaviour,' said Vera, who would throw every reproach at the girl but the true one. 'They see someone coming out of this house and meeting Terry round the corner, who should

they think of but me? I've always been with Terry – I – I have . . . '

Judith's eyes were on her aunt in amazement. 'Oh, no,' she said. 'No one could. No one could ever think you would do that, Auntie Vera. Not *you*.'

'Oh, don't put on that shocked baby face to me,' said Vera violently. 'You're deeper than you look. Terry's been taken in by you just as I was. You're deceitful and depraved. If I'd known what you were I should have refused the care of you. How far has this affair gone? Has he kissed you?' she said brutally, twisting the knife in her own wound.

Judith's head sank lower, her hair fell forward, covering her face.

'Tonight. Not before.'

There was a silence, in which she stood bowed with shame, exposed.

'I suppose you think he's in love with you?' said Vera with scorn.

'He said so,' said Judith in a whisper.

'Go away. Get out of my sight,' said Vera in a choked voice, putting her face against the hand clenching the mantelshelf.

But Judith stood there, weeping. 'Auntie Vera, forgive me,' she said.

'Never,' said Vera. 'Precocious, over-sexed – that's what you are. I suppose you take after your father. Go away. D'you hear?'

Judith turned and went blindly from the room. She went upstairs. She turned the handle of the bedroom door very quietly. She felt her way to her bed and threw herself down

beside it, stifling her tears in the eiderdown. Sarah must know nothing. Depraved. Over-sexed – oh, was it true? Was that why she had let him kiss her so easily? Was that why she wanted him to? She pressed her face closer into the eiderdown. She mustn't wake Sarah. She mustn't cry.

With a click the lamp with stars went on and Judith lifted her wet face to see Sarah sitting up in bed. The two girls stared at each other, Judith piteous, Sarah grave, her eyes searching her cousin's face.

'Have you been out with him?' she asked.

Judith looked away. She looked sideways to the floor.

'Has he been making love to you?' asked Sarah.

Judith looked at her, her eyes beseeching her cousin to spare her.

'So you do the same,' said Sarah. She turned her back on Judith, lay down in her bed and remained motionless.

Judith's face changed. The strangeness of that remark struck her. She got up from the floor and went over to Sarah's bed.

'I do the same?' she said. 'What do you mean?'

'The same as she does. He makes love to her.'

'To whom? Whom do you mean?'

'To Mummy, of course,' said Sarah.

There was silence. Then Judith leaned over until she could see Sarah's face half-hidden in the pillow.

'Sarah, is this true?'

'Of course it's true.'

'How d'you know?'

'I've seen them. I've seen them kissing each other in the

sitting-room. He comes back here at night when they think I'm asleep. I've heard them talking in the night. I've – I've listened . . . ' Sarah suddenly pulled the sheet over her head and burst into tears. 'And then you go and do the same. You let him make love to you too. People I love – first Mummy and then you. There's nobody any more. Nobody good, nobody to believe in . . . '

'Sarah, listen.' Judith pulled the sheet from Sarah's head and put her arms round her. 'Listen, Sarah please, please listen. I haven't done anything really wrong. Tonight I kissed him. No, I don't think I even kissed him, but he kissed me and that was bad enough, I know. Oh, Sarah, I'm ashamed. But why didn't you tell me about her? It would have saved everything – and I never dreamt of anything like it. She said such awful things to me tonight, and that's why. I see now. It wasn't only what *I'd* done . . . '

Over Sarah's head, Judith stared at the situation. She felt sick. But what must it have been for Sarah?

'Sarah,' she said, putting her cousin's hair back so that she could see her face plainly. 'You believe me, don't you? You can believe me, you know.'

Sarah looked at her, a long look.

'Yes, I believe you.' She threw her arms round her cousin's neck. 'Oh, Judith, I'm so glad it's all right,' she said, crying again. 'It's been so awful. But nothing can be so bad if you're all right.'

Judith rocked her in her arms.

'Oh, Judith, why is everything so horrible? Why do people do such awful, hideous things and lie about them and go

about pretending they're not doing anything? Why is everything so ugly?'

'It isn't,' said Judith. 'There's lots of goodness and beauty
in the world, or there wouldn't be so many books about them.
And there are good people. Look at Auntie Lucy and Uncle
William. Love between them isn't ugly; whatever it is, it's like
them, it's right.'

Sarah kept her tear-streaked face pressed against Judith's
shoulder, considering that.

'You know, we're both in the same boat,' went on Judith.
'You've seen too much for your age, and so have I, of a
different sort. I might have been as miserable as you, if it
hadn't been for Auntie Lucy. But all the time, she sort of kept
it in front of me that there was another side, that there *was*
goodness and beauty. And that's what I should have done for
you, but I came here and made it worse for you. Oh, Sarah,
I'm sorry . . . I'm so sorry.' Her tears fell on her cousin's face.
Sarah wiped them off with the sheet and then solicitously
wiped Judith's eyes too.

'It's all right now,' she said, comforting in her turn. 'It's
going to be all right now.'

But Judith was crying not only for Sarah but for herself.
How could he? she asked in secret. She wouldn't speak of him
to Sarah, she wouldn't burden Sarah with her bitter disillusionment. She must bury it deep, never speak of it. Yet in her
heart she believed him when he said he loved her. He did love
her, and if she stayed here, in spite of what she knew about
Vera and him, she might not be able to stop herself from
loving him more. She might fail Sarah after all. She felt she
might not be able to trust herself.

'Why d'you look like that?' asked Sarah. 'What are you thinking about?'

'I'm thinking about something very serious,' said Judith. 'But listen! What's that?'

'It's Mummy coming upstairs,' whispered Sarah, and put out the light.

They waited. Vera passed on the stairs, went into her room and closed the door. Sarah put the light on again.

'Sarah, I'm not going to stay here,' said Judith.

Sarah started to her knees in the bed and clutched her cousin.

'I'm coming with you, if you go. I won't stay here without you,' she whispered fiercely.

'No, I don't think you can,' said Judith. 'I think we both ought to go.'

'Where to?'

'Auntie Lucy's.'

Sarah stared at her, taking it in.

'It's all beyond me here,' said Judith. 'I can't deal with it. After what Auntie Vera said to me tonight, I can see she's going to send me away. Without you, of course. She'd probably send me to Auntie Lucy, but I must get you away. We shall have to go. Auntie Lucy will know what to do.'

'When shall we go?'

'At once. Tomorrow. Auntie Vera has an appointment with the masseuse tomorrow morning, hasn't she? We must go then. We can only take what we can carry. Thank goodness, I've got some money.'

'Judith, you won't let them separate us, will you? You won't let Auntie Lucy keep you and send me back?'

'She would never do that. But I won't be separated from you, I promise.'

Sarah reached up and kissed her.

'Auntie Lucy will tell us what to do,' said Judith comfortingly. 'The great thing is to get there. Sarah, it's nearly midnight. You must go to sleep. Lie down and let me cover you up. I'll undress very quickly and then we'll get the light out. Lie down, darling.'

'I shall never go to sleep,' said Sarah, lying down all the same.

'You must try. Don't let's speak another word. Good night, darling.'

'Judith . . . ' said Sarah.

'Sh . . . ' said Judith.

When the lamp was out she lay still, trying not to toss about and disturb Sarah. She closed her eyes, but the dark was crisscrossed with darts of light, like yellow rain against her eyelids. Her heart throbbed so loud she could not bear her ear against the pillow. Every nerve jangled from the encounters of the evening; the long wait for the signal, the brief, breathless meeting when she had found herself in his arms without knowing how she got there. He had never spoken of loving her before, never kissed her. And then the discovery by her aunt and that awful scene in the sitting-room, then this last flash from Sarah, revealing the whole ugly situation, and finishing it off for ever.

She had to go, and of her own free will never see him again, never feel that wild joy she had felt when he kissed her. It sounded very easy, just to go away and take refuge with

Auntie Lucy, but it was the hardest thing she had ever done. The only way she could do it was to set her face towards it and keep on. Auntie Lucy said you really always knew what was right and what was wrong, and she knew it was right to go and take Sarah with her. But oh, Terry, she thought, why had it to be like this? If only it could have been different . . .

In her room, lying fully dressed face downwards on her bed, Vera was saying the same thing. And in the big empty house across the park, even Terry was thinking it too.

CHAPTER TWENTY-SIX

I

Lucy was in the orchard, feeding the hens. They clustered round her taking tit-bits from the palm of her hand. She liked her hens. No domestic scene would be complete to her now, she told herself, without them. None of her hens ever appeared on the table. She had far too many old retainers. When one got beyond further enjoyment of life, it had to be smuggled away by William to a farmer. Lucy brought up hens and ducks and found them good homes round about as if they had been cats. The village benefited from this peculiarity, though they smiled at it.

She went to take a broody from a nest-box. The misguided creature was so faithful to two pottery eggs that she would not feed or drink until made to. She had plucked the feathers from her breast to lay it warm against the unresponsive china.

'Poor silly thing,' said Lucy, bringing her gently out. 'It's all so pathetic and absurd, you know.'

But were women any wiser, she thought, putting the broody down before her dish of food? Had Charlotte been? Was Vera? The men they chose to lavish their devotion on, to

lose everything else for, were poor things, in Lucy's opinion; decidedly of the pottery variety.

She stood in the orchard. The sun had sunk out of sight, but the sky was banded with yellow behind the great elms on her right. On her left the moon was a pale china globe waiting to have its light turned on. This lovely world, she thought, and alas! so threatened. This time next year, William said, they'd be at war. She had always felt the village, these fields, this little house protected her, but now she felt she must protect them. She knelt down and put her hand in the grass. It was cool, living. Overhead the apples hung secret among the leaves. The unchangingness of grass and apples contented her. Her thoughts left the threat of war. The strength and variety of life in the small space of the orchard struck her with wonder. She knelt on the grass, drawn into the evening quiet. In this country place, the presence of God seemed a thing to be expected, to be taken for granted as the old holy men took it, the Desert Fathers, for instance. The well-spring of happiness, which she could never trace exactly to its source, rose within her, ebbing and flowing, ebbing and flowing.

When she got up from the grass she saw, over the hedge, two figures, two girls coming across the green with suitcases. People didn't come this way unless they were coming to the church or the house, and since no one took a suitcase to the church, they must be coming to the house. But who could they be? It was too dark now to make them out. She went through the door in the old wall and came out on the front path. Then she saw it was Judith and Sarah.

'Children!' she cried.

Relief lit Judith's face. 'Oh, Auntie Lucy,' she said, running forward.

Lucy knew at once that something was wrong, they looked so tired and serious. 'Sarah, dear,' she said, kissing her. 'Give me your case. Is your mother all right?' she asked swiftly.

Sarah looked at Judith. 'Yes,' she said.

'Does she know you're here?' Lucy asked, realising that they must have run away.

'No,' said Judith. Their eyes were anxious on Lucy, but her face reassured them.

'Come in, darlings. We'll talk later. Have you been a long time on the way?'

'All day,' said Judith, smiling at her aunt, but wanly. 'We just went to the station and took the first train, but it was evidently the wrong one.'

'And then you had to wait for the bus to bring you out here,' said Lucy. 'But even if you'd telephoned, we had no car to fetch you with. Uncle William is away tonight. What have you had to eat?'

Two buns and two cups of tea, it appeared. 'You must be famished,' said Lucy, in an indignant voice.

As they came into the hall, Janet appeared in astonishment from the kitchen.

'Supper for these two as quickly as possible, Janet, please. They've had nothing but two buns all day.'

'There isn't enough fish for two extra,' objected Janet, but her mistress sent her a warning look from the stairs.

'They must have supper first. We'll see about ours afterwards,' she said firmly, continuing upwards with the girls. She

434

was in no mood to stand any nonsense from Janet. The girls must be made welcome; they were welcome and let anyone beware of implying otherwise, she thought fiercely.

Judith took off her hat with a sigh as they went into their room. This was coming home.

'I feel very gritty,' said Sarah, taking off her hat too. How she had grown, thought Lucy, but she was too thin and pale. Neither of them looked as if she had had any sleep, and they were both pathetically anxious and uncertain.

'You go and wash first, Sarah,' said Judith.

'Yes, come along and let me give you your towels.' Lucy went with Sarah to the bathroom and came back to Judith, who was standing in the middle of the room, waiting to get the ordeal of telling over.

'Darling, I can see something is badly wrong,' said Lucy. 'What is it?'

'Well – it's . . . ' faltered Judith, her lips pale and dry. She didn't know what Lucy would think of her. She would perhaps think she was depraved and deceitful, as Vera had said. Oversexed. Her eyes anxious, she plunged into the tale. Halfway through, Lucy, aghast, moved to close the door, but Judith stopped her. 'Don't shut Sarah out, Auntie Lucy. She knows all about it. She told me. We must never shut Sarah out. . . . Sarah!' she called from the door. 'Sarah!'

Sarah came slowly, drying her hands unnecessarily on the towel. Judith put an arm round her shoulders and continued to talk. 'We can't go back,' she finished, looking to Lucy. 'Auntie Vera doesn't want me, but Sarah can't go back. What can we do? We don't know what to do?'

'You can stay here, of course. You can stay here for ever, if need be.' Lucy kissed first one and then the other. 'Don't worry. The first thing is supper. We can talk while you're having it. Then you need a good night's rest, both of you. But don't worry any more. I'll ring up tonight, and I'll go to Trenton tomorrow, if necessary.'

But before supper was over, Vera rang up herself.

'I suppose they're with you, Lucy?' came her voice over the wire.

'Yes, they're here,' said Lucy.

'Well, they'd better stay there for the present,' said Vera coldly.

'Vera, come here too,' said Lucy earnestly. 'Do come. Give up that house for the present and come here.'

'No, thank you,' said Vera. 'And please leave me to live my own life, Lucy. You may not approve of it, but that's because you can't understand.'

'Darling, I only love you and want you to be happy,' said poor Lucy.

'But you won't agree that I should be happy in my own way.'

'I don't think you are happy. I feel you're unhappy now,' said Lucy.

'But you're wrong,' said Vera's mocking voice. 'As a matter of fact this incident, unpleasant though it was, has cleared the air. Judith behaved abominably. Abominably, Lucy. I never want to see her again. But Terry's explained everything.'

Lucy's heart sank. These men who can explain everything. And alas! the women who believe them, or perhaps don't

believe, but persuade themselves that they do because they want to! 'Never kid yourself' had been the young Vera's tough maxim, but it wasn't now.

'So long as everything is right between Terry and me, I don't care about anything else,' said Vera over the telephone. It sounded fantastic, even fatuous to Lucy. That Vera, once cool and clear-sighted, should talk like this, saddened and bewildered her.

'Leave me alone, Lucy,' Vera went on. 'That's all I ask. Now you've got Sarah, I suppose you'll admit I'm free to do as I like?'

'The damage is done, certainly,' said Lucy gravely.

'Well, it's no good going on with this conversation,' said Vera. 'So I'll ring off. Goodbye, Lucy . . . ' her voice broke suddenly. 'Don't judge me too harshly, darling.'

'Vera!' called Lucy in despair. 'Vera . . . '

But the telephone clicked in her ear; Vera was gone.

Lucy stood in the hall. She didn't want the girls to see that she had been distressed by the conversation. From where she was, she could see them at the supper-table in the lamp-light, not eating, their faces turned to the door, waiting for her to come back. A deep desire to banish anxiety from these young faces possessed her. 'I wish I could,' she thought. 'I hope I'll be able to.'

She went back to them. 'It's all right,' she said reassuringly. 'You're to stay here. For the time being, anyway. So just settle in, darlings, and don't worry any more. Now I must go and make up your beds. Judith, you serve the apricot cream, will you?'

She called Janet to come upstairs and Janet came, with pinched lips.

'Are they staying here permanent?' she asked stiffly, bringing the sheets.

'I don't know yet,' said Lucy.

'Because if they are, I'm not,' said Janet.

'Very well,' said Lucy. 'But I warn you, Janet, that I can't concern myself with you at present. Think the situation out and come to your own decision and then let me know. But don't visit your displeasure on me or on the girls. They have enough trouble of their own. Pass the pillow-slips, please.'

Janet pinched her lips still tighter, and mistress and maid finished the beds in silence.

'The sheets always smell of lavender here,' said Judith, with a sigh of satisfaction as she got into her bed a little later.

'Oh, I'm so sleepy,' said Sarah, getting into hers.

'Well, sleep then,' said Judith. 'You can, tonight.'

'What a good thing we've got Auntie Lucy, Judith,' said Sarah. 'Where should we have gone if we hadn't her?'

'Goodness knows,' said Judith.

II

When Lucy heard the car coming home the next night, she went out to prepare William. She was so afraid he might do or say anything to make the girls feel he didn't want them. But William took the news surprisingly. He listened as they stood together in the garage and then said briskly: 'The best thing Vera can do now is to take herself off and leave the girls to you.'

Lucy was both relieved and alarmed. She was relieved that he would accept the girls, but she was very alarmed in case Vera should do as he wished. Once he had put the idea into her head, she could not get it out, and after supper, she rang up the house in Burnham Road, fearful of getting no reply. But Vera's voice came coolly in response.

'What is it, Lucy?'

'Oh, Vera, are you all right?' said Lucy. 'I had to ring up to know.'

'Of course I'm all right,' said Vera. 'What did you think I'd be? Did you think I'd throw myself into the river or something because the girls have come to you?'

She meant to make Lucy's anxiety seem foolish, and for the moment she succeeded.

'Have you come to any decision yet?' asked Lucy.

'Decision?' said Vera. There was a pause. 'Oh, about the girls? Well, they're all right with you, aren't they? You always wanted Judith, at any rate. You ought almost to be grateful to your sisters for providing you with the children nature, or whatever it is, denied you.'

'You've said some bad things to me in your life,' said Lucy, goaded. 'But that's about the worst.'

She knew Vera. Vera purposely made you angry so that you would withdraw and leave her alone; and it nearly always came off.

'I'm simply stating a fact,' said Vera calmly now. 'It's hard lines that the only one in the family fit to bring up children, shouldn't have had any. But I'm very busy, Lucy. I must go. Good night, darling, and don't worry about me. I'm

perfectly capable of looking after myself. I'll write in a day or two.'

So they had to wait. Judith felt as if she had spent her life so far in waiting-rooms on the line. Sometimes she was allowed to go a little farther, but before long she had to get out and wait again, until someone decided what was to happen to her next. She suffered in secret. She could not forget Terry. She looked so unhappy sometimes when she was off her guard, that Lucy's heart ached for her. But she didn't say anything. No use telling the young that time heals everything; they would only be indignant at the suggestion that they could ever forget. Better suffer than forget, they feel. They think that ultimate release from suffering means that the suffering wasn't anything in the first instance; and they know it is.

Judith suffered and hid it, because of Sarah. She wanted Sarah to be happy, and the waiting was worse for Sarah, she thought, than anybody. She herself was sure to be allowed to stay at Underwood, but Sarah couldn't know what was to happen to her until her mother had decided. Sarah, for her part, tried to hide her feelings too. She was anxious and she wasn't as completely at home at Underwood as Judith, but she was so grateful to her cousin for bringing her away from Burnham Road and so glad to be with her, that she set herself to amuse and interest Judith as if she were the elder.

'They're an improvement on their mothers in one way at least,' said William. 'They obviously think of each other instead of all the time of themselves.'

Lucy was touched.

'You do think you're going to like them then? You won't mind if they come to live with us for good?'

'Oh, no,' William conceded, and was rewarded by one of the hugs which, after twenty years of married life, she frequently and abruptly bestowed on him.

Lucy's mind was at rest about William, but not about Janet. In spite of conciliatory enquiries about her cousins, Janet refused to be brought round. Silent, grim, she was cleaning like a fury. The house was perfectly clean already, Lucy remonstrated, but Janet took no notice. Bed-covers were ripped off and washed, carpets were taken up and put down, silver that was never used was brought out, cleaned and put back again. Sighing heavily, Janet went up to bed late, and got up at dawn to begin again. Sighing too, Lucy could but wait for the fury to abate.

But one morning, earlier than ever, Janet came down in her hat and coat and carrying a case. She looked at the kitchen clock. She'd plenty of time. She'd lay the breakfast. She'd done the grates and laid the fires the night before. When she had set the table, she found she still had time to dust the dining-room, so moving about in her hat and coat, she dusted. No good standing at the bus-stop for all to see, giving rise to talk. There never was such a place for talk as the village; it would fairly buzz today when the news got out that she'd left for good and all.

Well, time to go now. She'd left everything straight. Nothing to be ashamed of in the look of things; boot cupboard done out and everything. Ever since the girls came she'd been getting ready to go.

She took a piece of paper from the drawer where she always kept paper and pencil handy to make notes of what the mistress wanted from the shops. She bowed over the kitchen table in her ponderous hat, wondering what to write. The words wouldn't come. She didn't know what to say. She licked the stub of pencil to help her and then laboriously wrote. She laid the pencil on top of the four words, took a last look round the kitchen, picked up her case and went out of the back door. She would not risk passing Cora's kennel in case the sight of the old dog should be too much for her resolution. Carrying her heavy case, she went round the side of the house.

Lucy, who had been awake a long time, heard stealthy footsteps on the path below and sprang out of bed. She looked through the curtains and saw Janet's stocky figure going down the lane. So this was it! This was the explanation of the furious cleaning. Thrusting her feet into her slippers and snatching her dressing-gown, Lucy ran down and opened the front door. She ran out on to the green, but Janet had disappeared. Lucy turned back into the house and went forlornly to the kitchen. There on the table was the paper. 'Gone to my cousins,' she read. She laughed but only ruefully. She had never thought it would really come to this. A prop of the household had been removed and Lucy felt it must collapse. 'What shall I do without her?' she thought unhappily. She stood about in the kitchen, which seemed very empty without the familiar bustling figure in blue print. Then, sighing, she went back upstairs. She must dress quickly and see to breakfast herself.

But putting her hand to the curtains to draw them, she gave a burst of laughter, quickly stifled so as not to waken

William. Janet was coming back up the lane. Lucy dropped the curtain and hurried to get back into her bed, to make it appear that she had not been out of it.

Janet, on the way to the bus, had seen the milk-boy coming over the fields. He'd left them a pint short yesterday and with so many people as there were now in the house they'd been put out all day. He'd do the same again if she wasn't there to watch him. She'd have to go back. Besides, Cora was barking. She'd be waking the mistress and after all the bother she'd had, she needed her sleep.

Coming into the kitchen, she snatched the paper from the table and threw it into the grate. In a moment, the applied match lit the fire for the day and reduced the message to ash. She took off her hat and coat and hid them in the wash-house. By the time the milk-boy arrived at the back-door, she was tying on her apron and ready to tell him what she thought of him.

III

That morning, at breakfast, Vera's letter arrived, and when Lucy opened it, she murmured an excuse and left the table. She went out into the garden, round the side, where no one could see her. The letters that arrive at breakfast! The coffee that goes cold in the cup, the bacon that congeals on the plate because of them! Vera's letter came from London and had the address of the hotel torn off, she was running no risk of being appealed to by Lucy.

She was going to South Africa, eventually, with Terry

Crawford, she wrote. They were going to live a simple life far from the world. They both hated the life they'd had to live at Trenton. Terry wanted to go back to his own country, had always wanted it, and if he were happy there, Vera wrote, she would be happy too. She had made arrangements for the transference of Sarah's legacy from her grandmother to Lucy's care, and Judith's guardianship too. The furniture was sold, the house too. The girls' things had been sent on. 'The children will be better with you,' she wrote. 'I'm not fit to have charge of them.'

Lucy couldn't read for tears and when William came out in search of her, she could only hand him the letter.

'I've never known such an example of self-deception,' said William. 'How on earth does Vera imagine that she can live the simple life? And in the wilds too?'

'But he doesn't love her,' said Lucy, bewildered. 'Why does he take her with him?'

'Didn't you say he has no money? Her seven hundred a year will be very useful.'

'Oh, William,' cried Lucy in distress.

'And yet she loves him, you see,' she said in a moment. 'And I'm afraid Judith does too, in spite of everything.'

'Well, they say there's no reason in love. It looks as if it must be true. But Judith will get over it.'

'I can see nothing but misery for Vera, though,' said Lucy.

'I've just had to stand by and watch both my sisters destroy themselves,' she said.

'For Vera, at least, the epitaph should be, "Nobody to blame but herself,"' said William.

'That only makes it all the sadder,' said Lucy.

William drew her hand through his arm.

'Come in and tell the girls. Get it over and start afresh,' he said. 'Strange that after almost thirty years you should have had the same task put into your hands, isn't it?'

'I hope I manage better this time,' said Lucy. 'But perhaps I shall. I'm older and I've got you to help me. You'll supply plenty of salt and sense, I know.' She pressed his arm and smiled at him.

Her sisters had been like two fair ships with no hand on the wheel; one had foundered and gone down, the other was racing before the wind, headed for disaster. Lucy, grieving that she had not been able to help or save them, never thought – she had no idea – that she herself had been the beacon to bring their children to harbour.

AFTERWORD

In dicussing English writing, the word 'middle' is a term of abuse. If a phenomenon can be defined as middle-class, middle-brow or mid-life, let alone pertaining to the Midlands or to middle England, its significance is immediately denied. Indeed, there is an implicit sneer in the word, a subtext of culpable privilege. At an authors' event in Oxford, I once heard a young literature student demand of another novelist, 'Why do you write about the middle-classes?' The author swiftly defended herself by explaining that she herself came from a working-class family. So that was all right then.

Middle-phobia is a uniquely British phenomenon, so, luckily for the reading world, authors such as John Updike, Gustave Flaubert or Sinclair Lewis were never inhibited by it. These authors recognised how rich a field the middle ground is for a writer, who can give her readers a ringside seat to watch opposing cultural forces fight for control of the lives of millions. Extremes of poverty or wealth may not be found here, but extremes of hope and despair, of courage

and pain, are certainly felt by the people whose hearts and minds have to be won if a new morality is ever to become mainstream.

For Dorothy Whipple, the middle-class Midlands in mid-twentieth century was simply the world she knew. Her own life as a wildly popular novelist still had its share of prejudice; in her home town of Blackburn there were people who assumed that her husband must have written her books for her. She was acutely aware of injustice in the lives of less privileged women, saying, "I feel a woman, any woman, should *fight*." She undoubtedly shared the recognition that the great social upheavals of her time were going on around her, but had no ambition to become a polemical novelist. She wrote to please women like herself, who were intelligent, with an acute sense of justice but fundamentally loving and committed to all their relationships.

Her ambition was simply to 'wring the truth out of my people'. Her characters are buffeted by the huge social storms of the mid-decades of the twentieth century in Britain but the author only momentarily breaks the flow in her narrative to lecture the reader. Successfully wringing the truth from her characters, however, meant drawing daily lives which inevitably dramatised the struggles of feminism and the collapse of the class system. *They Were Sisters* is more domestic in scope than the extremely successful novels which preceded it, *They Knew Mr Knight* and *The Priory*, both of which offer a wider social panorama of Britain between the wars, at the start of the transition from an imperial and industrial society to a post-imperial and commercial one.

They Were Sisters is about Lucy, Charlotte and Vera, three daughters of a provincial lawyer and his wife. Lucy, the eldest, is eighteen when their mother dies of influenza and she puts aside her ambition to study at Oxford to assume the role of carer, housekeeper and companion to her father. Only when her sisters are married and her father has died is Lucy free to accept a husband herself. She has no children of her own, and her concern for her sisters seems partly a habit of nurturing but also the product of thwarted promise.

Most of the story takes place in the Thirties, as the three marriages mature and the children of them grow up. Charlotte, described as a woman who loves too much decades before those words became the title of a book about women drawn to dysfunctional partners, marries Geoffrey, a boorish, hard-drinking salesman who swiftly evolves into a domestic dictator. His blood-curdling sadism towards his wife and children is evoked without any physical violence or the use of a word stronger than 'damn'.

It is a great strength of Dorophy Whipple's writing that all her characters, even the players of cameo roles like the maids and the neighbours, are sketched with depth and endowed with vitality. She even finds empathy for Geoffrey, vile as he is. Long before the dynamics of domestic violence became a staple of kitchen-table psychology, she took care to reveal Geoffrey's underlying insecurity and fear of abandonment and explain the tyranny of an ego whose hunger for attention could never be assuaged.

Added to this emotional perspective, Whipple also depicts the complete helplessness of Charlotte, and the other women,

before a man who had, at that time, automatic social support for his actions, however psychotic. In a rare moment when Lucy speaks with author's voice, she says to herself, 'It was monstrous that such a man as Geoffrey should have such power, but there was no appeal against it.'

No sense of powerlessness afflicts Vera, however, because she was born a beauty, which allows her to become sublimely selfish. Like her contemporary, Scarlett O'Hara, she makes off with her sister's beau without a twinge of conscience. Vera wafts through the first half of the book trailing chiffon gowns, a team of male admirers and the scent of hot-house flowers, dazzling her young nieces. Sexual hubris, however, was always punished by social nemesis in heroines of this era and Vera's downfall would have appeared inevitable to Whipple's readers, especially when coupled with the ultimate crime, disinterest in her children.

The low status of women in the society in which the sisters live is apparent from the very first pages of the book. It is taken for granted that Lucy will abandon her academic ambitions when her mother dies. None of the sisters is educated for any kind of career. When Geoffrey arrives in the neighbourhood and starts leading the girls' brothers into heavy drinking and anti-social behaviour, the boys are saved by being given 'large lump sums' and sent to Canada, while Charlotte is allowed to follow her admiration for him to its fatal conclusion. Once married, Charlotte and Lucy can only visit each other with their husband's permission, and can only spend freely the money they are lucky enough to have inherited independently. Lucy's husband is considered

kind and wise, but she automatically blames herself for their infertility and probes, unsuccessfully, to find out how much he 'minds'.

Coupled with their financial dependence, but largely taken for granted because it would have been a fact of life for Whipple's readers, is the bitter truth that a middle-class women of this time had almost no chance of freeing herself from a bad husband. In the early Thirties, divorce was possible only on the grounds of adultery, which had to be substantiated by witnesses. Not until the Matrimonial Causes Act of 1937 were the additional grounds of three years' desertion, five years' insanity, and cruelty introduced, and even then a divorced woman suffered grave social disadvantages.

These are bitterly dramatised in Vera's fall from grace. Her husband, prompted by his dragon of a mother, contrives to divorce her from America and keep custody of one of their daughters. Vera's income is dramatically reduced, she moves to a smaller house and her luxurious way of life comes to an end. Their friends desert her, finding it 'awkward to fit in an odd woman at a dinner table – there were so many odd women'. Indeed there were – so many men had died in World War I that the British population was nearly 65% female at this time. Even her admirers disappear, afraid of the taint of scandal which surrounded a divorcée whether or not she had committed a matrimonial fault.

Dorothy Whipple considered herself a writer who was better at characterisation than at narrative construction. 'I don't like having to concoct plots, I like doing people,' she protested in her memoir, *Random Commentary*. An executive of

Gaumont British Pictures, negotiating for the film rights to *They Were Sisters*, complained that there wasn't enough 'love, romance, slap-up rows and reconciliations' in her books. She told him she didn't write that sort of book.

If sex and violence constitute action, then it is definitely missing in Dorothy Whipple's work. Her novels also owe nothing to the conventions of romantic comedy and are short on soap-opera devices. They are, however, works of extraordinary compulsion. The drama in *They Were Sisters* is entirely emotional and assumes a strong maternal consciousness in the reader. Dorothy Whipple mastered, evidently by instinct and by good reading, the most powerful techniques of story-telling. From the moment we learn that there is considered to be a 'strain of wildness or weakness' in the sisters' family, we wait for it to emerge and wreak havoc. We fear for Vera from the minute we fall under the mesmerising spell of her beauty but see that she lacks the strength of character to transcend it. And Charlotte, from the day she announces her engagement, is simply a tragedy waiting to happen.

The final character who sets a strand of fate unravelling is Judith, the youngest child of Charlotte and Geoffrey, a girl of so many virtues – wonder, intelligence, sensitivity, prettiness and aunt-appeal – that the reader immediately hopes that she will be saved from the train-wreck of her mother's life. Vera's daughter, Sarah, is a much less lovable child but so clearly the victim of emotional abuse that she eventually wins the readers' sympathy, especially when it becomes clear that she has a talent.

They Were Sisters is a story told in the language of mother-hood. The narrative is built on the values of nurturing and

self-sacrifice, and progresses as characters move towards personal fulfilment. The over-arching narrative strand is drawn out of Lucy's latent maternal instincts. Cheated of ambition, denied children, unable to save Charlotte from Geoffrey or Vera from herself, Lucy is finally fulfilled by her ability to rescue Judith and Sarah and set them on their own path towards independence. The message, which Whipple never spells out but her readers undoubtedly understood, is that there will be hope for the next generation.

Lucy's husband, whose age is never given, is loving but socially inept, a man of few words, most of them uncomfortably truthful. The author, whose first love died in World War I, married a man twenty years older than herself. Like Lucy, she had no children although she clearly adored them and idolised her young nieces. She never emphasised the autobiographical qualities of the book, although there are obvious parallels between her own life and that of her central character. She even chose to illustrate the companionable tolerance of Lucy's marriage by an incident that she recorded in her diary, in which her husband obliviously finished all the marmalade at breakfast. 'May I have just a *little* marmalade?' Lucy asks, by way of gentle complaint. 'As little as you please,' her husband answers, passing the empty dish. Lucy finds this funny, and a 'sensible' response, while recognising that her sisters would have disapproved.

They Were Sisters was a work which began with high enthusiasm. 'Suddenly, out of the blue, about six o'clock in the morning, an idea for a novel hit me,' the author recorded, early in 1939, and rushed to make notes and drafts. The

immense success of *The Priory*, whose pre-publication sub-scription sales in the summer of 1939 were up to 15,000 at a time when 10,000 alone made a No. 1 bestseller, meant she thought she could count on having a clear two years in which to work on a new book. The original focus of the story seems to have been Judith, because she went on to say: 'Now, my little girl, materialise with all your troubles, the aunts, the cousins, the worthless lover and that house!'

Events quickly turned this glorious dawn into a nightmare day. On a personal level, Dorothy's husband retired; they regretfully moved from Nottingham to Kettering, and her mother became terminally ill. On the world's stage, Hitler and Mussolini were on the march, fear and anxiety took hold of Europe, and in September 1939 Britain and France went to war. Dorothy struggled to write after sleepless nights in an air-raid shelter, listening to the Luftwaffe roaring overhead.

Many lives were lost among her family, friends and neighbours. By day, she was often forced to put aside her work and cater for a stream of visitors, relatives, billeted Canadian airmen and evacuee children, all of whom had to be fed somehow with rationed food and the couple's garden produce. Her publisher urged her to write a short book, because the shortage of paper meant that he could not produce a long one. The novel went to four drafts, and languished. The diary simply says: 'I can't write. Fiction seems so trivial. Fact is too terrible.'

But the traumas of war did not diminish the public demand for Dorothy Whipple's work. If anything, her status was confirmed as her readers' yearned for the tranquil normality of the years before 1939 and longed to escape to a stable world

defined by marriages, children and husbands. *The Priory* had sold over 27,000 copies in its first few months, and the magazine editor who had serialised it wanted more. By 1943, when her early elation had long drained away, Dorothy sent her the first fifty pages and a 'muddled' synopsis. By that time she still had no clear idea of how the book would end.

Soon she was rewriting the early chapters for serialisation in *Homes & Gardens* and trying to finish the work at the same time. Her confidence was at rock bottom and she castigated herself for not having thought through the novel's themes at the outset. No doubt this chaotic completion accounts for the small but uncharacteristic flaws in style and gaps in the narrative. The pressure of the serialisation was enough to renew her energy, and the ideas began to flow freely once more. When it was finally finished she still felt disappointed in it, but then, she usually felt deflated at the end of a book and was relentlessly critical of her own work until the customary rave reviews arrived to cheer her.

The advance sale of the book exceeded all the others, and when it was published it was swiftly reviewed as a 'masterpiece'. With the film of *They Knew Mr Knight* already in production, the screen rights to *They Were Sisters* were immediately sold to Gainsborough Pictures, who rushed the film out in 1945. Ironically, James Mason, who was cast as Geoffrey, stole the picture; he delivered a performance full of the chilling sexual magnetism that had already made him one of Britains biggest box-office stars.

Celia Brayfield
London, 2004